THE KISS
OF THE
CONCUBINE:
A STORY OF ANNE BOLEYN

JUDITH ARNOPP

First published in 2013 by FeedARead.com Publishing

Copyright © Judith Arnopp

A CIP catalogue record for this title is available from the
British Library.

Cover by Covergirl

For Sally, with love

THE KISS
OF
THE CONCUBINE

<u>28th January 1547 – Whitehall Palace</u>

It is almost midnight and January has Whitehall Palace clenched in its wintery fist. The gardens are rimed with frost, the casements glazed with ice. Like a shadow, I wait alone by the window in the silver-blue moonlight, my eye fixed on the bed.

The room is crowded, yet nobody speaks.

I tread softly among them. The flickering torchlight illuminates a sheen of anticipation on their faces, the rank odour of their uncertainty rising in a suffocating fug. Few can remember the time that went before, and both friend and foe balance upon the cusp of change, and tremble at the terror of the unknown.

I move through the heavily perfumed air, brush aside jewelled velvet sleeves. At the high-canopied bed I sink to my knees and observe his face for a long moment. He is changed. This is not the man I used to know.

They have propped him on pillows, the vast belly mountainous beneath the counterpane, and the yellow skin of mortality's mask is drawn tightly across his cheeks. There is not much time and before death can wipe his memory clean, I speak suddenly into his ear, a whisper meant only for him. "Henry!"

The king's eyes fly open and his eyeballs swivel from side to side, his disintegrating ego peering as if through the slits in a mummer's mask.

He knows me, and understands why I have come.

5

He whimpers like a frightened child and Anthony Denny steps forward and leans over the bed. "Your Majesty, Archbishop Cranmer has been summoned; he cannot be long now."

Henry's fat fingers tremble as he grips the coverlet, his pale lips coated with thick spittle as he tries to speak. I move closer, my face almost touching his, and the last rancid dregs of his breath engulf me. "They think you fear death, Henry. But you fear me more, don't you, my Lord?"

"Anne?"

The sound is unintelligible, both a denial and a greeting, but it tells me what I need to know. He recognises and fears my presence. Those assembled begin to mutter that the king is raving, talking with shadows.

I sink into the mattress beside him and curl my body around his bulk. "How many times did we share this bed, Henry?" His breathing is laboured now and sweat drips from his brow, the stench of his fear exceeded only by that of his festering thigh. I tighten my grip upon him. "Did you ever love me, Henry? Oh, I know that you lusted but that isn't the same. Do you remember how you burned for me, right to the end?"

I reach out to run my fingertip along his cheek and he leaps in fright, like a great fish floundering on a line, caught in a net of his own devising. One brave attendant steps forward to mop the king's brow as I continue to tease.

"Poor Henry. Are you afraid even now of your own sins? To win me you broke from Rome, although in your heart you never wanted to. Even the destruction of a thousand years of worship was a small price to pay to have me in your bed, wasn't it?"

Henry sucks in air and forgets to breathe again. A physician hurries forward, pushes the attendant aside and with great daring, lifts the king's right eyelid. Henry jerks his head away and the doctor snatches back his hand as if it has been scalded.

Even now they are fearful of him. Although the king can no longer so much as raise his head from his pillow, they still cower. How long will it take for them to forget their fear?

Mumbling apologies, the physician bows and backs away to take his place with the others. As they watch and wait a little longer, the sound of mumbled prayer increases. "Not long now, Henry," I whisper like a lover. "It is almost over."

A door opens. Cold air rushes into the stifling chamber and Archbishop Cranmer enters, stamping his feet to dislodge the snow from his boots. He hands his outer clothes to a servant before pushing through the crowd to approach the bed, his Bible tucked beneath his arm.

I playfully poke the end of Henry's nose. "Time to confess your sins, my husband." Cranmer takes the king's hand, his long slim fingers contrasting with the short swollen digits of his monarch. As he begins to mutter the last rites, I put my mouth close to Henry's ear to taunt him. "Tell the truth, Hal. Own up to all the lies you told; how you murdered and how you cheated. Go on …."

But King Henry has lost the power of speech, and cannot make a full confession. Gasping for one more breath he clings tightly to Cranmer's hand, and I know there is not long to wait before he is mine again. A single tear trickles from the corner of his eye to be lost upon his pillow.

"It's time, Henry," I whisper. "And I am here, waiting. For a few short years I showed you Paradise and now, perhaps, I can do so again. Unless, of course, I choose to show you Hell."

PART ONE
DAUGHTER

<u>1521 – Hever, Kent</u>

England seems small after the glories of the French court, and my father's house cramped and inconvenient. I am horribly bored kicking my heels in the country, and long for company. Mother is distracted, Father wears a face like a thundercloud, and neither of them pays my arrival home as much heed as I would like. There is no one save George, who is home for a few days.

My brother is always glad to listen to me and pretends to delight in the stories of my adventures overseas. "You do look fine, Anne," he says, admiring my fine French-styled clothes. I have grown used to admiration and whereas once I would have blushed and dismissed his words, I am far too elegant to let my discomposure show now I am older. George takes my arm and leads me inside, the interior of the hall suddenly dark after the brilliance of the day. "Have you heard about Mary?" he whispers.

My sister, Mary, has ever had the knack of stealing the attention from me, and is the centre of things once more. She almost brought disgrace on us by sharing the bed of the French king, but Father has recently managed to marry her off respectably to William Carey. We all imagined that now she was safely wed to a good man, she would settle down to provide Will with a string of infants. But although my parents have not spoken to me of it, I have lately learned that Mary is now enjoying a passionate 'flirtation' with King Henry. My sister, it seems, accumulates kings as one might collect butterflies, or compliments.

After supper, George and I closet ourselves in a small chamber where I poke the slumbering fire back to life. "You can't blame the king for fancying her, she is so pretty. Not cursed with my long nose and bony chin."

George laughs and stretches his feet toward the flames. "If I didn't know you better, Anne, I'd think you were fishing for compliments when you know very well that what you lack in looks, you make up for with wit."

He is right; my face does lack Mary's softness. Her expression is meek, just as men prefer. To make it worse, she boasts a nature twice as soft as mine. Although I tell myself I'd rather have brains than looks, I don't want to hear confirmation of my lack of beauty, even if it is only from the lips of my brother. I throw a cushion at his head, but he catches it deftly and laughs at me.

"Poor Anne," he teases, "is it a sweetheart you are lacking? Don't worry, sister, soon there will be courtiers aplenty fighting for your favour."

I try to stop the hot blood from burning my cheeks. "I don't need a sweetheart. Father is arranging my marriage as we speak, as well you know."

I am intended for James Butler, the heir of the Ormond estates, but his father and mine spend overmuch time quibbling over details, protracting the arrangement and leaving me in limbo. Although I have never set eyes on James, I am content with the match. He is young and rich enough to make a good husband, and I have heard no ill stories of him. I trust my father to choose well for me.

George leans forward and offers me a handful of nuts. I pop two into my cheek, continuing to speak with my mouth full. "Can you imagine Mary in the arms of the king? I am surprised she can think of a thing to say."

"He won't care what she says as long as it's yes." George laughs, his eyes glinting in the firelight. He watches me, aware that he has planted unmaidenly pictures in my mind. I have heard that my brother has a way with women, and I can believe the tales. He is good looking, dark like myself but with Mary's features; a goodly combination for a man.

Both Mary and George, it seems, are irresistible to the opposite sex, while I myself have not yet been tempted by any, despite the licentiousness of the French court. Perhaps my reluctance shows; perhaps there is something about me that promises rejection. Whatever the reason, I have never been tempted or even yet kissed; perhaps if I had been, I would have a little more understanding of my sister.

If I were indelicate enough to imagine Mary in a dalliance with any man, I could not visualise her ever refusing. She isn't the sort to say no. And by that I do not mean that she is in any way cheap, only that her gentleness makes her wary of hurting a fellow's feelings.

"Anyway," George continues, "as I said, you can't blame a man for trying, not when the prize is so full of sweet promise." Trying to ignore George's crude inferences, I force my thoughts toward Mary's husband.

"My sympathies are with poor William. How hard it must be for him to be made so publically a cuckold. What must he be feeling? They've only been married a few months."

"Well, be fair, Anne. He isn't the first man to be so used and besides, we don't even know if the king has so honoured Mary. She might well fend him off and cling to her reputation yet. Although, on the other hand, a romp with the king might be good for all of us. The Carey purse isn't a long one, and Henry usually looks after his concubines and pays well for a maid's honour."

George cannot have forgotten that Mary's honour was lost some time ago at the French court, but I don't remind him. Instead, my mind drifts back to the king.

I glimpsed him once or twice when I was a young girl, and have never forgotten his overwhelming presence. I cannot imagine ever having the wherewithal to resist such a man. The king does not look like a man who has ever been denied anything. Poor Mary, I'd not be in her shoes, not for all the jewels in the world.

George cracks another walnut in his palms and begins to separate the flesh from the shell. "We will be better able to assess the situation in a week or two when I accompany you to court. You will find it very different to life in France."

"So I've been told. I really need new gowns, but Father says his purse will not stretch to it and I am to make do with what I have." I pout and look up at George through my lashes, but if I was expecting sympathy, I am sore disappointed. Instead, he gives a shout of laughter that wakes the dog from his slumber. The old hound lifts his head and thumps his tail on the floor.

"Anne! You have more sleeves and headdresses than all of the queen's ladies put together. Believe me, you will not look ill-turned out beside even Queen Catherine herself."

He is right and I find myself cheered. I sit up straighter and stretch out my toes, admiring the jewels upon my slippers. "And there will be none with gowns cut in the French mode. I might not be the prettiest of the queen's ladies, but I can probably manage to be the most stylish."

"That's it, Anne, my girl. Astonish both king and court with your style and wit, and perhaps the gossips will leave Mary alone for a space."

22nd March 1522 – York Place

The Cardinal's house is crowded. I am drowning in a babble of voices, a thousand candles burning, a crush of bodies, the leaping shadows of the torches on the walls. As Mary helps me into a white satin gown and fastens on my headdress, I am in a fever of excitement.

To my relief, her liaison with the king hasn't altered her; She is still my gentle elder sister, overseeing my arrival at court, ensuring I am happily settled.

Tonight there is to be a pageant to honour the Emperor Charles of Spain, who is visiting court to discuss his future marriage to Princess Mary who is, as yet, but a child. There have been jousts and feasts and today, to mark the beginning of Lent, we are putting on a production of Chateau Vert. Mary and I, together with the other court ladies, are to play the eight feminine virtues. The king's sister, Princess Mary, is to represent Beauty, while my sister is Kindness, and Jane Parker, my brother's betrothed, is Constancy. I am to play Perseverance.

From behind the slits of my mask, I can see the other girls. They are all dressed identically and are as brim-full of excitement as I. They peek from behind the heavy fall of brocade that screens us from the assembly.

"Chateau Vert is enormous!" shrieks Jane over her shoulder, "it looks like a real castle." The other girls jostle her aside to get a closer look, and I follow them, elbowing past the Countess of Devonshire who is playing Honour.

At one end of the hall stands a glittering castle, all painted green, adorned with red roses, the battlements shining with green foil, the whole thing brightly lit by flaming torches.

The musicians are concealed behind the wooden walls, and the other girls and I, playing the feminine virtues, will soon be taking our places in the towers. Defending us along the battlements will be the contrary feminine vices; Danger, Disdain, Jealousy, Unkindness, Scorn, Sharp tongue, and Aloofness. Eight little boys, choristers from Wolsey's household, will play these vices.

To gain our hearts, the eight male Virtues, led they say by the king himself, must break a way through the Vices to win Fair Maiden's heart. The men will represent Amorousness, Nobleness, Youth, Attendance, Loyalty, Pleasure, Gentleness and Liberty.

"I wonder which the king will play?" Mary breathes in my ear, her face close to mine as we peek through the arras. I turn to look at her, my eyes level with her chin, and see a pulse beating at the base of her throat. She licks her lips, a blush upon her cheek.

"Sir Loyal Heart?" I quip, but then, feeling remorse for my teasing, I add, "I'm sure we will know soon enough, there is no disguising the king, after all."

Henry is more than six feet tall and towers over all his court. His fiery red hair, broad chest and well-turned leg cannot be disguised, although that doesn't deter him from such games of pretence. I have been instructed that we must all be surprised when he reveals himself at the unmasking.

The Countess claps her hands and we all scramble to finish dressing. "Tie on your mask," I cry to Mary who, realising she has mislaid it, upsets a pile of silk wraps in a fever of searching. With fumbling fingers I help her tie it over her eyes then, giggling and gossiping, we take a secret back passage into the hall and conceal ourselves within the wooden castle tower.

Silence falls within the hall. I can hear Mary's rapid breathing as the pageant spokesman steps forward to address the gathered company. It is William Cornish who, as Master of Choristers in the Chapel Royal, thinks up all these splendid pageants for the amusement of his king. Clad all in crimson satin, embroidered with burning flames of gold, Master Cornish opens his arms and looks toward the battlements where we are waiting.

"Ladies," he cries. "I am Ardent Desire and I beg you to surrender yourselves and come down to me."

We titter and hide behind our hands as two of the chorister boys, playing Scorn and Disdain, sneer a derisive and rather rude refusal.

"Then," Ardent Desire's voice rattles the rafters, "we must take your chateau by storm and force you down."

A great burst of cannon fire sounds from outside, and the women scream in pretended terror. Mary jumps into my arms, laughing and shaking with excitement, her head thrown back, her long white neck exposed. The court is in uproar and even the severe features of the Emperor are screwed up with laughter; beside him even the queen is smiling, for once.

The men come charging into the hall. The king's gentlemen, splendid in blue velvet and cloth of gold, hurl oranges and dates at our defences. As the hail of missiles falls, amid roars of laughter, I grab a handful of sweetmeats and launch them at the encroaching foe.

I recognise George despite his mask. He has one leg hooked over the battlements, his cap is lost, and Unkindness is bashing him with a cushion. The other men are in a similar predicament as Feminine Virtue puts up a sturdy fight. Dodging a hail of oranges, I lean over the battlements and scream encouragement.

Then, a giant of a man, who can only be the king, chases Jealousy and Scorn from their position and breaches the inner wall. At this a triumphant cheer erupts from the spectators, and I see Charles Brandon making off with Princess Mary over his shoulder. She clings to his doublet, her mouth wide with delighted terror. By rights Sir Loyal Heart, played by the king, should rescue Beauty first, but instead he heads for my sister. King Henry, whom we must not recognise, scrambles up the wooden wall, roaring like a bear, and lunges for her as she scurries away. Not noticing his mistake, his hand fastens like a vice about my wrist and he gives a grunt of satisfaction. I try to pull back but he is too strong for me, his determination not to be refused.

I find myself flung over his shoulder, the jewels on his doublet cutting through the thin stuff of my gown. As he runs away with me, the breath is forced from my lungs. My headdress slips and I grab for it as he bears me from the castle, his great hot hand gripping my upper thigh.

I am dragged from his shoulder, my hair cascading about my face as I slide down the king's body. He is very close, his breath in my face, his heart beating frantically against my own. I tilt my head to look up at him and for a long moment he returns my stare before deftly removing my mask. His eyes widen; eyes that are as brilliant as the summer sky.

"You are not …."

"Mary? No, Your Grace, I am not. I am Anne; Anne Boleyn."

With my hand still held fast between his fingers, he hesitates before bowing slightly. I sink to my knees before him.

After a long pause he raises me to my feet, opens his mouth to speak. "I am pleased to meet you, Mistress Anne." Transfixed by his face, it is some seconds before I can tear my eyes from him and turn them to where Mary still waits within her tower. The fight is diminishing around her, all are vanquished. She has removed her mask, her hurt and disappointment plain for all to see. She is no longer smiling.

I shake myself; free myself from the snare of Henry's eyes. "You must return to the battle, Sir Loyal Heart. A fair maiden still awaits you."

After a moment, in which his blue eyes bore into mine, he bows sharply and, with a brave battle cry, turns once more into the fray.

As the battle continues, I watch him for a moment before giving myself a mental shake and turning away toward the hall where the spectators are gathered. But before I am halfway across the room, my step is halted. "Mistress Anne?"

Harry Percy makes a leg before me and asks if I will join him in the dance. I curtsey, and with my fingers balanced on his palm, allow him to lead me to the floor.

The minstrels strike up a tune and the king, partnered now by Princess Mary, joins the dance. As we begin to move to the music, I cast a sideways glance at my partner.

Harry, his face flushed scarlet, returns my smile before darting his eyes away again. I have, of course, spoken with him before. He is part of the Cardinal's household and often accompanies him to court. More often than not, while the Cardinal is closeted with the king, Percy comes to the queen's apartments to pass the time with her ladies.

He does not speak much or push himself forward at all, but hovers in the background, listening and smiling and flushing every time our eyes meet, as they do … often.

I do not underestimate how much courage it has taken for him to invite me to dance.

"So, how did you like our pageant, My Lord?"

"I liked it very well, Mistress," he stammers, as we promenade before the dance forces us apart.

Now and then, the serpentine steps lead us toward other partners; I touch other hands, exchange pleasantries with other men. But all the while, I am aware of Percy watching me. The knowledge makes me lift my chin a little higher, my feet become lighter, and I toss my head with more spirit. When at last we are drawn together again, and he engulfs my hand in his palm, my pulse races and my smile becomes a little too welcoming.

When the music slides to an end, he makes his bow. I notice tiny spirals of curls at the nape of his neck. My tummy gives a little leap when he rises and fixes me with a look that is a little less nervous now.

"Can I get you a cup of wine, Mistress?"

My answering smile is as wanton as Mary's.

Later, when the court revellers are settling to sleep, George and I share a nightcap. Something about the ill-lit chamber urges us to keep our heads close together as we speak in whispers before the hearth. At first we merely gossip, revisiting the uproarious pageant, exchanging notes on who was flirting with whom. After a while, George sobers. "You would do well, Sister, to remember that your hand is pledged elsewhere."

His words force my head up. For a moment, our eyes lock together while I decide whether to be frank or to feign innocence.

"You mean Percy, I suppose. He is just a young man playing the game of love ... as our betters do."

"The game is dangerous, Anne. You don't want your name bandied about ... like Mary's. It won't do to have you both linked to easy virtue. Think what Father will say if you jeopardise the match with Ormond."

"Oh, George." I tuck my feet beneath me on the settle. "I did but dance with him and share a cup of wine."

It is not easy to lie so blatantly. I concentrate on the way the firelight is playing upon his hair and try not to think of Percy.

"You like him, I can tell. Never before have I seen your cheeks blush beneath a fellow's gaze. He is betrothed, you know. Has been since childhood."

"Everyone knows that. I don't know why you are making such a fuss. It was nothing."

I lower my face to my cup, close my eyes to remember again the softness of Harry Percy's hand brushing mine, the fine cut of his leg, the way the Adam's apple bobs in his throat when he laughs. I have no idea why I am deceiving George, who is party to all my secrets. Perhaps the silent pledge that passed between Harry Percy and me is not for sharing. I want to hug the knowledge to myself and run it over and over in my mind. The king is forgotten and I can barely wait for the next day, when Harry Percy is bound to call at the queen's apartments. But I have not fooled George and slyly he probes my motives further.

"Of course," he continues, "should his betrothal with Mary Talbot be broken, he would be as fine a match as you could ask for ... but I fear such an arrangement will never be revoked."

Percy is the son of the Earl of Northumberland, and will one day come into a vast inheritance. A prize indeed were he to ask for my hand, but I know – we both know – that such a thing is impossible for such bonds cannot be broken. And our cause is doubly hopeless since we are both promised elsewhere.

Nevertheless, George's words grate on my senses; I do not wish to hear that our suit is hopeless. For the first time I am made aware of how little control I have over my own destiny. I don't want to hear it. I untangle my legs and place my cup on a small table. "I am going to my bed. Where is Mary? Have you seen her?"

"She entertains the king, no doubt." He gets up and leaves a kiss on my forehead, places a finger beneath my chin and forces me to look into his eyes. "Tread carefully, Sister."

Impatiently, I shrug off his hand and march across the room. I throw open the door, almost colliding with Jane Parker on the threshold. "Oh," she says, "there you are, Anne. I thought you were never coming to bed."

She peers past me to where George is quaffing the last of his wine. He makes a knee to his betrothed and she flushes and bobs a knee in reply. While her head is lowered George blows me a mocking kiss, making me long for something to throw at him.

I turn on my heel. Grabbing Jane's wrist, I whirl her along the corridor to the chamber we share with Madge Shelton and Margery Horsman. The girls are in various stages of making ready for bed and when I suddenly throw open the door they look up, their faces opening like flowers in surprise. I cross the room swiftly and turn suddenly, the draught from my skirts making the candles dip and dance.

"Anne?" Jane is inquisitive. She follows me to my bed, perches on the mattress and watches as I try to quell the internal storm. In the end, her unspoken questions breach my defences and I burst out, "I could wish that George did not know me so well. Am I a book to be read, or a cypher to be broken? Sometimes, as much as I love him, I wish he would pay more mind to his own affairs."

She says nothing but she doesn't have to. It is fast becoming obvious that George is less than satisfied with his own betrothal, and does all in his power to avoid Jane's company. But she is resolute. She slides from the bed and begins to remove my cap. "Don't worry, Anne. George will have enough to occupy him once we are wed. I will fill his house with children, and he will lack both the time and the energy to pry into your affairs."

She pauses and picks up a brush, begins to smooth the tangles from my hair. "I saw Tom Wyatt watching you dance with Percy. You will have those two fighting like a pair of mastiffs if you are not careful."

"Cocks on the midden, more like," I quip, shrugging off her inference.

We laugh, but at the root of it, she comes close to the mark. Since I arrived at court, and for the first time in my life, I find myself with more suitors than I can handle.

Tom Wyatt is a gentleman and a poet, whom I have known since childhood. Despite his handsome face, he moves me little. Not like Harry.

When I am with Harry Percy, the blood runs faster in my veins and my very soul seems to tremble with delight. It is not something I have felt before … unless I count those fleeting moments I spent today in the presence of the king.

September 1523

I stifle a yawn and surreptitiously stretch my limbs. We have been sewing for hours, making garments for the poor while the queen works on an embroidered shirt for her husband. My eyes are tired, my brain screaming with boredom. It is as dull as ditch water in the queen's apartments. Where I had expected lively court entertainment, I instead find only stifling piety. She prays more often than she eats, although God doesn't show any sign of hearing. Queen Catherine's constant prayers for a child have so far only brought her Mary, a useless, fox-faced girl instead of the son and heir the king craves.

I watch her furrowed face as she pleads with God to bless her barren womb. She might do better to get up off her knees, lighten her expression, and make some attempt to lure the king back into her bed. Why would any man want a woman who behaves more like his mother than his wife? The king might blame her for not providing him with an heir, but that doesn't mean he is prepared to forego the charms of my sister for the queen's chilly embrace. She should fight for him. I would if I were queen.

It is a pity Mary's womb is not as unreceptive as Catherine's, for already my sister's belly swells with a royal bastard, although none acknowledge it as such. Poor Will Carey is paid well to play surrogate parent to the king's baseborn child but everyone, even the queen, knows the truth of it.

Each time Mary places a kerchief to her mouth and turns a little green, Queen Catherine casts an envious eye on her. Poor Mary. She is loath to leave the king, but at the same time longs for his permission to retire from court to await the birth. He is not yet tired of her but she knows that once her condition is plain for all to see, he will drop her like a glowing coal.

Meanwhile, in the queen's airless apartment, we bow our heads over our sewing and try not to notice the sunshine flooding through the window. Catherine sighs again, drops the embroidered sleeve she is working into her lap, and closes her eyes. Above her nose, two lines deepen, and her mouth droops. It is hard to reconcile this woman with the tales of the young Spanish princess who travelled to England to marry Prince Arthur – Henry's long-dead brother. In those tales she was a golden-haired beauty, winning the heart of king, prince and commoner alike. Now she is faded, worn out with fruitless confinements. She opens her eyes and sees me watching her. I slowly turn my eyes back to the seam I am sewing.

"Shall we take a turn about the gardens?"

Six white faces open in delight at the queen's suggestion. The women turn toward her, nodding and chattering in relief. While Jane runs to fetch the queen's wrap, Mary and I begin to tidy away the threads that are scattered across the table.

Queen Catherine's pace is maddeningly slow as we follow her from the privy apartments, through the outer chambers, and along the corridors toward the garden door. When we step outside, I close my eyes and turn my face up to the sun, inhale the glorious air like a felon released from chains.

21

We have been only a few moments in the garden when a footstep falls beside me. Before I look up, I know it is Percy. "I must see you, Anne. I've been loitering all day and don't have much longer …."

I glance at the queen's back as she turns along another path, her ladies following like baby ducks. Percy grabs my wrists and drags me into an arbour. "We must be quick …."

I had expected by his urgency to be swept into his arms but, cautious as always, he merely lifts my hand and kisses my fingers so gently I can scarce feel his breath on them. I know there must be more to a liaison than this. We have been meeting secretly for weeks now, but I am no closer to being kissed.

I step closer, our upper bodies almost touching, and look up at him, silently begging for his kiss. I am desperate to be kissed, to know the strength of his arms. I am trembling within, my limbs weak with longing, but he steps a little back so that I want to scream with frustration.

"Anne, I wish I could make you my wife."

This is more like it. This is what I long to hear. My mouth widens with delight.

"And what is to stop you?"

He slumps onto a grassy seat, keeping mastery over my hand. His head is lowered and I see again the neat cluster of curls at the nape of his neck. I long to throw off this polite restraint and twirl them in my fingers, kiss them, and let my fingers stray beneath the collar of his doublet. He looks up, spoiling my imaginings.

"Everything is against it. My father. The Talbots. Your betrothal to Ormond. Love plays a small part in such a comedy."

Suddenly I wish he were older, strong enough to throw off the restraints upon us. One day he will be powerful enough to stand up to everyone, apart from the king. If he were already made Earl, there would be few who could gainsay us.

"If you truly loved me …."

He puts his finger against my lips, stopping my words, and I resist the urge to bite the tip of it.

"Don't ever say that, Anne. It isn't for lack of love, it is lack of power ... or lack of backbone, if you will."

"If we stood together we could thwart them, and if we pledged ourselves before witnesses, our betrothal would be binding."

I see him hesitate. He wants to believe me. I clasp two of his fingers, rigid in my palm, in an attempt to imbue him with some of my own self-belief.

"Would it? Even before my father and the cardinal? I am not so sure." He stands up again, unwittingly pulling me with him.

"Be sure, Percy," I murmur. I push a little closer, crossing the invisible barrier, my small breasts tight against his chest. I can feel his rapid breath in my face, and with great daring I rise on my toes and let my lips touch his.

"Anne." At last, I am in his arms, his mouth is on mine, the abrasion of his cheek, the strength of his hands, and the heavenly man-smell of him. I am drowning in him.

But, too soon he lets me go, drops his eyes and his arms, leaving my senses swimming. "I – I beg forgiveness, Anne ...."

Now it is my turn to stop his words. I shake my head, finding it hard to speak.

"Don't be sorry, Harry. If you can, come back to court this evening. Look for my brother. I will be with him."

Then I turn and run from him, skimming along the gravel path to catch up with the queen and her ladies. I meekly take my place beside Mary, who looks at me askance. "Straighten your cap, Sister, and try to drive that flush from your cheek or Her Majesty will notice."

I clasp my hands, tuck them up my hanging sleeves, lower my head and meekly follow my queen.

***

I should be in bed but I am alone in an anti-chamber, the sounds of the revel far off. A fire burns in the grate. I hold out my hands to warm them and wonder for the thousandth time when he will come. Footsteps in the corridor make me raise my head, still my breath, listening … but they pass on, male voices fading into silence. I return to my vigil, letting my mind relive those few short moments in the garden this afternoon.

Each time I recall his touch, the heady passion of his welcome declaration, my tummy flips and delicious sensations swamp my limbs. I close my eyes, swaying on my feet as I prolong those feelings, reliving them in my mind again and again. I am so engrossed in the recollection that when at last the door opens and George and Percy join me in the ill-lit room, I am taken by surprise.

From the corner of my eyes, I see George make a graceful knee to me. My eyes are on Harry. He is dressed in blue, embellished with silver thread, his eyes full of the enormity of what lies ahead. An enormity that has turned the brave hero of my imaginings into a fawn afraid of the sound of hounds baying in the wood behind him.

By rights he should approach me, but he hesitates for so long that I am forced to cross the room, offer him my hand. His lips are cold and when he rises, I lead him toward the flames to warm himself.

After a few moments of polite conversation, George, seeing that his presence is unheeded, makes himself scarce although I know he will not go far. I lower my chin, keeping my eye on Percy as I pour and offer him a cup of wine. Our fingers brush as he takes it and places it untasted on the table. "Anne … today in the garden. I shouldn't have …."

"Then, why are you here, My Lord?"

He doesn't notice the teasing laughter in my eyes.

"Why am I here?" His face is white with tension, his lips drawn up and his eyes full of uncertainty that I long to soothe. I reach for him and let my hand travel up his shoulder, as if I am a draper testing the fine nap of his doublet. I part my lips, moisten them with my tongue.

"I wish you would kiss me again."

He doesn't need a second asking and once more I am swamped in his embrace. Just like the last time, my senses whirl, just as I remember it, stealing my breath, making my heart race. This time, with no queen to hinder our passion, we linger a little longer, exploring new territory. His lips stray from my mouth to my neck, his hands wandering to my bodice. This must be how Mary feels when she is with the king. For the first time, I begin to understand her wanton ways and wonder if perhaps I am made of the same stuff.

He pushes me a little away, his face slack, his eyes dark, and begins to fumble at my lacing. It takes all my willpower to stop him. "No, Harry, no. We cannot go further. Not until we are wed."

He groans and turns away, runs a hand through his hair. "But if we consummate our love, our bond will be harder to break."

I step away, smooth my hair and adjust my bodice. "If you take me before we are joined, I jeopardise my soul. If you want me, Harry Percy, you must first confront your father and the cardinal. I will fight them with you, but I intend to enter marriage as a maid. Do you give me your pledge, as a gentleman?"

"Oh, you know I do. You know I do." He tries to take me in his arms again but I hold back, unsure if I can trust myself. Although it kills me to do so, I keep him at arm's length, allowing him one chaste kiss on the cheek before turning back to our wine, which is warming by the hearth.

When the door swings open and George enters with a wide, devilish smile, Harry flushes like a girl. "So ...." George pours himself a glass and saunters across to join us. "I am soon to call you brother." He raises his cup. "Welcome to the family."

While Percy looks anxiously on, George tosses back his wine and slumps onto a chair, his legs sprawling toward the flames. "All you have to do now is convince your father of your suit ... and, of course, the king."

Two days later, I am sent on an errand for the queen. Not quite by accident, I encounter Harry en-route. He lures me into a niche below the stairs where the light of the torches does not quite reach. His lips, when they graze the corner of my mouth, cause the now-familiar stirring, but I clasp his hands and push him from me. I have no wish to be caught like some harlot in the shadows.

"I had not thought to see you here today."

"No, and I had not thought to be here. The cardinal has some unexpected business with the king, and I am not complaining."

"Nor me, My Lord."

He towers over me, his look menacing. On allowing him to sample my lips, I have unleashed a kind of monster. I gasp as he clamps a hand upon my rump, but I grab his wrist none too gently. "Have done, Percy," I hiss. "Now is not the time." I try to disentangle myself from his grasp. There is a kind of madness in him, an insatiable desire to possess me. If circumstances were different I would relish it. For now, however, I must keep this lion caged.

"No, Harry, please, don't …."

"You would do well to listen to her, boy." A quiet, controlled voice demolishes our conversation and Percy lets me go so quickly that I almost fall. We both turn, guilt staining our faces as the cardinal bears down upon us.

"Henry Percy. Mistress Anne." His small eyes dart from Harry to me, and back again. "You will come with me, now. The pair of you."

As if drawn on invisible strings, we follow after him. I hurry forward, try to slow his pace. "My Lord Cardinal, the queen is expecting me in her chambers."

His step does not falter. "If Her Majesty can be made to wait while you dally with my secretary, she can wait a while longer."

Harry, who has turned from a randy lion into a mewling kitten, makes a face at me, begging me not to argue further. When the cardinal turns suddenly up a sweeping stone stairway, we both follow like miscreant children.

Wolsey storms into his chambers and slams a book on the table. His aide quietly gathers his papers and melts into the tapestried walls, as if used to this kind of interruption.

"Well, explain to me, Percy, what you are doing dallying with this girl when you are betrothed to marry Mary Talbot in the spring."

Percy's face turns as red as the cardinal's robes. He flaps his arms helplessly, decides to engage the cardinal's mercy. "My Lord Cardinal, I have known Mistress Talbot for years, I have no wish to wed her, nor she to be joined with me. Anne and I ...."

"Anne and I? Anne and I? There is NO Anne and I. There is only Mary Talbot and Henry Percy – the match is made, all is settled. You will marry in the spring!"

Percy makes a strangled noise in the back of his throat. "But I've promised ...."

"Then you had no right to promise ... and neither did she." He waves his arm rudely in my direction. "She is intended for Ormond. That too is decided. It is not your place to decide."

Not our place to decide? The rage is bubbling inside me. Who is this fat priest to tell me what I should do? What I should feel? With the anger still rising, I take a step forward.

"We are pledged."

The accent I picked up in France becomes more pronounced when I am upset, and even I can hear the foreignness of my voice. He slowly turns his head, fixes me with his liverish eye. "Pledged?"

My knees begin to tremble. I creep closer to Percy, hoping for his support, but he says nothing, his hands hanging limply at his sides. I am forced to speak out to try to save the both of us.

"Yes, My Lord Cardinal, pledged before witnesses to be married."

He turns his face back to Percy. "Is this so?"

Percy stammers and sweats, shifts from foot to foot. His face works as he thinks up a reply, he bites his lips, loosens his collar until, at last, he discovers his courage.

"I love her, My Lord."

"Love? You are Northumberland's heir. It is not your place to love. If you continue with this … this folly, your father will disinherit you. And then what will you do? Feed her on worms?"

I can see Harry's bravado diminishing. He is easily beaten, but there is yet a little fight left in me.

"We had hoped you would speak for us, My Lord Cardinal. My father has much love and respect for you as, I am sure, does the Earl …."

"If Boleyn … if your father wasn't in Europe, he would have spotted this misbegotten attachment and stopped it in the bud the moment it began! Percy here would be safely married and you'd be at Hever nursing a sore arse."

He turns back to Percy. "I will summon your father to court. He will put you straight. Meanwhile, you are not to look upon this … this girl, again."

I turn to Percy, who reaches for my outstretched hands. Wolsey steps between us. "Or touch her!" he roars.

He swivels his head toward me, his eyes full of venom. "Get you to the queen, Mistress, and don't let me see or hear of you in this boy's company again."

"Percy!" I wail as Wolsey edges me toward the door. He won't look at me. His head is lowered, his eyes on the floor, The cardinal stands between us, ready to block any move I may make toward Harry.

My eyes fill and Harry seems to dissolve, his features blurring as if I am looking at him through a rain-washed window. I see him shatter and his cheeks grow moist and, as I look, I realise that he is really just a boy. I try to hang on to the passion we have shared, the love we pledged, but it is shifting into something more resembling pity.

Winter is losing its grip, although the wind still bites. Green shoots are showing in the garden and lamb's tails shiver on the hazel trees. Within the house the servants are throwing wide the casements, shaking out the bedding while Mary huddles before a lazy fire, her belly too swollen with the king's child for her to move around and warm herself. It is mid-morning, and if I do not stir myself Mother will set me some menial task as a way of punishing me further for my wilfulness.

"Why can't you be more obedient, like your sister?" she says. Like my sister? My ears can scarcely credit it. They wish me to be more like Mary, who bears a child that is not her husband's? For all the benefits Mary's immodesty has bestowed upon the family, I shall never be like her.

I tie on my cloak and slide out the kitchen door, duck through the yard where they are unloading apples from a cart. A boy, struggling with a heavy load toward the storeroom, pauses to let me pass. I reward him with a wide smile, thankful I am not born to toil.

In March the garden is bare, tidy. The paths are swept, the shrubs trimmed, burgeoning buds depriving the early bees of nectar. The gardener whips off his straw hat and pulls his forelock. "Fine mornin', Mistress," he mumbles but although I nod my head, I do not tarry. I make for the orchard, duck beneath lichened limbs, through the gate and into the meadow.

Here, the spring grass has not yet re-coloured the faded windswept clumps of last year's uncut hay. Several times I stumble, turning my ankle. I put out a hand to stop myself from falling and my veil slips, my cap askew. I drag it from my head, tuck it up my sleeve and struggle on with the wind in my hair.

Now I am free. I can breathe again.

I have always loved the meadow. When we were children, Mary, George and I would crawl in the long sweet grasses, making hideaways, sharing stories, embarking on adventures. Today, the ghost of our memories follows me, our childhood spirits dancing at the periphery of my vision, laughing like wind in my ears. They were happy times, although we did not know it then. We never know happiness until it is gone.

At the top of the rise I pause beneath a stand of trees and scan the horizon with a hand to my ribs to ease the pain in my side. I am slightly out of breath, the winter has robbed me of my usual vigour. The wind is blowing my hair over my face. I must look like a Gorgon. I put up a hand to trap it, sweep it back.

"I knew you'd come!" A man leaps suddenly from a branch above my head, making me squeal.

"Thomas! What are you doing here? You scared me half to death. Why aren't you at court?"

"The king took pity and sent me home to nurse the megrim I've been suffering."

I cast an eye over his robust frame, his rosy cheeks and fair windswept locks. He is the picture of health.

"You look very well to me."

His eyes are as blue as the king's. They bore into mine, a hint of laughter disguising something deeper.

"Now I have gained the thing I lacked, I am fully restored."

Disconcerted, I turn away and begin to walk along the ridge where the grass is shorter beneath the trees. He follows, a little behind. "I've written a verse." He fumbles beneath his doublet and draws out a parchment. The wind takes it, threatens to whip it from his fingers.

"Another one? I hope it's better than the last."

"You are a cruel mistress." He clears his throat. "It isn't quite right yet, but I have the gist of it. Are you going to listen?"

I slow my pace and, spying a fallen bough, I move toward it, perching on the rough bark while he praises me with gentle speech.

"The flaming sighs that boil within my breast,

Sometime break forth, and they can well declare
The heart's unrest, and how that it doth fare,
The pain thereof, the grief, and all the rest ...."

Poor Tom, he is nothing if not faithful. How can I not be touched by such lines? His face as he reads betrays his sincerity.

At court it is fashionable to love in vain. All the young men strut about the palace with their hearts on their sleeves, weeping and wailing over some married woman or another. But Tom, I fear, is different. He has made the mistake of loving sincerely ... albeit in vain.

His voice trails off and he folds his verse, tucks it back inside his doublet. "Of course, it still needs something. I may rework it ...."

"It's lovely, Tom, but you are your own worst fool. You are not free to love ..." I get up and begin to walk away, but he grabs my wrist.

"Anne ... one kiss and I will be silent. You used to let me kiss you, when we were children."

I look at my feet, smile ruefully. "You never kissed me, Tom. That was Mary."

"Well, it was you I wanted to kiss. I've never wanted anything so much ..."

"Try telling that to your wife."

I have known Thomas Wyatt since childhood. His family seat is but a little way from Hever and they were regular callers in the summer season. He is part of my childhood, part of me, but I cannot love him. Kissing him would be like kissing George. He is too familiar, too close; almost kin.

He is very near now, my forehead level with his jaw. He puts a finger beneath my chin, forces me to look at him. "You are so fair," he whispers, and I open my eyes wide.

"No, I am not. No one has ever called me fair. You are mistaking me again for Mary."

"Well, Mary may be fairer but what you have, Anne, shadows her like the sun outshines a torch. The king can keep Mary; it is you that I want."

It is not easy to rebuff the poetry of his words, but I have to for both our sakes. He has a wife and I, well, I have my virtue and intend to keep it. Since the disaster of loving Harry Percy, I am done with men.

"Just one, Anne, please? Call it payment for the verse."

I consider for a while. I like Tom and hate to be the cause of such hurt. His pursuit of me has been long and as yet, unrewarded.

"Just one little one, then. On the cheek."

I close my eyes and tilt my face. After a moment I sense him coming closer, his head shadowing the glare of the sun. I am swamped with the scent of apples and summertime.

His lips are warm on my skin, he leaves a gossamer touch on my mouth, a kiss so gentle that I relax, enjoying the chaste sensation of his salute. Perhaps I am wrong, it is pleasant to be kissed by Tom after all. Then suddenly, he pulls me closer, driving the breath from my lungs, our bodies tight, his mouth swamping mine as he injects all his passion into me as if he fears it will be his one and only chance.

When he finally lets me go, I stagger, almost fall, and while I gasp for breath and equilibrium, he spins away from me and goes leaping and bounding down the hill toward the house, like a thief who has successfully made off with the crown jewels.

"God bless you, Anne Boleyn," he calls over his shoulder, his jubilance dissipating in the wind. Inwardly I am laughing, refusing to acknowledge the sudden passion that sent the blood surging through my veins as it hasn't done since I was sent down from court.

"You are a rogue and a devil, Thomas Wyatt," I call after him. But as I make the slow journey home his kiss stays with me, and it lingers in my mind for many a day.

When I arrive back at the house, Mother and the servants are all in a scurry and no one notices my muddy skirts and flushed face. Mary's pains have started early and she has been borne to her chamber to await the birth.

In the parlour, William Carey paces the floor until Father, who has little patience with such things, suggests they have the horses saddled and go out on the chase. Once the household women are left alone, we all begin to relax a little, except Mary whose screams echo all around the house and can even be heard in the bailey.

I hover on the landing, watching the women dart in and out with bowls of warm water, piles of linen. When Mother emerges, I step forward and indicate I would join them in the chamber.

"Go to your room, Anne. It is no place for a maid."

I bite my lip and turn away, but do not argue that Jenny, Mary's servant, is a maid also. There are different rules for women like me and the likes of her.

It is no more restful in my chamber. My fire has gone out and, due to the scarcity of staff, I try to light it myself, struggling with the tinder until finally, a tiny flame takes hold. At first it licks at the kindling, a tongue of flame that grows ever more passionate until the wood flickers and is consumed, writhing in the heat. I add more fuel, quenching the blaze, cooling the ardour, grey smoke, the embers simmering. I lie back in a chair and gaze into the hearth, trying to make sense of my fickle feelings. First it is the king, and then it is Percy. Now it is Tom, whom I have known all my life. It is as if my body has a mind of its own. It grows demanding, difficult to manage.

Along the corridor Mary's screams grow frantic, and I kneel at my prie dieu and beg God not to let my sister die. She is young. She may be wicked but she cannot help it; she is kind and soft-hearted, not a bad bone in her body. I am afraid for her, for truly, I have never heard her make such a fuss over anything before. For the first time I begin to suspect the reason why women dread childbirth.

Another anguished scream, followed by scampering footsteps, banging doors. I can bear it no longer and rise from my knees, hurry onto the landing and listen, clutching the carved oak bannister with white fingers. Jenny's head appears from the lower floor; she starts when she sees me waiting in the gloom.

"Oh, Mistress Anne, you made me jump out of my skin." She is carrying a tray of victuals, a jug of ale, a platter of bread and cheese.

"How is Lady Carey? Is her child safe arrived?"

"Oh, yes, Mistress, it's a little lass, the bonniest thing you ever saw. I daresay your lady mother will let you in now her travail is over."

The door opens and Jenny disappears inside. Over her shoulder I see my sister sitting up in bed, looking down like the Madonna at a bundle in her arms. Suddenly, I feel shy of her, as if motherhood has altered her in some way, as if she is no longer my ruddy-cheeked elder sister. I hesitate in the doorway, wondering if I should stay or go, but she looks up and sees me.

"Oh, Anne," she beams. "Do come and look. Isn't she the loveliest thing you ever saw?"

Confident now that maternity hasn't altered her, I approach the bed. She pulls back the blankets and disturbs the child's slumber. The babe pulls a face, screws up her eyes and opens a milky mouth. A tuft of red hair stands up on her crown, her nose a shiny red button as she gnaws hungrily at her own fist. She is like a hobgoblin from a fairy story.

"She is lovely," I lie. "What will you call her?"

"Catherine," Mary replies, "after the queen."

After the queen? I wonder what Queen Catherine will make of that. It is one thing to have your husband producing bastards under your nose, and quite another to be their namesake. Oblivious to the hurt she may cause the queen, whom Mary likes and respects, she croons over her newborn. What would Catherine give to be in her shoes?

Time slides by so slowly, days, weeks of limited company. The proposed match with Ormond is not progressing well, and George and Father have returned to court to try to deal with it, leaving me kicking my heels at Hever with a houseful of women. Mother, usually to be found in her stillroom, is distracted, a faint frown on her forehead, her greying hair tightly concealed beneath her coif. Mary is engrossed in her child and has little time for me. As for Grandmother, she is bedevilled with age, her mind as winsome and as changeable as a wisp of wind. Always cold, she clutches a wrap about her shoulders and complains about the smeeching fire in the parlour.

Her thin, imperious summons eventually brings a houseboy who settles the wood further into the grate and works the bellows to invigorate the flames. "That's better." She coughs weakly and her rheumy eye, following him from the room, catches sight of me standing by the window. "Mary? What are you doing up and about so soon after childbed? Stupid girl, if you were mine I'd have you whipped for the trouble you've brought upon us."

I step forward, lean into the noxious odour of her body. "I am Anne, Grandmother, not Mary. She is still abed where she should be."

She chews her gums, the lines of her face shifting and quilting. "Oh yes, so it is. The plain one, I see that now."

She retreats into her thoughts and for a fleeting second I wonder what old women think about. They have no use for fine gowns or suitors and, due to her lack of teeth, even her dinner has to be ground to a fine mince and can bring her no joy.

Yet Grandmother was once my age, balanced on the cusp of life and full of hopes for the future. How must it feel to be at the end? To retire to bed at night not knowing if your eyes will open on the morrow?

Something shifts on her lap and her dog, Merlin, emerges from the recesses of her many layers. He opens a pink mouth and stretches, his tail beating against her thin chest. As he leaps from her knee, Grandmother grabs but fails to catch him, and he lifts his leg against the hearthstone. She emits another feeble cough. "Take him outside, child, before he fills the room with the stench of his shite."

Grateful for the chance to escape I grab the dog, who snuffles and snorts, trying to lick my face. His breath is ripe with all the things he has eaten that were better left untasted, and I avert my nose and hurry outside.

In the garden, I drop him to the ground. While he leaves a ripe curling turd on the gravel, I begin strolling among the emerging flowers. Spring is here now, warmer days interspersed with sudden unnecessary showers that leave the fresh grown leaves bejewelled with diamond rain drops. From an open casement I hear baby Catherine begin to wail, and shortly afterwards her nursemaid begins to sing gently in an attempt to lull her back to sleep.

Poor Mary is still kept close in her chamber until such time as she can be churched. It seems a shame to be incarcerated indoors on a day like this, when the sun is shining and the world is waking up to the joys of love.

I visit Mary in her chamber every afternoon, and most days I find her deep in the megrims of motherhood. A wet nurse has been engaged and my sister's breasts are tightly bound to stop the milk. Yet she complains of pains, and her nose is red and beginning to peel from too much weeping.

She thought the king would come, just once, to look upon her daughter, but there has been no word from him. Will, who spends his time wearing out his mount by dashing to and fro between court and his wife at Hever, brings royal congratulations but that is all. We all know there will be no acknowledgement. Not now.

"If he just came once, to ensure all is well with us, it would be something." She weeps again, bringing her knees up beneath the bedcovers, curling into her own misery.

I peer at her child and decide she looks a little better today. It is as if one of the maids has smoothed out her wrinkles a little bit. She is more like a human now, and less like a monkey. She peers at me through slit eyes and lets out a bubble of wind, a trickle of milk on her chin. I have yet to see a new born babe I admire. Perhaps it would be better if they came into the world at a few months of age, when they have grown into their skin a little and can look around, pay more attention to what is going on about them.

I turn my attention back to Mary.

"For goodness sake, Mary. Crying will get you nowhere. And suppose the king did decide to call? All he would find is you with your hair like a hayrick and your nose as red the queen's ruby. Look, sit up, dry your eyes, and take a drink. Why not get dressed? There is no need for this … this sloth."

I had hoped to spur her into action, but I fear I make things worse, for Mary opens her mouth, tears spout from her eyes again, and she dives beneath her pillow. Exchanging glances with the nursemaid, I raise my eyes to Heaven and stand up. "I will come back tomorrow. Hopefully you will be recovered by then."

With Mary's megrim taking up most of Mother's time, I am left alone to wander the gardens and meadow. Sometimes of an afternoon I climb the hill and linger beneath the trees at the summit, remembering Tom Wyatt and that kiss. He hasn't been back for more and the memory of our sudden passion is fading, just as my thoughts of Percy have dwindled.

Henry Percy is married now. Safely ensconced on his Northumbrian holdings where no doubt he forgets about me, too. I put a hand to my brow for from my vantage point on the hilltop, I spy a horseman riding toward the house. Squinting, I recognise Father's man, Ned Baines, and guess he brings messages for Mother.

I do not shorten my walk to greet him, for the news he brings will not concern me. Instead, I lift my skirts a little and tiptoe through emerging spring grass with the sun on my back. The only thing missing is good company. If George were here, the silence would be filled with his talk of politics and theology. He is very learned and has never hidden his knowledge from his sisters. Although with Mary it goes in one ear and out the other, I hoard the information so that I can bring it out one day and use his arguments against him. Of all the things and people I miss while rusticated here at Hever, it is George I miss the most.

Suddenly full of restless energy, I begin to skip downhill, startling a huddle of sheep that look up from their grazing and scuttle off en-masse to the far side of the meadow.

When I reach the bottom, I tightly grasp the orchard gate, breathless. My cap is crooked and my veil stained with lichen. It takes a little time for my breath to steady and then I straighten my cap, smooth down my skirts and wipe the worst of the mud from my shoes before hurrying through the garden toward the house.

"Anne, there you are. Where have you been?" Mother doesn't wait for a reply but thrusts a pile of linen into my arms. "Take that upstairs, all the servants are busy. Your father has sent word that he arrives tomorrow in the company of the king."

"The king?" My jaw drops. "But we are not prepared to receive the king."

"You don't have to tell me that, Daughter. Now, take those things to your Father's chamber and then find Jenny, she must assist the other maids to change the draperies in the parlour."

As I climb the stairs in a daze of disbelief, the parlour door opens and four male servants emerge bearing Grandmother aloft in her chair. Sparing nobody's blushes, she gives vent to her indignation at their chosen method of transport. "Am I a sack of coal or a bushel of apples to be carted around so? Put me down, you hedge-born foot-lickers, or I will have you whipped."

One red-faced boy pulls a comical face at me as they pass and I stifle a laugh, ducking my head into the pile of fragrant linen before scurrying about my business.

Jenny is chasing dust from beneath Father's bed, the casements are thrown open and the hearth is being hastily swept. "Mother is looking for you, Jenny," I say, and she turns a red, perspiring face toward me.

"What news, Mistress Anne! The king coming here? Your sister is beside herself and demanding that all her best gowns are made ready." She doesn't add, 'as if there isn't enough to do.' She doesn't need to.

As she runs downstairs to answer my mother's summons, I slip into Mary's chamber. Catherine is blue-faced and bawling in her crib, while her mother sorts through a heap of gowns and sleeves on the bed. "Where is the wet nurse?" I yell above the child's screams. Mary shrugs.

"Helping Mother ... she is sparing none of us the rod. Which sleeves go best with this bodice, Anne, the red or the gold?"

She turns to me, holding a garment beneath her chin, her face pale and anxious. Unable to bear the child's protests any longer, I lean over the cradle and, for the first time, gingerly lift her into my arms. Her head nods against my shoulder, her cries lessening a little.

Hesitantly, I jog her up and down and pat her back, turn my head toward her as I do so, inhaling the scent of her hair. The sweetness of her fragrance is new to me; she is replete with promise, as soft and fragile as a duckling. Something lurches in my breast and I close my eyes and inhale again, holding her a little tighter.

***

The king seems bigger now he is here at Hever, his frame fills the doorways and his laughter echoes to the vaulted ceiling. In bluff good humour that shows us his visit is to be informal, he lays an arm across my father's shoulder and congratulates Will on the birth of his child. He must realise we all know the truth, but if the king demands a game is to be played, who are we to gainsay him? Will is forced to conceal his scowls, and Mary flushes beneath his chilly greeting. The kiss he leaves on the back of her hand is not that of a lover, and when she summons a maid to bring her child, the eye he casts over her is disinterested. He gives a non-committal grunt before turning the subject back to hunting.

Mary cannot hide her stricken face. She shrinks into her chair, and as the conversation moves on to other things, she takes no part in it. She sits silently, her hands clasped in her lap as if all her grief and outrage are contained within them.

Father is boasting of the wild game that runs free across his lands, and King Henry declares that he must revisit very soon to sample it. Although royal visits have been the financial ruin of lesser men than Father, Mother tries not to look dismayed. She nods her head at the steward in a silent summons for refreshment to be brought in from the kitchens.

The cooks serve up fare far superior to what we are usually accustomed and King Henry smacks his lips and compliments Mother on her housewifery, making her blush with pleasure. Afterwards, he pushes his platter away and lays back in Father's favourite chair, his hands on his belly while Mother makes her excuses and disappears into the kitchens to organise supper.

"A turn about the gardens, Your Majesty?" Father asks, and Henry rises to his feet and looks about the chamber. When his eyes settle on Mary, they hesitate for a heartbeat before moving on to me.

"Since Madam Carey is indisposed, perhaps your other daughter will accompany me. Anne, isn't it?"

I leap to my feet, the blood rushing from my head as I open and close my mouth in confusion. I manage to mumble something, aware of the silent stab of Mary's outrage as the king holds out his arm. I smile, slide my fingers into the bend of his elbow, rest my palm on his fine slashed sleeves and allow him to escort me into the garden.

He is so tall that I feel like a child again, my head bobbing below his shoulder as we pass into the pleasance. The sun has blessed us today and still shines high in the sky, the clouds staying away as if unwilling to mar the monarch's pleasures.

"So, Mistress, when are you returning to court?"

I don't know how to reply. I was dragged from Greenwich at the behest of Cardinal Wolsey, and I have no doubt he will not be sorry should I never return.

"That is in my father's hands, Your Majesty. I await his pleasure."

Henry bends over and exclaims at an early rose bud, drawing my attention to the deep pink hue just peeking from its wrapping of green. "Summer is not long away, Mistress. That is good to see. I will speak to Thomas and tell him his daughter is missed. He will have you back in no time. I can't think how you amuse yourself all day, buried here in the country."

I wonder if he has such concerns for Mary who is likewise rusticated but, of course, I would never dare ask it. I pluck a leaf from the honeysuckle and begin to shred it. "Oh, I like to walk when the weather is fine and when it is not, I read. My father has a fine collection of books."

"Books? A little thing like you enjoys reading books? That is a thing I would not credit."

"Yes, Your Majesty, my brother George brings me things to read too, mostly so that he has someone with whom to share his wisdom of theology. I take great delight if I can best him at an argument."

King Henry bellows with laughter, his entire frame shaking with mirth. Then, when he has sobered a little, he wipes a tear from his eye and pats my hand.

"Oh, Mistress Anne, I had not expected that. I can well imagine your brother's discomfort at being beaten by a girl." Laughter is still rumbling around his frame, a dimple winking in his cheek. "I imagined your chatter would be of sleeves and buckles, and here we are on the brink of intellect." He turns and looks down at me, keeping hold of my hand. "I like you, Mistress Anne, and I believe you will amuse the queen too. I will instruct your father to bring you back to court just as soon as he can."

I bob a curtsey. He tucks my hand once more into his elbow and proceeds to conduct me around my own garden, pointing out primroses and a clump of Lent lilies beneath the hedge. As we turn a corner and duck beneath an arbour that will soon be smothered with roses, a movement from above draws my eye. I see my sister reaching out to slam her casement, and hear the tinkle of shattered glass fall to the gravel below.

<u>Autumn 1524</u>

I am glad to be back at court, and after my long, lonely time at Hever the queen's household seems less dull now. I welcome the other women's chatter as we wile away our days, sewing quietly or strolling in the gardens. The summer is just a memory now, although a few late flowers still struggle bravely against the encroaching season.

The gardeners are kept busy gathering up the leaves, the smoke from the bonfires drifting on the chilly breeze. Mary, after leaving her daughter in Hertfordshire, is back at court and in the king's favour once again. I find myself curious about them. I know that Mary is besotted with the king, but I am unsure if the feeling is reciprocated.

I watch from beneath my lashes and note how Mary seems to come alive when the king comes into the queen's apartments. She straightens her spine, her cheeks redden and her eyes brighten, but he gives no sign that he so much as knows my sister's name. But after dark, when she is summoned to his privy chamber, she gladly follows his messenger along the dim corridors to be with him. I am aghast that after the neglect he has so recently shown her, she can find it in herself to be so forgiving.

"What has changed?" I whisper to George when we are alone. "He would barely look at her a few months ago."

George thrusts a hot poker into a jug, making the ale hiss and bubble. He pours it out and hands me a cup. "The king is not alone. Some men are squeamish, prudish even, when it comes to sleeping with mothers, and although he craves a son, I think he draws the line at co-habiting with a woman who still bears the marks of maternity."

I am puzzled. "What marks, George? Does a woman who has borne a child wear some hidden badge denoting her condition? I don't understand."

He laughs and flushes a little at my directness. "There are minor signs on her body and, well, … other small things. But what I really meant was that Henry would not find any allure in a woman who smells of wet linen and is still leeching milk. He is delicate – fastidious even. Now that Mary has left baby Catherine at home, the king is able to see her in a new light."

"If it were me, I'd not be able to forgive him. As soon as her condition began to show he turned as cold as stone and was sniffing around other women, making no effort to hide the fact. And when he came to Hever, he paid her no mind at all!"

George wipes froth from his top lip and examines his sleeve for dampness. "I can imagine. If you were Mary, you'd call Henry to heel and make him do as he is told, king or not."

He is laughing at me. I make a face at my brother for being so rude and turn my attention to my own ale. George shifts to a more comfortable position, tilts his head back in his chair.

"What do you make of the king's decision to make Fitzroi his heir?"

"What do I make of it? You'd do better to ask what the queen makes of it."

Henry Fitzroi is the king's illegitimate son. At just six years old, the boy has been showered with titles and honours. Now, given the royal titles of Duke of Richmond and Somerset, and the offices of High Lord Admiral and Warden-General of the Marches, it looks very much as if Henry's intention is for his bastard son to rule in the place of his legitimate daughter, Mary.

I hardly know what I think, but both the queen and my sister Mary are inwardly furious that he is making such a show of the child they delight to call 'Bessie Blount's Bastard.'

Of course, no matter what traditions they may keep in Spain, the Princess Mary cannot rule in England. When she is married, it will be to a foreign prince who will take precedence over her. The English would never tolerate a foreigner ruling over them. All the same, it must hurt Queen Catherine to see her own legitimate daughter passed over in favour of a bastard, especially when she has lost so many beloved sons. But I can see Henry's point.

The lack of a legitimate son, or even a younger brother, to inherit his throne, could mean the end of his dynasty. What else can he do? The Tudor dynasty was begun such a little time ago, putting an end to years of civil war. Henry will move Heaven and Earth to keep the Plantagenet heirs away from the throne and to do that he needs a lusty male heir. Yet his hopes of begetting one in wedlock are fading fast.

Although nobody voices it, we all know there is little hope that Catherine will now produce another child. The queen is growing elderly, her body thickening and stiffening, her youth draining into the cup of time. Although Henry is discreet, and the queen turns a blind eye to his many mistresses, that doesn't mean she isn't silently suffering. I don't know how she stands it, but like many things, marriage is a mystery to me.

George is looking pensively into the flames, his eyes brooding, his mouth downturned. He looks as if he hasn't had sufficient sleep.

"And how are things with you and Jane?"

My words startle him from his reverie, and I do not fail to notice the dislike that instantly curls his upper lip at the mention of his wife. He fidgets, shrugs his shoulders. "I cannot like her, Anne."

He had not 'liked' her when they were betrothed, but I had hoped marriage might bring a softening. I sigh and reach out to put my cup on the table.

"What is it about the Boleyns? I wish one of us were happily wed. Mary is no more content than you are, and she treats poor Will Carey like a lapdog. And as for me, well, I sometimes wonder if I will ever marry."

George is fumbling with the poker again, and still on his knees shuffles toward me, gropes for my hand. "Of course you will, Anne. You will make the gladdest bride of all."

"Will I?"

"Of course you will, Father will see to it. Is it so hard to remain a maid for a little longer?"

My face is burning but there is no one else to whom I can speak so freely. "Of course it is, George. Everyone around me is indulging in some liaison, legitimate or otherwise. I crave affection and … sometimes I feel like some ugly old maid whom nobody desires enough to marry. Wyatt is my only serious suitor, and he is already wed!"

"That's ridiculous. They all want you. It's just that they know they can't have you."

Before I can stop it a little sob erupts from my throat, surprising even myself. George, still on his knees, grips my hands tighter. "Anne, Anne, my silly Anne. Don't you know how … how … brilliant you are? Give it time. You have lots of time before you. Be patient."

He buries his head in my skirts, his breath warming my lap. I look down at his dark, close clipped hair, a glimpse of scalp beneath. With a deep sigh I lay my hand upon it, promising myself that I will wait. George is right, I am young yet and marriage will come when I least expect it.

***

Before the year is out, Mary confides that she is once more with child. When her condition can be hidden no longer, she is packed off home. While she kisses George and I goodbye, Will Carey waits to assist her into a carriage "Take care, Mary," I say, trying not to notice the tear that escapes her control to trickle down her cheek. "Just think how lovely it will be to see baby Catherine again."

She tries to smile, her mouth quivering as George secures a fur about her knees. Will leaves a brotherly kiss on my cheek. "Take care of her, Will," I murmur, "she may carry your heir this time."

He flushes scarlet, and wary of giving himself away, does not meet my eye. I watch him mount his horse, gather the reins and prepare to ride off. None of us, not even Mary, can be sure if the child is her husband's or the king's, but this time I pray for Will's sake that the child will not be branded with the ruddy complexion of the Tudors.

As they drive away, Mary leans from the window, waving while her husband rides stony-faced beside the carriage. As the dust of the road settles around us, I lay a hand on George's arm and he leads me inside.

It is quiet and rather lonely without Mary. Although I am surrounded by women, there are none whom I can call a real friend. The next day, I trail in the queen's footsteps as we promenade around the garden. If I feel a pang on passing the arbour where Percy and I first kissed, I do not dwell on it but keep my eyes turned firmly away. I might lack a sweetheart, but I realise now that the feelings I once had for Percy were nothing more than calf-love; a practice for the real thing. All the same, I long to be kissed again.

When will I have a real sweetheart?

Tom Wyatt's laughing face swims like a naughty secret in my mind. There is always Tom, of course, who remains as devoted as ever, but I cannot forget his wife. Although she is kept far away from court, she represents an unbreakable barrier. No matter how sweet his poetry, or how ardent his kisses, I will allow myself to be no man's concubine.

And there is the proposed match with James Butler, but I don't believe that will ever come to anything, not the way he and Father are wrangling over who should have the Ormond estate. Father and I want a man who is free to love me. I dream of a handsome knight with a song on his lips and a glint in his eye. Sometimes after supper, as we listen to the songs of the minstrels, I sigh for love but I have to acknowledge, love does not seem to be sighing for want of me.

February 1526

The king no longer comes to the queen's bed. The ladies of her privy chamber report that she prays constantly, begging for a child, for her husband to come to her, for her courses to begin again, but we all know that none of this will ever happen. Even a queen cannot turn back time, and to Henry, who is by several years Catherine's junior, she is an old woman, a dried husk who has no chance of proving fruitful.

"The king says the marriage is cursed," George whispers to me when we are alone. "Yesterday he was quoting Leviticus, saying God wills him to be childless because he married his brother's widow."

In her youth, Catherine was indeed wed to Henry's brother, Arthur, who, had he lived, would have been king in Henry's stead.

"But, George," I say. "Their marriage has been blessed many times. The queen has borne him many children; it is not her fault they did not live. And what about the Princess Mary? Isn't she living proof of God's blessing on the marriage?"

George smiles, folds his arms across his chest, looks at me sideways. "Mary is a nine year old girl and doesn't suit the king's purpose. He wants out of his marriage before it is too late for him to beget a son, but he is very tightly stitched into it. Before they married, Catherine vowed before God that she was a maid and the Pope gave them a dispensation. The marriage is valid, there is nothing the king can do about that. Wolsey is beside himself."

"I don't care about the cardinal but ... poor Catherine ... how dreadful it must be for her."

Daily, I have seen and wondered at the queen's proud, white face, her reddened eyes, and had put it down to the megrims of her age. Now I see perhaps there may be more to it. George interrupts my thoughts.

"I don't think the king has told her that he seeks an annulment …."

"Maybe not, but perhaps she has heard of it. She weeps and prays constantly and has scarcely looked at me … not since …."

"Not since our gracious majesty has been seen so often in your company." George finishes for me, a wicked gleam in his eye.

"Our company, you mean."

It is true, the Boleyns are in high favour of late and the king has been spending much time with us. Yet it is not just me he favours, he honours all of us with his attention. In June last year Father was made Viscount Rochford, and George, after having manors and lands heaped upon him, is now a gentleman of the privy chamber and hopes to rise further.

Henry enjoys our company. We are young and fun-loving, and while devoted to God and the church, not overly pious. Delighted that my brother's sporting talent does not stretch to besting his sovereign, he and his closest friends play tennis and bowls with George daily. As for myself, if I encounter him in the garden and he offers me his arm, I walk with him and make him laugh. He seems to enjoy my wit, my intellect, and often shoots a remark to me at a gathering. Yet he is in no way seeking me for his mistress. I would know if he were. Wouldn't I?

"You are ridiculous, George."

"Oh, yea, I know that, but in this instance I believe I am right. I have seen the king smitten with one sister, and have no doubt that having done with Mary, he now transfers his allegiance to the other."

That is disgusting. I get up and walk to the window, look across the garden where dusk lies like a muffler around the castle. I cast my mind back to my encounters with the king. I close my eyes, remember the last time I was with him; his soft laughter, the light hot touch of his hand on mine. I hear him say my name again, "Anne," caressing the word as if it were a prayer. I wonder what it would be like to be kissed by a man like King Henry.

I snap open my eyes, the blood rushing to my cheeks, and turn back toward the fire. George is watching me over the rim of his wine cup. "Well, Anne, am I right? Has the king been wooing you all along without you even noticing?"

He leans forward, his eyes mocking, his tone teasing. I shake myself, draw my wits together and take a deep breath before taking a stool opposite him at the hearth.

"And what if he has? Many times you have heard me swear that I will not be like Mary. I will be no man's mistress, not even the king's."

***

At Shrovetide there is a great joust, and all the court are present to enjoy the celebrations. The lists are a dangerous playground, and the queen and those about her watch in fascinated terror. The ladies cover their eyes as the massive horses gallop forward, a great clash of wood on metal and a cry of dismay. We all rise as one, the better to see the fallen body that is sprawled in the dust. The horse runs free, reins trailing, tossing his head, snorting. He comes to a halt at the end of the field and begins to crop the grass, shaking his head, harness jingling.

When the crowd parts I see that the man bested is my cousin, Francis Bryan. He is not moving. With great care they remove his helmet and expose his bloody face to the air. We watch in silence as he is borne away on a stretcher and then take our places again, instantly forgetting him and ready to applaud the next contestants. It is an everyday occurrence, something to enhance the tension of the lists.

As they prepare to mount up, gossip trickles back to the royal stand that Francis is badly injured and likely to lose an eye. He is a rogue who has a way with the ladies. "I do hope his looks aren't spoiled," a voice beside me murmurs. I turn to Margery, another cousin, and pull a rueful smile.

49

The babble of chatter rises and falls again when the king appears, the brief hush followed by a great cheer. I raise my kerchief, wave it in the air until the crowds part and I see King Henry before me. A little frisson of excitement passes over my body, leaving me chilled although my cheeks are burning.

He is dressed all in splendour, his helm thrown back. He wears a smile as wide as the ocean, and emblazoned on his chest are the words Declare I Dare Not. As speculation licks like flame through the stand, I know not where to look. It is as close to a declaration as he has come, and although I am innocent in the matter, I glance guiltily at the queen.

Catherine is staring stony-faced across the tiltyard while all around us people whisper behind their hands. Despising their gossiping tongues, I can feel my face growing even hotter. Emulating the queen, I lift my chin and pretend I do not care.

Henry rides up close to the stand and throws up his visor, his eyes flashing blue in the sunshine. I keep my face as non-expressive as the queen's, and imagine nothing is amiss. Why should anyone, let alone Queen Catherine, believe that his brazen declaration is for me?

"Wish me luck, ladies," he calls. Obediently we all clap, flutter our kerchiefs and titter behind our hands. He is like a big baby, craving the adoration of everyone around him, but he is the king, how can we not adore him?

I watch him manoeuvre his caparisoned destrier into position, taking his stand at the tilt barrier. Loving and hating him at the same time, I watch our prince of chivalry hoist a lance the size of a young tree beneath his arm and prepare to ride against his foe.

Charles Brandon, similarly equipped at the opposite end of the yard, holds his horse in check until the signal to ride is given. Then they are away, the company holds their breath, and the huge pounding hooves pummel the ground. I can feel their echo in my heart.

Time seems to slow. I watch in a kind of delighted horror. Henry is covered head to toe in white armour; he could be anyone but I know it is he and he is in danger, just as he is every time he takes the field. As they come together and the clash is imminent, I cover my eyes and pray, whispering beneath my breath for him to triumph. I do not look up again until my ears are beset by a tremendous roar and the crowd erupts into celebration. All around me the ladies are clapping, smiling and laughing in relief ... all except the queen who just looks tired ... and rather bored at her husband's playacting.

Afterwards, although we are all tired out by a day spent outdoors we assemble in the great hall, waiting for the evening entertainments to begin. Giant shadows cast by the mammoth fire joust on the walls, dipping and dancing with those cast by the torches. The hubbub of voices and unsuppressed excitement lifts my spirits, the high-pitched tinkling laughter of the women echoed by the deeper rumble of the men.

Up in the gallery the minstrels are making discord, tuning their instruments in readiness for the king's enjoyment. I turn to speak to George as a serving girl passes with a tray of refreshments. George grabs her elbow and relieves her of a cup, and although she is far beneath him in status, she smirks and simpers beneath his smouldering appraisal. I scowl at him but my displeasure goes unnoticed when a clarion of trumpets announces a royal arrival.

Everyone sinks to the floor in a back breaking bow. My skirts pool around me as I crouch down to honour the queen passing among us to take her place on the dais. The women fuss around her, arranging her skirts, fetching a low stool for her feet. Once she is settled, she flicks her hand, freeing us to resume our conversation. Beside me, my cousin Margery is flirting with George, as she does with any man under the age of fifty. George leans on a carved screen, his eyes fixed on her generous bosom, and proceeds to see how far he can lead her before she remembers they are close cousins. We are of the Howard line and as such are related to everyone. There are too many cousins at court, our tangled bloodlines often tripping the unwary.

I clutch a cup of wine and let my eyes play across the company, noting who wears a new gown and who is playing cuckold to whom. Of course, the gossip is all of the king's secret matter, but none dare speak of it here. In the presence of the royal couple we all pretend ignorance; it is just another of the king's games but this time none of us are certain of the rules, not even Henry.

Another clarion announces the arrival of the king, and all except the queen sink to our knees again. He pauses at the door and I turn my head slightly that I might watch him enter, full of bonhomie, a beam slashed across his ruddy face, his arm thrown around the neck of Henry Norris. As he moves on I lower my eyes again, bow my head, the back of my neck aching as I watch the royal feet approach. To my surprise they falter before me and I find myself staring with some confusion at the king's square-toed shoes. They are made of the softest kid and are encrusted with pearls. Eventually, realising he is waiting, I lift my head, my cheeks hot with embarrassment.

The king and Norris are smiling down upon me. Blushing like a fool, I keep my chin tucked to my chest as graciously as I know how. The king clears his throat and shuffles his feet until I look up at him. He doesn't quite meet my eye as he utters my name, his voice loud in the silent room. "Mistress Anne," he says, and I am forced to reply.

"Your Majesty." I curtsey again, try to get closer to the floor, but I am as low as I can go. My bodice is digging deep into my flesh but I keep my eyes on his feet and sigh a great sigh of relief when, eventually, he passes on.

We all stand. My heart is thumping in my chest and I know my cheeks are scarlet. A murmur surges around the room. Everyone is staring at me. Whispering, insinuating, and speculating. I feel hot breath on my neck and realise, with no little relief, that George is standing close behind me.

"Well, well, Sister," he whispers. "Acknowledged by the king before the court. Whatever next?"

Across the room my father is standing in the shadows, conversing with my uncle, Norfolk. He raises his cup and smiles, as if I have done something favourable, while close beside him, Henry's sister, Mary, and her husband, Charles Brandon, do not hide their dislike.

Cold floods through my body, followed by an internal heat; sweat breaks out on my brow. My father and uncle will make me replace Mary if they can. I clench my fists, trying to resist the urge to run from the room, but before I can move, there is a flurry of activity at the dais.

Catherine and her ladies are on the move and as they sweep past in a flotilla of disapproval the music dwindles away, the conversation ceases abruptly and everyone drops hastily to their knees again. Taken unawares, I do not have time to respond, and the queen passes me by without acknowledgement. I look across to Henry who is seated on his throne, looking at me standing alone with the royal court spread at my feet in a carpet of stolen obeisance.

He gets up and comes toward me. I do not move but my heart is banging like a drum. As he draws near I sink into a curtsey, but before I am half way down, he seizes my elbow and stops me. "Mistress Anne," he says. "You cannot spend half your life on your knees. I am come to ask you to accompany me in the dance."

He makes an elegant knee, holds out his arm, and what else can I do? I can hardly refuse. The jewels on his sleeve are sharp beneath my cold fingers as I follow him onto the floor where they are forming for the first dance.

Although I have spoken to and walked with the king many times, there is something different about dancing with him in public; the implied passion of the storytelling feels too intimate for safety. He seems bigger now. He dwarfs me and if I look straight ahead I can see nothing but a breadth of jewel-encrusted doublet. And so I keep my head turned a little to the right to where, beyond the dance floor, the company are putting their heads together, whispering behind their hands. They think I am his mistress. The shame swamps me but I lift my chin higher, swallow the dread, and pretending to be unconcerned, I paste on a smile and concentrate on the steps.

Henry's body is anointed with rosewater, his breath tinged with spiced wine. He plays the part of a pivot in the wheel I tread around him, my fingers quivering in his palm.

Each time I chance to raise my eyes they are met by his laughing blue ones, his small mouth is a slash of red in his happy flushed face. Even were he not my king he would be handsome, and I am overwhelmed by such public notice. More to the point, the pressure of his fingers and the light touch of his hand on my waist, is affecting my feet which I must not allow to falter as we follow the prescribed movements of the dance.

Everyone in the hall is watching us, speaking in whispers, nodding knowingly as they witness another Boleyn girl fall beneath her monarch's unassailable charm. I smile brazenly as if I do not care but, indeed, my knees are trembling and my mouth is quite dry. When the dance brings us so near we almost touch, I glance up at him again and find that he is looking down at me, our faces close, our breath mingling, his lips almost kissing. My breath falters, my eyelids begin to flutter.

But the music takes him from me and for a time he is forced away from me to weave among other women. I ignore my partner to watch him laughing and flirting with others before, his face growing serious, the steps lead him back to me and I am lost again.

Everyone is wilting from the heat and exhaustion of the dancing. Servants have begun to clear away the remnant of the feast, when a page approaches and whispers in my ear. With great stealth I am ushered along dim-lit corridors, through chamber after chamber, deeper into the king's private world where I have never been before.

He is not alone and I wait with banging heart while his companions, Henry Norris, Charles Brandon, and others melt away into an outer chamber. Among them I spy Will Carey who, as he closes the door, shoots me a look of compassion before leaving me with the king. For the first time, the king and I are completely alone and I am bereft of words, my wits fled. My lips are dry, my breath unstable in my throat. Feigning nonchalance, I go boldly forward to meet him.

He has thrown off his doublet and the light of the fire plays on his snow-white shirt sleeves. When he looks up and sees me, his smile is gentle, his soft ruddy hair glowing in the candlelight.

"Anne," he says, rising from his chair and drawing me closer to the warmth. I am so nervous that my palms are perspiring, but he tucks my hand into his elbow. "Come, take a cup of wine with me."

I don't know what to say. How is it that when I meet with the king in public, I am full of wit and a host of ready answers runs tripping from my tongue but now, in the privacy of his closet, I am quite dumb? "You make a fine partner in the dance, Anne. I don't know when I have enjoyed it quite so much. You are so light of foot."

"Your Grace is kind." I keep my eyes lowered, too terrified to look at him.

"And are you kind, Mistress Anne?" His tone is low, as if he fears my answer. The inference of his words brings my chin up, our eyes meeting for the first time since I entered his private chamber.

"I-I hope so, Your Majesty." I am stuttering like a fool. I usually despise those who hesitate over their words.

"When we are alone, you may call me Henry."

He puts down his cup and picks up my hand, examining it, turning it this way and that, looking at my nails, the shape of my fingers. "Such pretty hands," he murmurs, lifting it to his lips.

At the touch of his lips I give a little gasp. Just as smartly as one of the royal Fools, my heart turns a somersault.

I cannot snatch my hand away.

I cannot move.

I am ruled by the red-hot emotion of the moment. He is the king. I cannot stop him. He pushes back my sleeve, his lips working their way along my arm, coming to a stop at my inner elbow. I feel his tongue on the place where my heart's blood runs closest to the surface, and I swallowing deeply, tilt back my head and close my eyes.

"It is lonely to be a king." He sounds like a little boy and I straighten my head and look down at him, seeing him differently. Bareheaded in the light of the fire, without his sumptuous tunic to remind me who he is, he is a little less terrifying, a little less king-like. I let out a long breath, unaware before now that I was holding it.

"I can be a friend to you, Your Majesty. I can dance with you, comfort you when you need me. I can warm your days but, Your Majesty, I can never warm your nights. Although the honour you do me is very great, I am not like my sister Mary, and can be no man's mistress …"

He looks up, his hair dishevelled, his eyes belying my words. "Not even mine?"

"Not even yours."

I withdraw my hand.

"Not even one kiss?" he says, unknowingly echoing the words of Thomas Wyatt.

He stands before me, as tall as a young oak tree, and there is nothing I can do to stop it. The kiss is inevitable.

A moment's hesitation before I am swamped in his arms; lost in the deep, wide chasm of his embrace. His mouth is hot, his tongue searching and desperate, his hands roaming over my body, pulling me deeper into him, awakening all the longings that I have fought so hard for so long. The hard nub of his codpiece is digging into my belly and I am foundering in a wild oceanic storm. I don't want it to stop. I never want him to stop.

PART TWO
MISTRESS

I plead sickness and beg permission from the queen to escape home to Hever. She is glad to be rid of me and I am grateful for the fresh air, the tranquillity of the countryside in which to breathe properly and, hopefully, clear my head. If I stay at court I will be lost, and I do not want to go the way of my sister. All my life I have dreamed of a husband and a home, a litter of small children – I have no wish to be any man's property but my husband's, and I would go to him a maid, not sullied by the whims of the king.

My mother has no patience with me. She harangues me for my niceties. "You cannot refuse a king," she says, "not if you care one jot about your family. Think what it would mean for us, and for George. Think what it would mean for your children …"

I lose my temper. "And what would it do for my children? What has he ever done for Mary's? Neither she nor Will know who their children should call 'Father.' It is madness. I intend to enter my marriage as a maid and neither you, nor Father, nor the king will prevent that."

Her face retreats into puckered resentful lines as she begins to shred her kerchief in her lap. By the hearth, Grandmother is snoring gently, oblivious to my predicament. I could wish I were an old woman, freed from the betrayals of my own body, my own heart. Mother will not let it rest. "What if the king should follow you here? You will not refuse to see him?"

I sigh and look from the window where a sprightly breeze is making the catkins dance. "Tell him I am sick, that should cool his ardour."

Henry has a great fear of infection and makes himself scarce at the least sign of plague.

"Many parents would shut you in your chamber until you relent."

"Many parents wouldn't try to coerce their daughter into whoredom."

"Anne, don't dare speak to me so!"

I spring up from my seat. "Then don't treat me so. I have told you that my conscience will not allow me to bed a man who is not my husband. You should not chide me for that. It is God's teaching."

She gentles. "Anne, how can you not love him?"

"Mother! I do love him. He is my king, he is a man above all others, but he is not free to love me. What he offers me is … is specious – I cannot give him what he wants."

She gives up for the time being and retreats into her stillroom, where I hear her crashing bottles and slamming doors. Thereafter I stay wisely close to my grandmother, safe in the knowledge that her noxious fumes will keep all but the most determined of bullies at bay.

And then the letters start arriving. Beautiful letters penned in Henry's own hand. Knowing how he hates to pick up a pen, preferring to dictate to others, this says almost as much for his regard for me as the words themselves.

He is missing me. It is evident in every ardent sentence, every passionate request for my return. He could, of course, order me back to court, but instead he requests it quite gently, and enclosed in each missive is a gift. Sometimes he sends me a purse, sometimes a jewel. Once, knowing my taste for it, a fresh slaughtered hind is delivered for my table, killed by the king. Sometimes he sends a verse, penned by his own lovesick hand.

O, my heart!
And O, my heart,
It is so sore!

Since I must needs from my Love depart;
And know no cause wherefore!

Finding me reading it in the garden, George slumps
onto the grass beside me and snatches it from my hand. After
one scan of the page he lets out a loud guffaw. I hide my
mouth behind my fingers. It is cruel of us to laugh but the
king is not greatly skilled at poetry, and spoiled as I am by
Wyatt's pretty lines, I cannot help but smile at Henry's.

"At least the sentiment is there," I say, snatching the
paper back again and tucking it within my bodice. George
lies back in the long grass, plucks a stalk and puts it in his
mouth like a peasant.

"What is going to happen, Anne? How long do you
think you can resist him? You make trouble at court, you
know, whether you are there are not."

"How so?"

George rolls onto his side, props his head on his hand
and watches my reaction to his words. "The king continues
to seek his divorce. Wolsey is tearing out his hair looking for
a solution, and the queen simmers with resentment ..."

"And who can blame her? She has been legally wed to
him for years and now he is tired of her, expects her to retire
gratefully."

"And Wyatt too makes trouble."

"Tom makes trouble? In what way?"

"He glowers every time the king mentions your name,
and that is often. Henry suspects something between you,
and each time Wyatt is absent from court, he enquires as to
his whereabouts, as if he is afraid it is your bed he is keeping
warm."

I frown, shake my head. "Why would the king think a
thing like that?"

"Tom has made no secret of his affection for you,
Anne. The pretty rhymes he pens are circulated at court. Half
the queen's ladies are in love with him, yet it is you he
desires. At least he and the king have that much in common.
When did you last see Tom?"

59

I cast my mind back a few weeks, lower my gaze and answer him quietly. "He rode over with some strawberries in July."

"Ha! I knew it. The sly fox. Did he try to make love to you?"

"He may have, but I assure you, he made no headway."

This last is a falsehood. I had allowed him one kiss, more to test if it had the same effect upon me as Henry's than anything else. It was pleasant, lingering and sensuous, but there was none of the thrilling, alarming sensations I had felt with the king. Poor Tom, I'd give so much to make a man like him happy.

I am in limbo, a strange phantom-like existence that has no direction, no goals. I know not where I am going, or how I am going to get there, but I am waiting for something. I tell myself that when it happens, I will know. The moment it arrives I will recognise the end of limbo and the beginning of my life.

And then, quite suddenly, the moment does arrive. The next time I raise my head and look out across the gardens, I see Henry riding along the road toward me.

Attended only by Brandon and Norris, the king's horse clatters into the bailey. Oblivious to the confusion that his unannounced arrival has inflicted upon our house, he tosses the reins to a groom and jumps from the saddle. I sink to my knees at his approach, feeling the warmth of his hand like a blessing on my head.

"None of that, none of that." He raises me up, smiles into my eyes, and my heart soars like a falcon.

"You are well, Your Majesty?"

"I am now." He beams about the courtyard as we pass through it, and doesn't notice the household falling like skittles as their king passes so unexpectedly among them.

"My father is from home, as you know, and I fear you find us in much disarray."

"No matter, no matter. A jug of ale is all I require, and then you can show me those roses of yours again. Did you get my letters?"

"Every one of them, Your Majesty."

"Enough of that, Anne. What happened to 'Henry?' Call me Henry."

"Very well ... Henry." I feel a laugh fermenting; soon it will erupt, burst from my throat in a fountain of joy. I usher him into the parlour and summon refreshment. Shortly afterwards a red-faced girl arrives, and with trembling hands places a tray on the table. She curtsies clumsily and at a jerk of my head hurries from the room. I begin to pour but stop when Henry steps up behind me, slides his hands around my waist, his breath warm on my neck. "Now we are alone, sweetheart ..."

I spin away from him, laughing. "But we are not alone, My Lord." I indicate Grandmother who is, as usual, asleep at the fireside. Henry raises his eyebrows, a comical furrow on his brow.

"Who in God's name is that?"

"My Grandmother. I trust a deaf, half-blind crone is chaperone enough."

"Will we wake her?"

"I doubt an earthquake would do that."

"Then come here, and kiss your king."

"I thought you said I should think of you as Henry."

I dip my face to my cup, taste sweet wine, looking at his over the rim as I do so. When I do not move, he comes closer. "Fie, you are a troublesome wench." He takes my cup, puts it on the table with a bang, and draws me into his body.

Today, after his ride, the sweet scent of his perfume is overlaid with horse and sweat, a male tang that torments my senses. I lay my head on his chest, his doublet as soft as a kitten on my cheek. "Oh Henry ..." I sigh, closing my eyes and enjoying the solidity of him.

"Did you miss me?"

I make no answer but nod my head while we sway tranquilly back and forth, half-embracing, half-dancing. "Then, will you not kiss me? I have waited so long."

Keeping my eyes closed I raise my face to his, sense his closeness, his breath on my cheek as, very softly, his lips touch mine.

Even if I am entertaining the king of England in my workaday gown, at least the gardens at Hever are looking their best. He leads me along the paths where the scent of roses fills the air, and daisies sprawl across the gravel. Our footsteps make a soft crunching sound, my skirts swishing along behind. As we walk he talks of his past; tales of his mother, the gentle queen of York, and the strict regime imposed upon him by his father, the first Henry Tudor.

I picture my Henry as a boy, round-faced and flushed from play, inwardly rebelling against too much time in the schoolroom and not enough in the tiltyard. "He would not let me joust," Henry exclaims in remembered outrage. "He wanted me in the schoolroom where there was no danger of me outshining my brother."

"Prince Arthur? What was he like?" I accept his offering of a daisy and tuck it into my bosom.

"According to my father and our tutor, Arthur was the perfect prince. I am a poor substitute."

I can see the old sibling rivalry still bites deep. Henry's brow is lowered, his mouth tight as he continues. "But I could always best him on horseback, or in the dance. It's a shame Father can't see me now, that would make him eat his words. Never, in all my youth, did I hear a single word of praise from his lips …"

"But I am sure your mother was different?"

"Oh yes. She was as different from my father as chalk is from cheese. She had an inbred kindness … empathy. Although I tried to hide it, she always knew when I was hurting. She would appear at my side, take my hand in hers and suddenly, the world would be less bleak. She never said it but I knew she preferred me to Arthur. I am like Edward, you know, her father, and Arthur was just like the king … my father, I mean. After my brother died, quickly followed by Mother, I was left alone with him, the old king. He wanted Kate for himself, you know, but I got …"

"Kate?" For a moment I do not know who he means, but as the colour rushes into his cheeks and he begins to bluster an explanation, I realise that he means Queen Catherine, the woman from whom he longs to be free. For a moment he had forgotten the rancour he feels for her, had forgotten the queen is now old. By remembering the old days he recalls her as she was; young again, young and pretty, and apparently fertile. I draw my hand away and walk on without him, surprised by the injury his words have inflicted.

"Anne." He catches up with me, snatches at my hand. "I wanted to talk to you about Catherine."

"What about her?" I cannot inject any warmth into my voice and I keep my eyes on the flowers behind him.

"You know I seek a divorce?"

I nod, still refusing to look at him.

"I never visit her now, especially at night, and have not done so for a long time."

Feeling the warmth in my cheeks, I shrug my shoulders, as if it is of no moment to me.

"Anne." He draws me into the arbour and sits down, pulls me beside him, our knees touching, hands clasped. If I didn't know any better I would think he was ready to propose. "If you will be my mistress, I swear to forsake all others. You would be my official mistress, I would give you honours, make you wealthy in your own right."

I snatch away my hand, wounded beyond measure by the inference. "Like a court official, Your Majesty? Would I have apartments next to Wolsey's? Where his sign would read 'The King's Lackey', would there be one above my door with the words 'The King's Whore – Keep Out'?"

"Anne!" He is astounded for no one has ever dared speak to him like this before, but I am trembling with rage.

"Just what do you think I am, Henry? How can you claim to love me when you hurt me so very much?"

Tears wash down my face. I fumble for my kerchief and see that it has mud on it where I wiped my dirty fingers this morning. To my relief, he hands me his own. It is edged with the finest lace and I recognise the embroidery as Queen Catherine's own. I put it to my nose and blow hard, filling it with snot. Then I turn to him.

"Henry, if I am not good enough to be your wife, and it is not meet that I become your mistress, then I fear we go no further. I know from experience what becomes of your cast-off women, and I must avoid that fate at all costs. Perhaps from now on we should only meet as friends."

He snatches back his filthy kerchief and thrusts it into his doublet. "Friends be damned!" he cries, leaping to his feet. "If I can have you no other way, then marry you I will and may the rest of the world go to hell."

"Don't be silly. How can that ever be?" I sniff, blink away more tears and look up at him, silhouetted against the sky, the biggest, bravest prince in Christendom.

"We must work on it, Sweetheart. I will win Wolsey over, get him to speak to the cardinals. The Pope must be persuaded that my marriage to Kate is sinful, unlawful. I must be free, Anne, I must be free to be with you and get myself an heir."

He sits down again and draws me onto his lap. "How will you like that, Sweetheart? Will you make a prince with me?"

My breath catches in my throat and I blink away more tears, half-laughing, half-crying. "Oh yes, Henry. Yes, yes, I will."

Swamped by his arms, his mouth clamped upon my throat, I am faced with the task of keeping his courtship within modest bounds. He hoists me higher on his lap, knocking off my cap, and I let out a shriek. "What are you doing?"

He looks up from my bosom, his mouth wet with kisses, and his face red with desire. "I thought we could make a start," he laughs, and I throw back my head, bursting with happiness. I twine my arms around his neck.

"Not yet, my love," I cry, "but soon, very soon we will be married and then, I swear, I will fill your royal nursery with sons."

Early Summer - 1528

"I am not sure how much more I can take." I burst unceremoniously into the room, waking George who has fallen asleep by the fire. He stretches his arms, uncrosses his legs, and still yawning, mocks the abruptness of my greeting. "Good morrow, Brother. How goes your day?"

I plump into a seat and scowl at him. Suddenly realising I am in earnest, he sits up and shakes the sleep from his weary head. "What is it now? You haven't fallen foul of the king, have you?"

"Of course not," I snap, maintaining my pout. "The king is fine. It is the rest of the court that is the problem. They hate me and do everything they can to drive a wedge between Henry and I. I know Catherine is behind it …"

"Well, you didn't expect her to just roll over, did you? Run off to a nunnery like a tame pup? She will fight you, Anne, with every inch of her soul."

He throws a log on the fire and puts a hand to his belly, which is rumbling loudly. "What time is supper? I am starving."

I shrug. "I am eating with Henry in his privy chamber."

"Alone?"

"Yes, alone. If I can free him from his council. They give him no rest. George, I just know Wolsey isn't doing all he could to secure the annulment. He hates me. I know it, ever since he …"

George stands up, still stretching and yawning. "Anne, there are many names I might be tempted to call Wolsey, but I would never label him a fool. He knows that to keep the king's favour he must do as the king wishes. I am sure he is doing all he can. It isn't a simple matter. There is Spain to consider, and Rome is in no position to act against the Emperor's interest. You must be patient."

"You don't know what it's like," I whisper, lowering my head so he will not see my ready tears.

"No," he says. "I don't suppose I do, but I do know what it's like to be wed to a woman who hates me, who accuses me of betraying her with every female in court."

Distracted momentarily from my own problems I look up at him, note his bloodshot eyes, his dishevelled clothing. The constant harping of his unhappy wife is driving him further away from her, and everyone whispers that he keeps undesirable company. Jane is always complaining of him not returning to their chambers until the early hours. I wonder that she wants him home at all when all she does is berate him once he is there. "And do you?"

"Do I what?"

"Sleep with other women."

He flushes and shrugs, his eyes focussed on the wall behind me. "Sometimes. I am a man, Anne, and I get no such comfort at home."

I lay back in my chair, fiddle with my girdle chain. It is a fine one, made of pearls and rubies, it was gifted to me by the king. It makes a satisfying sound as I pass it from hand to hand.

"Jane needs a child, George. Motherhood will soothe and gentle her. You will not get a child on her by sowing your oats all over the court."

"I know."

He scowls into the flames as we sit in silence, listening to the crackling flames devouring the fresh fuel. Beneath it, the embers of the spent logs are glowing red and black. It is like looking into the mouth of hell. I remember how, as a child, I would stare into the fire and imagine monsters and demons and fill myself so full of fear that I could not sleep at night. When they heard me crying, Mary and George would creep to my bed to comfort me.

But that was long ago. I could do with such comfort now, but George has his own problems and Mary is still in the country, raising the children of the man I will shortly wed. She must have heard by now of the king's intention and I wonder what she thinks of me. I fear that after what I have done, she will shun me and I will have lost a friend.

The evenings I spend alone with Henry are always difficult, for although I want to keep his love, I must also ensure our relationship remains chaste. Once he has had me, my enemies will say I am no better than a whore, no better than Mary whom I have scorned for loving him.

But when Henry kisses me, I burn for him, and in burning, I understand my sister better now. Yet when all is said and done, Henry is squeamish when it comes to women, and I must be careful not to offend his sense of propriety. I must not give my need for him too much rein. He may desire to know me carnally, but should he suspect that my own craving matches his, he will cease to love me and think me immoral. Henry will never wed a whore; he likes his women innocent, untouched. As long as he knows me to be unsullied, the gossips can whisper as much as they like.

So, when his kisses begin to burn me up inside, I pull away and pretend to be overwhelmed, confounded by the insistence of his passion. Yet all the time I am screaming internally for him to take me, and let the consequences go hang.

Other men avoid me now. They are pleasant, polite, but none seek to woo me, for who would dare pay court to Henry's intended queen? I am even denied the honeyed words of Tom Wyatt, whose devotion has warmed me for so many years. Henry, losing no time in ridding himself of a rival, has sent him on a mission overseas, away from court, away from temptation, depriving me of another friend.

Henry sends his servants away, picks up his lute and begins to play one of his latest compositions. His fingers skim across the strings, his face flushed more from a surfeit of food than any embarrassment at the lyrics. I paste a look of contentment on my face and sway my head gently to the music. As the final note dwindles, I sit up straight and clap my hands enthusiastically. "Wonderful, Henry. Is it about me?"

He puts down his instrument, laughing gently. "Of course, who else should it be about?" He opens his mouth to continue when someone scratches at the door. A shame-faced page enters to tell us that Cardinal Wolsey is without and craves a word with the king.

Henry throws me an apologetic smile. By the time Wolsey enters a few moments later, I have already withdrawn to a corner where I tinkle the strings of Henry's lute as if the presence of a cardinal is unworthy of my notice.

There is something about Wolsey that brings out the worst in me. Some inner demon prompts me to don my haughtiest, most disdainful manner. George tells me I am foolish to act so in the cardinal's presence, for Wolsey's power almost matches that of the king. Yet there is one part of me that cannot forget the cruel manner in which he wrenched Percy and I apart.

Even though I have come to realise that what I felt for Percy was nothing more than youthful folly, I resent the inference that I was not good enough for the son of an earl. I am good enough for a king, for Heaven's sake, and one day, I swear, I shall enjoy watching Wolsey eat his words.

"Thomas!" Henry gets up, and flinging an arm about Wolsey's shoulder, ushers him toward the fire. "What news, Tom? What did the Cardinals say?" He slops some wine into a cup and hands it to Wolsey, while I try to look as if I am not hanging onto his every word.

"Your Majesty, I managed to persuade His Holiness that the case can be heard here in England. He is sending a legate without delay and he and I will officiate. So, between us we should have the result you desire within a few months."

His eyes sweep the chamber, his smile fading when he notices me waiting in the shadows. He makes a small bow, my nebulous status making him uncertain how to greet me. The king's mistress demands no special etiquette, but the king's future wife? A future queen? That is something different. Both he and I know that one day soon he will greet me on his knees.

"Did you hear that, Sweetheart? Wolsey promises it shall be a matter of months!"

"I will do my best, Your Majesty." Wolsey is as red as his robes, his laugh nervous. He fumbles at his cassock. "Your Majesty, there are other matters I need to discuss with you, erm … in private."

Henry, pleased with the news from Rome, slaps him on the back. "Of course, Thomas, of course, but the morning will suit us better."

Now it is Henry who is blushing, embarrassed at the unintended inference of his words. Taking pity on him, I put down the lute and glide to his side, place one hand on the king's sleeve and hold out the other for Wolsey's salute. "Good night, Wolsey, the king and I appreciate your efforts on our behalf very much."

Dismissed by the king's concubine, Wolsey's colour increases, but there is nothing he can do except bend before me to leave his salute upon the back of my hand.

"My Lady," he murmurs before turning to Henry. "Your Majesty." And he takes his leave, disempowered by a slip of a girl … at least for the moment.

My satisfaction does not last long. All the next morning Henry is closeted with the cardinal, while I am left to wander the palace corridors at a loose end, anxious to know what the next step in the king's Great Matter will be. When at last the door to the privy chamber opens, and Wolsey hurries away bent upon the king's business, I slip inside. "Henry, what took so long? I thought your council would never end."

He turns to face me and I notice he looks a little pale. "Shall we take a turn about the gardens?" I ask, anxious that he should have some fresh air, but he holds out his hand.

"No, Anne. Come here. I must talk with you. Come, sit here, on my knee."

I rush to his side, perch upon his lap, glad to feel his big hands slide about my waist, his kiss upon my cheek.

He speaks hesitantly, thinking over his words before uttering them, but five minutes have not passed before I leap from his embrace, pulling my hand away from his. "Go back to Hever? Are you mad? Why should I do that? I will lose what little status I have managed to gain in your court. You mean to reinstate Catherine, don't you? Wolsey has persuaded you!"

"No, no. Don't be foolish. Wolsey thinks ..."

"I don't care what Wolsey thinks," I sob, "and you ... you should care what I think, not some fat old priest."

Henry is shocked. He looks about him as if he fears Heavenly forces will strike me dead. His lips narrow, he tucks his chin into his neck, his blue eyes piercing and severe. He clears his throat. "I invited the cardinal to speak his mind. He is my chief advisor and as such is at liberty to do so. Anne, what he says makes a lot of sense. He says it will not sit well with the Pope or the cardinals if I am seen to be estranged from Catherine. He says I must at least be seen to be doing my best to be a faithful spouse."

"So you are going back to Catherine! I can't believe you would do this to me ... after all I have given up for you!"

"I am not going back to her. I am just putting distance between you and I, for the sake of our future, and it breaks my heart to do so."

He does indeed look distraught. There are two straight lines above the bridge of his nose which I have learned only become visible at times of great stress.

"How long for? Won't I see you at all?"

He crosses the room and takes my hands in his. "Not for long, Anne. I couldn't bear it if it were long. As soon as the annulment comes through I shall summon you back to my side – as my betrothed."

That sounds a little better and I draw some comfort from his reluctance to be parted from me. "I couldn't bear to be away from you for long."

He is delighted by my admission and lifts my hands to his mouth. His lips are hot on my fingers, sending snakes of desire through my belly, feelings that I must hide lest he think me wanton.

***

I am awoken early, George's wife pulling urgently at my bedcovers. "Anne, wake up. Alys is sick."

I sit up, blink blearily about the chamber. The casement is open and I remember waking in the night, finding the room starved of air, and throwing it open. I recall leaning on the sill, inhaling the scent of roses from the moonlit garden. Now the blue-black dark is replaced by bright sunshine, the birds are singing, and a fat bumblebee is beating his head against the window.

"Anne, did you hear what I said?"

I blink at her stupidly, shake my head to chase away sleep. "No, Jane. I am sorry. What did you say?"

She is still in her nightgown, her hair tied in loose braids, a robe thrown across her shoulders. "Alys. You recall she retired to her bed early with a headache? Well, now she shivers and sweats and calls out in delirium."

Now Jane has my attention. Fear runs like icy water across my body. "Is it the Sweat?"

"We fear so."

I slide from the mattress, thrust my feet into slippers, tie on my wrap. "Where is George? Perhaps it is as well we are leaving for Hever today. Has the king been told?"

Jane is pulling on her stockings, thrusting her hair beneath a cap. She looks up at me. "The king has already gone, Anne. He and the queen left as soon as the news was abroad."

"Without saying goodb –"

Her look of triumph cuts short my sentence. I swallow my sudden jealousy as the picture of Henry hurrying his wife to safety sends a twist of grief deep into my bowels. He protects Catherine from contagion and leaves me to cope as best I can, because I am nothing but his concubine.

71

The sweating sickness is a dreadful thing; striking suddenly and leaving its victims dead in just one night. Few survive it. Henry, who lives in fear of infection, always flees at the merest suggestion of an outbreak. I am not surprised he has gone, but I am surprised he has abandoned me. I must look to my own safety.

"Go and find George," I say. "Tell him to order the horses made ready. We must leave as soon as possible."

For once, she doesn't argue. The door slams behind her and I hear her feet scurrying along the passage. Her obedience is indicative of her own fear. She would usually argue that she is not my servant but my sister-in-law, and demand that I summon a page.

As my things are gathered together I try not to think of Catherine's triumph. She will feel she has won him back and that I have lost. I know that none of her household will be sorry to see me parted from the king. Those about court who have gravitated to my side will be left in limbo, afraid to speak out in my defence and reluctant to sneak back to Catherine's faction.

Faction. What a word that is. I had never dreamed it would come to it, but Henry's court has divided in two. Those loyal to Catherine and her particularly mundane method of worship shun me whenever they can, and I resent their temporary return to prominence. Those who prefer my more liberal approach to life and Christianity will now be left out in the cold.

But only until I return. Wolsey must convince the legate to find in the king's favour, and Catherine can go to a nunnery where she can pray in peace for the rest of her days. Then, and only then, can I finally take my place as Henry's queen. It is what the king deserves. It is what I deserve and I will have it, if I can only escape this contagion.

We take horse across the countryside toward Hever. It has been a dry summer so far and the fields are parched, the roads thick with dust that rises in great choking clouds, stinging our eyes, coating our clothes, laying like a mask across my face. To avoid it, I spur my mount forward so that I am at the head of the party. George, enjoying the chase, joins me, hallooing as he raises his whip and tries to take the lead.

My skirts billow in the breeze and my hat bounces on my head but I lean further forward, feeling my horse's mane flick against my chin. Laughing aloud I risk a glance at my brother, whose face stretches in a grimace of exhilaration, his laughter lost in the wind. He brings down his whip again and his mount surges forward, forcing me to dig in my heels harder. Behind us, Jane bumps along unsteadily, her cries for us to slow down ignored. She will be unforgiving later, and George will suffer.

We pause on the rise to look down upon the rooftops of Hever, and the gardens laid out like fine embroidered handkerchiefs. The chimneys are smoking, the windows glinting in welcome. As we reach the meadow the sheep raise their heads, ruminating slowly, their big eyes blinking. Exchanging glances, George and I dig in our heels and our horses take flight again as we hare through the grass, scattering sheep and raising dust.

By the time I have washed the grime of the road from my face and hands and changed into a fresh gown, I realise I am exhausted. I long to sink into the mattress and lose myself in sleep, but a meal is waiting, a reunion with family and traditions of old. We sit around the old table just as we did as children, and I try not to mind Grandmother slurping at her soup. Despite the exertions of the ride, I have little appetite. I toy with my food and try to concentrate on the conversation. Mother is speaking, suggesting that she should come with me on my return to court. "I think you are in need of a proper chaperone now, Anne."

A comic picture flits through my mind of her valiantly defending me from the hot advances of the king.

Rumours about her have circulated for years, linking her name with Henry's in their youth. She was and still is a good-looking woman, but Henry swears there was nothing between them beyond a few dances. I choose to believe him;

it is hard enough to imagine Mary in his bed, let alone my mother. Poor Henry, what is it with him and the Boleyn women? I wonder what he makes of Grandmother.

The whole situation suddenly strikes me as ridiculous and a bubble of laughter escapes me, making everyone look up from their dinner.

"What is so funny?" George asks, his eyebrow quirked, ready to share the joke.

"Nothing, nothing at all." I look into my bowl where slices of carrot swim like fishes, the candlelight dancing like sunshine on the surface of a lake.

"Are you all right?"

I drop my spoon, splashing soup over my bodice.

"Yes, yes. I am fine, just a little headachy after the ride."

George leans toward me. "Anne, are you sure? You look hot, and your hands are trembling."

He is right. I clench them together for a moment before trying to pick up my spoon again. It is heavy, as heavy as lead. I drop it again and slump back in my chair. "Perhaps, George, I am not myself after all. Could you help me to my bed? I do feel suddenly so very tired."

I stand up, my chair falling backwards, and sway on my feet, grabbing for the table. Everyone leaps from their places. George's hand is instantly beneath my elbow, and Mother calls for a servant to stoke the fire in my chamber. Father stands anxiously at the door, dabbing his mouth with a napkin, his face white, his own hands shaking like one palsied while my brother ushers me from the room. Only Grandmother remains at table. Unaware of the drama around her, she stoically spoons up her soup, slurping like one of Father's hounds.

I suddenly feel very tall, as if my head is several yards from my feet and my knees do not belong to me at all. Although my head feels light, my neck is not strong enough to hold it up. Just as the room is about to tip over my head, George whisks me into his arms. He takes the stairs two at a time, yelling as he goes for someone to summon a doctor.

Rivers of ice run through my veins and I cannot control my shaking limbs, not even when they tuck warm bricks beneath the blankets. I am so very, very cold, and I know I will never be warm again.

I throw back the blankets, my mind teeming with demons, the people around me made monstrous by my imaginings. "Henry," I cry, and grasp his hand tightly when he comes to me. "Henry, don't let them hurt me."

"No, hush," he replies in George's voice, and I remember Henry is far away, cowering from the fever with his accursed wife.

For an instant I recall I am at Hever and I am ill, and then I plunge once more into the nightmare. Thin spiteful fiends are torturing me, they prod me, pull me. They tie a metal helmet about my skull, a helmet that seems to grow ever smaller, shrinking, pinching my brain, my head pincered in a huge claw – excruciating pain.

Someone places a damp cloth upon my brow, I smell lavender and marigold and I am in the garden with Henry again, his big laugh filling my ears, his hand warm on my arm.

"She is hotter than ever."

The cloth is removed, another applied. I toss and turn like a lost soul at sea, my bed heaving and lurching beneath me.

"She will never be queen," someone sneers, "she is just a whore, like her sister …"

I sit bolt upright, yelling at Henry to lock them in the Tower. But he laughs at me and the whole court joins in. Queen Catherine looms over me like a giant while I grow very small, as small as a beetle to be crushed beneath her shoe.

"Did you really think he would make you queen?" she laughs as she raises her foot.

"He is here!" someone cries. "Dr Butts is here."

Dr Butts? Henry's physician? Why is he here? Is someone ill?

Cool fingers touch head, pulling down my lower eyelid, probing my throat, the back of my neck. They wrench open my mouth, scrape my tongue, making me gag.

I am so hot I feel I am burning, but they heap more covers upon the bed. "Punish her," someone cries, "burn the witch …" I tumble back into the nightmare to be prodded by red-hot pokers; demons scream at me from the bed hanging, leer at me from the sweat-soaked pillow. They pull my hair, pinch my tender skin, light tapers and drive them into my eyes. Then, through the crowding fiends, I hear a voice I do not recognise. A voice that is calm, and in control. "Let her drink as much as she will, we must flush the fever from her."

Cool water bathes blistered lips, a damp cloth soothes parched skin. I hear murmured voices, my mother weeping, my brother shouting, Jane's voice tart and hostile in response and then, at last, a cockerel crowing, piercingly loud outside my window.

Is it dawn already?

I open my eyes.

"Water." They bring me a cup of cool ale that slides down my throat, quenching the fires but not the thirst. Cup after cup I drink until my belly is bursting. I feebly let them know I have to pee. Jenny helps me, my limbs trembling so violently that she half carries me across the room and supports me on the close stool. The piss pours forth in such a gush that it sounds like a horse in a stream. The relief is immense. She pulls down my gown and helps me back to bed, and with eyes full of fear puts a hand to my brow. "Are you better, Mistress Anne? Shall I fetch your mother? She has been in bed but an hour."

I shake my head and a tear slides from the corner of my eye to fall upon the pillow. I am as weak and pathetic as an infant and there is a great pain within my breast that makes breathing hard. She brings the cup again and again, feeding the insatiable thirst that will never be broken, and I drink deep.

A letter comes from Henry, written in his own hand. I am still so weak that Jenny has to break the seal so I might read it.

There came to me suddenly in the night the most afflifting news that could have arrived. The first, to hear of the sickness of my mistress, whom I esteem more than all the world, and whose health I desire as I do my own, so that I would gladly bear half your illness to make you well. The second, from the fear that I have of being still longer harassed by my enemy, Absence, much longer, who has hitherto given me all possible uneasiness, and as far as I can judge is determined to spite me more because I pray God to rid me of this troublesome tormentor. The third, because the physician in whom I have most confidence, is absent at the very time when he might do me the greatest pleasure; for I should hope, by him and his means, to obtain one of my chief joys on earth that is the care of my mistress yet for want of him I send you my second, and hope that he will soon make you well. I shall then love him more than ever. I beseech you to be guided by his advice in your illness. In so doing I hope soon to see you again, which will be to me a greater comfort than all the precious jewels in the world.

Written by that secretary, who is, and for ever will be, your loyal and most assured Servant,

Henry has signed it with our entwined initials. I kiss it, hold it briefly to my breast, relieved and reassured that I am not yet replaced in his affections. His fear and longing are evident in every stroke of his pen. Mind you, I think, glancing in the mirror, if he could see me now so peaked and wan-looking, I am not sure his heart would still be mine.

It is but a week since I lay so close to death, and I am still a long way from full recovery. The household is silent, the servants creeping as they go about their tasks, for George and Father have also fallen sick. We were glad to have Dr Butts so conveniently near, and thanks to his ministrations Father and George are past the worst and growing daily in

...ength, as I do. Though yesterday came news that poor Will Carey had not the strength to withstand it and has given up the fight, leaving Mary widowed.

I wonder what she will do now. The lodging she shared with Will at Greenwich will now be forfeit, her only income the rents from Will's Essex manor and an annuity from Tynemouth Priory. Without a penny of her own, Mary will now be in a sorry state.

"Father will surely bring her and the children home," I say to George as we sit together in the late June sunshine.

My brother is not so sure. "I doubt it very much. Our sister has done little to gain Father's approval. I fear Mary is on her own."

"If that is the case, I shall speak to the king. Mary may be wilful but she is still our sister, surely she has learned her lesson."

George shrugs and tugs the blanket higher about his chest. We are both still frail since the sickness and the summer breeze is sometimes a little too brisk.

"If you think it wise to draw his attention back to Mary, then do so by all means. There is no harm in her, she is just ... erm ... easily persuaded."

A robin red-breast perches on the garden wall, cocking his beady eye, looking for crumbs. I obligingly sprinkle what is left of the wafer I'd been nibbling onto the grass. Unafraid, he hops down, pecks at one or two pieces, looks up at us again before deciding we are harmless and finishing his meal.

"I am so bored, George. How will I ever pass my days until Henry sees fit to call me back to court?"

"There was a time you hardly had your nose out of a book. Don't you have anything to read?"

"Nothing I've not read before. I've tried re-reading Father's books but I can settle to nothing. I am as restless as ... as a –"

"A bitch on heat?"

"George!" I punch his arm playfully but do not take umbrage. It is hard to be offended when his words are so near the truth.

I miss Henry more than I had ever dreamed possible. It is weeks since I saw him last, and distance and the debilitation of the Sweat makes our romance seem like a lingering dream. "He writes to me often but I wish he would visit. I have a need to see him … in the flesh."

"He will come," says George, "just as soon as he is sure all risk of contagion has passed. You know what he is like when it comes to sickness."

I know only too well how Henry fears illness. He has shown me his stillroom, where he likes to concoct remedies and unguents. And should any of his household suffer a cold, he likes to minister to them himself, ordering them to keep to their chambers until the malady has passed.

When Henry does come he is full of concern, raining kisses on my face and on my hands. "You are thinner," he says. "Are you eating properly? Did you get the stag I sent you?"

He doesn't wait for my answer but continues to speak, holding tight to my hand as he greets my father and brother and nods reservedly to my mother.

We walk ceremoniously about the gardens, my hand on the king's sleeve while Father talks expansively of his plans for improvements to the house. Henry places his hot hand over mine, tracing my fingers, every so often giving me a little squeeze to show he is glad I am there. It is some time before we are alone. He pretends he wants me to show him the fish ponds and politely extricates himself from my family's company, bearing me off toward the meadow.

As soon as we are out of sight of the house he stops and draws me into his arms, swamping me with the scent of rosewater and underlying horse sweat. My smile is wide when I pull away a little and look up into his face. There, in his eyes, I see all the love and concern I had feared he had forgotten.

"Anne," he says, pulling off my peaked cap to let my hair fall loose. He buries his hands in it, his fingers digging into my skull, his lips hot and searching on mine. A sensation erupts deep in my belly like a scattering of red hot cinders. My breath grows short, the hammering of my heart loud in my ears. When his mouth slides from mine and I feel his tongue lick like a flame along my neck, his hands sliding down my bodice, I grow dizzy with desire, remembering just in time to be chaste and a little frightened. I pull away and drop my head, willing my lustful blood to cool. "Henry, My Lord, please."

With a hand to my mouth I pretend to be overcome by his demands, and he is instantly contrite. "Anne, forgive me. I could not help …"

"No matter," I say with what I hope is great compassion. "I understand." Then I shake myself, smile into his eyes and lead him to a fallen bough. "Let us sit here and enjoy the view to the house while you tell me how the divorce is going. When can I come back to court?"

He rubs his kerchief across his face, the bough creaks and bends beneath his great weight as he settles beside me. "Before too long, Sweetheart. Cardinal Campeggio is on his way from Rome but he is an old man and, so Wolsey tells me, suffers from the gout which forces him to make more stops than are desirable. We must concentrate on the future, on our marriage and the sons we will have."

"Sometimes I dream of the son we shall have, Henry. I imagine him as a tiny babe, a cap of red hair like yours, and I see him older too, dressed like a little man, forceful and strong like his father." I do not confide in Henry that I also see him years from now, taking his place on the English throne. Sprung from the loins of a Boleyn, he will be the best, most powerful king the world has ever seen. It is a happy dream and one that I cling to as I drift unhappily in the limbo that is my present.

"A happy dream indeed, and one that is too long in coming to pass." Henry shifts uncomfortably on the branch, his thigh pressed against mine. He takes off his hat and mops his head with his kerchief. "Are you not too hot, Anne?" he asks, and with a short laugh I shake my head.

"Since I was ill it is all I can do to keep warm. I crave the sunshine for it is so much warmer outside than indoors."

My eyes follow his as he examines my hands, the tracery of veins beneath the skin, the bones of my wrist standing out. I have never been plump and the sickness has left me thinner than ever. He turns his gaze back to my face. "You must put some meat on your bones; a plump woman is healthier, more fertile so they tell me than a thin one."

A pulse of fear beats in my throat. I swallow it and feign nonchalance. "Don't worry, My Lord. I am eating like a horse at the moment and my strength grows from day to day. By the time I return to court I will be as fat as a cook."

His big laugh fills the sky, sending up a crowd of rooks from their roost. "Don't overdo it, Sweetheart. I want you plump, not portly. If I wanted to bed a pig I'd look in the royal pigsty."

Our laughter merges, trickles away until we are solemn again. We stare at one another for a long time. "Can you stay the night, Henry?"

He flushes, hesitates, shakes his head. "Nay, Sweetheart. Think what the court gossips would say about that."

"Oh, I didn't mean that we should …"

His hand covers mine again, drawing me closer. "I know what you meant," he says, and I lay my head against his padded coat. For a long time we sit in silence, watching the light change as the day dwindles into dusk.

September 1528

It has been a wet month, and cooped up indoors all day my temper is short, my patience frayed. I have just summoned Jenny to tease the parlour fire back into life and she kneels at the hearth, vigorously poking the embers, looking for a glimpse of flame. Grandmother snores in her chair, her cap askew, her mouth open, a trickle of drool on her chin. Emitting another gusty sigh, I get up and begin to pace the floor, one moment looking from the window, the next sifting through some sheaves of paper on the table.

I pick up a poem written for me years ago by Tom Wyatt. On the day he presented it I made light of the honour, teasing him that it didn't scan. Now, the gentle words, so full of honesty, make me smile sadly, longing for those happier times.

I let the paper drop from my fingers and it floats gently to the floor, coming to rest on the rush matting that flanks the hearth. Jenny picks it up, scrambles to her feet and places it on the table. "Can I get you anything, Mistress Anne?"

"What? No, no, thank you, Jenny. I am just bored with being indoors for so long."

"I expect it will clear up later, like it did yesterday. Then you can walk in the gardens."

"Perhaps."

Jenny has no idea how dull it is at Hever compared with the goings-on at court. She can have no concept of how much I miss the king, how I worry that I will be replaced in his affections. Greenwich is full of girls clamouring for the honour of a romp in the royal bed and it is imperative I am there at his side, keeping his eyes and his hands away from them.

Buried here in the countryside I am starved of news. I know that Campeggio has not yet arrived at court, and Henry seethes as much as I with frustration at his tardiness. A snail could have travelled faster from Rome, and it seems to me that our most urgent business is in the hands of the slowest and most ancient cardinal they could find.

I know that Henry's patience is wearing thin for George brings me what news he can, often carrying letters and love tokens from the king. He is due back today but it is now past twelve of the clock. Knowing he may arrive any moment, I am unable to relax. At last, after another hour of floor-pacing and chewing at my fingers, I hear the sound of hooves on the gravel and raised voices in the yard. Within moments I am at the door.

"George! How tiresome you are, I had expected you long since."

"Well, that's a fine welcome," he says, handing his reins to the groom before kissing me and allowing me to lead him into the house. "The weather is awful for September. I am wet through."

He holds his hands out to the flames, which are now beginning to lick along the outer edges of the fuel, and when Jenny enters with a tray of refreshments, he selects a pastry, takes a huge bite.

"Did Henry send me anything?"

George nods, speaking with his mouth full. "There is a letter in my luggage, I will fetch it presently. I need to get out of these wet clothes. I have something for you, too. Something to keep your mind active even when your body is not."

Still taking bites of his pastry, he quits the chamber and begins to mount the stairs. I follow him, sit on his bed and rummage through his pack while he strips off his sodden clothing. He tosses his jacket and shirt onto the floor and begins to peel off his hose.

After much searching I seize Henry's letter, tear open the seal and unfold the parchment, my eyes quickly scanning the laboriously hand-written greeting. I let the letter drop and give a stifled scream. "It is infuriating! He says the Legatine court will not now sit until October at the earliest, and he insists that I stay here until it is done. He cannot risk my presence undermining all the hard work he has put in."

George turns, decently clad now, tying up his sleeves. "Your Henry is putting on a good show. The other day he was declaring before all in hearing distance that the impediment to his marriage with Catherine was a great trial to him, and if the great clerks could only clear his conscience and prove that his marriage was acceptable to God he would be glad of it, for if he were to marry again he would surely choose Catherine above all other women."

83

"He said what?" I am on my feet, shouting, outraged at such a betrayal. George holds out his hands, placating, begging me to be silent.

"Hush, hush. He did not mean it, we all know that. There was not one among us who believed him. His words were an act, designed to be carried to the Pope to persuade him that Henry has no intention of marrying elsewhere."

"Huh!" I shake off George's hand. "And you can be quite sure his words were carried straight to Catherine, and that she is gloating over them in triumph. By Christ, George, I wish he were an ordinary man, married to an ordinary woman. Any other wife would go meekly when asked for an annulment, not dig in her heels like a mule."

George slides his arm about my shoulders, kisses my head. "Would you?"

I scowl at him. "Certainly not, but that's different."

He laughs quietly.

"Would you like your gift now?"

I nod. My eyes are moist and my nose is beginning to run, but I cannot find my handkerchief. When he notices the lack, George gives me his own and I dab my eyes, blow my nose. Through my tears I see him haul a large parcel from his luggage and dump it on the bed. Despite my misery, I am intrigued.

"What is it?" I sit down again and begin to loosen the ties, tear off the wrapping, revealing a pile of books. "What are they?" I begin to turn the pages.

"Banned, mostly, so keep them out of sight. Only read them in the privacy of your chamber, and for goodness sake don't let Mother know you have them, she wouldn't approve. Oh, and don't tell Henry about them either ... not yet, anyway."

I squint at the pages in the dim light. "Are they blasphemous?"

"No, I don't think so, but there are those who wouldn't agree."

"Father has some books that he keeps locked away ... he won't let me read them. Are they books like this, do you think?"

George circumnavigates the bed and sits beside me. "Undoubtedly. It was Father who first perked my interest in reform. The Church is corrupt in so many ways, but their power is such that it cannot be broken. These men, the authors of these words, show there is a way to loosen the Church's hold on men's souls."

"Which should I read first?"

"Erasmus; his skill in setting out an argument is unsurpassed. Now, go conceal them in your chamber and meet me downstairs. I have much to tell you."

I spend much of the wet autumn studying theology, the reformist section anyway. As I digest the words of Erasmus and Lefèvre, I begin to see that the Church as it is now has many faults, and as I absorb the words, my mind is no longer entirely taken up with the king's great matter but also with the idea of religious reformation and change. I no longer think solely of becoming the king's wife, I now think of my future role. For the first time I realise that as Henry's queen, I will have a voice and, more importantly, the leverage required to implement real and important changes.

December 1528 – Hever

I angrily jab the needle into my sewing, fumble at the back of the fabric, pricking my skin. I drop the material, suck the tip of my finger and swear violently, making Jenny gasp. She flushes. "Sorry Mistress Anne, you took me by surprise. Does your finger need binding?"

"No, it is just a scratch. What I need, Jenny, is diversion. I am dying of boredom. All summer it seems I have been shut away here, while the king ..." I tail off, remembering belatedly to whom I am speaking. I shake my head. "No matter."

"It will be Christmas soon. You will enjoy that, you always do."

She picks up a tray of empty cups and moves across the room. What can she know of the joys I am missing? She has never been anywhere but here. All her life has been spent as a servant at Hever, the heady joys of a royal court are impossible for her to imagine, and she probably has no idea of Henry's plans to marry me, make me his queen. To Jenny, I am probably just another royal whore, like my sister.

Mary has still not returned to us. Although she writes frequently, complaining of penury and misery, Father will not let her come home. She is soiled goods, mistress to two kings, a penniless widow with two of the king's bastards in tow. Not a marriageable prospect and so of no use to Father. All his attention is on me. He envisages honours and property if only I can be securely married to the king. He has no use for my sister.

Soon, Mary writes to me privately, asking me to intercede for her with the king, begging for a return to court. I tuck her letter away. She will have to wait until my own position is more secure and I am ready to have her flaunting her charms around Henry. It is bad enough having him sharing lodgings with Catherine again, but an ageing barren wife is one thing. I can deal with that, but a pretty, ex-mistress is something else altogether. I do not want Mary back at court, at least, not until I am there to keep her in check.

It is cold, wet and dismal. Grey slush is piled in the corners of the yard and lies in pockets across the meadow. I have no zest for the day but with my hands tucked firmly in my fur-lined sleeves, I walk briskly about the bleak garden, sucking in air. The wind is bitter, peppered with specks of snow; it batters my cheeks, almost whipping the hood from my head. My eyes might be streaming from the cold and each breath cuts painfully at my lungs, but I am so tired of the dark, smoky rooms that I cannot face returning to the house just yet. Fed up to the teeth with Grandmother's wheezing cough and whining voice I cannot even lose myself in reading, and to make it all worse, I have read every book in the house, even the forbidden ones.

The last time he was here George promised to bring me more, but he has not come. "The roads are impassable," Mother says, making excuses for him. "You can't expect to see him until the thaw."

Well, now it has thawed. The streams are running lush and loud in the valleys, and the snow that has mantled the countryside is now giving way to floods and mud. I know George well enough to realise he could get here now … if he wished to. I put a hand to my veil that is whipping like a whirligig in the wind, and scan the horizon, watching, waiting for someone to rescue me. My desire to escape is so great that if the devil himself were to ride over the hill and offer me freedom, I would take it.

The skyline remains empty. I remember other times when I have looked up to see George or Henry galloping toward me, and the need to see them now is so great that the image is conjured up. I see them hallooing down the hill, hats waving, mounts snorting and steaming. Then I blink and the landscape is empty again, empty of everything but the drab shades of winter, and dirty woolly sheep.

Cross, I turn away to make two more swift circuits of the garden before heading for the door. The warmth of the hall engulfs me. I kick off my pattens, my frozen fingers struggling with the ties of my cloak. I am making it worse, the knot becomes tighter, and almost in tears, I yell for Jenny.

She comes running, her soothing words doing nothing to calm me. Yet soon I am seated at the fireside with a steaming cup in my hands, and the heat of the flames is making my nose run. Grandmother is fingering through the dog's wiry coat, searching for fleas. Every time she discovers one she squeezes it between her nails with satisfied pleasure and shows me her gums. I watch with distaste, my nose wrinkled and my lip turned up.

Jenny pops her head back around the door.

"Mistress, your brother is come, and the king is with him."

"The king?" I leap from the chair, spilling warm ale down my skirt. "I must get changed," I cry. "Oh, my goodness, what a time for him to pick! Just when I am looking my worst."

We make hasty reparation to my appearance and by the time he is dismounting at the front of the house I am waiting in the hall, seemingly as calm and collected as he could wish.

Mother and Father go forward to greet him. They fuss and fawn before him, apologising for being so unprepared for his arrival. I can see his growing impatience, for they are hampering his approach, his steps necessarily slow to accommodate them. I smile as his eyes scan the company looking for me. His face lights up and he sweeps off his jewel-studded hat, tossing it to George who catches it in one hand.

"Anne." Henry takes my hand, his mouth moist on my fingers, his eyes brimming with love for me. All the trials and miseries of the past months seep away.

"Good day, Your Majesty," I say, sinking to my knees in obeisance.

"Oh, get up, get up, we will have none of that," he says, taking my wrist again and smothering my fingers in kisses. When Mother suggests we move into the parlour, he tucks my hand beneath his arm, keeping me close. I know that soon he will see to it that we are alone but for now we must bear with the company, as tedious as it is.

For a while, talk is of the commonplace; the winter weather, the state of the roads, the hope that the cold will chase away the sweating sickness for good. At the mention of the Sweat we fall silent for a space, reflecting on those we have lost to the pestilence. Indeed, of all of us present, it is Henry who has suffered the most since the fever took not only his good friend, William Compton, but also Will Carey, who was his good companion as well as our brother-in-law. I send up a little silent prayer of thanks that God saw fit to spare my father, George, and I. Henry, seeing my closed eyes, whispers, "Pray it will never come again." His chin wobbles as he grips more tightly to my hand.

To lighten the sombre mood I suggest refreshments, but as soon as Mother has gone off to arrange it, Henry jerks his head at George who, correctly interpreting the silent command, diverts Father's attention while Henry and I slide from the room and into the privacy of a side chamber.

I immediately fall into his arms, and he pushes me flat against the panelling while his soft warm lips rain kisses on my face. His hands travel deliciously over my body, skimming my breasts, reaching down to cup my buttocks and pull me against his jutting codpiece. "Henry," I gasp, but he smothers my protests with kisses, issuing little grunts of desire as he pulls my cap from my hair, tangles it in his fingers. "Henry!" I protest, louder this time, and at length my anxiety intrudes upon his business. He pulls back, his red hair ruffled into damp spikes, his blue eyes wide.

"I must have you soon, Anne, or die of it."

Henry doesn't like to be made a figure of fun, but I risk a laugh. "You won't die of it, My Lord. And imagine if I were to submit and you were to get a child on me? He would be derided as a bastard. You would not want our prince to be base-born, would you, Henry?"

He sits down, runs his hands through his hair, making it stand up even more. "No, but ... there are ... ways of preventing conception ..." He looks at me sheepishly and I feel the blood surge into my cheeks at his inference.

"I would not know about that, My Lord, and I am sure no virtuous woman would allow such a thing." Despite my words I am indecently curious to know how one goes about preventing pregnancy. I make a note to ask George the next time we are alone.

"Anne." He takes my hands again, pulls me closer. "There would be no shame in being my mistress, my sole mistress. It would be an honour ..."

"No. I've told you. I will be no man's mistress, not even yours. Not if you were king of the world."

"We could still be married, when the time is right. Once I am rid of Catherine, there is no other who will do for me, but Anne, I am burning. I am a man, in the full flush of manhood. I am not made for abstinence."

I snatch my hand away. "Divorce her, then! Force their hand. Stop pussyfooting around Wolsey and demand that he gets a result. He is your servant, isn't he?"

His mouth opens and closes like a fish as he searches for a reply. I forestall him.

"They are playing with you, Henry, can't you see that? Campeggio is taking his time on purpose, shilly-shallying. He is afraid to say 'no' to you, and afraid to say 'yes' to the Pope. And as for Wolsey, well, he has no love for me and would sooner see you wed to the barren, toothless mare you are presently keeping in your stable. He would rather see you childless than happy, Henry. Force his hand. Make them act in our favour and I will be in your bed sooner than that."

I snap my fingers.

For a long moment we stare at each other, my breast rising and falling with the passion of my words. Henry is white-faced, his cheeks drooping, his mouth defeated. At this moment, the picture he presents is not that of a renaissance prince but rather a small child, refused his sweetmeats.

If the king's visit to Hever serves to reignite my desire for him and increase my frustration, it also brings about a change. My days of pining at Hever are done and Henry orders me to return to court. Before I agree, I demand certain conditions.

I tell him I want my own suite of rooms, the finest in the palace, and I want them close to his. I want the running of my own household, and I want my place in his court acknowledged, not as his mistress but as his future queen.

And to my surprise, I get it.

I hear him coming long before he arrives. I am in my apartments with my women, our heads bent over our sewing while in the corner a lutenist plays for our delectation. I hear a muffled thump and my head jerks up. The doors are thrown open, guards snap to attention, courtiers fall like harvested wheat at his approach. I stay where I am, waiting for him to come to me, and when he finally bursts into my chambers he is roaring and blustering like a lion.

He has returned from the Blackfriars sooner than expected. At a nod from me, my women put down their needlework and bow silently from the room, leaving the king and I alone. Henry paces the floor, his cap pushed back on his head, his cloak billowing behind him.

"What is it, Henry?" I move toward him but he makes a sharp, violent movement and I flinch away. Henry is famous for his rages but I have never yet seen him this angry, so furiously out of control. He snatches off his hat and throws it onto the floor, where the jewels shimmer like fallen stars.

"That blasted woman!"

I exhale as silently as I can, relieved it is not me who has displeased him this time. I move forward again, gently persistent. "Which woman, Henry? Come and sit down, tell me all about it."

But he is not ready to relax. His anger is so great it cannot be contained, cannot be soothed so readily. I turn away, pour him a cup of wine, hold it out to him. He almost snatches it from my hand and tips it down his throat as if it is a foul tasting medicine. While he drags his sleeve across his wet lips, I refill the cup and hand it back to him.

Once he has quaffed the second draught, he looks at me for the first time, his eyes almost desperate. I let him see my empathy. "Which woman, Henry?" I softly repeat.

He removes the lute from a chair and lowers himself onto the seat. "Catherine," he snaps, as if I hadn't guessed. "She has shamed me in front of everyone. Her words will

91

already be travelling around the world like a dirty secret. I spoke of her to the court in the gentlest of terms, outlining my doubts, my guilt that I have been living in sin, against God's teachings. I had them all in the palm of my hand, but then it was her turn and she refused to be judged. 'I am the Queen of England …'" he mocks in Catherine's thick Spanish accent, "'and, as such, this court is not fit to judge me.'"

"What? Surely the court didn't listen to her."

He looks up at me, his brow wrinkled.

"Oh, yes, they listened. She has been well-advised." He rubs his face, the jewels on his fingers winking in mockery of our quest for happiness. His lips form a snarl. "And when I discover just who it is that offers her such advice, they will swing from the highest gallows."

Catherine's ally has to be Eustace Chapuys, the Spanish Ambassador who is so often in her company, but I have other suspicions too. There are those about court who will risk even the king's wrath to be rid of me.

"What does Wolsey say, and Campeggio?"

"What do they ever say? They prevaricate and dissemble. Not one of them dares look me in the eye. Anne, Anne …" He reaches out, grasps my wrists, pulling until I am on my knees before him. "Who can I trust, Anne? Why can they not see what is best for their king, best for England?"

I do not answer him for my thoughts are still with Catherine who, I now see more plainly than ever, is a dangerous enemy. The purpose of the legatine court is to listen to the testimonies of both the king and Catherine so that they can come to a just decision … a decision that Henry has made quite clear to Wolsey is to be in his favour.

I make an angry noise at the back of my throat. "Just who does that woman think she is? What else did she say?"

"Very little. After pleading with me that she was my true-wed wife, and accusing me of treating her badly, she got up and left the court."

"You can't just leave the court!"

"You can if you think you are the queen. They called her back. 'Catherine of England, come into court,' but she refused to come. To have her dragged back, kicking and screaming, would have only worked in her favour. She is martyring herself, wanting to be seen as the wronged woman. She begs to be allowed to appeal directly to Rome."

"For God's sake, Henry." I slump against his legs, my fine silk skirts spread across the floor. "What will happen now?"

***

At my invitation, Mary comes to see me at the palace. At first she is sulky and refuses to look me in the eye, but ignoring her reticence I place a kiss upon her chilly cheek and show her a basket of kittens. "Choose one," I say, "whichever you like." I can see she wants to refuse but in the end, seduced by their soft eyes and tiny tails, she reaches out and picks up a tabby.

I lead her to a seat at the window where, with her cat tucked beneath her arm, we look unspeaking across the gardens. Courtiers are taking the air, their heads together in gossip. "I wonder who they are talking about today," I say, in an attempt to fill the silence.

She immediately bridles. "I have done nothing to cause fresh scandal."

"I wasn't suggesting you had." I look at her pinched face, the brittle glistening of her eyes betraying how close her tears are to the surface. "Mary, can't we be friends, as we used to be?"

She looks down at her linked fingers, shrugs her narrow shoulders, but makes no reply.

"None of this is your fault, Mary, I know that, but neither is it mine. I am your sister and want to help you in your widowhood. It must be so hard for you."

Her head jerks up, her face working as she fights to contain all the bitterness that has been building up inside her for so long. "You have no idea how hard. My income has been severed, Will's annuities stopped, and Father will not even speak to me. I want to go home to Hever but he will have none of it ..." She stops, her throat working as she fights for self-control. "I am at my wit's end, Anne. I know not where to turn."

I reach for her hand. "Did you think I would not help you? I have spoken to Father already, and when I received no encouragement there I took the matter to the king."

The colour drains slowly from her cheeks. I know Mary well enough to realise that she would spurn help from him if she could. For a moment a mulish expression clouds her face, but then it passes as she reconciles herself to the inevitable. "And what did he say?"

I inwardly quail at revealing Henry's decision, for I know she will not like it. I straighten my back, tame my demeanour and say, as casually as I can manage, "The king desires that the wardship of little Henry should pass to me."

Her head snaps up, her eyes wide, her face pale, lips parted. "To you? But I ... I ... that will give you control of him, you will have all the revenues from his lands. How will that help me?"

I get up, smooth my skirts and reach for a jug of wine on the table, but I do not pour. I put the jug down again, turn back to look at her. "You will have peace of mind, knowing your son will be properly cared for, that his future will be in the hands of the king. Once Henry and I are wed ..."

"Anne!" She jumps up, thrusts her face toward me, her whole body atremble. "Surely you don't still believe he will ever marry you. How long has he been promising that now? Don't you yet realise it is just a ruse to get you to his bed? He is nothing if not persistent."

I want to yell back that he'd not needed much persistence to land her in his net, but I have sworn not to argue with her. The divorce is certainly lagging more than either Henry or I had believed possible. To the king's fury Campeggio has adjourned the court for the summer, and our wait continues. Pushing the thought away, I close my eyes against Mary's fury and remind myself that I am the king's beloved. I take a deep breath and dive back into the fray.

"I am also determined to persuade the king to assign an annuity of one hundred pounds to you. This will ensure that you and Catherine are not penniless. Henry has not agreed to do so just yet but he has promised to speak to Father about allowing you to return to Hever."

Mary slumps suddenly into her chair, the kitten floundering on her lap. "They don't want me there."

I sit close beside her, our skirts overlapping, the fine quality of my cloth overshadowing the shiny worn nap of hers. "If the king demands it, they will have no choice." My words are as gentle as I can make them. I remind myself how hard it must be for Mary, her fall from the king's favourite to a penniless nobody difficult enough without having to see me, her younger, plainer sister, take her place.

Were I in her place I wouldn't relish returning to Hever. It is a household of women; a hostile mother, a witless grandmother, and a four-year-old child. What allure can that have for Mary, who has tasted the delights of court, both here and in France? But it will be better than starving.

"Mary, try to be thankful. Henry doesn't have to help you. It is the king's way of ensuring that you and your children enjoy a financially secure future. You will be taken care –"

"I will be safely out of sight, you mean. You are stealing my son, and Henry is paying me and his daughter to stay out of his way, as if I am some guilty secret."

"That is not true at all, and it is ungrateful of you to say so."

Her tears are falling now, splashing down her cheeks, dripping from the end of her nose. Disgusted, I thrust a kerchief into her hand and look away while I wait for her to pull herself together, although in truth, I long to give into the desire to deliver her a long overdue slap. Why is it so hard for her to accept help?

A sudden shower of summer rain rattles against the windows, and the people in the garden hurry toward the hall. As she calms, Mary's sobs subside into shudders. Miserably, she mops her wet face with my kerchief.

"You must try to make the best of things, Mary, for little Catherine's sake. With a small income of your own and your children independent, who knows, you may yet make a good second marriage."

She glares at me, her wet lashes parted like stars, the tip of her nose red and moist. "Nobody will marry me now, Anne, you know that. I am soiled goods, and everybody knows it."

I open my mouth to answer but at that moment the door bursts open and George enters, throwing his damp jerkin over the back of a chair.

"Sisters!" he cries, coming swiftly toward me, leaning over me to kiss my cheek, his hand squeezing my waist. "How are you, Anne? And Mary ..." He bends over her hand. "Still snivelling, I see."

I frown and shake my head at him, silently warning him to not to begin teasing her. He picks up a cushion and sinks into the opposite chair. "It has started to rain." He shakes his wet hair to demonstrate, scattering drops that spatter Mary's gown. "The king was with me, but Wolsey called him away."

The very name makes me shrivel inside. "Wolsey," I spit contemptuously, "that toad. I wonder what poison he is whispering into Henry's ear now."

George puts his feet up on a stool, crosses his ankles and tucks his fists beneath his armpits to warm them. "I had some speech with that fellow of his, Cromwell. I had no idea he was for Church reform."

"That dark-haired man who follows Wolsey around, as soft-footed as a sloth?"

"That's the fellow, yes. The draper's son. He isn't as callow as he first appears; you should nurture his good will, Anne. He could help us in our cause."

"Perhaps." I pick at a loose thread on my sleeve while George turns his attention to Mary.

"You have a cat, Mary. How are you? I've not seen you in a while," he asks, for all the world as if he has a care for her affairs. "And how are the little ones?"

She does not deign to answer but picks up our former conversation. "Which cause do you refer to, George? The reform of the Church, or our sister's entrapment of the king?"

"Entrapment? That is a harsh word for it, Mary. I suppose, were he our friend, the fellow could help with both. I know he is a reformer but were he to champion Anne as future queen, I can think of no one better placed to influence the cardinal."

I fidget in my seat, drawing George's attention. "What is it, Anne?"

"Oh, nothing. It is just that I have been trying not to think of it, the divorce, the Pope, the cardinals. I want it to be all over and done with so that the king and I can get down to the business of breeding our prince."

"I am sorry to have brought it up again."

"It is never very far from my mind. I keep trying to find ways of distracting myself. I need a worthy cause to fight for. All I ever seem to do is rage in vain against Catherine and the Pope, and all the while I have to battle to keep Henry's affection within the bounds of decency."

I cast a guilty look in Mary's direction but she is tempting the kitten from beneath the table and appears to be paying me no mind.

"What did you make of that book I gave you?"

"Tyndale? Oh, he is a wise man, expresses himself so well that even the most catholic of men would come round to his point of view."

"Did you show it to the king?"

"Good Lord, no. He wouldn't like it at all. He found me with a copy of Luther's On the Bondage of the Will and swore it was blasphemous. I had to lie to him and pretend I had found it lying around, picked it up out of idle curiosity. I don't think he would like Tyndale any better, especially since he is against the divorce."

George casts a quick glance at Mary, who is still engaged with the kitten. He leans forward, his arms resting on his knees. "I was thinking of the section where he speaks out against popes, and advocates that kings should answer to no one but God."

"Oh but, I mean … the Pope is indispensable …"

"Is he?" My voice trails off as George shuffles even closer. I lean toward him, our heads almost touching. "Just imagine, Anne. If Henry were head of the Church and not the Pope ... what then? What difference would that make to him, and to you?"

I sit back, a frown upon my brow as I try to imagine the world that George's words are painting. No Pope, just Henry standing betwix God and the English people. No Pope, no Roman Church to lord it over us. Henry is a great king, but with the Pope out of the way he would be ... I gasp and sit up straight, my eyes boring into George's.

"Do you see, Anne? Do you see what I am saying?"

I nod slowly, my stomach churning, my head reeling as if I am balanced on the edge of a great chasm. Can I risk his anger and persuade the king to read Tyndale's book? Henry hates the man, swears his words are blasphemy, but now I wonder if he can be brought to see how Tyndale's beliefs can serve him, serve us both. Can I get the king to change his mind?

It is as if the door keeping Henry and I apart has opened just a chink, and a blinding light is shining on the other side, tempting us forward. I grip my brother's hand and he lifts our entwined fingers to his mouth, covers my knuckles with kisses. "You can do this, Anne," he whispers. "If anyone can, it is you."

September 1529 –Greenwich

The royal barge cuts through dark green water, the expert oarsman making scarcely a ripple on the surface of the river. It is the perfect autumn day. I lie back on cushions, screened from the public gaze by curtains, while around me my friends are gathered and a little way off, a fellow with merry brown eyes strums a lute. We are on our way to Greenwich and I am inwardly burning with excitement. Beside me, reclining at the feet of our cousin, Madge Shelton, I know George is burning too.

His wife, Jane, sits a little way off, scowling at their blatant flirtation. I should kick George, make him sit up and behave, but today I am too excited. The thing for which my brother and I have striven is finally coming to pass. The cardinal is to be arrested and charged with Praemunire. For the first time, Henry has decided to take action to stop Wolsey in his crusade against us.

I raise my eyes to the calm, pretty face of Nan Gainsford, a newcomer to my household. I discovered shortly after her arrival, that we both share a zeal for reform that made us instant friends. It was Nan who let my copy of Tyndale fall into the hands of her betrothed, George Zouche, and as we had guessed he would, he carried it straight to Wolsey. The cardinal, eager to denounce my household as a breeding ground for heresy, lost no time in showing it to the king. Closing my eyes, I lie back on my cushions, and as the smooth green water carries me onward I recall the encounter that followed.

"I was intrigued, Henry," I pleaded, "for I've been told his wisdom and had to read it for myself. Are you not also curious?" Clutching the banned book to my bosom, I maintained his gaze for a few moments, opening my eyes wide. Then I held out the book. "Read it yourself, My Lord. Be your own judge, do not let others determine what you shall or shall not read. You are the king, and you should be the one to decide what is heresy and what is not. Why should anyone dictate to you?"

His nostrils flared, his eyes narrowed, but he slowly reached out and took the book from me. He turned away, loosening the catch and opening the cover. For some time the only sound was the crackling flames in the grate and the soft hush of turning pages.

I watched him from the corner of my eye. It was the first time I dared to lure him toward reform; before this, I kept my opinions of religion to myself. As he became further engrossed in Tyndale's words, his breathing slowed, became audible. He settled more comfortably into his seat, turning the pages with his jewelled fingers while I waited, poised on the edge of a stool, my hands twisted in my lap, barely daring to breathe.

When he finally looked up from the page, he was pensive. He made as if to speak to me but hesitated, bowed over my hand, took his leave of me and disappeared from the chamber with Tyndale's book clasped tightly beneath his arm. I waited in my apartments, biting my nails as to the outcome of the revelation.

It was a big risk, the book could either sway Henry to our cause or turn him fully against it. But slowly, over the next days and weeks, Henry's arguments become tinged with Tyndale's philosophies. When the Pope retracts his permission for the divorce to be tried in England, Henry's rage is peppered with questions like: Why should the Pope hold sway over the English people? Shouldn't a man's conscience be between himself and God alone? What right has Rome over the governing of England?

Hiding the gleam of triumph in my eye, I allow the king to believe he has worked it all out for himself. And now, within just a few weeks of planting the first seeds of reform into his mind, Henry has struck the first blow against Wolsey and the power of Rome.

Cardinal Wolsey was a rich man. Now, stripped of his offices, he retires to York while Henry appropriates his property. Among them is York Place, the house where Henry first laid eyes on me all those years ago, when we both played a part in the Chateau Vert. That fateful day when he mistook me for Mary and hefted me over his shoulder and ran away with me seems so long ago now. Had anyone told me then that Henry and I would be planning to build a house together, I would have laughed in their face. Then, I was a silly untried girl, but now, just a few years later, I am soon to be queen. How strange is fate?

One afternoon in late October, Henry and I, closely chaperoned by my mother who now rarely leaves my side, go upriver to examine the house and see what use we can make of it. It is to be a pleasant, informal jaunt with only a handful of attendants. We have left royal pomp and ceremony behind us at Greenwich.

As soon as we climb the river steps and pass through the garden and look upon the house in its river setting, I realise that it is perfect. It owns a prime position on the Thames, offering easy access to Greenwich and Richmond, yet is still close to Henry's favourite hunting country. The friendly façade welcomes me. It is like coming home.

Every one of Henry's palaces shows evidence of Catherine. Her initials are everywhere, entwined with Henry's; her heavy Spanish influence in the furnishings, the cushions and hangings fashioned by her own hands. I have a hankering for our own palace, a place where I can make my own mark, and have my own emblem emblazoned on the walls, the hangings of my own choosing.

We spend a pleasant afternoon strolling arm in arm through the rooms, our footsteps echoing in the empty house as we note the richness of the fabrics, the fine carvings and finials.

"We can hold court here, without Catherine," I say, disengaging Henry's arm and beginning to investigate each cupboard, nook and cranny.

"It isn't big enough, my sweet," he replies in his most indulgent tone and, turning to face him, I place my hands on my hips and let the enthusiasm blaze in my eye.

"We will make it big enough. You are the king, you can do anything. We can add private apartments and wine cellars, extend the kitchens and build a great hall big enough to house half of Europe."

"Only half?" He is laughing at me but I don't mind. Now that we no longer have to rely on Wolsey's bumbling over the divorce, I know that my time is near. Catherine is on her way out and I will soon be queen. I spin around happily.

"Just think, Henry. Our son will be born here, and all our children. These halls will ring with the sound of their laughter."

"Anne." He crosses the room in three strides, takes my hands in his, his eyes awash with hope. "Do you really believe so?"

"Oh yes, My Lord. I know so. I can feel it in my bones."

"In that case, my love, we will turn it into a shining white palace fit to house King Arthur himself!"

The gap left by Wolsey in the administration of the realm is quickly filled by my adherents. My father, soon to be made the Earl of Wiltshire, becomes Lord Privy Seal, and Uncle Thomas is made Lord Treasurer. Together with Suffolk, who despite having no love for me shares a dislike of cardinals, they step into Wolsey's red shoes and do battle to obtain the king's desires.

With the cardinal fallen, they take the opportunity to whip up a frenzy for Church reform while I whisper into the king's ear that, just as Wolsey was not his superior but his subject, so the Pope is no friend to England. As we had wished, Henry launches an attack against the clergy, forbidding them from keeping taverns, prohibiting them from gambling, hunting and whoring. He passes a law against plurality of office, ensuring that each parish has a permanent cleric in residence. Henry has learnt that, as a divinely elected king, the Pope holds no sway over his decisions. From now on, England's king will be ruled by no one lower than God himself.

At this time, two other men step from the shadows of obscurity. One is a man whose soft tread and sharp ears quickly prove invaluable, both to my cause and to that of Church reform.

Thomas Cromwell is a discreet, unassuming man. He listens quietly to counsel and then, without seeming to do so, demolishes a presented proposal and replaces it with one of his own. His face is long, his methods are subtle, and his desire for reform cold-blooded. I do not like Master Thomas Cromwell, his origins are far too evident, but he is clever, and soon becomes indispensable. Unlike many at Henry's court, he treats me as if I am already his queen.

The other fellow, another Thomas, this one by the name of Cranmer, is altogether more likeable than Cromwell. He is a clergyman, keen for reform, and is already the Boleyn family chaplain. Henry is impressed when he meets him and shortly afterwards raises him up, sends him on diplomatic business overseas in the company of my father as part of his diplomatic entourage.

The stage is set, I am acknowledged by all who are wise enough, as Henry's future queen. My family's fortune is in ascendance and I am happy ... all but for one thing.

***

Henry orders Mother to wait in the outer chamber. She cannot argue with the king, but she frowns a silent warning as I pass blithely into his inner sanctum. The room is softly lit; the glow of candlelight reflecting from the mirrors, the firelight dancing seductively on the walls. A table is laden with a sumptuous repast.

With a flick of his hand he dismisses his page. The boy bows and backs away, leaving Henry to serve me himself. Leaning close, he bubbles wine into my cup, his now familiar fragrance filling my head. With a great sigh, he puts down the jug, runs a finger along my face. In response, I tilt my head toward him, trapping his warm hand against my neck.

"It is not food I hunger for, Anne." His eyes are soft and sad. His tongue appears briefly, moistening his lips before disappearing again.

Alone with him in the firelight, the danger sends a shiver of anticipation through me. I close my eyes, savouring the painful pleasure of the moment. It is times like these, when he is less a king and more a man, that are our most precious … and our most perilous. For a little while I can cast off my brittle armour and become soft and womanly, but it is dangerous.

I lean against his doublet and his hand moves to my head, pulls off my hood to let my hair fall free. His fingers trickle across my hair, his rings snagging, pulling my head back. I look up at him, baring my throat, and swiftly he stoops to place his lips against it. With a gasp I push against his chest, knowing I should fend him off, but he is like a hungry hound, licking and biting, sending delight stabbing deep, deep into my belly.

When he draws away, his hair stands up in a red halo, his lips are wet and slack, his eyes dark, his breath rapid. Keeping hold of my hand he pulls me toward the fire, pushes me down upon floor cushions. I lie back, afraid, but wanting. I cannot fight him. I don't want to fight him.

With a grunt he falls down beside me and burrows his face in my neck again, his hands fumbling at my bodice. I can scarcely breathe. I crane back my head, my limbs squirming, pushing my body closer to his. He is making little headway with the lacings and, with a roar of frustration, he tears them apart, freeing my breasts. Then he pulls back a little while he feasts his eyes upon me. Then slowly, he reaches out and cups them with both hands. His thumbs roll across my nipples and I give a small squeal at the waves of pleasure surging through me. "Henry," I gasp, but he doesn't heed me. He is busy at my skirts, his great hand upon my knee. "Henry!" My warning is unconvincing, I feel his fingers on my thigh, upon my … "Henry!" but he is deaf and I am defenceless. I slump upon the pillows, my armour stripped away. I let him have his way.

So this is what the touch of a man feels like! This is the thing I have been yearning for. With clumsy fingers the king invades my secret places, penetrating my innocence and tearing away my dignity. I could not stop him, even were I strong enough. I am embarrassed, yet swamped with desire. I don't want him to stop. As his fingers explore further I grow wanton, opening myself to him, no longer caring if our prince should be born out of wedlock.

I am sprawled before the hearth with my skirts about my waist, my inhibitions fled. Henry kneels before me, fumbles with his codpiece, his jaw tight, his eye as wild as I have ever seen it, his face almost puce with desperation. When I hold out my arms he falls upon me again and we melt into each other, welded as one, his chest rasping against my face, my hands pulling at the back of his shirt, sliding against the slick skin of his buttocks.

At my touch his expression freezes, his body stiffens. With a roar, he thrusts himself against me. For long moments I am suffocating, crushed beneath the weight of his body. A terrific heat gushes suddenly upon my thigh, and then he goes limp and falls against me, breathing hard and fast like a wounded bear.

After a while, his breath having slowed, Henry rolls away and sits with his back to me, his head in his hands, panting heavily. My body is still screaming for his attention. I need him to do to me whatever it is that comes next; something, anything, to relieve the shivering need that consumes me.

"Henry?" My voice is hoarse. I reach out and place a hand upon his lower back, tug at his shirt tail. "Come back to me, My Lord."

He springs to his feet, looks down at me, sprawled dishevelled on his floor, his eyes darting immediately away again. With a swift movement he stoops, pulling down my skirts to cover my nakedness. Then he holds out a hand to help me rise.

"I am so sorry, Anne. I had not meant … I am so sorry, treating you like a tavern wench."

His voice breaks as, wracked with remorse, he struggles to find a way back to how we were before. How can I tell him I don't mind? How can I tell Henry, whose prudish side is now back in control, that all I desire is for him to throw me down and use me so again?

With a heavy heart, I know I must play the sympathetic lady, not the demanding whore.

"I understand, Henry. I know it is difficult for a man to remain chaste for so long. When we are married …"

Words fail me, and while Henry disguises his humiliation by pouring out two cups of wine, I tuck my tingling breasts into my chemise and begin to lace up my bodice.

February 1530 -Richmond

"Tell me it's a lie!" The words hiss from between my teeth, making George draw back in alarm. He holds out his hands.

"Hey, don't shoot the emissary. I am merely reporting what I've heard."

"Then I will see Henry and ask him." I storm across the chamber to the door, but before I can open it George grasps my upper arm, spins me round.

"Don't be a fool, Anne. You need to tread carefully. Pretend you are glad he and Wolsey are reconciled; and should he return to court, receive him graciously. There are many ways to kill a cat."

Anger surges through my body, but inside my head a wiser voice advises me to listen to my brother. My shoulders sag and I slump onto the bed, pluck at the counterpane with nervous fingers. "It is true Henry has missed him. He says no one gives him such honest counsel as 'his old friend, Thomas'. But to go in secret against our work and reinstate Wolsey's archbishopric …"

"Well, if he is wise, perhaps Wolsey will now seek to get the king what he wants, instead of putting Rome before England."

I raise my hand and let it fall again, punching the stuffed mattress with all my might. "Why does the Pope have to be so against this? What concern is it of his who is queen?"

"Hush, hush. He is doing his job, protecting the Church, and he knows Henry fears a war. Catherine has powerful friends, and with France making peace with the Emperor, and stirring up the Scots against us, the king's hands are tied. All we need do is continue to persuade Henry that the Pope is his enemy, and that he needs to break free. Our hardest task will be to make Henry feel justified in taking the matter into his own hands. Just look upon this as a set-back; that is all it is. Wolsey will be his own ruin."

I cover my face with my hands and sob silently for a few moments, although no tears come. "It is so hard for us, George, hard for Henry but harder for me. I know he has other women, he has to seek release somewhere, whereas I ..."

I do not need to speak the words. George knows to what I refer. He gets up, puts his arms around me and I lie upon his chest, the old familiar smell of him reminding me of happier days, youthful days at Hever, before my world was ruled by Henry.

He kisses the top of my head.

"We will get there, Anne. I promise. You will be queen, and your son will sit on the throne, and your daughters will marry with the great princes of Europe. All will be as we want it. It is our destiny, written clear in the stars."

I smile into his jerkin, my courage temporarily restored.

Autumn 1530

In reality, Wolsey is not the master of his own ruin. It takes all our efforts to oust him from favour again. Although he claims sickness and stays away from court for much of the time, his influence with the king remains too great. My brother works closely with Cromwell and Cranmer to undermine his strengths, and magnify his weaknesses.

107

But with new friends come new enemies, and Suffolk, the friend of Henry's youth, turns against me and my cause. It is his wife, Mary, Henry's sister, who is behind his *volte face*, and she makes no secret of her triumph. She has always hated me, resenting the precedence that I, as a mere commoner, am given over her, a Tudor princess and former queen of France. She snubs me publically, looks down her hooked Tudor nose and makes no secret of her championship of Catherine.

"She defies you, Henry," I rage at him. "If it were anyone else, you would have them in the Tower!" But although Henry blusters and threatens her, I cannot make him take action. Not against his sister; not against a Tudor.

And so her husband, Suffolk, takes her side, whispering gossip into the king's ear, gossip about an imagined past affair between myself and Tom Wyatt that, thankfully, the king takes no heed of. Instead of punishing me, Henry turns upon them and sends Brandon and his sulky wife to rusticate at their country seat until he sees fit to recall them.

It is less than they deserve, and although Suffolk may be out of sight, he is not out of mind. I know he continues to work against us, and now that he and his wife are openly my enemies, all I can do is man my guns and defend my rights.

December 1530 - Richmond

"How does this look?" My sister, Mary, whom I have recalled from Hever to bolster my flagging retinue of friends, holds up her embroidery.

"It is a little cockled, Mary. That gold thread needs to be unpicked and re-stitched."

Mary sighs and resigns herself to the task. We are busy designing a new device for my household and I have decided on the phrase;

Let them grumble: this is how it is going to be.

It is a fitting sentiment for the way I feel and will show my enemies, once and for all, the spirit of the woman they are dealing with. They would do well to remember that one day soon I will be their queen.

Mary and I bow our heads to our work again and do not look up until the door opens and the king enters, followed by Norris and George.

"Henry!" I throw away my needlework and rise to greet him. He drapes an arm about my shoulder, kisses the top of my head, and keeps hold of my hand while George pulls up a seat beside mine. We sit ourselves down. Norris perches on the arm of Mary's chair and George stands at the hearth, surreptitiously lifting his doublet to warm his behind.

"What are you working on, Mary?" he asks and she flushes, uncomfortable to be in the presence of the king.

"It is Anne's new device," she murmurs and holds it up for him to see. George, who has just taken a draught of wine, almost chokes.

"You can't use that, Anne. What are you thinking of?"

"Why not?" I stick out my chin and glare at him while Henry leans forward to take my own work from my lap. He frowns at the golden lettering and when he sees what is writ there, his eyebrows shoot up beneath his cap.

"Indeed you cannot, Sweetheart. It would cause a riot."

"Why so? I am fed up with pussyfooting around everyone. I am soon to be their queen. They should respect me for that."

Henry sighs, kisses my fingers, his brow lined with trouble. "We must tread carefully with the people, Anne. We must woo them to our cause, not trample them underfoot."

I look down at my handiwork, the words that had seemed to say it all, and I know he is right. I have known it all along. It is the frustration of my situation that makes me so heavy handed. It is not the first time I have made such a mistake. These days, George is always accusing me of pride and arrogance. "You win yourself no friends," he says, but he doesn't realise how hard it is for me. I am neither one thing nor another, never knowing from one day to the next who at this topsy-turvy court is a true friend, or an enemy.

I should be happy now Wolsey is dead. The hard work of my adherents was unnecessary in the end, for just as they managed to get a warrant for his arrest, word came to us that the old man had died. Of a broken heart, the king believes. Henry wept when he heard the news, and for a long time since has been listless and sad. I fear he blames me for the loss of his friend.

I try to comfort him. I perch on his knee, place my lips on his whiskery cheek. "With Wolsey gone, the way is now clear for us, Henry. At last we can make some headway with the divorce. The cardinal was working against it; secretly he was Catherine's man …"

He looks at me oddly, pushes me from his knee and stands up, moves to the window to look across the wintery gardens.

"Have a care, Madam," he murmurs, "lest I come to believe other rumours that are abroad."

"Rumours?" I stand at his side, my cap just level with his shoulder. "What rumours, My Lord?" I know very well to what he refers, for although I had no hand in it, the death of Wolsey has brought me new enemies. Each time I walk into a room the chatter ceases, and I know they have been talking about me. George says I must brazen it out, so I stick out my chin, gird myself in an armour of steely arrogance, although I know they love me even less for it.

For every ten people who pretend to love me, I warrant there are three who would see me fall, and no matter what I do or how I act, no matter how many churches or colleges I endow, or widows and orphans I give aid to, I will never be beloved … as Catherine is.

Only the king shields me from my enemies, and sometimes I suspect that even Henry grows tired of me. Oh, his eyes follow me still, his gaze lingering warmly on my breasts, his big warm hands coming to rest more often than is seemly upon my waist, or upon my thigh. It is my tongue he does not suffer gladly.

I am skimming along the corridor toward his apartment when I encounter a man from the king's privy chamber bearing a spotless pile of linen. As soon as I see him, suspicion destroys my peace of mind. I stop and click my fingers at the fellow. "Where are you going with the king's linen?"

He flushes, makes as if to bow, remembers himself and merely inclines his head politely. "The king bid me take this linen to the queen's chambers so that she can make up His Majesty's shirts as is customary."

"He? She ...?" I am blustering like a fool, disbelief robbing me of coherence. I turn on my heel, and leaving the man standing open-mouthed, march on toward the king's apartment. The guards, seeing my approach, throw open the door and I pass through the outer chambers, through the presence chamber, and into the privy chamber where I surprise Henry at his midday meal.

"So," I storm without bothering to bid him good day. "You run to Catherine for your new shirts, My Lord. Do you think I am incapable of stitching a few sleeves? Are my needle skills so inferior to hers that you go behind my back for her services? I wonder what other services she continues to offer you. God's teeth, I wish all Spaniards were at the bottom of the sea!"

"Anne!" He gets up from his table, throws down his napkin and bellows at me, his face as red and angry as a baited bull. His attendants keep their eyes on the wall but they cannot hide their shocked, white faces. I suddenly remember to whom I am speaking. It is as if I am looking down from a great height at a picture of myself, a termagant, railing at a king. I see in his small round eyes and tight mouth the man who, pushed too far, will stop at nothing to gain vengeance.

All anger drains away, leaving me shaking, spent. I fall to my knees, my skirts spreading around me.

"I beg pardon, Your Grace. I – I forgot ..."

"Forgot what, Madam? Forgot your place? Forgot the respect you owe your betters – the obedience you owe your monarch?"

I had imagined he was more than just my monarch. I look upon him as my betrothed, my soul mate … perhaps I am wrong.

"Forgive me, Henry." I lift my face up to him, stretch my neck, feel the weight of my hair, my hood, the whole world, dragging it backward, dragging me down. I close my eyes, swallow tears before letting it crash forward again, with a sudden wrenching pain at the top of my spine. "Oh Henry …"

He cannot mistake the despair in my voice. He takes a step forward. "Get up, Anne." There is no love in his voice, just a weary resignation, and I fear I am losing him.

I can't seem to get close as I once did. It is so long since we have been properly alone. Those long heady evenings in his chamber when he would play with my 'duckies' and call me 'sweetheart' are far away. I know I must be gentle, make him love me again, for there are a hundred girls, younger, prettier, and merrier than I waiting to take my place. I cannot lose him now, not after we have come so far. I must win him back, and fast, but a chasm has opened between us, a vast, ugly gulf, and I have no idea how to cross it.

January 1531- Richmond

There is bad news from Rome and Henry is in a towering rage. His courtiers cower in his presence, the women scuttle away at his approach, heads down pretending they don't see him coming. Only I am there to bear the brunt of his fury against the Pope. He waves the communication in the air and yells like a furious child.

"He forbids me, at the request of the queen, to remarry until the decision of the case, and …" Henry stabs the letter with his stubby forefinger, "furthermore, he declares that if we do marry all issue will be illegitimate."

I take the letter from him and quickly scan the page. As I read, the sickness in my belly grows, kindling anger in my heart. The Pope forbids any one in England, of ecclesiastical or secular dignity, universities, parliaments, and courts of law, to make any decision in the affair because the judgment of it is reserved for the Holy See.

I look up at the king, who continues to storm up and down the chamber, his face puce, his lips clenched so tightly they have all but disappeared. "Excommunication?" he rages on. "Does he think that will stop me? I am done with popes and cardinals, I am done with Rome! Send for Cromwell, he will have the answer to this if anyone does."

A page creeps from the corner where he has taken refuge, and after a hasty bow quits the chamber in search of the secretary. While we wait, Henry continues to simmer. I can't find the words to soothe him, for my own spirits are as battered as his. On days like this I wonder if it is all worth it. Had he not laid eyes on me, I could have been wed and become a mother by now.

I might have been happier.

I wonder if Henry feels the same. His quest of me has blown his cosy world asunder. His wife and daughter are estranged from him, half the court murmur against him, and even his friends are turning their backs. And now the Pope threatens to sever all ties with Rome.

Henry is a pious man, a devout Christian. It is not so many years since he earned himself the title 'Defender of the Faith' for his treatise on the defence of the seven sacraments. But the days when Henry was young and brimming with youthful ideology have passed. These days he barely listens to anyone as he single-mindedly pursues his own ends.

I pick at my finger, tear a strip from the side of my nail, making it sore. As I pop it into my mouth Henry sits down, his hands on his knees, his eyes on the floor. Then he gets up again and begins to pace about the room. It seems a long while before Cromwell is announced.

Cromwell's advice has been sought more and more of late. He is an astute man, putting the desires of the king before everything else, even his own wishes. We are affected by his presence, his cool detached manner, as soon as he enters the room. As always, he is clutching a sheaf of papers. He bows to the king and then graciously inclines his head to me, not as reverently as he will when I am queen, but low enough. I give him a brittle smile before his dark-lashed eyes swivel from my face to the king and back again. "How can I be of service, Your Majesty?"

Henry thrusts the balled up letter into Cromwell's chest. He takes it, slowly smoothes out the creases, and begins to read. "Ahh," he says. "It is as I expected."

Henry sits again and fixes the secretary with his eye. "If you expected this then I assume you have already concocted a remedy."

Cromwell smiles slowly and inclines his head again. "Indeed, Your Majesty, I have a remedy of sorts ... although I am not sure you will find it completely pleasing."

Henry gestures him to continue, the jewels on his fingers flashing in the firelight. "Go on, go on, don't hedge, man. I don't bite."

I raise my eyebrows at this but Cromwell doesn't flinch. He places his papers on the table and takes a seat, presses the tips of his ink-stained fingers together. "Your Grace, I have discussed the remedy with my colleagues and, with one or two exceptions, we all agree that it may be possible ... or even necessary, for you to dispense with the services of Rome altogether and become sole protector and supreme head of the Church in England ... and its clergy."

Henry straightens up, narrows his eyes. I can almost see his brain assimilating the information and envisioning making it so. "As a sort of Pope, you mean? Head of the state and the church?"

"Yes, Your Majesty."

"I would no longer need to consult Rome on any matter ecclesiastical?"

"No, Your Majesty."

"And the revenues from the churches, that would no longer go to Rome?"

"No, Your Majesty."

Henry looks across the room to me, a gleam in his eye, a half smile playing on his lips. "That would be a blow, to both Pope Clement and Spain. I can be free of Catherine, free of the Pope, and free to marry as I see fit and get myself an heir. Can this really be done, Cromwell?"

Cromwell inclines his head, and as the full implications of what this might mean filters through his mind, Henry slaps his thigh in satisfaction. He holds out his arms. "Come here, Sweetheart. Cromwell, my man, sort this out for us and you shall be richer than a Jew. Go now, don't make me sorry."

As the secretary bows from the room, Henry nuzzles into my neck, his tongue sending shivers of delight along my spine. For the rest of the afternoon he is my Henry again, our enemies are all but vanquished and all the old passions are rekindled.

Less than a month later, the deed is all but done. Henry declares himself Head of the English Church and clergy, although it takes every inch of Cromwell's acumen to do so, and even then he has to concede to their reservations by adding the codicil 'as far as the law of Christ allows."

Although Henry and I are happy, Cromwell is happy, and my father and George are ecstatic, not everyone is as delighted as we. There are some courtiers who oppose the move, and even more who oppose our marriage.

Suffolk, as I had guessed, speaks out against me, as does my aunt, the Duchess of Norfolk. More, I suspect, to spite her unfaithful husband than me. Bishop Fisher dissents, of course, as does Henry's oldest and heretofore mentor, Thomas More.

I fear Henry's heart will break at the defection of 'Dear Tom', as the King calls him. I hold the king's hand as he weeps, and try to help him steel himself to accept More's resignation as Chancellor and look about for a replacement, more sympathetic to our needs.

As word of our plans spreads, discord breaks out in the streets. We begin to hear tales of a lunatic nun, whom the common people refer to as the Nun of Kent. She defames me in the streets, declaring from the town cross that should Henry marry me, he will die shortly after and that his place in Hell is already marked.

She has long been a thorn in our flesh, speaking out against reform, renouncing Lutherism and naming me a whore and a disciple of Satan. I would have her hanged, but Henry, although he will not admit it, is afraid. In some parts of the country she is more popular than the king himself, and he is reluctant to stir up rebellion.

To take my mind off it, I turn my attention to renovating York Place. Soon my chambers are heaped with fabric and hangings as I select the best for our new home. I send for tapestries from Florence, glass from Venice, and as the pile of sumptuous trappings grows, so does the bill from the drapers.

Mary and I are engaged in the vital decision of what colour draperies I should choose for the bedchamber when Henry arrives. I am not expecting him and as I scramble to my feet, a swathe of priceless silk slithers to the floor. "Henry!" I hurry toward him, rise on my toes to kiss his whiskery cheek, while Mary stays where she is sorting through a pile of samples. By rights she should rise and greet her king in the proper manner, but neither Henry nor I reprimand her.

He leads me into the antechamber and holds out a roll of parchment. "What is it?" I ask, unsure if it be good tidings or bad.

"Open it and see." He is smiling, so guessing the news is not bad, I break the seal and unroll the missive, begin to scan the contents. As I read, the colour rises in my cheeks, the heat builds up in my face, and my ears begin to ring. "Henry!" I gasp, and look up at him, a hand to my throbbing heart.

He is like a benign uncle, his mouth stretched into a smile, his cheeks as flushed as mine. "I thought it would please you."

"Please me? Why, it's, it's … oh Henry!"

Throwing decorum away, I fling my arms about his neck, kissing him over and over. For a while he flounders, trying to capture my lips as they fly about his face, until finally he seizes my head, clamps it still and kisses me properly, his mouth fastened over mine and his passion as uncontainable as it has ever been.

I have won him back, I think, with a huge surge of relief. I had feared that all was lost but he wants me still. We stumble backwards onto a settle, almost overbalancing it, my skirts tumbling, my legs bared to the knee. As we grapple together like a child wrestling a beast, I laugh as loudly as he. He is a bear of a man, there is nothing I can do to control him, but I don't want to, not really. But then I remember our prince, and how vital it is that he be born within wedlock. I reluctantly seek to put an end to the tussle.

"My Lord," I cry, "is this how you would treat a marchioness?"

After a moment Henry sits up, and I hastily straighten my garments, catch my breath, and tuck my hair back beneath my cap. He looks at me sideways as I adjust my garters. "It pleases you then, to be Marchioness of Pembroke?"

My smile is like the sunshine. "It does indeed, my love. It does indeed."

June 1532

Henry and I are alone. Ostensibly, he is listening to the new piece I have been practicing on my lute but in reality he is plucking his bottom lip, deep in thought. I hate it when this mood takes him. He retreats so far into himself that I have no clue to his feelings, I am not party to his problems. When he

117

sighs for the hundredth time, I cease mid-tune and put my instrument down. "What is bothering you, Henry?"

"Hmmm?" He looks up, dragging himself back from wherever he has been. "What did you say, my dear?"

"I asked what it is that troubles you."

"Have you spoken to George today?"

"George? No, I had a glimpse of him this morning but he was waylaid by his wife. Since I had no wish to be involved in another of their marital disputes, I beat a hasty retreat."

The king smiles, and sighs again. "There is more trouble, I fear."

There is always trouble. Catherine is behind it all, I have no doubt about that. She is always harping on about her penury and tribulation, although she is housed in luxury with more than three hundred retainers and no less than fifty ladies in waiting, not bad for a woman who is no longer queen.

I feel my features harden as I think of her, and it takes some effort to shake away the tension and present Henry with a calm, gentle face. I fail miserably and when my words tumble from my mouth, my voice is full of bitterness and frustration.

"And what does Catherine want from us now, my love? A liveried servant to exercise her dog?"

He looks up, surprised at my venom. "No," he says, "it isn't Catherine, not this time."

"Then what is it, Henry?"

He shifts in his seat, turns his eye upon me, his gaze so penetrating that I can feel my colour begin to rise.

"Your dealings with young Percy ... how far did they go?"

I open and close my mouth, my cheeks flushing deeper. "I don't know what you mean, My Lord. It went nowhere at all. The cardinal saw to that."

"Oh come, Anne. There must be more to it than that. Were you not in love? Did you not meet in secret, hold hands? Did he never kiss you?"

I stand up, afraid now. Unsure of where he is leading me, unsure what answer he requires, but certain he must never know the truth. "Our meetings were brief. He kissed my hands and my cheek, but no more than that. I was an honest maid. Does Your Majesty think I would refuse the bed of my king yet succumb to the fumblings of an untried boy?"

It is only a little lie, there was very little more to it really, but Henry's jealousy is sometimes out of control and I am not prepared to risk losing him now. He stares at me for a long moment, his slitted eyes darting about my face, looking for lies, searching for deceit.

"So there was no contract?"

"No! Nothing more than the pretensions of a pair of silly children. Wolsey was right to intervene; it was nothing more than folly."

Henry seems to relax a little.

"Why do you ask, Henry? What has brought this on?"

I hold out my hand and he takes it, pulls me closer, and I perch on the arm of his chair.

"Percy's wife is seeking a divorce. She claims that a pre-contract with you before witnesses makes their marriage illegal."

Dread creeps like a spider up my spine but I try not to shiver. "And what does Percy say?"

"We shall find out very soon. I have summoned him to appear before me. Let us hope his story is the same as yours."

Henry looks at me from the corner of his eye, judging my reaction. I keep my expression bland as I have learnt it is best to do. I toss my head and smile at him, for all the world as if my belly is not churning with fear.

"Well then, there will be no problem. Mary Talbot is clutching at straws, seeking any way to be free of him."

Outwardly, I am calm, pretending indifference, hoping with all my heart that Percy will have the sense to lie. Any hint of a pre-contract between us will put an end to my marriage with the king, and Henry's wrath will be terrible, for both of us. Percy cannot be unaware of the danger in which we both stand, or so I hope, but as I recall, he was never the sharpest blade in the king's armoury.

"Let us hope so, Madam. His arrival is expected any time now, and then we shall know the truth of the matter."

"Then, I shall make myself scarce …"

"No. No, Anne. You are to stay here and receive him with me. I would watch his reaction. I will know from his demeanour if he dissembles, just as I will from yours."

And so I stand at the king's right hand, and wait for Percy to be shown into our presence. I have no idea how it will feel to be face to face with my old love again. I try to remember what he looked like, what it was I felt for him, but it evades me. All I remember is my banging heart, my throbbing pulse and the secrecy, the excitement and the sense of danger our dalliance evoked. It was never real. Poor Percy was nothing but an outlet for my youthful longings, and I hope with all my heart that what he felt for me was equally as fabricated.

A sound outside the apartment alerts us that our conversation is at an end. Marching feet, a thump on the door and the guards snap to attention; Percy's arrival is announced. The man who used to make my heart race stands just inside the door, twisting his cap in his hands. When Henry beckons him closer, he shuffles forward and makes his bow, first to Henry and then to myself, as if I am already queen.

As he straightens up he glances at me, whipping his eye quickly away before I can acknowledge him, and thereafter concentrates on the face of his king. Although he is the Earl of Northumberland and one of the most powerful men in the kingdom, he looks pale, but whether this is due to illness or the impending wrath of his monarch I do not know.

How puny he is, I think, how very feeble. His father, the great Earl, must have been sore disappointed in his son. He continues to twist his cap, the fine velvet will be ruined, the teardrop pearls loosened and lost if he carries on. I notice how bony and white his fingers are. He has bitten his fingernails to the quick and I remember, with a sudden shudder, those fingers tangling in my hair, his palms cupping my breasts, and those trembling blue lips biting and sucking at my throat. I swallow and turn away, disgusted at the laxity of my younger self. It takes a great deal of determination to thrust the picture away and remember who I am. I am Anne Boleyn, and soon to be Henry's queen. I take a deep breath and try to still the fear in my gut.

Percy's voice has not changed at all. He clears his throat, swallows, and in shaking, high-pitched tones denounces his wife as a liar and a scold.

"Our marriage has not been a happy one, Your Majesty," he says. "From our first day she has made it her mission in life to make me miserable. I will be as happy as she to see an end to it, but I will not let her lies slander a good woman's character, nor impinge on Your Grace's future happiness. There was no contract between the Lady Anne and myself. We shared a few dances and a walk in the gardens; that is all."

That is well said, Percy, I think, looking on him with new, approving eyes. He is sweating. I can see it popping from his forehead, trickling down the side of his neck, dampening his collar. Beside me Henry leans forward, his mean mouth tight and threatening.

"You swear that to your king and, should the need arise, will you swear it before the court?"

Percy stands tall, no longer shaking so much, his chin firmer, his eyes curiously bright as, for both our sakes, he calmly perjures himself.

"Before God, Your Grace."

Silence in the room, apart from a fly banging its head repeatedly against the mullioned window. I am abruptly aware of how very hot it is in this stuffy chamber, and I wish I could push the walls and the ceiling away and feel the sun on my face and the wind in my hair.

I long for the meadows of Hever, the days of my youth. After so many years, Percy's presence reminds me of all those times of pleasure and laughter, and I realise I am growing old in the king's company. When I first came to his notice, I was little more than a girl. I was in demand, courted by many and flirting with any, yet all these years later, although laden down with jewels and property, I am still a maid. Still not wed, still not a mother.

1st September 1532 - Windsor

I am up with the lark on the morning I am to be crowned Marchioness. The early September sun streams through the casement, the light flashing and flicking upon the surface of my bath like bright water nymphs. One of my women brings a jug and trickles warm fluid through my hair, the steam rising and infusing the air with the scent of roses.

Warmed by braziers, the room is busy with my attendants. Mary, who perches nearby watching the proceedings, quirks her brow. "Quite a ceremony," she sniffs as she tests the nap of my new velvet gown between finger and thumb. "I hope you will not forget us once you are of the nobility."

"As if I could ever climb so high as to forget you and George," I say, squeezing a sponge along my arm, watching the trickling water glisten. "I intend to raise you both as high as I can. We will find you a handsome nobleman of your own, Mary. How would you like that?"

Her pretty cheeks flush but she shrugs her shoulders, doesn't meet my eye. She slides from the bed and moves to the window, leaning across the sill to inhale the freshness of the morning. Windsor is one of Henry's favourite palaces and each summer, to avoid the pestilence that season can bring, the court adjourns to the leafier pleasures offered by the castle. With a prime hunting ground on his doorstep, Henry mounts up most days and rides from dawn to dusk, coming home tired and famished. But not today.

Today is special, for it marks my ascendency to the nobility. My new title of Marchioness of Pembroke will not only offer me new property and vast wealth, but also marks another step on my passage from commoner to queen.

I have never been more popular with my family. Their gifts come flooding in; some from my closest kin, but many from cousins and second-cousins I have not spoken to in an age, most of them by way of angling for preferment. Of all the gifts, the one presented to me by William Brereton is my favourite. It is a puppy, an Italian greyhound who I've named Urien, from the tales of Arthur. He is a timid little thing who, when he cannot seek the warmth of my skirts, hugs the hearth in search of comfort. He is chewing on a jewelled slipper that was part of a gift presented to me that morning by the French ambassador. The whole chamber is piled with sumptuous frivolities.

In a spurt of generosity I make a gift of some of their offerings to Mary. "I have so much," I say, "and you have so little." But instead of gratitude, a look of irritation flashes across her face. She tries to hide it but it is too late, I have seen it, and some of my euphoria dwindles. "I want us to be friends, Mary, that is all."

She stands up, the hoods and bracelets she has been holding falling to the floor. "You don't have to buy me, Anne. I am your sister. If you want my advice, I would concentrate on winning the love of those about court who would do you harm." She sighs, puts a hand to her forehead, her brow wearily furrowed. "I must make ready for the ceremony," she says, her voice dull but still vaguely irritated. "I will come back once I am dressed."

"I thought you wanted to borrow a hood ...?" I call after her, but she is gone. I shrug my shoulders, not sure what I have done now to upset her. She is so prickly, and the more I try to regain our former friendship the further she slips from me. Deciding to speak to Henry at the first opportunity and get her a good husband, I let the matter slip from my mind.

A little later while my ladies are lacing me into my petticoat, George pokes his head around the door, his demeanour as different from Mary's as chalk is from cheese.

"Can I come in?" he says, and without waiting for confirmation he makes his way across the room, picking his way through dropped linen and abandoned sleeves. He places a protracted kiss on my cheek, inhaling deeply as if I am a buttercup. "Mmm," he says, "you smell heavenly."

"Thank you." I hold out my right arm while my woman fixes on a sleeve. "What are you hiding behind your back, George? Is it a present?"

He winks gaily at one of my servants and she giggles, smiling shyly back at him. We are all merry today but I flick my hand, bidding her get on with the task of picking up the clothes from the floor. Despite my silent reprimand, from time to time she cannot help casting an eye in his direction to see if he is still watching. But George has forgotten her.

He perches on the edge of my bed, holds out his hand and opens his fingers. "Of course, anything I give you will be overshadowed by the jewels that Henry brings, but I thought you might like it."

Moving forward, wearing only one crimson sleeve, my hair as yet loose, my bodice not properly laced, I lean over his outstretched hand. "Oh George," I say. "It is exquisite. I love it."

"You are just saying that." He watches as the girl bends over to gather an armful of shoes and when she rises again, he smiles appreciatively. I can never fathom my brother's intrigue with the lower classes. To give him credit, although I know his relationship with Jane remains cool, his name has never been linked in scandal to anyone. I begin to wonder if his wife wears a long face because he prefers to spend his nights curled up with a hearth wench, or vice versa.

"You are silly, George. Of course I love it, but you know I cannot wear it today. I must please the king and wear the jewels he has sent me."

"I know. I am sorry I cannot afford to give you gems fit for a marchioness." He gets up, kisses my neck where it meets my shoulder and I duck my chin to my collarbone.

"Don't, it tickles," I laugh, pushing him away. "I shall wear your jewel tomorrow. I may even wear it when I accompany the king to France. I may wear it on the day I am introduced to King Francis himself."

I hold the single drop pearl to my throat and turn my head this way and that, admiring myself in the looking-glass.

"If you do that it will be all around Europe that Henry is a miser and keeps his future queen in penury."

"I am hardly in rags!" I wave my arm about the chamber indicating the furs, the velvets and fine silk. "I have more finery than the king himself. He has demanded that Catherine hand over the royal jewels ... and look, George, look at the robes I am to wear this afternoon."

I summon Nan, who hurries forward to hang the ermine-trimmed robe about my shoulders. My hair is loose, falling to my waist like a dark silken shroud. I raise my chin, assume a haughty demeanour and look at George from the corner of my eye. I expect to find him laughing or mocking, but instead his face has grown sombre, his eyes dark and kindling. "Oh Anne," he whispers, "my little sister. You have climbed so high." He comes closer, lifts my fingers to his lips. "I am so proud; it almost makes me want to weep."

Our heads are close together. He leans his forehead on mine and I raise my eyes, but he is so near his face is blurred. "God bless you, Anne," he whispers, and the kiss he leaves upon my forehead is as soft as summer rain.

Henry, enthroned in splendour, seems like a stranger. As I am led toward him amid a great clarion of trumpets, he keeps his expression neutral. All around me the courtiers jostle for a better view, the crush and the atmosphere is heavy with the solemnity of the moment. In raising me to the nobility, no one can doubt the sincerity of his intention to marry me, and realising that I am soon to be queen in deed, they are all come to do me honour. And soon they will all be vying for the privilege of seeing me crowned queen.

They are all here, or at least, those that matter. Now that I am to be the highest peeress in the land, many noses are out of joint. Henry's stubborn mule of a sister has stayed away, feigning illness, but her husband, Suffolk, has reluctantly agreed to attend. My father is there with my uncle of Norfolk, his eagle eye darting about the hall, no doubt marking all who are absent, including his own wife, my aunt Elizabeth, who continues to obstinately champion Catherine's cause. But I do not care. I am winning the battle, while the old queen shivers in her draughty exile. I, the new queen, am in ascendancy and no one can stop me.

We approach the throne and the trumpets cease. I curtsey low before the king and then kneel upon the steps as the hall falls silent, waiting for Bishop Gardiner to read out the patent, conferring upon me and all my offspring the title of Marchioness of Pembroke.

As Marchioness in my own right, no one can take it away from me. Even after my death, those rights will pass to my sons and to their sons, forever more.

Henry comes forward and as he draws close I recognise the gentleness, the warm affection in his eyes, and also the hint of a tear. I bow my head, look down past the jutting royal codpiece to his well-turned calves and jewelled square-toed shoes. He places the coronet very lightly on my head, letting his hands run softly down my hair as I rise to stand before him. He briefly clasps my shoulders, and without moving my head, I raise my eyes to his and discover a smile quirking the side of his mouth as he drapes the crimson mantle about me. He is so close I can detect the aroma of rosewater, the underlying musky scent of his body.

In his grandeur he looks all powerful, invincible, and I am suddenly full of wonder that I have this man's love. This man, who is almost a god, has seen fit to endow me, a nobody from Kent, with his heart and his hand in marriage. I close my eyes, trembling with emotion, and thank God for it. I thank God not just for Henry the king, but for Henry the man too, and I silently swear to be a good wife, a noble queen and, just as soon as I am blessed with Henry's son, I will be a mother fit to rival the Virgin Mary herself.

"Did you see Tom Wyatt today?"

Mary and I are walking along the *chemin de rond* – the walkway behind the battlements. We can see for miles across the choppy waters of the Channel, and it is strange to think that England lies somewhere across those waters. All the people we have left behind are there, continuing their lives. I spend some time considering the implications of Mary's question before deciding she is too guileless to mean anything by it.

"I saw him but did not speak to him, since you were both nattering away nineteen to the dozen."

She flushes. "We haven't seen each other for years, not since …" She squints, trying to recall, but in the end she gives up. "Oh, I don't know, but it is a long time."

"How is he?" I ask nonchalantly, leaning on the cold stone of the battlement.

"Well in health, I think, although not happy in his self."

"Why is that?" I ask, although I know the answer before she gives it.

"As I understand it, he mislikes his wife, and she him. He says he hasn't been home to Kent in a long while."

"That is because Henry keeps sending him overseas. There is nothing wrong with Elizabeth Wyatt, as I remember her."

"Well, that is as maybe, but you don't have to live with her."

I laugh and, calling Urien to my side, link arms with my sister as we continue our promenade. It is early afternoon and I am missing Henry, who has been visiting King Francis in Boulogne. I imagine, from what I remember of the French king, that the carousing will have been thorough. I expect Henry to be tired on his return, and probably rather tetchy. Of course, had our plans not gone awry I should have accompanied him to the French court, but Francis' new wife had other ideas.

At first, when I heard that Queen Eleanor would not agree to meet me, I was angry and wanted Henry to refuse to meet with them at all. And, to be honest, the injury went deeper because my dear friend Marguerite, Francis' sister, with whom I had been great friends during my youth in France, also declined to be introduced to me. She claims to be too ill but I know she fears to undermine her queen's staunch support of Catherine. I suppose queens must stick together, but instead of blaming Eleanor and Marguerite personally for their slight, I add it to the list of Catherine's other crimes.

Why is that woman so stubborn? Why couldn't she just retire gracefully? Why, oh why, does she have to cause us so much trouble? Does she not want Henry to be happy, or to have a legitimate son? These are the questions that constantly jostle in my mind. She spoils so much; she is like a great blot of black ink upon the perfect snowy page of mine and Henry's relationship.

Yet not for one moment do I let my disappointment show. Not even Mary or Jane Rochford, who are constantly at my side, know how deep the insult cuts. What care I for the love of the French king's wife and sister? —I have other friends. There is no doubt I am loved. For the ten days we've spent in Calais so far, I have been treated as if I am already Henry's queen, and it is a feeling I like very much. Everywhere I go I am accompanied by a train of thirty ladies-in-waiting, all of whom are overwhelmed by the courtesy we receive. The soldiers stationed at the garrison battle to outdo each other in gaining our attention, and twice I have had to call Mary away from unsuitable company and reprimand her.

"You must remember who you are," I tell her. "If we are to find you a good husband, your reputation must be unsullied." Or as unsullied as a girl with two bastard offspring can be, I add silently.

Mary shrugs and doesn't apologise. Without a hint of regret she says, "They are harmless, Anne, and far from home. They are glad of the company of English ladies, it is not just me. Nan was getting along very nicely with a certain fellow last evening."

I cannot prevent a little ire from creeping into my voice. "That's as may be, but make sure you remember that you are a lady, and soon to be sister to the queen."

"As if I can forget that," she snaps. After a few moments, which pass in silence, she makes an excuse to leave my presence and I sulk for a while, as at odds with her as she is with me.

What is wrong with her? Surely she isn't still jealous? She can't still be pining for Henry. It has been years now since they were together. I bite my inner cheek and wonder what it is that ails her. I am still lost in thought when a herald arrives to inform me that Henry is on his way from Boulogne, and that the king of France is in his train.

I don't know when I have attended so sumptuous a feast. Never one to waste an opportunity to show off, Henry ensures that everything is done to impress the French king. The servants stagger in with course after course of fine food, and the wine flows forth in a stream of ruby-red celebration. The last time I saw King Francis I was still a lady-in-waiting, a green girl with her life as yet unmapped. This time, after a meagre span of years, I am introduced as Henry's intended queen. Life truly is a great leveller.

My ladies and I have spent the last few weeks putting together a masque for his entertainment. And since the first thing he did on his arrival was to present me with a diamond the size of a baby's fist, I intend to entertain him well.

With my ears still ringing from the three thousand gun salute that was fired in his honour, I join my favourite ladies on the floor. A gasp eddies about the hall and both kings put down their knives as Mary, Jane, Nan, Elizabeth, Lady Fitzwater, Lady Lisle, Lady Wallop, and I, masked and clad identically in cloth of gold, burst into the hall. After a few dainty circuits of the floor to the accompaniment of hoots and whistles of appreciation, we each choose a partner to lead into the dance. I, of course, prowl laughingly toward

King Francis, who gets up, takes my hand and drools like a dog over my naked arm.

From his place at the table, Henry watches, his eyes narrowed and brooding, but I have a job to do and I mean to do it well. It is imperative that I woo Francis onto our side; he must support us in Rome, stand fast with us against Spain. Without France as an ally, England will be isolated, forced to stand alone against the whole of Europe. So, trying not to stare at his nose that rises like a pinnacle in the centre of his face, I smile and simper and make a great friend of him.

He stands too close to me, squints down at me. "I could not believe when I heard of the English king's infatuation for a commoner, Lady Anne, but now I have met you, all becomes perfectly clear."

"But, Your Majesty, we have met before. I spent my youth at your court with my sister, Mary."

He looks blank and I can see he has no recollection of me, no recollection of taking my sister's virtue, and I am fuelled with sudden anger. How dare this vain, ugly – yes, ugly –French pig have ruined my sister's reputation and then forgotten her very existence! It takes all my wits to maintain my smile as I must do to ensure his allegiance. As the evening continues, somehow I tolerate his slimy attentions and focus upon my goal.

As we dance and make merry together, Henry watches, as if uncertain whether my admiration is an act or not. I inwardly despair at the conceit of these kings, so different in appearance yet so alike in vanity. It is quite clear that once I have snared Francis' friendship and made a slave of him, I will have Henry's damaged pride to soothe. It is a delicate path I tread, juggling the demands of both kings.

It is late when the evening finally draws to a close and I am able to prise myself from the attentions of King Francis. At first, when Henry and I are alone in his chamber, he is quiet, withdrawn. Dispensing with their services, he chases his yawning attendants to bed and I move from the warmth of the fire to stand beside him as he draws the shutters.

The pale pink stripe of morning is snug against the horizon, and the cold blue day set to begin, but we are alone and drenched in weariness. I stretch and yawn.

"The evening went well, I think."

"Yes, it did, thanks to you and your coquettish ways."

He draws me close and I tuck my hands beneath his fur doublet, feel the warmth of his body through the lawn of his shirt. I smile into his chest.

"The French king is less a man than you, my love. You must know I was only play-acting to bind him to our cause."

He sighs deeply, rests his chin on my head and holds me so tightly I can feel the thud of his heart, the rise and fall of his breathing. I am safe and I am warm, and I am cherished. I have no wish to leave his company for the loneliness of my maiden bed. I raise my face to his, close my eyes, my pursed lips asking for his kiss.

At first he is gentle, his touch as soft as a baby's, but as I press against him and let him feel my nakedness beneath my loose chamber-robe, he grows more ardent. We have been here many times, he has had me naked to the waist, he has spent his ardour many times upon my thigh, but tonight something is different. His hands roam over my body until I am breathless, desperate that this time there should be more. He draws away a little, looks down at me, his face dark and serious. Even though no words are exchanged, we both know that tonight there can be no turning back.

Not tonight.

He takes my hand and leads me toward the bed, stopping just short of it to kiss me again and slip my robe from my shoulders, leaving me in nothing but a thin chemise. With great daring I pull his doublet apart and begin to tug at his shirt; the cuffs and collar of which have been lovingly embroidered by his discarded wife.

His hands are large and strike cold through my shift. He cups a breast, making me gasp. It is lost in his palm but he rubs and massages, teasing my nipples until they stand proud. When I am almost ready to swoon I place a hand

131

either side of his head and drag his face down, cover his mouth with mine, but he pulls away. He lifts me bodily from the floor, carries me to the bed and throws me onto the mattress.

I am panting, the secret place between my legs is throbbing and twitching. I want him so badly I can hang onto virtue no longer. All my self-imposed chastity is forgotten as I scramble up to rest upon his pillows and open my arms.

With great grunting and struggling, Henry wriggles from his hose, casts his shirt to the floor and leaps onto the bed beside me. It is like wrestling a bear. He tosses me from side to side so I can scarcely catch my breath. Some part of me remembers that I must not offend him with undue lust, so I become pliant. I keep my eyes firmly closed, and resist the urge to slow him down and guide his hand to where I need it most.

But as soon as I get comfortable and begin to relax, he shifts position again. One moment his mouth is slurping like a child at my breast, the next he is biting and sucking at my thigh. Then he turns me over, his great hands massaging my buttocks, his fingers prodding and penetrating, making me wriggle and squeak. I want him to slow down, to stroke me, love me gently, and ease me into the experience but, like a ship lost at sea, I am at the mercy of his storming passion.

He bites and nibbles at my quaint. I throw my head back, melting into the heavenly sensation, but just as I feel I am drowning and my breath becomes deep and slow, he pulls away. I open one eye in time to find him sliding up my body, his blue gaze gleaming with intent.

He is bathed in sweat and something hot and hard is nudging at my thigh. I instinctively part my legs. He rolls heavily upon me, my face squashed between the pillow and his downy chest, my mouth full of hair. As he lifts both my knees and plunges into me, I cry aloud at the sudden shock and grab his shoulders, digging my nails deep into royal skin.

Thereafter I hold my breath, astonished and out of control. As he moves rhythmically upon me, I open my mouth, my breath knocked from my lungs while Henry's voice rasps hoarse in my ear. His grip becomes more painful as his thrusts grow deeper and more rapid. And then he ceases, stiffens, shuddering deeply, setting the whole bed aquiver, before slumping upon me like one dead.

Henry rolls away, sits on the edge of the bed, his chest heaving, his skin slick with sweat. He turns to look at me, his red hair stuck darkly to his head and in his eye I recognise gratitude, mixed with more than a little shame.

Was that it? The wondrous thing everyone whispers about? Is that the act that people have killed for, men have started wars for, women have died for?

"Did I hurt you?" He comes back to my side, picks up a strand of my gnarled and knotted hair. I shake my head. Feel a tear trickle toward the pillow.

"No," I whisper and it's true, he didn't hurt me. Not really. He surprised me, shocked me, exhausted and overwhelmed me, but my overriding emotion is not one of injury or anxiety. It is disappointment.

In the morning he takes me again, and later that afternoon, when the rest of the court are taking the air, he locks his chamber door and begins to raise my skirts. I put out a hand, clasp his wrist. "Henry, suppose I have a child. What then? We do not want our prince denounced as a bastard."

Not to be deterred, he tips me backward across the counterpane and begins to untangle my legs from my petticoat. "Don't worry." He looks up from between my thighs. "We will be wed the moment we reach the shores of England."

I lie back and close my eyes as his lips brush the contours of my quaint. How can that be, I think, when he is still tied to the Spanish woman? But some remedy must be found for I can no longer keep his lust at bay. Indeed, it is a wonder that I have held him off for so long. Now that I am his wife in all but name, I swear for the sake of our unborn child that I will go to any lengths to secure him.

133

For days now a storm has been blowing, preventing our return to England. Fortunately the exchequer has beautiful gardens and a tennis court, and the rooms I have been given are sumptuous. My apartments adjoin the king's, a convenience that he takes every opportunity to enjoy. Since the evening of the revel I have not spent one night alone, and most afternoons have seen me in his bed. I begin to look forward to the days when state affairs keep him occupied and I am accorded some relief.

I lower myself delicately into a seat, my rump as tender as if I have been a week on horseback. Guessing the cause, George quirks his brow and chuckles as he leans over my chair to whisper in my ear. "Our king is treating you well, My Lady Marchioness?"

I punch his shoulder. "If it is any of your business, Brother. I am as well and as thoroughly serviced as a brood mare."

He sits close to me. "So, the rumours are true, our king is indeed a stallion. You are a lucky woman ..." He begins to laugh but something in my face halts him. "... or maybe not?"

I flush, feeling a sudden rush of tears. My chin begins to wobble and my mouth goes out of shape, making it difficult to form my words. He reaches for my hand.

"Hey, don't cry. It can't be that bad. These things sometimes take time to get right."

My breast judders as I dash the tears from my cheek. He is the only person I can confide in, for there is no way on God's earth I will ever tell Mary. She would not be able to hide her delight that her one-time lover has disappointed me.

"I had thought there would be more to it ..." My words fade as my confusion grows. I should not be talking this way, not even to George. It would be betrayal to speak this way of any man, but to defame a king's sexual prowess is tantamount to treason. While my cheeks continue to burn, George shows no such reticence.

"You went the whole way, then. He ...?"

"Yes, George. Spare me your questions, for Heaven's sake."

"So, what was wrong? You found him displeasing, you do not love him after all?"

George's hand is on my lap, the pressure of his fingers caressing the bony contours of my knee, his expression so concerned and loving that tears nudge behind my eyelids again. I take a kerchief, shake it out and begin to dab my cheeks dry.

"I love him very well, as much as I ever did. It is not that, at all. It is ... well, I had imagined ... I had been told that there was great pleasure in it."

For once, he doesn't laugh. He straightens his spine, tilts his head to one side, one corner of his mouth lifted in a sorrowful smile.

"Ah, poor Anne." He gets down on his knees before me and slides his arms about my shoulders, his voice muffled in my hair. "There is pleasure to be had, Sweetheart, with the right man, in the right circumstances. Very great pleasure that I cannot begin to describe." He sits back and, taking my kerchief, dries my eyes. "We can only hope that you will find it one day. In the meantime, concentrate on conceiving the king a prince. Often, it is when we are not looking for pleasure that we find it."

"Dear George, where would I be without you to comfort me?"

He stands up, stretches his back, and picks up a cup of wine. "We, all of us, have travelled a long hard road to get where we are. You most of all, and if a brother can't support his little sister in her travail, then who can ...?"

The door opens and Jane enters. "Oh, there you are, George," she says, letting the door bang behind her. "I should have guessed." She looks at me, her eyes kindling with barely suppressed rage. "Can I get you anything, Anne? A bite of supper, perhaps?"

I shake my head and gesture for her to take a seat, although I would rather she left us in peace. She perches

135

straight-backed on a stool, her dislike for me dissolving the former intimacy.

"I can see you've been crying; is anything wrong?"

I shake my head and try to smile. "No, I am fine, now. George has just been advising me on a private matter."

Her mouth spreads in a forced show of pleasure. "You are fortunate to have both a brother and a king to offer you comfort when you are unhappy."

I ignore her inferred insult, and shake my head. "I expect I am just tired from all the excitement, and I am finding the delay in our departure for England tiresome."

"Aren't we all?" George leans back in his chair, stretches his long legs toward the hearth and refuses to look at his wife. He raises his cup. "To a quick return of our Marchioness' smile," he says. "And here's to a hasty change in the wind."

As if George's words have some heavenly influence, by the next morning the storm has abated, and a few days later we are able to leave. Henry and I stand on deck and watch the port of Calais dwindle into the distance. I hold on tight to the rail and turn my head and look across the surging grey sea, focussing my sight on the coast of England, the white cliffs eventually emerging from the mist like a welcoming banner. As we draw ever closer to home, I remember Henry's words. "We will be married just as soon as we reach the shores of England," and I wonder if he meant them.

There is a priest waiting, and although Henry's divorce from Catherine is by no means certain, and I have some doubts as to the legality of it, we make a hasty vow before him. Henry promises a more public marriage when we reach London and, despite the vile weather, I am anxious to travel on. Yet Henry tarries and seems to have forgotten that, even now, I may be ripening with his prince. We stop at each and every manor house we pass to enable Henry to make full use of my newly available body.

PART THREE
QUEEN

I spend the night alone, or in as much solitude as I am ever afforded. As I slide from my bed and creep across the floor, my attendant raises a sleepy head from her pillow, but I hush her back to sleep. Used to my nocturnal comings and goings, she obediently turns over, thumps her pillow, her gentle snores resuming almost at once.

Knowing she would not relish the business I am bent upon, I do not wake Mary but tread even more carefully as I pass her door. Hurrying along the corridor, tying my gown as I go, my stomach churns with anticipation until I reach the side chamber where I have instructed Nan to wait upon me. She is fully dressed and waiting, and when I slide through the heavy door she dips a curtsey in greeting.

"I have your things ready, My Lady."

With great stealth she helps me from my night attire and into the gown I have selected for my wedding to the king. She bathes my face and washes my hands, and then I stand erect while she ties in my sleeves and fastens back my hair before placing a jewelled cap upon it.

I like Nan, and have come to rely upon her calm nature that ensures she never frets or fusses. She has never yet expressed any shock or surprise, even when I instruct her to carry out the most extraordinary things, and she did not bat an eye when I asked her to meet me here at dawn, bringing with her my favourite gown and jewels. I smile at her suddenly, glad to have her as an ally, and she grins back, curious as to our purpose but too well-trained to enquire.

"There," she says, "you are beautiful." She curtseys again and hands me my psalter before following me along the corridors of Whitehall. Our scurrying feet and lowered voices raise no alarms, for the guards have been forewarned to turn a blind eye to that which is none of their concern.

Outside the royal chapel I stop, catch my breath, and bite my lips to redden them while Nan ensures my French hood is straight. My fellow conspirator looks at me. "Wish me luck," I say, and her face blossoms.

"Oh, Lady Anne. I do wish you luck, all the luck in the world." And then she pushes open the door and stands aside to let me pass.

Dawn light filters through the narrow windows, adding to the illumination of the flickering altar candles. A choir boy, dragged recently from his bed, knuckles his eye and begins to sing, the initial discordance soon clearing to rival the tones of the early morning blackbird. A huddle of men look up from their conversation and one, larger than the rest, detaches himself from the group and comes toward me, his jewels winking in the half-light. He pauses halfway along the aisle. "Anne."

I glide toward him, lay my fingers in his palm and close my eyes as his kisses warm me. His companions follow: Henry Norris, William Brereton, and Thomas Henage. They incline their heads graciously and Norris ushers the king back toward the altar to take his place for the ceremony.

Dr Rowlands Lee, with sweat beading his upper lip, opens his book upon the lectern and calls down a blessing on those gathered. While I glide to stand at Henry's side, Nan, clutching my psalter, takes her place among the gentlemen.

It has not been easy for Henry to arrange this, and Dr Rowlands Lee, wary at the clandestine nature of the marriage, insists that we show him papal licence before he agrees to conduct the ceremony. But Henry, his eyes narrowing and his face darkening, draws himself up to his full height. "Blast you, man, the licence is with Cromwell for safe-keeping. I can show it to you on the morrow. I am damned if I am sending for it now. You would do well to do as your king asks, and let me deal with papal trouble if and when it comes."

He is not telling the truth, there is no papal licence, but Dr Rowlands Lee is not a sturdy fellow and is disinclined to argue, not with the king. He begins to speak the words that bind Henry and I together as man and wife, before God and before the church.

"In nòmine Patris, et Fìlii, et Spìritus Sancti."

Henry fumbles for my hand, squeezes it, crushing my fingers with his heavy rings. His nervousness spreads and, finding it contagious, my knees begin to quiver as the ceremony begins.

Dr Rowlands Lee's voice drones on, his words binding me to Henry, and he to me. The solitary voice of the choir boy rises, the aroma of incense fills my nose and my fingers grow moist in Henry's palm. Just a few moments more, I tell myself, just a few moments more and he will be mine. I will be the king's wife, and queen in all but name.

As we are joined before God, the sun breaks from the clouds as if in heavenly approval, an ethereal stream of light falling upon us. Henry leans forward to kiss me, then he raises our joined hands and his voice is hoarse with emotion as we face the witnesses to our union. "Behold," he says. "Gentleman, I give you your Queen."

As our friends gather round us, Henry grows anxious again, his brow lowering, his blue eyes piercing. "You are to speak of this to no one, not even your wives and sweethearts." He turns kindly toward Nan, addressing her gently but firmly. "And not to any members of the queen's household. I know how keen you ladies are for gossip."

Later, when we are alone and he has sated his needs upon my body, I shift away from him in the bed. "Am I not even allowed to tell George, or my mother?"

He rolls toward me, his face softened by love. "And would you listen if I were to forbid it?"

"Of course, you are my husband, whom I must listen to and obey."

"Ha!" He slaps me playfully on the thigh, making my body jerk in alarm. "You would do well to listen to yourself."

His open palm begins to massage my leg, his hand skimming across my skin. Intrigued by the exploration of his own fingers, as if he is not party to it, he keeps his eye fastened on the contact as he answers carelessly. "Yes, you can tell them, as long as you impress upon them the need for absolute silence." He pauses before adding, "But perhaps it would be best not to tell Mary just yet, my love. Not until we have finalised the arrangements for her own wedding."

The very next morning I am sick upon rising, losing my breakfast and unable to take any food until long past noon. Having missed my courses, I immediately suspect I am with child, but I daren't tell Henry in case I am wrong. Clutching the secret to myself, I smile through my nausea and pray that the day our secret can be revealed will come soon.

After a week of looking at my pale face and putting up with my listless lovemaking, the truth finally becomes plain to Henry. He hedges at first, unwilling to ask the question in case he is mistaken. "You are not well, Anne," he says. "How long have you been off your food now? Two weeks? Three?"

I keep my head lowered over my embroidery and glance at him through my lashes. "Almost a month, my love."

"And ..." He clears his throat, his face turning a little pink. "Have you missed anything that you should not have missed?"

A mixture of excitement and dread bubbles up in my chest, making it difficult to breathe, difficult to speak. What if I should be wrong?

"I ... I have, My Lord. My monthly flux is almost two months overd –"

Before I can complete my sentence he is on his knees before me, my needlework snatched away and thrown in the rushes, his hands circling my belly. "Anne! You are with child. You must be. We must call Dr Butts. We must summon the astrologers. You are carrying our prince. Oh, Anne, it must be a boy. It must be."

My mind quickly conjures up the unlikely scenario that I am carrying a girl, but I push the image quickly away and place my hands over his so that we are both cradling my womb. While he kisses my belly, I nurse his head. His hat has fallen to the floor and his close-cropped hair is burnished into slivers of bright gold by the torches.

A thought nags at my mind. "Henry," I say. "If we do not announce our marriage soon, I am afraid the people will claim our prince was not conceived within wedlock. I would not have him called bastard."

He looks up at me, his face glowing, his eyes alight with triumph. "I shall summon Cromwell and Cranmer, they can do what I pay them to and put their clever heads together and come up with an answer, so worry no more."

Satisfied, I lie back in my chair again while he continues to stroke and kiss my flat belly. I suddenly crave an apple, not the shrivelled fruit that has been stored since the autumn but a fresh, plump apple, just plucked from a tree, smelling of sunshine and … Tom.

The thought of apple trees and summer time always brings a fleeting memory of youth and the days when Tom would to ride over with a few bushels of apples. I sigh momentarily for those easier times.

"What?" Henry raises his head. "Did you say something?"

I push memory away and let my hands trickle down Henry's cheeks, playfully I pull at his nose. "I said, bid them be quick about it for we have little time."

My coronation, to be held on Whit Sunday, is but a few days away and the preparations are almost complete. The streets are scrubbed and adorned with arras, velvet and tissue of gold. There will be flowers everywhere, and my white falcon badge will be prominent above every arch and doorway. At the palace, new clothes and jewels, for both me and my ladies, begin to fill my apartments, and the guests begin to arrive.

The royal palace becomes crammed with dignitaries so rapidly that the lower orders are forced to look elsewhere for lodgings. Of course, there are those who refuse to attend, those who hate me and refute my role as Henry's queen. Although they decline in the prettiest manner, it is plain to see their loyalty to Catherine and Mary lurking behind their sorry excuses. Even Henry's sister refuses to come, pleading sickness, just as she did on our trip to Calais. "You should insist she comes, Henry," I hiss through tight lips. "Her excuses are an insult to both of us. She pays more loyalty to Catherine than to you, her monarch. She is your subject and should be reminded of that."

He lifts his shoulders, opens his eyes wide. "She is sick! What would you have me do, have her dragged from her bed to attend you?"

"It is an excuse, Henry. Plain and simple. Your sister despises me for a commoner and her pride will not give me the precedence I deserve."

"Oh, you women. Why must you always bicker? Come here, sweetheart, sit beside me and tell me how our son is faring today."

At the mention of our prince, my temper softens a little and I move toward him, allow him to caress my belly. "He grows apace."

Henry kisses the velvet bulge of my womb. "With our prince so much in evidence, there will be no refuting your fitness to be our queen. You are beautiful, virtuous and fertile, Anne, and you have my undying love. Remember that should your fears get the better of you."

He stands up and pulls me close, so that I am cradled in the softness of his doublet. Being in his arms is like floating on a fragrant cloud; I feel cherished, safe. He senses my fears even if he cannot understand them. Henry is used to being in the public eye, but I am less so and nervous about the forthcoming events.

The celebrations are to cover several days, beginning with a vast river pageant. All of London will be there. From the nobility down to the lowest whore, they will be watching … and judging, and it is hard to forget that not all of those eyes will look kindly upon me.

Urien, who has been asleep at the hearth, lifts his head. Hearing a scuffling outside the door, we draw apart as Brandon and Norris are announced. Henry Norris has some business with the king so, to give them some peace, I join my ladies in the antechamber. They are gathered at the window and I mingle with them, taking a place beside my sister-in-law.

Jane smiles her brittle smile. "How are my sister and her little prince today?"

"I am very well, if a little fraught with nerves." We both lean across the sill, admiring the green gardens, the courtiers moving slowly along honey-coloured avenues. Nan, soon to be wed to Lord Berkeley, hears my words and sets out to soothe me.

"You have no call to be nervous, My Lady. Everything is arranged down the smallest detail. Even the palace mice have been issued with tiny tables and napkins."

I nudge her with my shoulder, giggling in spite of my fermenting anxiety. Looking down I recognise Mary, who is wearing one of my discarded French hoods to replace her own that was growing shabby. As my sister, we cannot allow her poverty to show. Jane follows my eye. "Who is Mary flirting with now?"

The angle from which we are looking foreshortens the figures, making them appear stouter. "I'm not sure." I crane my neck, leaning to the right. "Oh, I recognise him now. He was at Calais, part of the garrison. I saw her with him when we were there, he must have come across for the coronation."

"Hmm, her laughter is too loud. You must find her a worthy husband soon, before her reputation is damaged for good."

Nan and I exchange faces behind Jane's back. She is renowned for giving vent to her opinion unasked, but I am not in the mood for discord today.

"Henry and I have discussed it, since Father is not prepared to do anything for her."

"Well, for goodness sake, make sure you find her someone virile and firm enough to keep her in hand."

The door opens and the king and his gentleman enter. Norris is laughing at something the king said, his head thrown back, earning Henry's approving smile. They come toward us and, as soon as I am within his reach, Henry slips his arm around my waist.

"All is set for the celebration, my love. Norris here was just telling me that the barge is ready and is looking splendid after the re-fit."

I clap my hands. "Oh, good, I was worried it wouldn't be ready in time."

The barge, which is the best in the land, used to belong to Catherine, but I refused to use it until every sign of her ownership was removed. Now, at great cost, it has been re-gilded and her arms replaced with mine and when I am rowed upriver to the Tower, it shall be in the finest royal barge to ever grace the Thames.

29th May 1533

I will always love the river in May, just because of this day when the whole world is twittering with joy. A little after noon, I am escorted to the waiting barge and settled upon soft downy cushions. My ladies spread the skirts of my cloth-of-gold gown around me and smooth my hair, which is left to hang loose. Mary is with me, and Nan and Madge sit to my left, but the rest of my women follow behind on another barge.

The craft bobs and dips on the water as the twenty-four rowers take their places at the oars. Beside me, Mary is pink with excitement, for once forgetting to begrudge my good fortune.

"Oh, Anne. Did you see that? Look!" She points across the river, and following the line of her finger I peer through the seething river-traffic. Flags and bunting flutter in the light breeze, the sun glaring on gold foil hangings and drapes. Across the crowded water, the most extraordinary thing that I have ever seen is gliding toward us. I draw in my breath, opening my eyes in surprise.

"Good Lord, whatever is that?" I crane my neck and squint into the sun, focusing upon the dragon moving majestically toward us. Surrounded by beasts and wild men as it goes on its way, the dragon slowly turns its head from side to side, every so often belching forth a blast of flame.

The first time it does so, Mary gives a little yelp. "How do they make it do that? Isn't it marvellous?" She turns to look at me, her eyes bright with pleasure, and it makes me glad to glimpse her old self. This is how she used to be. She could almost be sixteen again. I reach out and squeeze her hand.

"I don't know how they do it, but it is wonderful. Oh, if only George were here to share it instead of stuck in France on the king's business."

"We must just look forward to telling him all about it when he gets back. Oh look, Anne, look at that one, the launch coming along behind the Mayor."

This time I see a wherry bearing an enormous crowned white falcon, proudly roosting on a nest of red and white roses. All around the green cloth hill on which he rests are a group of virgins, whose sweet songs float across the river. Leaning forward in my seat I raise my hand and smile, and one little girl, forgetting her instruction, waves back.

145

Bolstered by her friendliness, I relax into the cushions a little, swallow my emotion and try not to think of the exhausting hours that still lay ahead.

For two hours we move through the joyous commotion, and I begin to think that whether the people like me or not, they all love a revel and an excuse for celebration. As my nerves recede I begin to enjoy myself. I sit up straight so that the crowd can see the proud curve of my belly, and share with them the comfort that our prince is soon to be born to England.

When the first of the gun salutes tears through the air, shattering my calm, the child leaps in my womb and I comfort him with gentle strokes. As we approach the bend in the river and the Tower looms in the distance, the guns continue, round after round of fire. Then the big guns sound, putting the previous din in the shade as a final crescendo of devastating blasts greets me as the barge glides toward the landing steps at Tower Wharf

Before Henry and I can be alone, there are official receptions to be borne. I nod and smile and try to be as gracious as I can, although sometimes it is difficult to remember who I am being introduced to. But at last we are ushered from the crowd and led along corridors, up twisted stairways to the newly-refurbished royal apartments. I sink gratefully onto the bed, kick off my shoes and roll into the pillows. A chair creaks and I open my eyes to see Henry settled at the hearth. He takes off his hat and tosses it onto the seat beside him. "You must be tired, Anne. How is our boy, has he endured the proceedings well?"

"Very well," I reply, rolling onto my back again so that my belly juts into the air. "He wasn't too sure about the cannon but he is quiet now, and I can enjoy some rest."

"Yes, you sleep, my dear. You will need to be fresh for the evening banquet." He picks up a lute and begins to quietly strum, every so often raising his voice in song, the high-pitched tone lulling me to sleep.

We are to spend the next few days here at the Tower, and tomorrow there will be further ceremony when the king

146

invests knighthoods and honours on our favourites, as well as our not so favourite. Henry says it is his way of ensuring that even our dissenters give an outward show of support.

"They are greedy," he sneers. "I will wave the honours beneath their noses like a giant carrot before a donkey, and they will not be able to resist."

He is right. They do come, dressed in their finest. Hiding their dislike of me, their pity for Catherine, and their loyalty to Rome beneath false smiles of bonhomie, they come to watch as I am crowned.

Yet there are still those few who stay away, and I mentally make note of their names. The Earl of Shrewsbury pleads a sick stomach and sends his son in his stead. Brandon, the Duke of Suffolk, is present but his wife, Henry's sister, Mary, and their half-grown daughter both stay away – surely they can't both be sick. But to our great chagrin, the most blatant missing person, and pleading no excuse for it, is the former Chancellor, Thomas More. This snub wounds Henry deeply for he is Henry's oldest and dearest friend.

31st May 1533 – The Tower of London

The filmy white cloth slithers over my head, moulding to my body to proudly reveal the contours of my blessed womb. My hair, left loose, cascades past my waist in a cloud of gleaming darkness, contrasting perfectly with the golden coronet they will place upon it.

"Oh, you are lovely, My Lady, quite lovely." Her hushed voice reassures me this is no idle compliment and I can see for myself that Nan's assessment is correct. The looking-glass reveals a woman quite unlike myself. Pregnancy has plumped not just my body but also my face, and excitement, together with a little fear, gleams in my eye as my cheeks are warmed by the heat of the day. My bosom is high, my belly replete with a royal prince, and the future stretches before me like a red carpet of opportunity.

147

Today marks the final step on my journey. By this evening I will be queen, and then my proper work can begin. With Henry's support I can make England a better place. I can aid George in his bid to redeem those whose philosophies have made them outcasts. I shall create a haven of new learning and theology, and lead the way in the reformation of our Holy Church. When the time comes, although I hope it will be long away, my son will rule a peaceful realm and head a Church scrubbed free of corruption and blasphemy. As from tomorrow, my battles will be over.

The litter in which I travel is swathed in white cloth-of-gold, the palfreys that draw it clothed in white damask. Over my head a canopy of gold flutters and snaps in the breeze, and behind me six of my ladies follow, my brother's wife among them, each one in a crimson velvet gown.

Mary is further back, with our aunts and cousins and other women of rank. Along the crowd-lined route the streets are alive with pageants and music, so many I cannot look at them all, and all the while the fickle crowd cries out a blessing. As we pass beneath a gilded triumphal arch bearing the entwined initials H and A, the words ring out again. "God save Your Grace!"

Although by the time we reach Westminster Hall I am almost dropping with fatigue, I am led by the hand to the high dais where my health is drunk with hippocras before I am allowed to retire. I am exhausted, my body aching, my mind so alive with images of the day that even when my head is on my pillow and the shutters are fastened across the windows, I cannot rest. I lie awake, watching the flickering shadows of the night's candle on the walls and relive the day over and over in my mind.

1st June 1533 - Westminster

The stone floor where I lie prostrate is cold, the child in my womb squirming beneath me, kicking at my bladder, making me want to pee. How George will laugh to learn that the most important moment of my life so far is spent longing for the close-stool.

Above me on the high altar, Cranmer prays, calling down God's blessing upon my reign. Forgetting to beg for my own salvation, I pray instead that he will make haste so that I can get up from the floor. My cheek is pressed to the icy stone and all I can see are his feet and the skirts of his robes, specks of dust and dirt from the procession still clinging to the hem. His voice drones on, the congregation murmuring a response where required.

The rise and fall of his voice is making me drowsy and I close my eyes, my mind slipping away. I think of George far away in France, and know he will be thinking of me, cursing the fact he cannot be here. Henry is here in the abbey, watching the proceedings from behind a screen, and I know how proud he will be, how emotional to be at last making me his queen. Yet at the same time his beady eye will be vigilant for any dissention in the congregation. In a few moments I will be his queen, and there will be nothing any of them can do about it; not Catherine, nor Bishop Fisher, nor Thomas More, not even the Pope in Rome, for God has put me here.

At last, Cranmer's voice calls for my praise to be sung and the notes of the choir fill the vast space of the abbey. As I am assisted to my feet for the anointing, he murmurs the blessing, marks the sign of the cross upon me before leading me, slowly and reverently, to St Edward's chair.

I am tired, my limbs numb from the cold floor, but I try not to stumble. Any mishap will be seen by my enemies as an ill-omen, and it is imperative that I tread carefully. Yet as we move on I step on my skirts and almost falter, but I hang on tight to Cranmer's arm. He pauses and allows me to regain my balance before moving on and I flash him a grateful smile. Then, with my spine threatening to snap in two, I lower myself thankfully into the seat upon which somebody has thoughtfully placed a cushion.

Now I can look about me, at the vaulted ceiling, the towering windows, heraldic flags swaying high above our heads. I see the abbey crammed with the noblest in the land, from Earls and Dukes to knights of the garter. They have all assembled to see me crowned and do me honour. I can ask for little more.

When Cranmer lifts the crown of St Edward high above my head, the congregation draw in their breath, slowly exhaling as he places the diadem on my brow. Then, with great solemnity, he offers me the sceptre and the orb, and I take them from him. In a sort of daze I look about the hall, the heaviness of the crown forcing me to keep my chin high and still. I look down on the gathering, upon those who love me and those who don't. I see triumph in the eyes of my father and mother, a kind of affectionate awe in the eyes of my sister, but only shadows in the eyes of Jane.

And then the Te Deum begins as my vision skims across the faces of those with little cause to love me. My joy begins to falter, but the voices of the choir soar so high that shivers of ice rush up and down my spine. My eyes prickle with unshed tears and I am comforted.

I am Henry's wife, Queen of England, and only death can take that from me.

25 June 1533

"Henry, what is it?" As soon as I enter his chamber I know something is wrong, for he has dismissed his attendants and the fire is sulky in the grate. I hurry to his side, kneel at his feet and press his cold fingers to my face. He looks up, his cheeks grey and drooping, and offers me a letter.

Rising ungainly to my feet, I carry it to the window where there is still just enough light to read by. My eyes scan the page and see from the thick rushed scrawl that the letter is from Westhorpe Hall, the home of Suffolk and his wife. 'It is with a heavy heart …' I skip the first few lines.

'…She was sicker than we realised, Your Grace, and on my return from the coronation I discovered her life to have all but dwindled away. Although we did all we could, by the third day she was gone and there was nothing left to do but weep.'

My heart thumps loud and heavy, regret twisting my innards. I glance up at Henry, who remains seated by the fire. I had thought her to be dissembling. I had accused her of pretending sickness to avoid doing me honour as queen. It seems I was wrong. Clasping the letter to my bosom, I take a step closer to him.

"I am so sorry, Henry."

When he doesn't reply, I move closer still and put the crumpled missive on the table beside him. "The fire is dying, my love. I shall call a servant …"

"No."

"No? But it is growing chilly."

He sighs, tugs at his lower lip. "I want to be alone, to think, to remember …"

"You want me to go?"

"No, no, stay but be quiet with me, that is all I ask."

"Very well, but the fire needs tending to; you know I must keep warm for the sake of our prince."

I kneel at the hearth, poke the embers back to life and toss on a few small logs. "That should last a while." I light a taper and move around the room, igniting the candles. Yellow warmth floods slowly up the walls, deepening the shadows, blackening the night sky outside the window. "There, that is better."

Henry blinks at me, his eyes shrunken and reddened, and I realise he has been weeping. "Oh Henry," I whisper and, moving closer, I draw his head to rest against my belly. "I am so sorry, my love, so sorry."

And I am indeed sorry. I try to imagine how it must feel to lose a sibling. In my youth I lost two brothers, but they were infants, not yet grown into people, they were not companions in my nursery. If it were George or Mary, I would be broken. I cannot begin to imagine how I would feel.

A sibling shares so much, sprung from the same womb, the same nursery, nursed at the same breast, taught to speak at the same knee. Siblings are each part of the other, and losing one is like severing a part of oneself. "Tell me about her, Henry. I never really knew her, although I was part of her household when she went to France to wed the old king."

He shifts beneath my hands, turns his face into my velvet skirt, his breath hot against my loins. Then he sits up and pulls me down to lounge awkwardly against him. The babe shifts, pressing against my ribs, but I do not move away, sensing Henry's need is greater than my own comfort.

"I remember the day she was born …"

Henry's voice is hoarse in the dim light as he recalls his infancy playing with Mary and Margaret at Richmond. "She was always a brave child, getting into trouble, earning us all a scolding. She was the baby and everybody's darling."

"I know she was beautiful …"

"It was said in her youth that nature never formed anything so beautiful …"

"Yes." To be honest I had always considered Mary's good looks to be spoiled by a proud and haughty expression, but since she never liked me, perhaps she kept that visage strictly for me.

"She was so cross when I insisted she marry the old king of France." He gives a little chuckle in remembrance and I am comforted that, as I had suspected, talking of her is leavening his grief a little. "She told me once that she led him such a merry dance his poor heart gave out sooner than it should have. She was a minx …"

I risk a giggle, and his hand tightens on mine, his rings digging into my flesh.

"And then, once she was widowed, she wed a man of her own choice, without your leave." I laugh through my words but he sobers, releasing his grip.

152

"Yes. And my best friend too. By God, I was angry with them. I shouldn't have been. I should have realised how they felt but how could I, when I'd not yet known you and what love can make a man do?"

We both fall silent, remembering our own battle, the obstacles we have overcome. The logs in the grate shift and settle, the embers glowing red in the growing darkness. I stretch my limbs. "Shall we go to our bed, my love?"

It is hours later, in the deepest darkness of the night, that I become aware that Henry is sobbing again. I turn to him and put my arm across his chest. "Shh, do not weep, Henry, do not weep."

His grip on my arm is like a vice and his voice sounds ghastly. "They are all dying, Anne, my parents, my friends, my sisters. Soon I will be the only one left. The last Tudor. I must have a son, Anne. You must give me a prince."

"Hush, My Lord, I will do. In just a few more weeks you will have your son, I swear it."

21st August 1533- York Place

As the time for my confinement approaches, I summon my household ladies and present them with a book of prayers. They are lovely little objects, the enamelled gold cover containing a wealth of devotional wisdom. Each lady sinks to her knees as I place the book in her hands and bid her be good and virtuous and, above all, pious in my service. "While it is good that we should be joyous and embrace life's delights, do not indulge in idle pleasures. Modesty is paramount. I will not tolerate unchaste behaviour in my household, so look to your prayers and embrace Christ's Gospel."

They stare back, glassy-eyed. Already I know whom I can trust, and whom I need to watch. "On the common table in my chambers you will find a copy of the English Bible. You are free to read from it each day ... as I shall."

153

The ladies form into groups, murmuring their pleasure and stroking the sumptuous covers of the books. I smile and settle myself in a chair, summoning a girl to bring a drink.

I do not let anyone know quite how exhausted I feel. My unborn son is sapping my energy, my ankles are swollen and I feel listless, especially in the summer heat. Henry suggests that we cancel the summer progress and stay at Greenwich instead, and I embrace the idea of giving birth in the palace where Henry himself was born. Today, I gratefully suck in the air that trickles through the open windows, knowing that soon I shall be confined within my chamber, shut away from the world, away from Henry, to await the birth of my son.

I close my eyes, lay my head against the back of the chair, and imagine holding him in my arms. His tiny fingers clenching mine; his little mouth; his closed eyes. I can picture it quite clearly and cannot help but smile. Once I have given Henry his heir, the people's attitude will change toward me. The mother to the Prince of Wales will be greeted with glee. Henry is already planning the celebrations that will be held throughout the land. A time of great joy awaits not just Henry and I, but all of England.

It is almost time for me to go. The chambers are hung in readiness with arras of gold and silver, and thick carpets have been placed upon the floor. I will be sealed in, the light dimmed, the air carefully controlled, just one window left ajar to let in a little fresh air. The high-canopied bed is hung with drapery, and the Royal Jewel house all but stripped of its finest cups and bowls and crucifixes. All has been prepared, but I don't want to go.

I am plagued with unbidden memories of Mary screaming as she battled to bring little Catherine into the world. She was young then, and I am old to be a mother for the first time. As the day fast approaches I spend more and more time on my knees, praying for my own safety and that of my son.

Over the next few weeks my peace of mind evaporates. There is something about being captive in this swollen body that makes me afraid, vulnerable. I detest being at a disadvantage, I cling to Henry, pine when he is gone, and look anxiously for his return.

I have been sitting here waiting long enough. I get to my feet, signal to my ladies to remain where they are, and go in search of him. I pass through chamber after chamber, guards snap to attention, doors are thrown open at my approach.

He is nowhere.

Panic begins to rise. I feel I am in a waking dream where, try as I might, I cannot get home. I pass along a little used corridor, up a sweeping stair and freeze, stand motionless, when I hear his muffled laugh. I know that sound. Many times have I heard that low, amused chuckle. A chuckle that speaks of desire ... and of lust.

I am panting slightly when I turn the corner.

Henry jumps away from her like a boy caught with his hand in the pantry. She sinks to her knees, her face almost in the rushes, and I am consumed with murderous hatred. I want to kick her, send her bouncing down the stairwell. My heart is thumping, the sound of it thudding in my ears, unbalancing me. For a moment I hover on the brink of consciousness.

"Anne ..." Henry steps forward, reaches for me, but I tear my hand from his grasp.

"How dare you?" I scream, when at last I find my voice. "How dare you?"

The white-faced woman doesn't get up, her hands are clenched together and I can see her veil trembling. "Get out," I hiss at her, "before I have you whipped."

As she skitters down the stair, I turn my rage back to my husband, my lips taught, eyes narrowed. At this moment I hate him, more than I have ever hated anyone. How dare he do this? The whole court will be laughing, making a mock of me, laying odds on how long it will be before he has her in his bed.

"Anne …" he repeats, but his tone is less contrite now. Struggling to assert himself he scrabbles for control. My whole body is trembling with rage. I thrust my face toward him, give him the full force of my fury.

"There is no room for three in this marriage, Henry," I say, making it quite clear that I mean what I say. For a long moment we glare at each other, neither of us willing to be the first to back down.

Somehow he is tarnished by his lack of faith. His blue eyes are less bright, his face slack, his self-assertion dented, but I know him too well. I can sense his fear but I know it is not for me, it is for his child, his prince, upon whom the continuity of his dynasty pivots.

I wonder if I mean anything at all.

He clears his throat, looks at me with distaste as he begins to bluster. "You would do well, Madam, to remember your place and learn to behave as your betters have done before you."

"Turn the other cheek, like Catherine, you mean?" I want to claw his face, gouge out his eyes, but some small part of me remembers my child, and I will not have him harmed. Besides, Henry is not just any man. He is the king and therefore unassailable.

Henry looks down his nose, as only a Tudor can. "I have raised you high but I can cast you down again, like that …" He clicks his fingers, the sound quivering in the outraged air.

There is no love in him, no remorse, no pity. His deception makes me worthless. I have never felt so low, so abused. I wonder how far it has gone, how long I have been sharing his affections unknown. I should have guessed that my matronly state would never hold his interest. I have lost him, and soon I must leave him and be shut away, closed off from the male world while I wait to bring forth England's heir.

Until I am churched I will be forbidden to leave my chambers. For the first time, I wonder how Henry will amuse himself while I am risking my very life for the Tudor cause.

26th August 1533

The Chapel Royal is hushed, only the sound of Lord Burgh, My Lord Chamberlain's prayer keeps me focused. Already I have the urge to clamber up from my knees and hasten to Henry, beg him to take me with him, back to our chambers, back to his hearth. But I am queen now; I can no longer give in to childish anxieties. I lift my chin, close my eyes, and pray for the strength to vanquish fear.

Afterwards, in my great chamber, they stand me beneath a canopy, bring me spiced wine, and the Lord Chamberlain leads us all in another prayer, asking God to send me a good hour. It is a prayer that I join in most devoutly, for the safe delivery of our prince is paramount.

Then the men in our company depart. As Henry kisses me, George bends over my hand, bids me farewell. The Lord Chamberlain bows low, his nose almost on my slippers. I am in a sort of daze. The heavy doors close and I am contained within a feminine world where there are no courtly games, no George to extinguish my doubts, and no Henry to convince me of his love. The walls are oppressive. I want to shrug it all off, escape into the country where I can breathe again. But with Henry's son big within me, all I can hope is that the child comes soon.

7th September 1533

Something wakes me. I stare at the canopy for a long time, wondering what is wrong. It is not quite light yet, the gentle tic-tic of my women's breathing is the only sound in the gloom. I long to throw open the casements and lean over the sill to fill my lungs with fresh night air. But there are rules even a queen must follow.

I fidget my legs, kick back the counterpane, and throw a pillow onto the floor. My throat is parched and I contemplate waking Nan to fetch me a drink, but I am so tired of their gentle company, I cannot bear to hear any more platitudes. Swinging my legs from the mattress, I lean over and grasp the handle of the jug and fill a cup. The wine is tepid and does not refresh me. I put the drink down again.

My belly juts forward like the prow of a ship. Placing both hands upon it, I stroke it lovingly. Come on, little prince, I urge silently. We are eager to meet you. But he makes no response.

Fumbling with my foot for my slippers, I creep to the window and draw back the hanging just a little bit. The grey striped dawn promises a fine day ahead. I lay my head on the mullion and reflect that soon, no doubt, Henry will be riding out with the hunt. I picture him galloping across the heath in the sunshine, his eye on the game, his blood coursing through his veins, his mind empty of me.

I sigh deeply.

"Are you all right, Your Majesty? Oh, come away from the window, the night air is full of danger."

I turn toward the voice and as I do so, I feel a little pop in some unspecified area of my anatomy. Warm fluid gushes down my legs, making me gasp and clamp a hand against my womb. We both look down at the spreading puddle on the floor. A slow smile blossoms on Nan's face.

"Let's get you back into bed, Your Majesty, and I will send for the midwife."

At first I congratulate myself that the pain is not so very bad, and I am relieved I will not have to resort to screaming. A brazier is lit and they burn ambergris, musk, and civet, fragrant herbs thought to soothe and aid me in my travail. Before they bring me some light refreshment, they settle me back into bed, and Mary, still in her nightgown, runs to fetch a cooler jug of wine.

"It won't be long now," she says as she pours it out and hands me the cup. She perches on the edge of my bed. "Your son will be here before you know it."

Her voice trembles with excitement and as she speaks I am aware of a tightening sensation in my back, the top of my thighs, my loins aching and grating. Since I have been experiencing such things from the moment my waters were breached I expect it to ease off soon, but this time it grows stronger, tightening until I can scarcely breathe. When I am certain my spine is about to snap in two, I thrust the cup at Mary and gasp, bringing up my knees as sweat beads my forehead.

Mary nods to the midwife, who takes her place and asks permission to lift my shift and feel my belly. Then to my horror she anoints her hands with goose grease and asks me to part my thighs. I glance at Mary, who moves forward and offers me her hand. While the midwife makes her examination, I cling to Mary as if she were a rock in a stormy sea. "It's all right, Anne. Don't worry. All will be well."

The midwife withdraws her fingers, pulls down my clothes, and smiles. "He'll be along anytime now. Just a few more minutes and you'll be pushing him into the world."

There is nothing ceremonious about this ritual. After the pageantry of my coronation, the grand ceremony of my confinement, I had half expected my child would come forth miraculously, sparing me the pain and the indignity that other women suffer. I am a queen, after all.

But if I thought the initial pain was bad, when the actual birthing begins I am helpless, tossed in a sea of misery. How did Mary stand this? Mary, who faints if she scratches her finger with a needle? Somewhere in the midst of my travail, a new respect for my sister is born.

"Come on, Anne," she says. "If I can do it, so can you. Think of Henry, and concentrate on how happy he will be when you present his son to him."

She gives no sign of resentment that the birth of her own son went unremarked by his father. She kneels by the bed, her hand my only hope, and I focus on her eyes, breathe when she tells me to, and pant when she orders it. My body is tortured, every muscle an agony of torment, until I think I can bear it no more.

Each respite is welcome and in between the pains and the pushing, I flop back against the pillow and wish I were somewhere else, sure that this birth will be the end of me. It

159

will pass, I tell myself, and I have to believe it. This will not last, not forever. I breathe deeply, cast my thoughts on other things but, just as I am imagining dining alone with Henry, or riding to the chase with George, or dancing in a pageant, the agony returns, slicing through my happy daydreams and lurching me back to reality.

Little by little, I can feel the bulge in my nethers begin to move. With each pain I groan like a heifer, strain with each sinew of my body, and focus my mind on expelling the obstruction from my womb.

Nan brings a flannel, dabs my forehead with cool, cool water. I stick out my tongue to try to moisten my mouth, but before they can fetch me a drink, the pain takes me again.

I am stretching, tearing, my mouth open, and my voice hoarse with yelling. My women cluster around the bed, each one trying to find a way to ease me; make an end to it. And then the midwife grips my upper arm. "Get up," she says. "Squat like a milkmaid."

With clumsy movement, I am hauled to my feet and helped into position. Immediately, the pain abates a little, the pressure off my spine. Something shifts inside. When I push again, I feel a jolt and his head pulsing between my legs.

The midwife forages beneath my petticoat. "That's it, push again," she yells, glancing up at me. Her face is red, her brow as sweat-drenched as mine, and there is blood on her veil.

I grit my teeth, hang on to Mary's hand, throw back my head and push long and hard, screeching as I do so. For long moments I hold my breath and strain to bring forth my child. And quite suddenly, in a great rush of limbs and liquid, my son slips from my body and into the midwife's waiting arms.

For a few moments I lie back, gasping on my dishevelled pillows, not really believing what I have done. My body is exhausted but my mind is alive with triumphant joy. Then the midwife takes the child, hands it to my women, and continues to fuss around my petticoats, prodding at my belly. I crane my neck, watching the women

160

rub my son's limbs and swathe him in linen. In the end I can bear the suspense no more.

"Bring him to me," I demand. Mary turns with him in her arms, hesitates. "Come on, I want to see him," I say, and she takes a step forward, stops again.

"Anne ..."

Only then do I notice that the expression on her face does not match mine; she is not sharing my joy. My body floods with horror. "What? What is wrong with him?"

I know he lives. I felt his lusty kick, heard his angry cries. I pull myself upright and bat away the midwife's probing hands. "Give him to me now."

Mary comes near, stoops over and places my boy very gently in my arms. I look down at his pale red hair, his snub of a nose, his hungry sucking lips and, with a great surge of triumph, I lay him on the bed and cast off his cloth to take a proper look at him.

The child is perfect. He is bawling in protest at the rough treatment he has received, and it is plain to see he has strong kicking legs, large grasping hands, and a rage as ripe as his father's.

There is just one thing wrong with him. Our precious little Tudor prince, upon whom all our hopes are pinned ... is a girl.

In a daze I sit propped upon my pillows, my child in my arms ... my daughter in my arms. Henry, when he hears the news, will be devastated. I had pictured my husband brushing aside the protestations of my ladies and entering the birthing chamber to greet his son for the first time. I close my eyes, imagining how it should have been. Henry adoring me, kissing me as together we look down upon our hallowed prince.

Now it will all be different.

I try to imagine his reaction. He might be raging. He might be cold and bitter. The one emotion I am certain he will not be feeling is delight.

I have let him down.

For seven long years he wooed me. He put away his wife, turned from his friends, and offended his Pope, all in the faith that I, Anne Boleyn, would provide him with the son he craves. Instead, I have produced a daughter. She is a beautiful girl whose Tudor origins are clearly etched in every outraged inch of her, but she is a useless girl nonetheless.

How our enemies will laugh. I can imagine the Emperor and Chapuys sniggering behind their hands. In my mind's eye I can see Catherine and Mary crashing to their knees to thank God for the curse he has laid upon us. Even Henry's sister, Mary, will no doubt be laughing in Heaven … if that is where she is. Oh, how I wish George was here to advise me, he would know what to do.

"The king is coming, Anne." Mary hovers at the foot of the bed. "Shall I take the child, or …" She does not finish her sentence. With one shake of my head I dismiss her and, reading my silent wishes correctly, she herds all the women from my presence, leaving me to face the wrath of the king alone.

He comes in quietly, his hat in his hand, as if seeking penitence. Where I had expected rage, I find sorrow, and where I had expected retribution, I find only defeat. His close-cropped hair is glinting, the candlelight forming a nimbus around his head, but it is the only bright thing about him. His shoulders are slumped, his cheeks sagging, his eyes unusually clouded. I clear my throat and speak softly. "It is a girl, My Lord."

"Yes," he says, after a long moment. "So they tell me."

When he doesn't look at us, I hoist her higher in my arms. "She is lusty, Henry, and has a suck on her like a piglet, and her brothers will be even stronger."

At last he raises his eyes, attempts to smile. "Brothers," he says hoarsely. "I like the sound of that."

Encouraged, I sit up straighter and try to keep the tremor from my voice.

"Come, Henry. Won't you hold her, or look at her at least? We need to think of a suitable name."

162

He comes reluctantly to stand at the head of the bed, and I tilt the child in my arms so that the light falls across her face. She screws up her eyes in protest and opens her mouth in a milky yawn before discovering her fist and beginning to chomp upon it. "She has red hair, like yours." I add.

"But not much of it," he remarks. For a few moments that seem to last a week, he examines her face, lifts the edge of the shawl to look upon her limbs. I swear I can see a softening of his expression.

"Here, take her, Henry, feel the weight of her, how well-formed she is."

With our child in his arms, he turns away, moves from the bed, and I see her tiny fist fly out to clench around his finger. "A good grip," he says, and his voice is a little lighter now. He turns back to me. "We have made a good start, Sweetheart."

Relief surges through me like a flooding tide, and I know I am forgiven. I know we will love and breed again. I have not lost him, and next time I will get it right. I have to get it right.

"What about Elizabeth?" he says, perching on the edge of the bed, making clucking noises at his daughter who sleeps blissfully on.

"After your mother?" I smile, for his suggestion shows favour indeed.

"And yours, of course," he says. I sit forward, peer over his shoulder at our sleeping child. "Yes, E-liz-a-beth." I enunciate the word, trying out the name. "That will do nicely, and we can name her brother Henry, after your father."

He looks at me, his brow quirked. "My father? I should think not. No, we shall name him Henry, but it won't be after him, it will be after me."

PART FOUR
MOTHER

"Watch over her, George. I am putting her in your care."

My brother laughs his big laugh. "She has all the king's men looking to her safety but, if it makes you feel better, I will not let her out of my sight."

I am piqued that Elizabeth's christening will take place without me but I have not yet been churched, and the customs of the lying-in chamber hold me captive. I would prefer to join in the ceremony, watch for those who dare to look askance at my daughter and question her legitimacy. I know there are those still loyal to Catherine and her bastard daughter, and it is good to know one's enemy. To appease my qualms, Mary and Nan promise to relate every detail of the day on their return and Henry, of course, will be present too.

The king has allowed no one the opportunity to scoff at our princess. She is his legitimate heir and he will allow none to gainsay it. Although the jousts and pageants that were prepared for our prince have been cancelled, the christening is to go ahead as planned, a magnificent ceremony fit for our daughter, our Elizabeth.

Everyone of note is to take part in the proceedings, even the Marchioness of Exeter, friend and supporter to Catherine, whom Henry has left with little choice but to attend.

"I'll show her to whom she owes allegiance," Henry mocks. "I will make her god-mother to our daughter and force her to bow the knee to her, and I will make her do so before all our friends too."

I smile luxuriously. "And she won't be able to resist carrying tales back to Catherine and your bastard either."

"No." Henry's smile fades, as it always does when I refer to Mary as 'bastard.' I do so often just to ensure that he does not relent, does not reinstate her in her place of honour. She is sprung from the loins of an illicit union, and as such has no place in the line of succession. She has no place in our palaces or in our kingdom, and if I disliked and resented her overt resistance to me before, I dislike her even more now that I have a daughter of my own.

Henry has removed her privileges, disbanded her household, but still she refuses to bend the knee and declare her parents' marriage invalid. She is as stubborn as her mother. How much easier everything would have been had Catherine only been willing to back down. Every misfortune that has sprung from Henry's struggle to be free of her can be laid directly at her feet. All the suffering, the risk of war with Spain; everything is Catherine's fault and I will not have Mary, who is cut from the same cloth, doing likewise. We will thwart her stubbornness. She will be made to bow to my daughter, and if she does not, she will suffer.

The decision is hers.

Just a few attendants wait with me in my chamber. They sew in silence, every so often breaking into my thoughts to enquire if I would like a drink, or if my pillows need plumping. I answer with a shake of my head, my mind with Henry and our daughter as she is embraced by God into the Christian Church.

It is a long time before I hear movement in the outer chambers and know that the christening gifts are being delivered to my apartments. There are further ceremonies, ritual blessings and prayers, and I grow quite fidgety with impatience, waiting for them to come.

By the time they return and Elizabeth is placed in my arms, my breasts are aching with milk. I immediately loosen the neck of my gown and she latches on to me in a frenzy of feeding, both of us relaxing at once, and I know without doubt that she is glad to be back.

Soon the time will come to find her a wet-nurse, and soon after that, Henry will establish Elizabeth in a household of her own. She will be raised far away from us in Hatfield, and the thought is difficult to bear. Even though I know our visits will be regular, the knowledge that we will necessarily be parted makes these few weeks all the more precious.

There are mothers who refuse the services of a wet-nurse, but I cannot allow myself that luxury. Everyone knows that a child at breast reduces a woman's fruitfulness and hinders conception. If I am to fall quickly with Henry's son, I will need a rapid return to fertility.

As I look down at my feeding babe I stroke her downy red head, and idly listen to Mary and Jane's chatter.

"I never saw such solemnity," Mary says as she and Jane settle at the hearth. Mary kicks off her shoes and wiggles her toes while the other women gather around and begin to discuss the day's events.

"I never saw such care taken over a child," Jane sniffs. "Her attendants were scarcely allowed to breathe on her."

Elizabeth, the daughter of me, Anne Boleyn, was for one day the centre of the world, the pivot around which everybody turned. I had heard that the walk from the Great Hall to the Church of the Observant Friars was covered in a thick carpet of green rushes, and hung with rich arras. The walls of the church, both inside and out, were swathed with hangings to keep out draughts, and for fear of contamination, Elizabeth's attendants were swathed in aprons and towels.

Everyone was present, the mayor and council, our closest friends and family and, bar one or two of the most obstinate, even our direst enemies. How I hope they will carry a vivid picture of the ostentatious display back to Catherine in her draughty castle. How I hope she will squirm.

"Everyone was there," Mary gabbles, her eyes wide, her hands enhancing her descriptions with a graceful dance. "Gentlemen, squires, chaplains and alderman, everyone was there. Mary of Norfolk bore the chrisom and the old duchess carried Elizabeth. She was swathed in royal purple and our father bore the train with Norfolk and Suffolk on either side. Suffolk's discomfort was plain to see but he dare not complain, not in this. Henry would forgive him many things, but not a snub to his precious princess."

I glance quickly at her to see if there is spite behind Mary's words. She must feel and resent the difference between her daughter and mine, born to the same father, in such different circumstances. I wonder if she believes she herself could have been queen had she only showed more cunning.

I prise Elizabeth's jaws from my nipple and she makes a face, squeals like a piglet when I sit her up and deprive her of sustenance. Like a drunken old man she slumps forward over my supporting hand while I rub her back until she belches. A trickle of milk runs across my wrist and I turn her around, bare the other breast, and she latches on again.

Jane raises her eyebrows. "She is a lusty feeder, Anne."

I smile, glad of praise for my offspring, even when it comes from those I do not favour. Usually Jane, who craves a child of her own, pays babies little heed, pretending they hold no charm for her. "You will have to find her a milch cow rather than a wet-nurse," she continues, spoiling the brief instance of camaraderie by reminding me that these halcyon days must necessarily be short.

My smile drops and tears prick the back of my lids, but I blink them away and turn my face back to Mary, who continues her tale.

"You should have heard the trumpets and seen the torches! I have never seen so many in one place, or heard so many cries of good-will from the people as they looked on. They love little Elizabeth already."

This last is satisfying, for rumours persist that the public hate me and resent my daughter for what is seen by some as her usurpation of Mary's place. Now that I have proved my fertility by giving them a princess, maybe the people will love me and, secure in the nation's love, I can bring forth a boy.

Just as Elizabeth's appetite is waning, Henry barges into the chamber. After kissing my hair, he holds out his arms for her. I hand her over. "She is sleepy now, My Lord, and in need of gentle handling."

"Gentle? Am I not gentle?" He holds her aloft and looks up into her red face, waggles her from side to side before placing her against his shoulder.

He supports her head, and father and daughter process about the room, Henry smiling on the company, making my women giggle with his indulgent remarks about his offspring. When he turns away from me toward the window, I see that Elizabeth has disgorged a goodly portion of her milk down the back of her father's doublet. I refrain from informing him of the fact. It serves him right for ignoring my instruction.

Mary sees it too and we exchange glances, suppressing our laughter as we continue to be bemused by Henry's infatuation.

February 1534- Hatfield

Accompanied by a small cavalcade, Henry and I ride across the frigid countryside to visit our daughter. We leave so early that a thick frost still rimes the trees, and our breath puffs from our mouths, the vapour hanging long in the air before dissipating.

I have spent a restless night, full of excitement at being with Elizabeth again. I cannot imagine how she will have grown. She will have settled into her new home, learnt new skills and, to my secret sorrow, found comfort from another woman's breast. This morning I feel alive, young and invincible. I dig in my heels, urge my palfrey into a canter, and Henry, ever one to love a chase, joins me with a loud halloo.

Although they do their best to follow, we leave our attendants behind. Henry quickly outstrips me, leaning low over his horse's ears, grinning at me as he passes, his thick fur cloak billowing behind him, the feather in his cap streaming in the wind. I have no hope of catching him but I raise my whip and follow, my hat bouncing on my head, my petticoats blowing about my knees.

The wind whips tears from my eyes as I chase him down a slope and through a stand of trees. We splash across a ford and into a village, where a band of peasants watch open-mouthed as their king and queen streak through the settlement.

He finally draws to a halt on the brow of a hill. Our mounts circle and snort, sides heaving, harness jingling. Our blood is up and we are both breathing hard. We exchanged smiles. I put up a hand to straighten my hat and he reaches out, takes my fingers, edges his horse toward mine. "You look like a young girl again," he says, leaning precariously from the saddle to kiss my knuckles.

"Do I?" It is ridiculous to be so flustered by the attentions of one's own husband but recently, since Elizabeth's birth, although we couple regularly on our never-ending quest for a male heir, real affection has been missing.

He squints across the landscape, pushes back his cap and scratches his head. "When we were courting I'd have lured you into the woods by now and tried to deflower you in the undergrowth."

In the silence that follows, I fumble for a reply. I open my mouth, feel my face flush scarlet as the words tumble unbidden from my lips.

"Is it not extraordinary that you no longer attempt to ravish me now I have no cause to deny you?"

He looks at me quickly, his face relaxing into serious lines, his eyes searching mine as the vapours of our breath mingle in the air. Oh God, now he will think me unchaste.

My heart feels as if it has ceased to beat. After a long moment he stoops forward, takes hold of my reins. "Come, Madam," he says and, kicking his mount straight into a

170

canter, steers me to the bottom of the hill where a lazy river loops beneath an avenue of trees.

My head crashes into the tree trunk, Henry's mouth hot on my neck, his hands rasping across my skin. He hoists my skirts and takes me rapidly, with all the pent-up passion I have missed. As his hot, urgent kisses increase I feel a warm, almost burning sensation in my loins. I cling around his neck, my mouth opening as my body melts and my limbs threaten to give way. This is it, I think, as joy takes hold of me. This is how it should be, this is what George meant.

I wrap myself around him. He hoists me higher, lifting me away from the tree so we become one living being, joined at the groin. I throw back my head and dissolve into him, as he touches the very root of my soul.

Afterwards, thoroughly shaken, my knees still trembling, he helps tuck my hair back beneath my veil and brushes the worst of the lichen from the back of my cloak. I feel alight inside, as if there is a torch burning in my groin, but I put away my wanton self and resume my role as queen. He stoops, makes a stirrup of his hands and hoists me back into the saddle, holds the bridle while I arrange my skirts. "Thank you, Henry," I murmur and our eyes meet. Mine are smouldering and grateful, his are guarded, embarrassed even. He flushes like a maid and, knowing my thanks are not just for his assistance in mounting, jerks his head in acknowledgment.

He knows it was different; he cannot but be aware that I have gained more pleasure from this encounter than any other, but he is too squeamish to mention it. As I follow him back up the hill toward our waiting party, who are craning their heads in curiosity, I watch his back, enjoy the way his body moves in perfect unison with his mount. I feel warm inside and sated, the residue of his love still moist within me. I wonder if we can prolong the pleasure next time, for surely that is the most pleasant way to make a child. For the first time in a long while, I feel confident in our marriage, and loved again.

Hatfield House slumbers, the windows a myriad of diamonds in the midday sunshine. We clatter up the hill and beneath the red-bricked arch into the courtyard, and grooms come running to take our horses. As I am assisted from the saddle I hear the crunch of footsteps on the gravel behind me, and turn to find Lady Bryan with Elizabeth in her arms.

Forgetting all dignity I swoop upon my child, cradle her tightly, scattering kisses across her cheeks. She screws up her face and mews in protest. Then a shadow falls across the sun and Henry is there too, leaning on my shoulder to examine his heir.

"She is growing," he remarks unnecessarily. "Come, let us take her inside out of this chill." We are ushered toward the hall, our attendants and Lady Bryan following in our wake. Even while my cloak and hat are removed I do not relinquish Elizabeth, but keep her in my arms as we are led toward waiting chairs and refreshment. I fire a barrage of questions and instructions at poor Lady Bryan.

"Does she feed well?" "Is the wet-nurse clean?" "Do not let the nurse dine on onions or her milk will curdle." "Does Elizabeth sleep well?" "Are her stools too hard or green in colour?"

In the end Henry throws up his hands. "Give us peace, my love. Here, let me take her for a while."

I reluctantly hand her over, tucking her carefully into his arms. He tests her weight, examines her face. "Support her head, My Lord, you must be most careful, the slightest jerk could harm her."

Henry wags his head at his daughter. "From hearing your mother speak, you'd think I had never held a child before, but I nursed your sister, and your brother, Fitzroy, too."

Elizabeth moves her head, opens her mouth. I snap to attention. "Is she smiling? Lady Bryan, was that a smile? You did not tell me she could smile!"

"I wasn't aware she could, Your Majesty. It must be her first attempt."

Lady Bryan beams with pride at the excellence of her charge, and although I am a little piqued that she has chosen to bestow her first smile on Henry, I too am beside myself with joy. It is turning out to be a good day indeed.

Elizabeth has smiled.

And then Henry spoils it all. "Where is the Lady Mary? Why is she not here to greet us?"

My happiness subsides. To our great chagrin, Henry's bastard, Mary, continues to refuse to acknowledge that her parents' union was flawed. She will not sign, nor even verbally concede that she is of illegitimate birth. Henry has disbanded Mary's own household and sent her here to Hatfield as part of her step-sister's retinue. Lady Bryan looks uncomfortable.

"The Lady Mary is in her chamber and refuses to come down, Your Majesty. I cannot get her to do anything. She does not eat with us or attend her duties. All she does is weep … and pray."

Henry sighs and hands Elizabeth back to me. I tuck her into the crook of my arm and amuse myself by counting her fingers one more time, silently exclaiming over the perfect nails, the miniscule creases on each knuckle.

"I will go aloft and speak with her."

I look up from the adulation of Elizabeth.

"No, Henry. You must make her do your bidding. Do not bend to her demands. You are the king, she is a bastard."

He looks uncomfortable, shifts from foot to foot. "I will go to her, this once. Maybe I can talk some sense into her."

He is gone a long while. I pass the time inspecting Elizabeth's nursery, looking over her linen and staff. "I will see that new hangings are ordered," I say as Lady Bryan follows behind me. All the time I am trying to concentrate on domestic matters, the problem of Mary nags like a fishwife in the back of my head. I have made friendly overtures to her, tried to lure her into our family nest, but she will have none of it.

173

"I know no queen but my lady mother," she retorts whenever I am given my proper title. "I will call the child sister, but never Princess," she replies when they demand that she give Elizabeth the entitlement she deserves.

Lady Bryan and I trail about Elizabeth's nursery until, unable to resist the urge any longer, I turn suddenly.

"Tell me, does the Lady Mary treat our royal princess with honour, or does she scorn her? Do you think it is safe to have her in Elizabeth's company? Should harm come to her because …"

Breaking convention, she reaches out and places a comforting hand upon my arm. "Rest assured, Your Majesty. I have known Princ—The Lady Mary since she was born, she would not harm an innocent child. She is simply angry with … circumstance, and … confused as to her new status."

"Things would go better for her if she just signed the Act of Succession. If she acknowledged the validity of our marriage and Elizabeth's rightful place as the king's true heir, we would find her a good husband. She is seventeen now, it's about time she was wed and out of our hair. If she is not careful, I will have her married off to some lackey."

Lady Bryan looks at the floor. "She is a resolute girl."

"Stubborn, you mean, like her Spanish mother."

"That is as may be, but I do assure you, she will not harm her sister. I have seen her edging her way toward the cot when she thinks no one is looking, letting Elizabeth grasp her finger—"

I turn sharply and almost squawk. "They are not, on any account, to be left alone together. Never, do you understand? Until she agrees to call me 'Queen' and name my Elizabeth 'Princess,' you are to watch her like a hawk. And there is to be no more skulking in her chamber either. She must eat with the rest of the household and she is to perform her duties. She is a bastard and to be treated as such."

Lady Bryan bows her head. "Yes, Your Majesty. It shall be as you say."

It almost tears out my heart to leave Elizabeth again so soon. I kiss her a thousand times, issue Lady Bryan with a list of instructions as long as my arm before I can be persuaded back on to my horse. I gather up the reins, not relishing the long ride back, and with tears on my cheeks, I look back to wave one more time.

As I do so I glimpse a shadow at an upstairs window, and instinctively know it is Mary. For a moment I think she has relented and is waving at me, but as I go to respond, I see Henry drop his own hand and realise the exchange was between him and his daughter.

He still loves her. With a twist of jealous anger, I tighten my reins and urge my mount forward, our former understanding marred.

April 1534 - Richmond

Urien leaps from his hiding place beneath my skirts and rushes across the hall, the high pitched excitement of his bark informing me who approaches. George ruffles the dog's ears, and when he rolls over and presents his belly for scratching, George doesn't hesitate to oblige. Eventually he turns his attention to me.

"You look well, Anne." George's lips are cool on the back of my hand. As he stands up I draw him closer, incline my head toward him and speak quietly into his ear.

"There may be a reason for that."

He does not mistake my meaning, and leads me away from the crowd toward the window that has been thrown open to admit the scents and sounds of spring.

"Are you certain?"

"As sure as I can be. It is too early to be definite."

"And you've told the king?"

I hesitate, glance around the room. "Not yet, no."

"Why ever not? He will be over joyed."

"I know, but he will also wrap me in gossamer, forbid me to hunt and …"

175

"And what?"

I can feel my face warming under the intensity of his stare. "He will stop coming to my bed."

George throws back his head, but his amusement is lost on me. Since our encounter in the wood, love between Henry and I has changed. No more fumblings leaving me discontent and frustrated. After making gentle enquiries of Nan, who enjoys a full and happy union with her own husband, I am discovering the skill to improve things in the royal bedchamber. I have learnt how to draw things out and invent new ways to please him, and I give it my utmost attention. The prudish side of Henry sees my games as sinful, but he is never repentant until after the act. I smile as my mind drifts back to the previous night.

Our bodies were slick with passion, our enjoyment full and vocal and, when I was done with him, he lay naked across my bed. "I declare, Madam," he panted, rolling onto his belly and kissing the sole of my foot, "you must have been corrupted during your time in France."

He was joking of course, but I know he is uneasy with what he sees as depravity, and his ever-prickly conscience shortly forced him to rise and take himself off to chapel to make his peace with God.

If I tell him that my courses are late, my breasts tender and my trips to the close stool increasing, he will cease his nightly visits, discontinue our games, and I am loath to do so.

I have never been so happy.

"So, can I gather from this that things have improved?"

George breaks into my thoughts and although I try to prevent it, I find I am blushing. Queens shouldn't blush or be discomforted by the teasing of younger brothers. I jerk my chin.

"Sometimes, George, you are just too nosey."

We turn back and face the throng, where one of Henry's fools is turning cartwheels along the length of the

176

hall. The onlookers clap appreciatively while Henry roars with laughter from the dais.

Soon the musicians will come on, and afterwards there will be dancing and entertainments. Just as I decide to join my husband, I become aware of Jane at my shoulder. I turn and welcome her and Henry Norris into our company, but George turns away.

Jane's face drops and she raises her cup. "Who will drink with me to the ridiculous fool?" she cries as he moves away. She drains her wine and I see she is a little drunk.

Her double entendre is not lost on George, who freezes and turns back to face us. They glare at each other. I wish things were better for them. If only one of them would make the effort to save their marriage. If they had a child their problems would be over, I know they would. But how can you get a child with a partner you dislike more with each passing day?

I open my mouth, hoping to find some common ground on which my brother and Jane can find mutual footing, but Norris forestalls me. Snatching a parchment from beneath his doublet, he begins reciting a verse he has written in praise of a secret lady's smile. Of course, we all know that the muse of both Norris and Francis Weston is my cousin, Madge Shelton. She is the target of the affections of many men, but their double wooing of her has been prolonged and is a source of great amusement to onlookers. When Norris has finished his ode, George puts his hands over his heart and begins to deliver his own rhyme, aiming mocking, lovelorn eyes upon his wife.

"Jane, my wife, my love, my bane ..."

The words trip unrehearsed from his tongue and with a look of fury she thrusts him aside and storms away, elbowing her way through the crowd. We laugh, somewhat guiltily, and I push George gently on the shoulder. "You are cruel. How can you hope to salvage anything—" I halt mid-sentence as my attention is captured by the sight of our sister Mary, who has freshly returned from the country. She said she'd been spending time with her daughter but ....

177

I nudge George in the ribs and he exhales suddenly, putting a hand to his side. "Ow, what was that for?"

With a nod toward our sister, I say through tight lips, "Mary is back. Come with me."

Mary lets out an exclamation of surprise when, without ceremony, I take her by the elbow and steer her relentlessly toward my privy chamber. George lumbers behind us like a spaniel, oblivious to the fact which to me has just become starkly clear.

Mary can barely keep pace with me; she scrabbles at her skirts in an attempt to lift them clear of her feet as we hasten along the corridors. Scullions press themselves against the walls to get out of our way; a bevy of gentlemen, on seeing our approach, bow deeply, but I do not acknowledge them. My fury is too great to be polite.

Once in the privacy of my chamber, I dismiss my staff with a jerk of my head and spin Mary round, my eyes scanning her body, taking note of her raised bosom and flushed cheeks.

"What's going on?" George slumps onto my bed, putting his shoes on the counterpane, but for once I do not care.

"I think Mary has something to tell us."

I want to be mistaken; I can't remember when I have ever wanted to be so wrong about something, but instead of looking puzzled, she flushes. I recognise from old the look of bravado she assumes as she stares me squarely in the eye.

"And what if I do?" she sniffs, her voice hostile, brittle. George, sensing something important in the air, sits up, attentive at last.

"Whose is it this time?"

Her face is white, her lips colourless, but she does not back down. I recognise that I share a similar stubborn streak. "Not Henry's, if that's what is worrying you."

George, beginning to realise what our conversation is about, lets out a whistle and looks at her stomach.

"Christ, Mary. You really do heap troubles upon your own head, don't you?"

"Shut up, George." Since she cannot speak as she wishes to me, she turns her venom upon him. "It's none of your business, and none of yours either, Anne. I am a woman grown and can make my own decisions."

Anger burns through me. I feel I am on fire. I want to slap her, cast her out of my life and let her starve on the streets. "No! You are wrong. You cannot make your own decisions. You are the sister of the queen of England, and look at you … a drab, a trull. The shame of it, Mary! How am I supposed to find you a decent husband now?"

She juts her face toward me, the sinews on her neck tightening, her mouth squared and ugly, spittle forming at the corners of her lips. "You don't have to. I don't need your assistance at all, and I have no wish for a loveless marriage. I have a husband already."

"What?"

In the silence that follows, George gets up from the bed and helps me to a chair, lowers me into the seat. "Remember your condition," he whispers, "no upsets, no violence."

He hands me a cup of wine and I gulp it, cough when it goes down the wrong way. Tears spring to my eyes, although I am not sure if it is from the wine or the situation.

If Mary has married against the express wishes of the king, things could go very ill for her. Henry and I have already entered negotiations for her marriage; we aimed high and were quite sure of our mark, no easy thing when the intended bride is soiled goods. George stands at my shoulder; I grasp his hand very tightly and blink at Mary through my tears. "What did you say?"

It is her turn to slump on the bed, her blooming breasts resting snugly on the bulge of her belly. Now that she is sitting, I realise she is further gone than I thought. She no longer seems so glowingly healthy; her eyes are shadowed by fear, her hands trembling slightly. Oh Mary, I think, why can you not keep out of trouble?

"I said, I have a husband already."

179

I swallow bile as the hope that she was lying dwindles away. "Who—" I croak, handing the cup back to George. "Who is he?"

She tosses her head, her former bravado wavering. Drawing herself together, she looks me in the eye, her voice challenging as she enunciates the name clearly so that there should be no mistake. "William Stafford."

"Good God!" George knocks over the cup, wine spreading like blood across the damask table cloth. "Stafford? Couldn't you have done better than that?"

"George." I shake my head, warning him to be silent, and cover my face with my hands. Stafford is of the knightly classes, the soldier I saw in her company at the garrison at Calais. I should have seen this coming but I have been so engrossed in my own affairs, so involved with Elizabeth and Henry and the forthcoming child that I forgot to worry what my sister was up to.

I groan inwardly, knowing the scandal will be huge. Henry will be furious. Father will disown her all over again. In all her life Mary has never made one good decision. She has lurched from disgrace to disaster and each time she lands in the muck, filth splashes up to mire the skirts of our whole family.

"Oh Mary," I manage finally, but I can't look at her. I have never been so disappointed in anyone in my life.

"Why are you so worried? William loves me, and I him. Is that so hard for you to understand? Just because you shunned love to marry a king doesn't mean the rest of us cannot find happiness unless couched upon a bed of jewels and power."

Is that what she thinks? That I have no love for Henry? Does she really believe I could have tolerated all the delay and self-denial if I had no love for him? She doesn't know me at all.

I wonder if anyone really does.

"The scandal will be too great, Mary," I say sadly. "You will be sent away from court, denied the company of your family, and all because you could not do the thing properly."

"You would never have let me marry him." She is on her feet now, hollering like a fishwife. "You would have insisted I be wed to some ageing lord with a long purse and a grotesque belly. I had to do it this way, don't you see? I had to take my life into my own hands before you ruined it!"

She is weeping as George escorts her from the room, but I cannot look at her. I cannot forgive her. Tomorrow, when Henry and Father find out, there will be Hell to pay, and Henry does not forgive lightly. I fear my sister is lost to me for good.

<u>June 1534</u>

I am amusing myself with Henry's cage birds where they hang in the window of our chambers. They accept my offerings of crumbs and regard me with bright beady eyes, hoping for more. One, braver than the rest, pecks at the bars. "You are a pretty fellow," I say, reaching for more food. Then a light cough behind me makes me jump so violently that there is little use in trying to hide it. I turn around. "Master Cromwell, you startled me."

Unruffled, he bows low, his eyes cool, a slight smile playing upon his lips. "Did Your Majesty not summon me to attend her when the king's business was concluded?"

"Yes, yes I did. I just did not hear you enter."

I look around the chamber for Urien, who is hiding beneath the table. When I call him he ignores me, his tail like a whip on the floor. Cromwell comes to stand beside me at the window, from which I have been admiring the ordered symmetry of the garden.

"I think your mind was far away."

"Yes, it was. I was thinking of my mother and wondering whether a visit to Hever soon would do me good."

"I am sure it would. You need rest and relaxation, for the sake of our little prince."

"Yes."

His eyes flick to my stomach, and my hand flies instinctively to the bulge of my womb. Cromwell's smile settles more comfortably into the contours of his face. Master Cromwell is as careful with his expressions as he is with his purse, and one can never quite tell what he is thinking. I move from the window and cross the room to where a table is laid out with papers and bills. Master Cromwell follows, his books clasped beneath his arm. I locate a sheaf of paper. "My sister's child, my ward Henry Carey, is approaching ten now."

His brow furrows and he runs an eye over the lines of script as I continue. "I want to engage a tutor and he has to be the very best. I wondered, what is your opinion of Nicholas Bourbon?"

Of course, I know his opinion very well and although he betrays no emotion, I know he must be delighted. Bourbon, known for his Evangelical leanings, is a great friend of Cromwell and has recently been released from prison at our instigation. He is presently installed in the home of Henry's friend and physician, Dr Butts.

Betraying no pleasure, Cromwell smoothes the papers and replaces them on the pile. His hands are square and strong, the clipped nails and clean, pale skin belying his early life as a tradesman and soldier. I have always found this man intriguing and slightly repellent. Maybe it is his deference, his economy with words, or the conviction I have that he is concealing something. I am certain that if I spent each day of the next twenty years in his company, he would remain a stranger at the end of it.

"I think he would do very well, Your Grace. He is a known reformer and will ensure young Henry's mind is not filled with too much popish nonsense. The future of reform lies with our young people, and Bourbon is a fine linguist and popular with his peers ... he will provide an all-round education."

"I have always found him most pleasant. As you know, my nephew is presently at Syon in the company of Henry Norris' son and Nicholas Hervey's boy. I think Bourbon's rhetoric will counterbalance the nuns' teachings a little."

He closes his eyes, inclines his head in agreement. "You have discussed this with his mother?"

I jerk my head toward him, surprised he should mention her. Mary has left the court and Henry refuses to allow her back. She has crossed and burned her bridges now, and no amount of shoring them up will bring her back to us.

"It is no concern of hers; you know that, Master Cromwell. My sister is dead to us."

My words trail away. I can scarce believe I am saying them, for I miss Mary more than I had ever imagined. Somehow, with George away so often on the king's business, she had managed to fill a gap in my life. Now, the family member most often in my company is Jane, and her sour face is sometimes enough to curdle milk.

Cromwell watches me. He puts down his books and turns toward me, pressing the tips of his fingers together, making a cathedral of his hands. "Madam, may I speak freely?"

I am surprised. Unless asked for it, Cromwell usually keeps his own counsel. My curiosity piqued, I nod and lower myself into a chair.

"Your Majesty, I suspect that it is the king who is most displeased with your sister's behaviour. Her actions have not only offended his sense of propriety, but deprived the king of a beneficial arrangement. You, I suspect, loving her as you do, would show leniency … after a suitable period of punishment, of course."

I nod again. My throat constricts with unexpected grief, and I have the inexplicable desire to lay my head in my hands and give way to tears. It is the child making me mawkish. I swallow, blink away emotion and turn away so he cannot see my sudden weakness.

"She has behaved dreadfully, but I would forgive her … eventually. Henry says she is not to return to court … not ever."

He is silent for a while, watching as I try to school my face and calm my agitated hands. Apart from anything else, I would like Mary with me at the birth. My child and the one she is carrying will be of an age, they could be raised together, cousins at court, had her choice of husband not ruined everything.

Cromwell gropes beneath his gown. "Your Majesty, I received a letter."

"From Mary?"

A pause. The logs settle in the grate, a puff of smoke drifts into the room.

"It is not meant for your eyes."

I hold out my hand and after a moment, several sheets of parchment crackle between my fingers. I scan the pages, reading quickly the first time, and more slowly the second.

"Well, a strange letter indeed …"

"Why strange?"

"One minute she pleads for you to intervene with Henry and I, and our parents, inferring that she and Stafford are destitute and that she is desperate to return to court. Yet the next moment she insults me. Listen to this bit. 'I had rather beg my bread with him than to be the greatest Queen christened.' It seems a strange way of engaging my sympathy."

He holds out his hand and I pass the letter back to him. "She did not intend you to see it, Your Majesty. In her words I read desperation, bravado, and a sense of exile."

I am cross, mulling over her letter, irritated and unsettled by her passion. I cast an eye over Cromwell. He is still standing, his shoulders hunched, his face turned toward the hearth where a small summer fire burns. He looks inscrutable, unapproachable—reptilian, in many ways. Mary must be desperate indeed to turn to Cromwell, and yet … many women of my acquaintance speak well of him.

Perhaps it is our relative positions that makes him so reserved with me.

"What do you think I should do?"

He turns his head slowly, raises his brows, eyes opening wide, the creases in his forehead deepening. He splays his hands.

"Help her, Your Majesty."

"Help her? Against the king's will?"

He smiles, a slight twinkle gleaming in the dark depths of his eyes.

"I suggest you use your, erm … charm to persuade His Majesty that perhaps she is deserving of a little help. In the meantime, perhaps Your Majesty would permit me, personally, to send her a little aid, out of my own pocket?"

My jaw drops. "Why would you do that?"

He shrugs. "She is the sister of my queen and she is not a bad woman, just rash and a little, shall we say, too eager to please."

I place both hands on my belly and stare into the lick of flame in the hearth. I remember Mary's tinkling laugh, the fall of her fair hair, the forgiving warmth of her embrace.

"Very well," I hear myself saying. "You may send her alms and I will speak to Henry, but not until I am sure he is ready to hear it."

July 1534

I enter the hall, Urien at my heels, and immediately spot George speaking with our cousin, Francis Bryan. Both men turn and make a knee to me, and I cannot help but note that Francis's handsome smile is unblemished by the loss of his eye. The jewelled eye patch adds a reckless charm to his previously smooth good looks. But beside George, of course, he is nothing. My brother is laughing.

"Anne," he says, "our cousin has been saddled with an unwanted gift."

"Look at my doublet." Francis lifts his arms to indicate the liberal spread of white hair that clings to it.

"Have you been grooming your horse in your court clothes, Cousin?" I laugh, knowing that is far from likely. He puts his head close to mine and lowers his tone.

"Lady Lisle has given me a dog, Your Grace, and as much as I adore them, this one is not the type I would choose."

"A dog? Where is it?"

Francis and George search the floor. "He was here just now. "Dog … doggy, where are you?"

"Is that his name?"

Francis pulls a face. "I haven't named him. I am hoping I won't have to keep him."

"There he is!" George swoops down and holds aloft a bundle of white fur. "You can see he isn't exactly a dog suited to the likes of a hero of the lists."

I reach out a hand, feeling the lick of a tiny, hot tongue. A pair of big brown eyes look up at me.

"Oh, the sweet thing!" I take him from George, who immediately proceeds to brush his own doublet.

"I see what you mean about the hair," he laughs.

The dog scrabbles at my bosom, longing to reach my face with his long lapping tongue.

"He is as eager to kiss you as the rest of us." Francis laughs. "I think you should do me the honour of keeping him, Your Grace, he is clearly made for you."

"Can I, Francis? Can I have him?" I am quite smitten, my cheeks wet with slobber, the jewels on my bodice already snagged and covered in hair.

"It would be my pleasure to present you with such a gift, my dear cousin." Francis bends over my hand, his relief clear to see. "I am sure Lady Lisle will understand when I explain that the Queen's Grace was so enamoured of him that I couldn't refuse."

Urien growls when I enter the chamber with my new pet. "Stop it," I say. "Don't be nasty, it is your new

186

companion." I hold the puppy close, let them sniff each other, and Urien, being the soft fellow that he is, is soon won over. By supper time they are fast friends, and I have no qualms about leaving them alone with the servants when I descend to the hall for supper.

"What have you named him?" Henry asks when I introduce him to the puppy.

"Well, you see how he puts his head on one side like that, as if he is asking a question."

Henry nods, and obligingly the dog cocks his head, looks at us questioningly. "Well, I thought I'd call him Pourquoi, you know, the French word for 'why.'"

Henry throws back his head and laughs. "That is perfect, my love, quite perfect. You couldn't call him anything else."

July 1534 - Hever

For a moment, when I tell Henry of my desire to visit Hever, he looks as if he has been stung by a wasp. "But what about the tournament," he cries, "and the pageant?"

"Oh Henry, there are so many pageants and jousts. It won't hurt me to miss one."

We have already had to postpone a trip to the French court because of my condition. He lowers his chin, pouts and looks at me through his eyebrows. "I suppose you would like me to come with you."

"No, no. You stay and enjoy the fun. All I shall do is sit in the sun and gossip with my mother. It is what our prince and I need just now, there is no need for you to be inconvenienced."

He rises from his chair and pulls me to my feet. "Won't you miss me?"

I poke the end of his nose, pull his beard playfully. "Of course, but it is only for a week or so. Then, when I get home, there will be but a month or two before the confinement."

187

He turns me in his arms, so my back is toward him. I lean against him and he rests his chin on my head, letting his hands slide down to caress my belly. "And then we will meet this little man," he murmurs. I cover his hands with my own, give his fingers a squeeze and don't let him know I have heard the rumours. My brother makes sure of that.

Of course I am acutely jealous, but George says it is natural for a man to seek solace from another when his wife is so close to confinement. "Look upon it as doing you a service," he says. "You wouldn't want the king's demands in bed to undermine the health of your prince."

My eyelids are pricking. I look down, shaking my head, and a tear drops onto my lap, followed by another. George's hand is instantly on my shoulder. "Anne, don't worry. Our cousin will ensure that Henry's eye does not stray too far. Once you are able to facilitate his needs she will hand him back, as good as new."

My chest feels as if it will burst open. My chin wobbles, my mouth turning upside down. "But I see them, George, inside my head. Horrible visions of them together …"

"Hush, hush." He draws me close, comforts me as only he can. "It is Madge, our little cousin, no enemy. She does not want him for herself, her affections lay elsewhere. You should thank me for putting her in the king's way once his eye began to wander."

It is true; George acted in my best interests. As soon as my pregnancy was advanced enough for Henry to begin to fidget and cast his eye upon the daughter of our enemy, he dangled our cousin like a carrot beneath the royal nose. "Look upon her as a wet nurse, caring for your husband until you are fit to see to his needs yourself."

George, being a man, doesn't understand the pain of handing one's child into the arms of another woman. He doesn't realise it is equally as difficult when it's your husband. But there is nothing to be done, so I square my shoulders and try not to think about it. Yet still the images creep up on me unawares; in the dead of night or in the middle of the afternoon, it makes no difference. I see them in disgusting clarity and in my mind's eye Henry loves her, far more than he has ever loved me.

So to get myself away from it and to prevent another dreadful row with Henry, I come back to Hever. And if not for the fact that the servants fall on their noses every time they see me, it would seem that I have never been away.

There is something relaxing about the lack of formality. It is nice to put on a plain gown and tie up my hair beneath an ordinary cap. I am in the garden, Urien and Pourquoi investigating the array of aromas beneath the hedges as I stroll along the path. The summer sun winks through the trees, warming my face as I spy a stray weed unnoticed by the gardener. Acting on a sudden impulse, I kneel on the grass, reach out and dig my fingers into the soil, grasp it tightly and tug it out. It comes away easily, the tap root sliding from the well-tilled earth. Then, hidden beneath the lavender, I spy a seedling of rosebay willowherb that will spoil the look of the border if left to grow wild. It comes up easily, and soon I have a small pile of wilting weeds on the grass beside me. It is sometime later when the dogs set up a commotion and, raising a hand to shield my eyes from the sun, I look up to see who they are greeting with such enthusiasm. My visitor, after fighting himself free of eager paws and tongues, whips off his hat and makes a bow.

"Tom!" I try to get up, but the size of my belly hinders me. Tom stoops down and offers me his hand, hauls me to my feet. I stumble, hang onto his sleeve and laugh up at him. "I am not very nimble at the moment."

"So I see."

I look down at my muddy hands and slap them together, sending out a shower of dirt. "What are you doing here?"

"Oh," he slaps his hat against his thigh, "I often ride over and see how things are … remember the old days."

His words evoke the memory of four children, two boys and two girls, running in and out of the flower beds,

189

tumbling in the meadows, playing hide-and-go-seek in the grain store.

"Those were happy times," I say, my face beginning to ache from smiling so widely.

"And now you have children of your own. How is Princess Elizabeth?"

He listens attentively, feigning interest, as I launch into a lengthy description of my daughter's virtues. "She is so clever, so forward. She toddles to meet me when I visit and can already say a few words. If her brother is half as bright, he will be a king to be reckoned with."

Of course, I see Tom from time to time at court. He has a prominent place in the household and is often around on the king's business, taking part in pageants and state functions. But when we meet there, by some unspoken agreement we are reserved, detached. Here at Hever it is as if the years have been torn aside like a curtain, and the sunshine of our youth is smiling down upon us.

"Will you walk with me?" He shows no sign of mischief so I lay my hand on his arm and he assists me slowly around the garden. We speak of ordinary things. He makes no mention of his former love for me and we are at ease; old friends sharing a precious afternoon. He laughs a lot, and even when he is serious there is a twinkle in his eye, a quirk to the side of his mouth where his laughter always begins.

Before he takes his leave, he tucks my hand beneath his, close to his heart. "Are you happy, Anne?"

I close my eyes, turn my face to the sun and nod. "Yes, very happy. And I will be happier still when my prince is born."

He raises my fingers to his mouth, presses his lips against them. "You know I am yours to command. I will serve you, even in the face of the king's wrath."

And then he is gone, springing into the saddle, clamping his hat firmly onto his head before gathering the reins and cantering away. As I call to the dogs and turn back toward the hall, I realise that perhaps Tom does still care for me, after all.

It is dark inside and I do not notice Grandmother until she speaks. "Was that the king I saw you with?"

I leap at the sound of her voice and with a hand to my breast to still my banging heart, I move closer so that she might hear my reply.

"No, Grandmother. It was Tom, Tom Wyatt."

She shows me her gums, the creases on her face moving and settling into new lines. "Little Tom Wyatt? Here all alone? Does his mother know he is out unaccompanied?"

It would be funny were it not so tragic. My smile is sad. "Grandmother, Tom is past thirty now! His mother is long dead."

"Eh?" She squints as if it will help her to hear, but I do not repeat myself, there is no point. Let her stay in her strange world that has no regard for the present. The past is a happy place, let her live it.

Poor Grandmother, I think, her life is almost over now and all her pleasures past. I can just recall how she was when I was young. A proud upright woman, mother to ten and given to interfering in her children's lives long after they were grown. She has been a widow now for thirty years, each year growing older, slipping slowly and steadily closer to infirmity, her mind as dishevelled as the bottom of a chicken coop. It will not be long before we lay her in her grave … I shake off the thought, thrust it aside. Even though it has long been expected, it will be a hard day for us when it comes.

"Here, look at this," she says, crooking a wizened finger. "Merlin has a canker; he needs a physic."

I reluctantly bend over the dog, the noxious fumes of Grandmother's skirts making me blench. She runs her fingers through his coat, parting the wiry hair to display a livid looking boil, or a rat bite.

"Give him to me," I say, "I will take him to the stables and get a groom to look at him."

191

She parts with him as reluctantly as I hand Elizabeth to Lady Bryan. He is an obnoxious little beast but it will not do to let the creature sicken and die. He is Grandmother's only remaining friend, and the only member of the household who does not mind the stench of pee and cabbage that seems to cling to her.

Mother is distracted, as if she doesn't know what to do with me. She is no longer comfortable having me home; it is one thing to entertain a daughter, a queen is another matter altogether. She is tense, awkward and nervous. In the end, when she continues to put on airs for my benefit, I can bear it no longer.

"Mother! I came home for some respite from royal etiquette. Just let it rest and come and sit with me, bear me company. Come; pick up your sewing."

She perches on the edge of a chair, lowers her head over a row of tiny stitches while I fasten an edging of swansdown to a tiny linen bonnet. For a while the afternoon ticks on, and we work in companionable silence.

From time to time I look up at her bowed head, the light shining upon her lined brow, cheeks that are beginning to droop. They say she was very beautiful as a girl, rather like Mary in looks. It has been my eternal regret that I resemble Grandmother. I have heard stories of how Mother danced with Henry when he was still the Prince of Wales, how their beauty and grace caused quite a stir.

"What was Henry like as a boy, Mother?"

She jumps a little, looks up from her work, a flush pinkening her cheeks. She shrugs, inserts her needle and fumbles for the point at the back of the cloth.

"Oh, you know. Handsome and gallant, very athletic and always with a song on his lips."

"I suppose all the women were in love with him – young and old."

She puts down her work, tips her head to one side.

"Oh yes. Court ladies are always in love with the Prince of Wales, whatever he looks like, but with Henry there was a genuine reason for fancying him."

"It's a mercy he doesn't resemble his father," I say. Not that I ever met the old king, for he was dead long before I was old enough to come to court. His portrait shows a closed, private man, the hooded eyes hiding secrets, plotting mischief. Of course, I could be influenced by Henry's aversion to him. He has never said anything good about his father, apart from once when he commended his father for ending the war between York and Lancaster. Although he is a Tudor and proud of it, I know Henry sees himself as more of York than Lancaster, and looks beyond his penny-pinching father to the grandeur of his grandfather, Edward IV.

We never know our parents, not really. We only ever hear the stories they wish us to hear. I know the tales linking Mother and Henry, and wonder again if there is any truth in them, but I do not ask her for fear I would not like her reply.

The king has always had an eye for a pretty lady and this does not sit well with his prudish nature. I know that sometimes, after a night of love with me, his lawful wedded wife, he creeps away to make confession to his God. I wonder how Henry excuses his consorting with my cousin to himself, let alone God.

To me, love between married people is a God-given right, and we should think ourselves fortunate to be so in love. Love and marriage excuses even the most inventive of intimacies, and it only becomes a sin when those same things are carried out with someone like my cousin; or an ill-spent hour with a Bankside whore. Such crimes cannot be forgiven, neither by God nor by me.

Madge is always on my mind. I look down at my swollen body and fat ankles and wonder if I will ever regain the attributes needed to win my husband back. It does seem the day will never come. I have two more months at least before the birth, and then a further month before I am churched. By then my pretty cousin could easily have won

193

him with her favours or, worse still, he may have moved on to fresher waters.

August 1534 - Whitehall

Although it is several weeks yet to the birth, I have set my seamstresses to making new gowns for after the confinement. Just seven months into my pregnancy, it is weeks since I have seen past my belly. As the summer grows hotter so does my temper, and I have to bite my tongue, remember that Henry is a man with needs and that Madge is doing me a favour.

He doesn't flaunt their relationship and she is discreet, keeping her eye on her needlework whenever he enters our presence. But I know, and it smarts worse than any wound.

At the hottest part of the day, Henry comes into my apartment to escape the heat. He smiles congenially at everyone, tells them not to rise, and after leaving a careless kiss upon my veil, takes his place beside me. Once, he would have made sure his lips made contact. He would have thrown my sewing aside and bade me sit upon his knee. It has been a long time since we shared such intimacy. I stab the needle into the fabric. These days, his affection is all for her.

The lutenist, Mark Smeaton, strums a relaxing tune while my ladies are gathered in small groups with the gentlemen, who are lounging, idling away an hour listening to the music and admiring the women. From the corner of my eye I notice Norris scrawl a note. When he thinks no one is watching, he slips it into Madge's hand. I see her secrete it away … and so does the king.

I glance up, immediately recognising the significance of his narrowed eyes, pinched nostrils. He is annoyed and his eyes dart from Norris back to Madge. My guts twist with jealousy and I cannot help but nudge him with my elbow. Henry turns his head and with a subtle shake of my own, I silently advise him not to make a fuss. He ignores my wisdom and leaps to his feet.

"With me, Norris," he growls, and stomps from the room, the guards struggling to throw open the doors in time. After a moment I put down my sewing and follow, my heart thumping sickeningly beneath my ribs.

I should turn around, go back to my chamber, closet myself away, draw the bed curtains, and bury my head beneath the pillows, anything to shut out the knowledge. I should be blind, as Catherine was before me. But something drives me to follow … and to listen at the king's privy chamber door.

Henry's voice is loud, his wishes clear. "Stay away from the lady, or I will have you sent from court, do you hear?"

Norris' reply is muffled, but I detect fear in his voice as well as pain as he begs the forgiveness of his king.

Henry cannot love my cousin, I know that. He loves me, and always will. Our passion that lasted, ungratified, for more than seven years cannot be quenched by the charms of an insipid girl. I am queen and I will not allow it.

Norris opens the door so suddenly that we almost collide. He is so upset that he forgets the respect due to his queen. Instead of pausing and making a knee to me, he pulls off his cap and speeds along the passage in the direction of the gardens.

I press myself against the wall, reluctant for Henry to find me here, and with the blood rushing in my ears I flinch as he kicks a stool furiously against the chamber wall, where it splinters into firewood.

Before I can escape, Henry is there. He towers over me, his face reddening with rage as he realises I have witnessed his petty jealousy. "Why are you here?" he yells. "Get you back to your own chamber, and mind your own business."

I cringe against the force of his anger and flee from his presence, lifting my skirts and literally running along the corridor. Even the guards, usually so immovable, are surprised to see my flight. I burst into my chambers, falling back against the door as the tears spill forth.

"Your Majesty?" Nan is the first to my side and she takes my elbow, calls for Jane as she steers me to my bed.

They lay me on pillows, ease off my slippers, and Jane bathes my face with cool water. Slowly my sobs cease and I look around, the sympathetic faces of my women shaming me. I have never let them see my vulnerability before, and I hate the pity that is so clear in their eyes.

A shadow at the bedside and Jane Seymour is there, her plain face stodgy with concern. She offers me a cup of wine then stands back, her hands clasped in her hanging sleeves as she watches me drink. She is a quiet girl, always watching and listening, not joining in with the others, but she is pious and well-behaved, so I tolerate her despite her cloying ways.

She fusses with my pillows but her hands are clammy. My hair sticks to her fingers, snagging and pulling, so I irritably pull away. "Leave me," I snap and she creeps away like a kicked spaniel. I lay back, emit a huge sigh and close my eyes, to battle with demons until I fall asleep.

It is pain that wakes me. I clap both hands to my stomach, holding my breath until the cramp has passed. Then, when I can breathe, I call out for Nan. Almost immediately her head appears around the door, her face draining of colour when she sees me contorted with agony.

"Your Majesty." She is at the bedside in seconds. I grab her arm, clench my fingers down hard.

"Help me," I croak, and slowly she assists me to rise. Abandoning all decorum, she screams for my ladies and they all come running, their pattering feet and murmuring voices dying away when the torches are lit and they see my soaked petticoats and the pink puddle on the counterpane.

"I will fetch the midwife …" Jane Seymour scurries from the room while the other women clamour to assist me.

Exhausted after hours of travail, I slump on my pillows as they hand me my child. My son is swaddled in linen, his little blue face closed as in sleep, his purple lips like a bow. I cast back the covering to examine his perfectly formed limbs, his minute nail-less fingers, the tiny proof of his manhood. Apart from the fact he does not breathe, our little prince is perfect.

They take him from me, creeping away, and I roll over and wish I could die. I can find no comfort. I have lost our son, the prince that we have fought for all these years. What has it all been for? The tears don't fall, they wash down my face, no sobbing, no thrashing. I am saturated in grief.

My attendants don't know what to say to me. They avoid my eye, speak in whispers and creep from my presence. When Henry finally deigns to come and face me I am quite alone, with only the terror of my thoughts for company.

He is deflated, like a child's bladder ball, his royal brilliance destroyed, his confidence quashed. I raise sore, wet eyes to him and for a long while we stare at each other, my throat working painfully, my breast burning. His face is flaccid and I can detect no anger, just unquenchable sorrow. In the end I hold out a hand, and after a long time of just looking at it, he eventually takes it and falls onto the bed beside me.

I curl myself around him, cling to the strong trunk of his body, my arms choking, my legs wrapped about his hips. If I could climb inside him I would, for there is nowhere and no one safe in this world but him; nowhere I can escape to and no way to put things right.

As we lie there together, his torso begins to quiver and then shakes as great heaving sobs begin to tear him apart. I weep with him; useless, wrenching tears that have no end and do not heal. Henry and I are the most powerful couple in all of England and yet, in the face of death, we are powerless.

<u>August 1534 – Hatfield</u>

When my body is sufficiently healed, Henry and I travel to visit Elizabeth. She knows me now and falls happily into my arms. I almost crush her in my grief as I give vent to starved motherhood. Anxious to hide my sorrow and my sense of helplessness from my enemies, I do not let my tears fall but weep inwardly, painfully internalising my unrelenting grief.

I know there are spies everywhere. Those who are against reform, those who persist in loving Catherine. Brandon, pretending to be Henry's friend, while all the time an enemy to me. More and Fisher, while continuing to campaign against reform, refuse to acknowledge that Henry's first marriage was invalid. They whisper lies, terrible lies, and wish me dead.

All these people hate me, but Chapuys and his cursed mistress are the worst of all. I know they plot with Spain to steal Henry's throne and put Mary on it, and still, after all our efforts, Catherine refuses to acknowledge me as queen. Mary, the bastard, takes her lead and will never betray her mother, not even to please her father and get back into his good graces. She is like some smug Christian, smiling as she is fed to the lions, and her martyred expression sickens me.

I want to slap her.

I have been cuddling Elizabeth for so long that she begins to squirm. I relax my hold a little and look up just in time to see Mary hesitating at the door. She wears a smile of satisfaction. She is glad my son is dead. That is treason, surely.

I turn to Henry with a protest on my lips, but already he is bearing down upon his bastard daughter, tears in his eyes as they embrace. She is like a child, lost in the circumference of his arms.

Fury is like a poison in my heart. I long to ride away and leave it all behind me; the hatred, the grief, the strain of retaining my status. I wish I could take Elizabeth and get away, away from all of them. These days I am even unsure of Henry, and George is now my only true friend. The only person in the world whom I trust.

Yet as I recover my health I begin to realise I have more supporters than I had thought. There is Nan Zouche, who is ever on my side, and even Jane and cousin Madge have proved constant in their care of me since the miscarriage. Cromwell and Cranmer are hot for the cause of reform, and then there is Mother who, despite her failing health, has ridden from Hever to be with me.

"The best thing you can do, Anne, is to have another child." She sits in my chamber handing out sympathy and clichés as if they are refreshment. As if I didn't know that I need to produce a child. Hasn't my whole adult life been taken up with trying to give Henry his prince?

Madge is gentle. "Don't worry, Anne. I won't keep him from you. He doesn't need me now."

I pat her hand and try not to mind the barbs that her gentle words drive deep into my skin. After the trauma of the last few months I feel I have been flailed. I am sore and bleeding, exhausted and sick, both physically and mentally. I don't even know if I have the attributes or the energy necessary to win Henry back into my bed. Not now.

But as soon as I let it be known I am likely to be fruitful again he comes, quite willingly, to my chamber. He stands at the edge of the bed in his nightshirt and we pray together, asking God to bless our union and deliver us a son safely, this time.

We have suffered enough, after all we've been through, surely we deserve to get it right this once. I hold out my arms and Henry climbs onto the bed, drags my shift over my head and begins to fondle my breasts. I close my eyes, snuggle into the pillow and give myself up to the joy of it.

But something is wrong. After a while I squint down at our sprawled nakedness, our entwined legs, mine smooth and long, his muscular and clothed in short golden hair. Our torsos are facing, our faces parallel on the pillow as his thumbs rub to and fro across my nipples. I can barely feel his touch. Frowning inwardly, I take a deep breath and force myself to relax, squirm a little on the mattress and part my legs, thinking lovely thoughts to try to nurture a little desire.

In the centre of the royal bed we curl like babes, trying so hard to please each other, wanting so desperately for it to work between us, for things to be like they used to be. But it is no use. I cannot stop imagining him with Madge, and what little excitement had begun to rise now dwindles. I cannot be stirred, and after a while I realise that Henry is also unmoved; his member is as flaccid as an empty sack.

"Perhaps it is too soon," I whisper into his beard, stroking his forlorn cheeks. "Maybe we are just too tired."

Maybe he is tired of me. But I do not speak the fear aloud as I continue to stroke and soothe him until his body relaxes and his head sinks upon my shoulder. When he begins to drool and his snores reassure me that he is asleep, I am not disappointed, just greatly relieved that the embarrassing fiasco is over … for now.

February 1535 - Windsor

"George!" When my brother appears suddenly in the great hall after so long away, I forget I am queen and almost run across the floor to launch myself into his arms. His breath is warm on my neck, his laughter soft in my ear as he swings me around. By the time he places me back on the ground, we are both breathless. I hang onto his arm and lead him toward Henry, who slaps him on the back, almost as delighted as I.

"How was the crossing? The wind got up last night, didn't it?"

"I've known worse, Your Grace, and I was so eager to reach home I would have swum across the Channel."

Henry laughs, the courtiers tittering in agreement. "If you hadn't come soon I think the queen would have swum across to find you." The laughter grows louder. It doesn't do to ignore the king's jokes, no matter how poor they are. I smile, still clutching George's sleeve, his hand warm on mine.

"What did Francis say about the match? Did he agree?"

George's face falls a little, and he glances about the room to see who is near. "I would discuss that matter in private, if Your Grace will allow." He makes a short bow and Henry, sensing disappointment, grows solemn.

"Come," he says. "Let us retire so we can speak freely."

The private chamber is dark and warm, the bright fire and gleaming torches reflecting in the black diamonds of the windows. Henry and George take their places about the table, but I move a little a way off to stand before the hearth.

"So, what did our friend the French ambassador say?" Henry leans back in his chair and clasps his hands over his belly while George glances at me and pulls a face.

"Erm … he was not helpful, I am afraid. He declines your offer of Elizabeth in Mary's place and prefers to keep to the original proposal. He offers Elizabeth his third son …"

"What? Francis said that?" I rush forward and George puts up his hands in self-defence.

"I am only the messenger, Anne, but I gather the ambassador passes on his master's wishes."

"But Francis is my friend!" My hands are shaking, my knees trembling from outrage. "How could he do this?"

"Shh." Henry reaches out for me, takes my hand and pulls me to his side. "There are no friends in politics, Sweetheart, you know that."

His pinched nostrils betray that his annoyance is only just contained, but he is not as hurt, not as offended by the snub as I am. George turns his back and begins to pour wine into three vessels. He hands a cup to Henry first and then passes one to me. I shake my head, and he places it carefully on the table in the ring of the candle's light.

"We can only assume that since he prefers to negotiate for Mary's hand, he sees her claim to the throne as the greater. This makes him our enemy."

Henry waggles my arm. "Not necessarily, Sweetheart, perhaps he prefers to negotiate for a grown woman rather than an infant."

"A bastard!" I almost spit the word, immediately regretting it when hurt spreads across Henry's face like a stain.

"But Mary is my 'bastard,' don't forget."

His voice is quiet as he withdraws his hand and pretends to pick at a loose thread on his sleeve. I know I have made a mistake, but sometimes it is impossible to keep everything inside. Sometimes I have to speak out and I want to scream truths, no matter how painful or distasteful they are.

Having just one daughter terrifies me. How can one weak girl stand against a world so hostile to women? Married to France, Elizabeth would have powerful allies, strong defences against Spain, who is our enemy. If the Dauphin weds Mary it will strengthen her claim, reinforce her cause.

We cannot let that happen.

I can only hope that the furore in France just now will keep their king's mind on more pressing matters. Across the Channel, the church reforms are not going smoothly and every week we hear reports of burnings and mutilations, and rumours reach us that the country is on the brink of disarray. King Francis will have his hands full. I hope he will forget about Mary.

Not that the situation is much better here in England. There is a new Pope in Rome, one in whom we had placed much confidence, but he has shattered all our hopes by upholding Catherine's claim and declaring our marriage illegal. That snub is so great that Henry, not troubling to disguise his anger, goes wild with fury and sends for Cromwell.

A light cough tells us of his arrival and we turn as one. Simply the presence of Master Cromwell has a calming effect. He enquires politely as to our health, suggests that I sit down on the most comfortable chair. His eyes linger a little too long on my waist and I know he is already surmising if I am yet with child. Henry, sitting opposite me at the hearth, clears his throat, puts a hand on each knee and leans forward, launching into a tirade against the Pope.

"And what is to be done about it, Cromwell, my friend? You tell me that."

And of course, Thomas Cromwell, who is as wily as he is willing, has the answer we require. As a result, Henry is now Supreme Head of the Church in England and, in addition to that, Cromwell hurries a law through Parliament making non-recognition of that fact treason. The penalty for denying Henry his title as Supreme Leader of the Church in England is now death. It has all happened so quickly and the resolution to our predicament, one that has confounded everyone for years, is simple to Cromwell. With one sweep he dispenses with Rome and with Catherine, but of course, we know that even now there will be consequences, and those who refuse to accept it.

I move to stand at the window, kneel on the seat and look up at the black night skies. The clouds pass across the moon, a sudden gust of wind sends arid leaves fluttering to the ground, and I am suddenly cold.

My skin retracts, the hairs on my arms and the back of my neck stand on end, and the voices of the men shrink to a murmur as I wrap my arms about my body and shudder at what I fear is to come.

May 1535- Whitehall

So many people have been put to death. Why can they not accept it? Why can they not just sign? First it is the Carthusian monks, seven in all; among them Newdigate, Exmew, Middlemore ... A few weeks since they were merely names on a slip of paper, but now they are felons, traitors, martyrs to their fallacious cause.

The people mutter against us, picking up the cry of Elizabeth Barton, a traitorous nun whom Cromwell hung last

203

year. She railed against us, decrying our marriage, denouncing our heir, and she named Henry as King Mouldwarp from ancient prophecy, whose miserable reign was destined to divide and bring down the kingdom.

She is dead now but as fast as Cromwell rids us of one rebel another appears, and among these latest foes is one of Henry's former friends.

Sebastian Newdigate is, or was, a former privy councillor. He was wise enough to sign the act of supremacy, but now refuses to acknowledge Henry as Head of the Church. Henry, sick to the stomach at the betrayal of his friend, visits him in Marshalsea prison, and later at the Tower to beg him to reconsider.

He refuses.

What else can we do?

There cannot be one rule for one man, and one for another.

Treason is treason.

There is nothing to be done.

Henry simmers with suppressed rage. He wants to be the beloved of his people; his whole life has been dedicated to nurturing his image as a golden renaissance prince. Instead, he is hated; we are both hated. He is Mouldwarp, and I have become Salome.

How did this happen?

Instead of the threat of capital punishment encouraging people to sign, it seems to strengthen their resolve to defy us, but we cannot back down. Next it is Fisher, a man whom Henry loved and looked up to in his youth for his wisdom and learning. A friend of Erasmus and More, Fisher is a good man … but misguided all the same. From the early days he has despised me, and despised reform, seeing in it the certain destruction of the Holy Church in Rome.

Why are these wise men so blind?

We don't want to destroy the Church.

We want to make it better, fairer, more accessible. But I never thought so many people would have to die.

<u>June 1535 – Richmond</u>

Henry is sitting by the window, his head in his hands. When he hears me enter, he looks up, his face bleak. "Anne …"

Encouraged by his welcome I move forward and perch on his knee, the attendants melting away into the darkness. I lean against him, tug his beard playfully, trying to cheer him, but he stills my hand and says in a small voice, "Cromwell was here, Anne. He says that More must die. There is no option …" His words break on a sob, and I slide from his knee to the floor and lay my head in his lap.

"Why don't you see him, Henry? Speak to him. He may listen to you, he loves you so much."

He pulls off my veil and his hand falls lightly on my hair. "Does he?"

I look up at him. "Of course he does. It is only his intractable religion and his affection for Catherine that makes him act against you."

Both More and Fisher have proved immovable when it comes to Catherine. When in my company, they are coldly polite but hostile. Or perhaps I should say they were hostile.

I keep forgetting that Bishop Fisher is dead and More is shortly to follow.

Soon, we will leave all this horror behind us and embark upon a summer progress. I have persuaded Henry to travel west, that we may inspect the reforms Cromwell has implemented there. We embark from Windsor, through Reading and onto Oxfordshire, and then to one of my favourite Gloucestershire houses, Sudeley Castle. We then plan to travel down through Wiltshire and Hampshire, to South Hampton, calling at Winchester on the way and, after a short stay in Portsmouth, journey back toward London. This should give Henry ample time to recover from recent upsets, and Cromwell, who plans to split his time between riding with us and continuing his investigations into the lesser monasteries, can bear the brunt of the responsibility.

Cromwell has temporarily become the power in the land, the hand that wields the knife to trim the diseased shoots from the Church. There is so much waste, so much corruption in these monastic institutions. I had never expected it to be so bad, but some of the stories that come to our ears make me weep indeed. Stories of corruption, immorality—and to think that these ... these people, supposedly devout and pious monks and nuns, seek to conceal their nefarious deeds beneath holy robes. Henry and I are determined to root them out, sort the good from the bad, the wheat from the chaff, and close down those foundations that are no better than houses of ill-repute.

***

"I will wear the purple, Jane." Purple is the colour of royalty and power and I wish to look my best as I face the public, and ride through the country over which I am queen. I will show them I am no Salome. I will smile upon them, throw them purses of silver to help them feed their children and pay their taxes. After this progress they will no longer speak of me as Anne the whore. I will become Anne the Benefactor.

Just as Jane lays the gown on the bed and I slip from my shift, the door opens and George enters. As I snatch up a sheet to conceal my nakedness, Jane squeals and throws a cushion at him, which he catches skilfully and slides into a chair.

"It's all right. I won't look," he says, screwing his eyes tight and grinning inanely.

The cool fresh linen slides over my arms, and Jane, who is fuming inwardly, begins to tie it at the neck. The other Jane, the Seymour girl, brings a selection of shoes and hats and I pick my favourites.

"You can pack the others. The men be here shortly to take the boxes to the carts." She bobs a curtsey and scurries off to do my bidding. "Are you ready, George? The king wishes to leave promptly."

As I lean over to pick up a slipper, the neck of my shift gapes wide. George flushes and tears his eyes from the fleeting glimpse of my breasts. When I straighten up, his wife begins to lace me into my bodice, pushing my bosom high, squeezing my waist tight. Then the sleeves are tied in place, the contrasting colours of my undergarments drawn through the slashes. As she works, Jane's eyes are averted, her jaw clenched. I can tell she is angry. She always is when George is with me.

When my girdle chain is fastened, I pick up my pomander. "I will join the king now. You two follow on after."

As I sweep from the room and the doors close behind me, the monotone of Jane's nagging follows me along the passage. I wonder how George bears it.

The king is waiting, the horses growing restless in the yard. His face lights up when he sees me and he tightens his reins. The grooms help me mount and as I settle myself in the saddle, I let Henry have the full force of my smile. I am Queen of England, Henry's wife. I am looking my very best and we have weeks of pleasure ahead of us.

The progress will keep us from London for the whole of the summer. By the time I see it again the leaves will be falling, the evenings growing darker and the sun lower in the sky. I plan to make the most of the ensuing weeks.

Even in London, which so far has been eager for Church reform, the crowds stand sullen in the rain. George tries to explain that they are sick of the suffering, of witnessing the public destruction of formerly great men, and as we ride by I cannot help but hear their mutterings of discontent. But when we reach the countryside and travel through villages and hamlets where news from London is slow to arrive, children run from their hovels to cheer us on our way. I toss them a purse, laugh to see them scrabble in the puddles, fighting over the coin.

"God bless Your Majesties!" someone calls, and I raise my gloved hand and salute their loyalty. As I do so the shower resumes, sending a scattering of raindrops across my face. I wrinkle my nose and George rides up alongside.

"Why don't you call for your litter and escape the shower?"

I shake my head. "No, George. The rain isn't much and the people need to see me if they are to learn to love me." I throw more coin, the cheers rise, and Henry bobs along ahead, the feather on his cap looking more like a drowned hen with each passing minute.

I've a mind to stop at Hook Norton, a property recently recovered from Henry Brandon, who has so displeased his king with his continuing support of Catherine. On a fine morning we set out from Langley Castle, en route to Sudeley, our hawks on our wrists, the hounds running free.

It is a rare dry morning in a wet month, and at the top of a rise we look down on the property nestled in a fold of the hills. Brandon, who owns it, claims to have renovated and improved it, but from what I can see of it, it is a dreary place, surrounded by trees, and I can tell from my vantage place that it will be chilly and damp. There is also a scarcity of game, although Suffolk claims the parkland to be well-stuffed with red deer.

I decide I don't want it.

Henry will have to let it rot.

Disappointed in the hunt, we reach Sudeley without the hoped-for meat for the kitchens. Even so, the retainers who have ridden ahead of our party manage to provide a royal feast. We are well received, the best apartments have been aired and cleaned, and we are entertained by the finest minstrels and players.

I love Sudeley Castle. It has a certain peace, an almost spiritual calm. The gardens are full of sprawling wet roses and vines and their scent, together with the lavender and lilac, make it smell like Heaven. The trickling fountains, the mossy seats, evoke memories of Hever and the joys of home.

We should visit here more often, bring Elizabeth I decide as, our arms linked, Henry and I glide along the honey-coloured paths.

We can forget things here, we can be ourselves; Henry and Anne, not the king and queen, not Mouldwarp and Salome. Our bodies relax, our smiles are more spontaneous, and that night the passion returns to our marriage bed.

I wake in the morning, roll over and groan at the ache in my limbs. Groping for my shift, lost in the night among the covers, I notice the bruises left by Henry's mouth on my thigh. What will my ladies have to say about that, I wonder? Smiling to myself, I fumble for and make use of the pot from beneath the bed.

Henry opens one eye and I smile good morning from my inelegant throne.

"Come here." He lifts his arm and I slide beneath it. His fingers walk across my belly until my breast sits neatly in his palm. His lips shift to my neck, just where it meets my shoulder, and shivers consume me. I close my eyes, let my head roll back, giving access, giving him permission. He props himself on his hands, rearing above me. He smells of sex and sweat, and last night's supper; his beard is damp from kissing me and his blue eyes are full of intent. I part my legs and lick my lips like a trollop, welcoming him home.

It is so different from the first time; so different from the months following the loss of our son. This time, just as he was last night, he is certain. Cousin Madge is forgotten.

"You are a witch, Madam," he whispers, the rhythm of our movements stirring the bed hangings, the ropes twanging and stretching beneath us. "You have bewitched me with your wicked wiles."

This is Henry's favourite bed-time game. He pretends I am a bad woman, or a witch, or sometimes a little girl. I have no need of such games myself but if it gets me a son, I welcome any invention that pleases him.

"I am indeed," I cry as he rolls over onto his back, clamping me to him. I am aloft, my thighs straining across

209

his loins. "I am Hecate, and you are under my spell, powerful under my control."

Riding him like a horse we gallop on, my nails scoring his flesh, my hair running like black snakes across my naked breasts. Henry grows rigid, I ride harder, my own pleasure mounting, pinching and scratching until, all of a sudden, he sits up, grabs me and smothers my face in his golden-furred chest. He bellows in my ear as we peak together, his groans, coarse and loud, mingling with my own kitten-like mews, his fingers tangled in my hair. He falls back on the pillows with his mouth agape and I slump forward, my breasts dangling in his face. "Anne," he gasps, "Anne, I swear you will be the death of me."

While Henry sneaks off to make his peace with God, I take a bath. Jane must notice the bruises, but she has the grace not to remark on them. I am tired and happier than I have been for a long time. If I can get Henry to make love to me like that more often, I will soon be with child. The need for a prince is never far away, even at my happiest times when I am dancing or riding through the woods with the hunt; the thought of a boy child hovers in the back of my mind.

After Mass, I watch Henry and George play tennis. They are close matched and it is a humid day. The rain outside is intermittent, but there is no air and soon both men are sweating. From the gallery I watch, not really minding who wins but knowing from experience that Henry will expect my cheers to be only for him. During the interval he mops his face with a large kerchief and scans the crowd, knowing he will find me in its midst. I wave and blow him a kiss, which he pretends to catch. He holds the imprisoned kiss to his lips and we both laugh. Even at this distance we are together.

"I swear you and the king are closer than you've ever been before." Nan takes a chair beside me, which Jane has recently vacated. "It does my heart good to see it."

To my surprise I find myself blushing, and in a sudden rush of affection I cover her hand with mine. "We are very happy, Nan, and I have every hope that soon we will be happier still."

She turns to me, her face pink with curiosity. "Do you mean …?"

I shake my head. "Not yet, but I am sure to be soon. The king keeps me … very busy."

"Busy? I am surprised he has the energy for tennis." Her dancing eyes belie the disapproval of her words and we are still laughing when Jane returns. As usual, she is looking disgruntled about something.

"What is so funny?" she asks, hurt to have missed a joke.

"Nothing, just a silly trifle, not worth repeating," I say, but as the tennis resumes I have to concentrate hard on the ball as it bounces back and forth about the court, for laughter is still rumbling in my belly and I cannot risk looking at Nan again for fear of bursting out afresh.

He seeks me out after the match. "I heard you cheering," he says, like a schoolboy showing off in front of his mother. His snow-white shirt clings to a torso damp with sweat, the open lacing at his neck revealing a tangle of wet red hair. I want to twirl those curls in my fingers, lick the sweat from my fingertips. It is hard to tear my eyes away.

"You were wonderful, Henry." I mop his brow with my own kerchief and as I help him back into his doublet, the unique scent of his body floats up to me. I step closer, reach up to kiss his earlobe. "I have need of you, My Lord," I whisper, trailing my hand down his chest to leave him in no doubt as to my meaning.

Then I walk away, leaving him stunned, looking back at him over my shoulder before calling to my ladies that I wish to retire to freshen up before dinner. As we take our seats at table, I am aware of him watching me. He seems preoccupied, anxious, and when I smile at him, his returning grin makes me hope I am the only one able to detect the lust that hides beneath.

His appetite is unaffected, but while he makes short shrift of his meal with his right hand, his left lies clamped on my thigh, intent upon an investigation of its own. While the minstrels play, he taps his jewelled fingers on the board and sighs impatiently.

I lean toward him, speaking quietly so none can hear. "You are king, Henry. You can call for a quick end to this."

As if remembering himself, he stands up, claps his hands, and the music dwindles into discord.

"The queen is unwell and wishes to lie down. You will excuse us."

Pink-faced from the blatant fib, he stands up, offers me his hand and leads me from the dais. When my ladies rise as one and make to follow us, he waves them away. "No, no. You can stay, ladies. Enjoy yourselves. I will see to the needs of the queen."

George's laughter still burns in my ears when Henry and I enter the bedchamber. "You couldn't have made it clearer if you'd tried!" I cry. "You might as well have said, 'You people stay here and have fun while I do husbandry service on the queen.'"

He kneels on the floor, his hands creeping up my skirts. Two huge palms cup my bare buttocks, drawing me closer. "Be quiet," he says, diving beneath my petticoats. He continues to speak but his voice is muffled, his tongue hot on my quaint, and I don't care what he is saying. I stumble a little, grab for the bed which luckily is within distance, and fall back upon it, give myself up to the pleasure of him.

We are taking a late breakfast in my chamber when Cromwell asks for admittance. He comes in, deferent as ever, asking after our health, remarking on the weather.

"Sit down, Tom, share a little wine. Have a wafer ..."

Henry calls for another chair and after some hesitation Cromwell lowers himself into it, although he does not partake of breakfast. "Are you enjoying the west country?" Henry asks, pouring honey liberally over a handful of wafers.

Cromwell closes his eyes and smiles. "I am, Your Majesty. The land is fertile, the game is good. The place leaves very little to be desired." He hesitates, looks from the king to me and back again. "I took the opportunity to ride to Hailes yesterday, to look into the matter we discussed a few weeks ago."

"The Holy Blood?" I look up, curiosity piqued. "Did you see it?"

He leans back in his chair. "I saw a phial with some fluid inside … whether it be the blood of Christ or the blood of a farmyard duck is anyone's guess."

Henry chokes on his wafer. I thump him on the back until the moment has passed. He emerges from the attack laughing, thinking it a joke. "A farmyard duck," he repeats, "I like that."

But I can see that Cromwell is in earnest and my hand stills on Henry's back. "A duck? You are not serious?"

"Madam." Cromwell's face is paler than usual, his eyes unusually restive. "If every relic were genuine, St Peter must have had several dozen fingers, Cuthbert fifty ribs or more, and our lady a mouthful of teeth that would grace a crocodile."

Henry wipes his mouth and puts the cloth on his plate. "You mean the monks are deceiving us?"

Cromwell nods. "I mean they may be deceiving us, yes. I would like your permission to look into it. Have the phial examined to discover if it is indeed Christ's blood, or simply a deception."

Henry leans back in his chair. "I don't know …"

"Henry, you must. If this is a trick then it has to be exposed. Pilgrims come from far and wide to see the Blood of Christ, it has healing powers. Oh Cromwell, how can it not be genuine?"

"As I said, Madam. It may be, but just to be sure, I think we should look into it."

I turn in my seat, grab Henry's wrist with both hands. "Henry, please! We must know the truth. Once we are in possession of the facts then we can decide what action, if any, is necessary."

I open my eyes wide, blink winningly, and he is unable to resist me. He sighs so gustily I feel it on my cheeks. He pats my hands, smiles at Cromwell.

"Oh very well, Cromwell, see what you can discover, but be discreet. Bring the findings to us and speak to no one else of it."

Cromwell bows from our presence, leaving us alone. Henry leans back, puts his hand beneath his shirt and scratches his belly. "Now, what shall we do today, Sweetheart? The rain is still falling, shall we return to our bed?"

The whole court is gossiping about how much in love we are. Jane says that bets are being placed on how soon it will be before I am fat with child. She sighs when she tells me this, and since I am in love and want everyone else to be, I reach out in sympathy.

"Jane, are you still at odds with George? Is there anything to be done?"

She jerks her shoulders, avoiding my eye. "It's too late for that. He prefers to take his pleasure elsewhere, and even should he bother to try to warm my bed, I'd have none of it."

"But a child, Jane. A child would make things so much better, even if you and George …"

"Pardon me, Madam," she says, snatching away her hand, "but do you think I don't know that? Do you not think I spend every waking hour longing for a child? But how can I get one when my husband prefers to sleep with hearth wenches?"

She is not easy to like, and very difficult to help, but I can see her pain. "I am sorry, truly, Jane. Shall I speak to George, see if I can persuade him to make an effort?"

She sighs, looks at the ceiling and then at the floor. "Your Majesty, how would you feel if your husband had to be 'told' to sleep with you? Would you then be filled with lust for him, or would you want to crown him with your chamber pot?"

I have a sudden vision of George with the contents of the night stool streaming over his shoulders. It would be his

214

just deserts. If the situation were not so tragic, I would laugh. I see her point entirely but, knowing George as I do, I see his also.

He craves soft loving arms, not the sharp acid tongue Jane has developed. What a shame their marriage got off to such a bad start, I can see no hope for it now.

Turning back to the mirror I grow quiet, pensive as Jane brushes the knots from my hair. She is gentle and I have always liked the way she teases the tangles instead of dragging at them as some do. I reach out and give her hand a squeeze. Our eyes meet in the looking-glass and I see her pain and self-pity, mixed with a little self-loathing.

August 1535 – Gloucestershire

We reluctantly leave Sudeley and move on across the Severn Valley to stop at Thornbury Castle, but our loving mood continues and the court, infected by our happiness, is gay. Even the rain relents a little and allows the sun to peek through the clouds. We all tumble outside into the gardens, glad of the respite from the weather.

My ladies and I have spread our skirts and are sitting on the grass listening to a minstrel's tale, when news reaches us of plague in Bristol Town. Henry's brows draw together. "We must rethink our journey," he says at once. "We cannot risk contagion."

In the end, the town fathers come to pay their homage to us at Thornbury, and they come bearing gifts. Livestock and victuals for Henry's table, and to me they present a parcel-gilt cup and cover which is filled with coin; a hundred marks in all.

The austere old men line up before me, sombre and reserved, but when I beam upon them, enthusing over their gifts, their hostility seems to dissolve, falling under my loving spell, blushing and stroking their grey beards in delight. At last, I am learning how to reach out to people. How I wish that everyone was so easily won.

All summer I have been looking forward to the next stop on our travels, for we are to visit the home of an old and dear friend, Nicholas Poyntz. For once I need have no fear that our hosts are hiding disloyalty to us, for the people of Acton Court leave us in no doubt as to where their loyalties lie.

The approach to the manor is lined with waving cottars, the bailey bedecked with flags, and at the top of the steps to the great hall, Nicholas and his household wait to greet us. As we ride in, the cheers are deafening. Henry and I smile widely, and so do the rest of our party.

It is only a year or so since Nicholas Poyntz lost his wife, but the loss doesn't seem to have affected him greatly. He skims down the steps, sweeps an elegant bow, and as soon as I am dismounted, takes my hand and anoints my wrist with a respectful kiss.

"Nicholas," I say, looking down at his dark curly head. "How are you? It has been a long time."

"Indeed it has, Your Grace, too long." He turns next to greet Henry, bowing low to welcome him to his home. Nicholas is more my friend than Henry's. He is a long term supporter of the reform, and George and I have known him for a number of years. He is intelligent, handsome, and sincere, and I hope Henry will come to love him as we do.

"How were the roads, Your Majesty?" Nicholas asks. "I was thinking of you only last evening and wondering if the recent heavy weather has made them impassable."

"I've seen worse," Henry replies, still a little wary as his eye slides about the bailey, taking in his surroundings. With great deference, Nicholas ushers us through the band of happy retainers who have come to greet us and into the hall, where Henry stands tall, assessing the wealth and opulence, little realising that Nicholas has probably bankrupted himself for the sake of our comfort.

"How lovely, Nicholas," I murmur when Henry makes no comment. Nicholas holds out his arm and with my hand on his sleeve, leads us through his house. I feel very much at home already. The renovations have been thorough, a whole new wing built just to accommodate our visit, and the rooms are designed to open into each other, in the way of a royal palace. Each chamber is brightly lit, draped with the finest tapestries and wall paintings, and in each hearth burns a fire large enough to roast an ox.

A suite of rooms are provided for Henry and I, each one more lavishly furnished than the last, and I am pleased to see a garderobe discreetly situated in each chamber. I look about me, unable to hide my grateful smile. "I shall be very comfortable here, Nicholas," I say with feeling, and in his answering smile I see a mixture of relief and gratitude.

When Henry and I are alone, I sit on the window seat and begin to draw off my gloves. "What did you think of Nicholas, Henry? Do you think you will make a friend of him?"

I have the desire that Nicholas should have a knighthood, status, a place at court. The king moves toward me, pulls a chair close and eases into it. We are both a little stiff from the saddle; riding in the rain is never comfortable. The leather chafes, the water finds a way beneath all but the most voluminous coverings, and my limbs are aching and sore. Of course, Henry hunts almost every day and is more used to it than I, but even he is weary.

"Hmm, I liked him well enough, and he certainly seemed to admire you."

From the corner of my eye I cannot be sure if he is teasing or not. I decide to be dismissive. "Oh, I have known him forever, since I was a girl in France."

"He seems enamoured of you, also."

"Not enamoured, Henry. Nicholas is playing the attentive host, that is all. I hope you are not going to be jealous and silly, it will spoil everything."

"Not unless you give me cause."

I slide from the seat, lean forward to kiss the end of his nose, tug his beard. I know he hates it when I tease him, but it is the only way to treat such foolishness. "I love you, Henry Tudor," I whisper. "Not the king, the man. The man I share my bed with every night, the man I stayed a maid for

217

until I was far too old to be so. There is no other man for me."

He pulls me onto his lap and lays his head on my shoulder, his damp hair further wetting my gown. A hand creeps up my bodice to tamper with my breast. We remain so for some time, watching the changing light outside the window. I listen to his breathing, regular and slow, and soon my eyes begin to droop. When dusk falls and the chamberer comes to light the torches, he disturbs our slumber.

I sit up and our cheeks, which have welded together as we dozed, tear apart. I put up a hand as we untangle our bodies, and see the red imprint of my face on his. As I rise from his lap, I look down in dismay at our fine velvet clothes, which are stiffening as the mud dries upon them.

That evening, the music is loud and merry. George makes us all laugh, playing the fool on the dance floor and spoiling the composure of his partner, Joan. We clap our hands, tap our feet, and Henry, unable to resist the lure of the melody, holds out his palm and demands that I partner him.

Soon we are all dancing, skirts swaying, feet stomping. We laugh, spinning, as we desperately strive to keep time with the musicians. I don't just dance with Henry. I partner every man in the room; George and Norris, and Nicholas more than once, growing quite rosy with exertion.

The other ladies dance as well—even Jane who, pink-cheeked from the wine and the activity, manages to look quite pretty. George deigns to lead her about the floor for a while, although he soon hands her on to Nicholas and partners Madge instead. He is never with the same partner for long, one after the other my ladies pass through his hands, subject to his teasing, his flirting.

As we promenade through a corridor of dancers, Norris whispers something daring in my ear and I burst out laughing again, quickly drawing Henry's eye. I try to contain it but the joke is too great and too rude to be shared. I clench my lips together, trying not to laugh, and with my hand in his, Norris and I weave in and out of the other dancers. He is light of foot, his eye twinkles and I respond because I am happy, because I am a queen dancing with my courtiers.

We are all quite drunk, both with the wine and the warm heady night, and when George moves in to claim his turn with me, Norris pretends to refuse to hand me over. "You shan't have her," he cries, in mock heroism. "I am not done with her yet."

And my idiot brother, drunker than the rest of us, lowers his head and charges like an angry bull. He knocks Norris sideways and grabs my hand. While Norris scrabbles to rise from the floor, amid shouts of laughter, George spins me round, hoists me over his shoulder, his hand clutching my thigh, and runs with me from the room. I shriek as he charges along the dimly-lit corridor, jolted and laughing all the way. I kick my legs, calling for help, but the sounds of the revel die away as he bursts into a side chamber and lets me slide to the floor.

It is dark within, a seldom used room that is musty with little traffic. There are no torches, no fire; just the darkness, and George and I. I lie back against the door, breathless, my laughter lingering, my bosom jerking. As my giggles subside and my eyes grow accustomed to the darkness, I can just make out the shadows of his face, the gleam of moonlight on his forehead. He sobers, reaching out to run a finger along my cheek, his thumb lingering on my wet lips.

My smile fades.

"Ah Anne," he whispers, as if I am not there to hear him. "If only you were not my sister, not my queen."

The joke is over. I don't feel like laughing now. I can hear the pain in his voice, the deep hurt of his words. He is drunk, I tell myself. He will remember none of this in the morning.

And neither must I.

The rest of the progress passes in a haze of merriment as we stop briefly at Little Sodbury, Baynton, and a little longer at the Seymour seat at Wulfhall. By mid-September we are in Winchester, where our revel comes to an abrupt halt as bad news reaches us. Once more, it is from Rome.

To my husband's fury, Pope Paul denounces us again, depriving Henry of his royal dignity and his right to the kingdom, and urging France to uphold this Papal brief. The Pope's influence is vast and we are used to obeying him. Our choices are clear; we can either do as he says, separate and let Henry take Catherine back as his queen, or we can hide in a corner, besmirched by Papal disapproval, or we can be audacious and show the world once and for all that the Pope's words are meaningless in England. We have our own Head of the Church in England, and Henry is both Pope and King rolled into one. I urge Henry to strike out, stand firm against Rome's bullying.

Due to the recent treasonous activities of some church members, there are bishoprics to appoint. It is our duty to elect new men to the posts and we intend to fill those posts with our friends, our supporters.

In a belligerent mood, on the nineteenth day of September, we hold a grand religious ceremony in which Cranmer consecrates three bishops: Bishop Foxe of Hereford, Bishop Latimer of Worcester, and Bishop Hisley of Rochester. In a show of defiance against the Pope, Henry and I, clothed in our best, attend the ceremony and bite our thumbs at Rome.

Afterwards, the council scrambles to please us, tearing out their hair to come up with ways to legally counter the Pope's actions. It is Gardiner, so wily with his pen, who composes a writ defending the Supremacy, finding words in the Scriptures to uphold it; words that simultaneously attack papal authority.

"No man," says the Bishop, "is bounden to perform an unlawful oath," and with these words he frees both the king and all Englishmen from the oaths once sworn to the Roman Church in good faith.

I should be happy, yet I am troubled. Something in the wording of the document bothers me. I frown at the spidery handwriting for a long time before taking the matter to George.

He is sitting alone in the dark, a jug of ale at his side, and he claims to have a headache. I light a candle, take my place beside him and show him the paper. He takes it from me and showing no sign of remembering his indiscretion at Acton Court, frowns at the script. I thrust the memory from my own mind.

It was nothing.

Nothing but a case of too much wine.

"That should do it," he grunts as he picks up his cup again. "What bothers you about it?"

I fumble with the papers, hurrying to the place where I have turned down the corner of the page. "It is this part, where it says, 'No man is bounden to perform an unlawful oath.' It seems to me that this act could prove convenient to our enemies. Is there not a recently sworn oath that many would like to see undone? The Oath of Succession?"

"I see what you mean." He takes the paper back again, his hand trembling slightly as he brings it close for examination.

"Do you think Gardiner works for us or against us, George? And why didn't Cromwell notice this flaw?"

After a long moment George slumps back in his chair, tosses the papers on the table. "You must speak to the king. He must have overlooked the loophole. It must be altered, speak to Cromwell. You can trust him. I'd lay my life on it."

October 1535 – Greenwich

"Henry!" I cannot wait; with the dogs at my heels I burst in whilst he is in council. The men look up from their business, scowling and grumbling in their beards, but Henry's face is surprised and friendly.

"What is it, Sweetheart?"

I take hold of his hand and tug it, and he laughs indulgently as I drag him from his chair. He casts an apologetic eye toward the assembly and opens his mouth to speak, but I forestall him.

"I must have a word with you, now Henry, and in private." He lumbers after me like a benign bear, thinking I am leading into one of our games, but my mind is not on a royal romp. The news I have is immense.

Once we are alone he tries to draw me into an embrace, but I grip both his hands hard and bid him listen. I lick my lips, mentally fumbling to frame the words. As emotion threatens to get the better of me, I swallow a sudden lump in my throat and my voice, when it comes, is hoarse with happy tears.

"I am with child, Henry."

His face lights up like sunshine. "Anne, are you sure?"

I nod, place my hands lightly upon my womb. This time everything will be perfect. This time our boy will live, I am certain. With a great sigh of relief, he slides his arms around me, rests his chin upon my head and cradles me as if I am made of glass.

"You must take especial care this time," he says. "For the whole while you must not fret or worry, or take exertion of any kind. You carry the hopes of England within you and this time … this time we must get it right."

My friends are excited, pleased for me. My ladies ensure that I do not exert myself at all. My every wish is catered to, the king has decreed it, and of course, perversely, I suddenly have the desire to hunt, to take long walks, to turn out all the cupboards in the royal nursery. When they find me kneeling on the floor surrounded by linen, they take me gently by the elbow and insist I rise.

"We will do that for you, Your Grace, you just sit there and oversee our work."

They bring me a footstool and a rug for my knees as if I am as old as Grandmother, and reluctantly I obey them. My son is more important than any whim of mine.

At first, Henry is attentive. He continues to come to my bed although, of course, we do not make love. He holds me, strokes me and we are both content with that, but soon rumours begin to reach me that he is paying court to another woman; of all people, the Seymour girl. It cannot be serious, of course, she is a pale, green-faced thing with not a scrap of spirit about her. Henry will be bored in an hour.

"He has given her a jewel," my sister-in-law Jane whispers one evening as she helps me make ready for bed.

"A trinket, no doubt," I reply tartly, still unable to believe that his affection is serious. Henry is always playing court to some wench or another—it is a game all men play, poetic wooing that has no substance. It is not real.

"A locket, so they say, bearing the king's image." Jane folds my linen, her nose pinched in disapproval, the gleam in her eye betraying her delight in my hurt. Refusing to let her know that jealousy is twisting my bowels, I shrug my shoulders, reach for my looking glass. It shows me a pale and aging face.

I am almost thirty-four. I lay my fingers on the tiny lines that mar the corners of my eyes, the creases that are developing beside my mouth. I am a poor shadow of the girl who stole King Henry's heart all those years ago. Pregnancy saps not just my strength but my beauty too, or what little beauty I ever possessed. It was always my wit that attracted him, but I find I have little energy left to be clever.

Climbing into bed I lie on cold white pillows, pull the covers to my chin and try not to notice the sinking of my heart. I keep it all inside; the fear, the sick, hollow despair that he is falling out of love with me.

Not now, I think, stroking my still flat belly, not now I am finally carrying our prince. Jane collects a bundle of soiled linen and approaches the door. As she opens it, I call her back.

"Where is George?"

"How should I know? He might be with the king."

Ignoring her rude manner I close my eyes, turn my face way. "Can you send for him, ask him to come when the king is done with him? There is a matter I wish to discuss."

She closes the door quietly and I am left alone, the flames flickering on the wall, the palace silent and cold around me. Where is George? I am beginning to fret, Jane's words returning, echoing, mocking. A jewel, I wonder. What sort of jewel? How deeply is he attached to this woman? Surely it is but a fleeting thing.

When George finally peeks around the edge of the door, I am just dropping off to sleep. I wake with a jerk and pull myself upright. "George …"

I fight off the edges of slumber and beckon him forward to sit on my bed. He lounges on one elbow and begins to fiddle with the tassels on a cushion.

"What is the matter, Anne? Can't you sleep?"

It is almost midnight, the candles are burnt low, outside an owl calls for his mate. In the outer chamber my ladies are slumbering; one of them stirs and mutters in her sleep. I lean closer to my brother and fumble for his hand.

"What do you know of the king … and Jane Seymour?"

He grimaces and waggles my hand reassuringly. "It is nothing, Anne. Don't worry. Henry is ever one to wander when you are with child, you know that."

"He gave her a jewel."

"What if he did? He is always giving people jewels."

"Not gems that bear his own likeness."

To give a likeness of oneself is akin to giving them your soul. It is a pledge … a promise. A look of annoyance flashes across George's face.

"Who has told you these things, Anne? Who would want to worry you like this?"

"Jane." My voice is quiet.

George emits a loud breath. "Bitch."

I have never heard such venom in his voice, and to hear it now makes me tremble all the more.

224

"Listen," he shifts closer. I look down at our entwined fingers. "Don't listen to gossip. It is true that Henry has been paying courtly service to the Seymour girl, but that is nothing new. He has done so before. It doesn't mean anything. I will have a word with Madge and get her to dangle her assets before him. She has served us before and will happily do so again."

I remember the agony of sharing him with Madge before, but it will be better than sharing him with Mistress Seymour. Her family are ambitious, her brothers edging ever closer to Henry's favour. They will damage me if they can. They are against the reforms and have little love for me. I had rather Henry played his little games with someone I can trust.

George has given me little comfort. I had hoped he would deny Jane's words, say it was all gossip, but his confirmation of my fears scores deep scratches into my heart. I can only trust that he knows what is best; he is the only one at court I can rely on … apart from Henry, and even he has betrayed me now.

"I don't have the strength to fight any more, George. I am tired, worn out with conflict, and I don't know if I can put a brave face on things any longer. I am in no condition to combat rivals."

I can no longer keep the misery hidden and my chin trembles, a sob rising in my throat. "Sweetheart, don't." George shuffles closer, clambering onto the pillows beside me, and I fall against him, weeping as if my heart will break. He croons deep in his throat, stroking my shoulder, kissing my hair.

And into this scene comes his wife. She enters without knocking, and after taking one look at us, turns on her heel and storms from the room, slamming the door behind her. Neither of us pays her any heed.

In the morning, boosted by George's advice and restored by a good sleep, I rediscover some of my resilience. I am still Henry's wife, his queen, and I am carrying his son. Nothing can change that. As if I am putting on armour, I call for my finest clothes. Nan combs my hair until it snaps and crackles, and then I pinch my cheeks and bite my lips to redden them. With my chin high, I pass through chamber after chamber on my way to the king's apartments.

I find him with Cromwell, the two of them hunched over a table littered with papers, quills and sealing wax. They both stand when I enter. Henry's kiss skims my cheek, Cromwell bows so low his head almost touches my knees.

"Henry," I smile as if nothing is amiss, as if I am not aware of his fluctuating affection. "Master Cromwell."

The secretary offers me a chair and I sit down, my hands in my lap, balancing my head attractively with a gentle smile playing on my lips. "I expect you have come to tell us of your findings, Master Cromwell."

I lean forward and pick up a sheet of parchment; *Valor Ecclesiasticus* is written large upon the top. The church values, all carefully calculated and costed by Cromwell's commissioners over the summer. It makes eye-opening reading.

The value is huge, and as yet only the smaller monasteries have yet been assessed. The plan is to close them, disperse the monks to larger houses, and take the monies raised from the dissolved properties for the Crown. It is an unsubtle plan, and one I do not agree with. It will do reform no good at all if we allow ourselves to look greedy, or grasping. The monies we raise should be channelled back into the Church. We should use it for charity and open up the monastic buildings as seats of learning.

But Cromwell, my erstwhile ally and friend, is set against me. He knows that Henry covets the treasures, and he seeks only to please his king in all things, which although a noble sentiment, is not always wise.

My eye scans down the page. I look up at the two men, one larger than life and glittering with gold and colour, the other contained and monochrome. Two men so very different, both bound to the same cause—a cause that opposes mine. To fight them both, I will need to wield a weapon in either hand. But I am disarmed; usually to win

Henry round I would take him to bed, make him greedier for me than for the ecclesiastical treasures, but I cannot do that now. He has foresworn my body for the sake of his unborn son. As for Cromwell, it will take a cleaver to make him change his mind now it is set.

The words blur on the page, the voices of the men drone around my head as my thoughts fly off in another direction. Jane, Jane, Jane. She will not leave me alone. Just as I had once been obsessed with Madge, now it is Jane Seymour I envision sitting on his knee, blushing beneath his kisses, his extravagant compliments, her coffers growing heavy with his expensive gifts. I must be rid of Jane, for the sake of my sanity, for the sake of Henry's conscience.

Henry's conscience. This, I suddenly realise, is the key to it all. He has ever been a slave to his conscience. I must make him guilty. I must tell him that God will be angry. He is putting his eternal soul in jeopardy. I turn my head sharply and Henry's voice abruptly stops.

"Where you going to say something, Anne?"

I stammer, my face growing hot. "No, no." I look down, fumble with my girdle chain, and Henry takes up his conversation again. I watch him argue a point with his secretary. To emphasise his words he prods the table with a stubby finger. Every so often he glances at me, his expression soft, his mouth quirking at the corner. He loves me still, that much is clear; why then should I share him?

A noise at the door heralds Cranmer's arrival. He bows to the king, bends over my hand, and tosses a nod to Cromwell. "How are you faring, Your Grace?" he asks, concerned for my health. When I reply that I am very well, he looks pleased. Cranmer is a good man, a gentle soul who manoeuvres through the jagged maze of court intrigues with a vaguely troubled air.

He takes a proffered seat. "You must look after yourself, Your Grace. Our little prince is precious. A quiet Christmas is planned this year, I think?" He transfers his glance to the king for confirmation, and Henry leans back in his chair.

"We will save our celebrations for the summer, when our boy arrives." Henry winks at me, sending a shimmer of fear through my body. Suppose I bear him another girl, I think, what will I do then? But I do not let the thought linger. I push it away and concentrate my mind upon masculine matters, afraid lest female fears allow a girl child to take root.

January 1536 – Greenwich

Although we enjoy the traditional pageants and feasting, the festivities are quieter this year. Just as the New Year celebrations are about to begin, news comes that Catherine is very ill and likely to die.

She has been at Kimbolton Castle for some time now, constantly complaining of the cold and damp, and Henry's neglect. Many times have I wished her dead, and my life would have been so very much easier without her, but now that she is about to breathe her last I find that, for the first time, I feel pity.

Guilty.

Guilty that Catherine, who was born to greatness, now dies in ignominy because of me. Had she only gone quietly to a nunnery we would have treated her better, endowed her monies and allowed her to see her daughter. But she was stubborn, foolish, pig-headed. It is not my fault that she dies alone, and in misery.

It is not my fault, I tell myself, but deep down I know that it is.

As a green girl, I could never imagine how it felt to be dispossessed, passed over for a younger, prettier woman, but now that I myself fear losing Henry's affection, I have a little more understanding. Had our roles been reversed, I would have acted no differently; I would have clung on to my husband and my position to the end. Perhaps Catherine and I are more alike than I thought.

228

So when I go to hear Mass, I spare a prayer for her. Not that she may live, but that her passing may be peaceful and her place in Heaven assured.

Henry, on the other hand, is remorseless. Excited by the prospect of peace with Spain, the relief of the imminent war, he swears she cannot die quickly enough. I cross myself, send up a prayer assuring God that he does not mean it. For all her faults, Catherine was once the woman he professed to love and, lawful or otherwise, she was his wife for many years. She bore his daughter and buried his sons … as I have done.

A letter arrives from Mary begging to be allowed to see her mother, just to say goodbye.

"Not unless she signs the act of succession," Henry bellows, making Cromwell cringe away in fear of a cuffing. Yet we all know she will not sign, not even if it means she never sees her mother again.

If I were Mary, I would sign it. I am not as brave as she. Perhaps it is because I lack her Spanish blood, her royal breeding. If it were me, I would swear anything for a last glimpse of my mother, even my own death warrant. For the first time I realise I am, deep down, a coward; to me, life and liberty is everything, and worth much more than pride.

It is a week before we learn that Catherine has passed. On the eighth of January, I am already dressed and ready for the feast. I have a new gown of yellow silk, the colour of renewal and fertility. I have had it made to celebrate my fruitfulness and to remind the king, and all who look upon me, that I carry his heir within. If anything will prevent him straying to another woman's bed, it is the lure of the prince I have promised. But when the news comes of Catherine's passing, I slowly begin to untie the sleeves.

"What are you doing?" George places his hand over mine, keeping my fingers from the knots.

"I must wear something more sombre; this shade would be an insult."

My ladies have paused in their tasks and are watching us. Jane is close by, her hands hovering over the jewel casket, pretending not to look at us. George manoeuvres me out of her hearing.

"Don't change. You must show the world that she was nothing. She was not queen; she was just the Dowager Princess of Wales, nothing more."

"Oh … but."

"Her death is a good thing, Anne. It frees us from Rome, frees us from war with Spain. Henry can now make peace with them. Catherine's passing liberates the country from danger, therefore you must act as if nothing has happened. You must not appear tainted by fault."

I look down at the yards of material in my skirts that are shimmering in the firelight. George's fingers knead my arm, his head is close to mine, his breath warm on my cheek, his eyes glittering with intensity. "Listen to me, Anne, I would never misadvise you."

"Some may see this gown as a mark of celebration; that would never do." I am uncertain, hesitant, and sensing this, he pushes his point home.

"Let them think what they will, but be sure of this. If you show remorse in any way, or mark her passing with mourning, your enemies will whisper that she was the true queen and your position will always be questioned. And so will Elizabeth's."

Henry wears a matching doublet and a yellow hat with a big white plume. We parade Elizabeth, who has been brought to court for the seasonal celebrations, between us, holding her high for the courtiers to see. Elizabeth sits on Henry's left shoulder, her plump hand clutching his right ear. She laughs at the crowd as they pay her the homage that is her due. No mention of Catherine is made; her passing only whispered of in corners. I try to be happy, to think only of the future. For the first time I am Henry's undisputed queen, but I cannot help but be aware of those who think us callous. And before long my enemies are accusing me, whispering of poison, and prophesising that Mary will be my next victim.

Cold blue light streams through the chapel windows where I kneel praying for the health of my son, the security of my marriage. The edge of the stone step digs into my knees, my neck aches, and behind me I can hear my women growing fidgety. I have been here too long. I must not become like Catherine. Piety is a virtue, but I must not let it consume me.

I am half way up, one hand on the altar rail, when I hear a shout in the corridor, a clattering of weaponry, a bang on the floor. As the door bursts open I hurry to my feet, wrenching my knee. I put a hand to my racing heart.

"Your Majesty!"

My uncle of Norfolk, still clad in armour from the tiltyard, scarcely takes time to bow. "It is the king," he cries, panting for breath. "He has taken a fall. We fear he is dead!"

The world dips and sways, and my bowels plunge sickeningly. His voice ebbs and flows, the high-pitched panic of my ladies twittering like a cage of birds. I push away encroaching darkness, force myself to remain standing as I search for words in a parched throat.

"Where is he?" The voice is unlike my own; panicky, strained, terrified.

"They are bringing him now, to his apartments. The physicians have been summoned."

Norfolk has removed his helmet, his damp hair standing in spikes about his head. I have never seen him less than calm. Now his eyes are wild, his face bleached of colour. He is unprepared for this, afraid of what Henry's death will mean. He waves his arm in the direction of the royal apartments and I find myself suddenly running, my skirts held high above my knees, my heart clanging in my chest like a great bell. I run faster than I have since I was a child at Hever.

The doors stand open and the guards outside do not move. They make no attempt to hinder me. "Henry!"

I burst in. A crowd is gathered around the high-canopied bed; a hubbub of voices, knaves running hither and thither bringing bowls and towels, taking away soiled linen; linen that is stained crimson with royal blood.

"Henry!" I push my way through towering male bodies with the stench of tiltyard sweat. They part unwillingly and let me close.

His body lays upon the bed, his armour partly removed, his chest laid bare. For a moment I feel a sharp rush of relief that it is slowly rising and falling. He is breathing. I close my eyes and send up a rapid prayer.

But then I see that his face is bloodless. His lips are blue, a trickle of blood oozing from his temple. Tentatively, I reach out and touch him.

Cold, clammy skin.

Like a corpse.

A hand slides across my shoulder and George is there. He grips my elbows, gives me a shake, urging me to stay calm. I turn into his body, lay my head on his armoured chest, seeking comfort from hard steel. With a great sob, I cry, "What happened?" my voice sounding as if it comes from afar.

"It was all so quick, I don't really know. One moment he was mounted, bearing down on his opponent, and the next the horse seemed to stumble. There was a great cry, a scream, and the king was thrown, his horse coming down upon him. We feared the worst right away …"

"Norfolk said he was dead." My voice breaks. I shake my head, unable to believe I am not in the midst of a nightmare. I do not want to leave the bedside, but George manoeuvers me away. "Let the doctors do their work, Anne."

We sit close by, hands clasped. I feel sick, unable to breathe properly, my lungs tight with unshed tears.

"George, what if he should die?"

His hand tightens on mine. "Don't even think it. God won't let that happen. He is the king."

But other kings have died.

While the doctors do what they can, I imagine a life without Henry. It is a bleak picture, so long has he been the pivot around which I move. George and I do not speak of the danger to us should Henry not survive. We do not speak of it, although the threat looms larger with each passing second. In my mind, the demonic shadow flickers and reforms into the image of Chapuys and his master, who will not hesitate to depose Elizabeth and put Mary on the throne. What hope has an infant against a young woman? No hope at all.

And then there is my uncle of Norfolk, his daughter conveniently married to Fitzroi, the king's bastard who has for so long had the expectation of being made heir. Before this day I had thought Norfolk my friend, but now I see that, if the worst should happen, it will be every man for himself. Elizabeth and I will have few allies. There are not many who would be prepared to stand against Spain, or even the power of my uncle, for the sake of a baby girl.

Henry must not die.

I am not asking God, not even begging him. I am bargaining with him. I will do anything, give up everything, if He will only spare my husband. For the sake of my daughter, for the sake of the English Church, and for the sake of my son, who is not, as yet, even born.

For more than two hours I wait, refusing both food and drink. I refuse to lie down. I even refuse a cushion when Nan brings one for my back. I am determined to sit here, without respite, without comfort, until my Henry opens his eyes.

A servant stokes the fires. The flames leap, illuminating the ring of faces that wait upon the comatose king. No one speaks; the silence is peppered with sighs, fidgeting feet, whispered prayers.

And then he sighs. A jewel glints as a finger moves and I leap to my feet, pushing aside the physicians to grasp the hand that is my lifeline.

"Henry," I croon, gently, willing him to speak to me.

He opens one eye and exhales, foul breath swamping my face. He squeezes my hand feebly and at last, he speaks.

"Jane?"

They are burying Catherine today. I wonder if she is laughing from her Heavenly seat? For while she escapes the cares of this wicked world, I find myself living her life, thinking her thoughts. Her trials are become mine. I wonder if it is divine retribution.

The child within me moved yesterday for the first time; another reason I should be happy. But how can I be? How can I rejoice in bringing forth a child whose very presence is the cause of my losing Henry's love?

He asked for Jane. I was there, holding his hand, yet he asked for Jane. I am full of anger. If I could I would have her whipped, have her burned at the stake, boiled alive as a traitor and a witch. I have never hated before and the feeling makes me ill.

I am unable to eat, unable to sleep, unable to even think straight. For the first time in my life, jealousy is corroding my sanity. Now I know how Jane Rochford feels, and how cruelly George has treated her. I must somehow persuade him to make amends.

It is a wet miserable day, as if the Heavens are mourning the death of the woman who called herself queen. I wonder if by some chance she is conscious that her body is to be interred, not in the Carthusian monastery as she wished, but in Peterborough Abbey, for the Carthusians are gone, put asunder by Cromwell's hand.

Does Catherine know that the marking on her gravestone will read 'Princess Dowager' and not 'Queen of England?' And will she hear Bishop Hisley's sermon claiming she acknowledged in the hour of her death that she was never England's queen? If, by some chance, she does know, the rumbles of her anger will thunder in the skies above us.

I am afraid, although I cannot show it. I keep to my chamber, pacing the floor, my hands on my belly. This child, this child who will ensure that Henry loves me still, may also be my downfall. I am rendered unable to fight simply by his occupation of my womb. I am disarmed.

"She will not sleep with him." I want to tell Jane Rochford to shut up but I cannot help myself. I tilt my head closer to hers, while her gossip lacerates me. "The king is beside himself with lust but she will have none of it; she is devout."

Or perhaps she is just clever, I think, remembering my own refusal to go easy to Henry's bed. Perhaps she has been instructed to tag him along, get out of him what she can.

I remember similar advice from my father and my uncle, even from George. At the beginning I was instructed to entertain the king, and I did so to appease my father. At what point did I stop pretending and begin to love him in earnest? At what point did the tables turn and I become the quarry?

The walls are high, the windows shuttered, and I cannot see the sun. Even the air I breathe is unfamiliar, stale. It chokes my lungs; my chest feels as if an iron band has been placed around it and someone is drawing it tighter ... tighter.

There are scuffles in the darkness. I strain to see, fumble along slimy stone walls in search of a friend, in search of human contact. I seek comfort, although I know I am alone. I seek enlightenment, although the sun has been extinguished. In this place, even God cannot reach me. My fingers scrabble against stone, tearing my nails, and I call out, my voice lost in nothingness.

I wake suddenly, my nightgown sticking to me, a stream of sunshine blinding me. I blink stupidly at Nan who is drawing back the shutters, her friendly smile welcoming me back. She glides toward me, placing a tray beside the bed. "Drink it up while it's hot, Madam. You've been asleep all the afternoon."

I drag myself up on my pillows, reflecting that Henry did not attend me although I waited until long past the appointed hour. Still half asleep I reach out for the cup, not really wanting it but too weary to fight such gentle concern.

It is then that I see the blood on my hand.

For a long while I stare at my fingers, the nails rimmed red, the iron tang of my own blood revolting my senses. My head reels as I slowly become conscious of the deep dragging sensation in my belly.

In trepidation I push back the covers and find my nightgown, my thighs, the sheets, all covered with gore. I open my mouth and begin to scream, and from all directions my ladies come running.

30th January 1536

George comes to me first, full of sympathy, full of assurances that I will soon be with child again. I do not believe him. I feel I am damned. Catherine has cursed me, somehow taken away my ability to give Henry what he wants. Misery sits like a stone in my stomach and I cannot rouse myself, not even for George.

"What did Henry say?" My voice is small, betraying my fear of his answer. George shrugs, his eyes full of sadness.

"He weeps, and prays. He will come to you when he is recovered." He strokes my fingers, his hand large and brown against my small white palm.

"I expect She comforts him. She has certainly not shown her face in here."

"Perhaps they told her to keep away. Your dislike for her is no secret."

"And who would blame me?" I snatch my hand from his and wrap my arms about myself. "She seeks to steal my husband."

George shifts on the mattress. "To be fair, Anne, it is your husband who seeks her, not the other way around."

Only George would be brave enough to say this and despite the jagged edge of his words, I do appreciate his forthright reasoning. I fidget my legs, rumpling the covers.

"What am I to do about it? I lack the will to live, let alone fight for him."

He sighs, running a hand through his hair, ruffling it so he looks like a boy again. "Perhaps you need do nothing but be yourself. Anne, Henry isn't the first man to stray and he won't be the last. Take it from me, she is nothing but a dalliance. Once you are back on your feet and the colour has returned to your cheeks, he will be eating out of your hand again. I warrant you will be pregnant before the year's end."

Pregnant, so he can wander off again? I do not speak the fear aloud; after all, my sole purpose is to provide England with a prince. I cannot neglect my duty, even should I want to. Maybe George is right, but privately, I resolve to be rid of the Seymour girl. I will send her from court at the first opportunity I get and if Henry tries to stop me—well, there are other ways.

It is two days before Henry comes. He is somehow smaller, shrunken, trying to disguise the defeat beneath bluster. I know him too well. He stands at the end of the bed, feet splayed, hands on hips, his chin tilted so that he is forced to view me along the length of his nose.

"How are you, wife?" There is no warmth, just husbandly duty in his request. To win back our old affection will be a test indeed.

I try to smile but it is false, brittle; it makes my cheeks ache. My eyes fill with ready tears. "I am well in body, My Lord, although my spirits … well ..."

"You must eat well, take plenty of rest, and you'll soon be up and about again."

"I am getting up tomorrow."

"Good, that's good." His eyes trail away from me. Like two strangers we have nothing to say. He clears his throat, turns as if to leave.

"Henry!" I am on my knees on the mattress, clinging to the bedpost. "Forgive me, Henry, forgive me. I will give you a prince, I swear it."

He takes a step nearer, reaches out and pats my hand dismissively as if I am a child, or one of his hounds. "Yes," he says in a distant voice. "Next time fortune will smile upon us, and God help us if it does not."

He doesn't linger. He turns to go, his head down, his broad shoulders filling the doorway for a moment, blotting out the light, leaving me with nothing, not even hope.

February 1536 – Greenwich

My legs are as unsteady as my mind when first I rise from my sick bed. I demand to be dressed in my finest clothes, and layer by layer, my status is reconfirmed as I prepare to fight the battle of my life. I am determined to win my husband back and defeat the insidious woman who creeps like a louse into our marriage bed.

George arrives in a gust of fresh air to escort me to the hall. He holds out his arms, lets his hands slap against his thighs. "Anne, you are magnificent. If you weren't my queen and my sister, I would woo you myself."

Ignoring his wife's scowl, I manage to laugh. I link my arm through his and we process to the hall. The court falls to its knees at my entrance, Jane Seymour included, and when I am half way to the throne, Henry rises and comes to meet me. His smile is warm, his eyes soft with concern. For the benefit of the court, I wonder? Or is his gentleness genuine?

He tucks my hand beneath his elbow, keeping it covered with his own, and leads me to my chair next to his. Together we sit and face the court. "You look beautiful," he whispers as he lets go my hand, and a shiver of hope flushes through my body. I feel warmer than I have in days.

His fool, Will Somer, begins to do his work, wandering about the room like a dotard, making jokes of the ladies fashions, blithely insulting the greatest lords of the land, safe in the king's protection. The hall fills with laughter and merriment, our lost prince forgotten. Life goes on.

When the music begins Henry leads me out and we dance before them all, our hands touching, our eyes locked, our feet much lighter than our hearts. When the musicians pause, he bows over my hand and leads me back to my place.

Jane is nowhere to be seen. I hope she has been dismissed and is snivelling somewhere en route to Gloucestershire; but perhaps she is ensconced in some secret boudoir waiting for Henry's return. Uncertainty and fear nibble at my mind, and my eyes dart constantly about the hall. But I keep a smile on my lips and George, the only person who knows that my hold on sanity is tenuous, hovers nearby, every so often leaning close to place a hand upon my shoulder or on my knee.

Henry behaves as if nothing is amiss, as if baby princes are as easily obtained as buns from a baker's shop. Determined that none shall think him vulnerable, his laughter is loud, his wit bouncing about the vaulted hall. Like George on my right, he often leans close to draw me into the revel.

I am in the midst of court. It is warm—too warm—the people are laughing, the music is loud, and I am surrounded by friends. And yet, I feel I am not really here. I have become a priceless relic, encased in glass, seen yet not touched, admired yet not used. A queen of ice, my feelings numbed.

That night, Henry comes to me. He draws back the bed hanging and without speaking, lifts the sheets and slides naked into bed beside me. He is huge and safe, and I am so glad. I roll into him, lay my cheek upon his furred chest and anoint him with my tears, his kisses light, like butterflies on my face.

He loves me gently. There are no games, no French trickery. I lay in his arms like a wounded hind grazed by his arrow, and beneath his kisses I begin to heal, the angry sore of loss is soothed; a scab begins to form.

As he loves me the numbness begins to gradually recede, and feeling creeps back. I stretch my limbs, open myself to him, delight in the ecstasy of his touch flowing like blood through my veins. My breasts, that have ached to nourish my dead son, now ache for him, my quaint leaping and throbbing beneath his fingers. He mounts me, his face serious, and fumbles between my legs. I gasp at his entry.

His movements, slow at first, grow rapid and I cling to him, my mouth open, my eyes closed. As we leave our cares behind and ascend to the stars, my tears begin to fall, releasing my sorrow and filling me with life.

Life that smarts and burns.

***

Jane Seymour has not left court, but she has the sense to stay out of my way. On the morning I encounter her in the garden, she sinks into a curtsey and stays there as I sweep past, her head low, her skirts spoiling in a dirty puddle. I pretend to be unaffected. She is as insignificant as the other small beasts that frequent the court; the rats in the cellars, the beetles in the wainscot, and the fleas on the court dogs. Yet my hands tremble and I need to sit down, but the turf seats are wet, the lawns soggy and dotted with worm casts.

Nan offers me her arm. "Don't let her worry you," she whispers, full of concern. "She is nothing. Carry on as if she does not exist."

But she does exist, and the king persists in his courtly game. My sister-in-law, Jane, delights to bring me news of it. I hear of every move or gesture the king makes toward her, and the knowledge consumes me. Yet it is to me he comes at night, we make love regularly and desperately as he battles to conceive his son.

To keep myself sane when he is away from me and I fear he is with her, I bury myself in work. I raise funds for charity, giving aid to the poor and needy, and I continue to work toward Church reform, although these days my ally, Cromwell, sometimes seems to be more akin to a foe.

He blocks my wishes, coolly countering my argument with his own as if he were my master and not my servant. "He is the king's servant," George says when I complain to him.

"And I am the queen. What better way to serve the king than to please his wife?"

George does not reply, his raised eyebrows say it all. He has removed his doublet and his shirt sleeves are white against the darkness of the chamber. "The problems with Spain persist," he says, joining me at the table. "The conditions they demand in exchange for peace suggest to me that it is not peace they really seek."

"I know. How dare they demand that Henry make amends with Rome, and that Mary be reinstated in the succession? I am confident Henry will never agree to that, so the Emperor is doing me a favour; the treaty with France is as good as signed."

"Yet Cromwell appears to be considering the Spanish treaty. Do you think he is stalling? Perhaps he has plans of his own."

I shrug. No one can be sure what Cromwell is thinking, or what he is plotting. His duplicity will never cease to astound me. His underhand politics were fine when I was sure he was working with me, but recently I am not so sure. There is something in his manner; his eyes slide away to dark corners and do not meet mine, conversations halt when I enter a room and another begins on a new subject of little import. It is as if he is squeezing me out, diminishing my influence with the king.

The greatest bone of contention between us is the use to which we put the Church lands and benefices from the closure of the smaller abbeys. I insist that the buildings would make ideal seats of learning; we could fill them with the best books, open schools of theology to educate future preachers of God's word. But Cromwell has let Henry realise the riches to be gained, the gold he could have to fill his coffers, the property he could sell to the highest bidders. Before the Bill is even penned and passed through Parliament, Sawley Abbey in Yorkshire has been sold to Sir Arthur Darcy. This is not the way forward, it is not the path to betterment; it is gluttony and makes our motives for reform questionable.

My arguments are lost. Male voices being louder than female, and my influence over the king less than it once was, I feel my feet slipping from beneath me, my hold on the reform policy picked from my pocket. Like everything else it undermines my security, increases my unease. Each time I enter a room I cast about for enemies, and more often than not find Jane Seymour's brothers hovering like wasps, with their stings at the ready.

At night when Henry comes to my bed, after he has loved me we lie in the dark and he speaks of his inner fears. In the black of night I can pretend that nothing has changed, that all is as it ever was. He places his hands on my belly, silently asking if there are any signs of pregnancy, but I have to disappoint him, tell him there is no hint that I have yet conceived. He falls back on the pillow and sighs.

"I am the last Tudor, Anne. Why does God not send me a prince? Have I offended him? Is he punishing me? Punishing us?"

I stroke his damp brow. "No, my love. There has not yet been time. We must give it a while, our prince will come."

I smother his face in kisses and urge him to love me again, but in truth, I fear he may be right. Perhaps I am barren. Cursed!

Whenever I can I pray, my knees growing stiff and roughened from kneeling. I am like Catherine, praying and praying to a God who does not heed me. But the difference between Catherine and I is that whilst she resorted to prayer alone, I am not content to do so. I am a queen and can indulge in politics just as effectively as Cromwell.

PART FIVE
TRAITOR

The caged birds at the window sing gaily of the spring, their song filling the chamber with brightness. I am being idle, teasing grass and pieces of stick from Porquoi's coat. He lies across my lap, from time to time licking my hand in gratitude. He is growing fat, and I make a note to feed him fewer treats and make the grooms exercise him more vigorously. The English tongues at court, making their usual chaos of the French language, have long since degenerated his lovely name 'Porquoi' into 'Purkoy,' and I find myself using it too. It suits him somehow. He is everyone's favourite, and I often have to seek him out when he has followed one of the servants from the room, or secreted himself beneath the skirts of one of my ladies.

Nan comes breezily into the room. "Good morrow, Your Grace. The king has just arrived back from the hunt, did you not hear the furore in the courtyard?"

"Thank you, Nan." I lift Purkoy from my lap. "Look after the dogs for me, please. I have something I wish to discuss with the king before he closets himself with his council."

I get up and move toward the door, the dogs following expectantly. "No!" I order them back to the hearth. "Stay." As I hurry along the corridor I can hear them creating a fuss, lifting their voices in a conjoined howl. I smile as I picture them with their noses pointing Heavenward, lamenting the fact of our parting, although I shall be gone no more than an hour.

243

Henry is distracted, his brow furrowed. We both need to get away, escape from court and the constant barrage of problems that beset us, if just for a little while. I try to get his attention, tear his mind from matters of state, but I fail. "Later, Sweetheart," he says, absent-mindedly patting my shoulder. "I will come to you later and we can talk about it then."

I turn away and march crossly back to my apartment. I am so distracted I do not notice Nan's red eyes, or the way the women tread so carefully around me for the rest of the afternoon. Neither do I notice that someone is missing from my household. I take myself early to bed and wait for Henry, promising that if he fails to come, I will go in search of him.

Yet he does come, much, much later, creeping guiltily through the door like a clandestine lover. He sits heavily on the bed, his sigh a gust of winter air.

"What is it, Henry? What troubles you?"

He doesn't answer right away but rakes his fingers through his hair, easing back onto the pillow, resting his injured leg carefully on the mattress. "Does your leg trouble you? Shall I call for someone?"

"No, no. It is not that. Anne … Anne, I have something to tell you. Something you will not like to hear … it is difficult …"

A wave of anger. It is her again. He has been misbehaving. "Maybe it is best I don't hear it, then." The tart words emerge from clenched teeth, and his hand tightens on my knee when he hears and understands my rising fury.

"Nay, it isn't that, Anne. It is your little dog, Purkoy."

"Purkoy?" Only then do I realise he wasn't there to greet me when I returned from Henry's apartment. Urien was there, but not his companion, not Purkoy. "Where is he? What have they done with him?"

I do not know what I mean by the question. I am only certain that some ill has befallen him. I see him in my mind's eye, his little white curly head cocked questioningly, his black eyes gleaming with mischief, the soothing feel of his soft coat. "Where is he?" I repeat with rising panic.

244

Henry takes hold of me, draws me close to him, but I pull away, forcing him to look at me as he tells me the news.

"There were none in your household brave enough to break the news. I am sorry to be the one to tell you but, Purkoy, well, he had an accident …"

"How? When? What happened?"

Henry sighs. "You know how he loved to bark at the cage birds? Well, he jumped up, barking, on to the sill and … and well, the window was open … and he fell … he broke his neck …"

"Fell? Oh, my dear God." Tears are pouring from my eyes, my heart breaking. "And I didn't even notice he was missing, I thought he was out with the grooms or something. Oh Henry, the poor little fellow …" I am in his arms, his chest soft beneath my cheek. He rocks me to and fro like a child, like a baby. My tears fall, absorbed into the priceless material of his doublet.

"Poor Purkoy … poor, poor Purkoy."

2nd April 1536 – Chapel Royal- Greenwich

As my almoner John Skip's voice echoes about the vaulted ceiling, the listening congregation sit in stunned silence. I risk a glimpse of Henry beside me, his hands on his knees, his lips compressed into a slash. The shocked stillness rings in the air, and then feet begin to shuffle, a cacophony of coughs, a murmur of voices. Henry stands up and I follow his example. Without taking my elbow in his usual manner, he stomps along the aisle and through the high-arched doors.

I follow after, afraid now of my bold action. I see George, he tries to smile, but I have no time to linger. I throw him a look of worried exasperation and hurry after the king.

As I follow Henry into his apartments, his attendants scurry out, and straight away he turns and points an accusing finger. "You are behind this."

There is little point in arguing, I have no defence, but I stand my ground, and raise my chin. "Someone has to try to stop him. Cromwell is at fault here, not me."

"But you cannot have him compared to Hamon, the evil wicked minister who deceived his king and oppressed the Jews."

I purse my lips, trying to stop my chin from wobbling and betraying my fear. I take a step forward.

"Henry, this thing is getting out of hand. Yes, some of the monasteries are corrupt and we need to take action, but we cannot condemn all monks on the actions of a few! We should seek to redirect them, not punish them. We must use the monies from the monasteries to educate, to change the way we worship. By stuffing their treasures in your coffers you make yourself look like an anti-Christ. King Ahasuerus at least was deceived by his minister but you, Henry, you are aware of Cromwell's intentions and seem to be in full support."

"Anti-Christ!" he bellows, his face purple with rage. "You forget yourself, Madam, you are not Esther. You are a nobody raised by my hand. I can just as easily strike you down again."

The threat hovers in the air between us. We stare at each other, his blue eyes open wide, his mouth narrowed. When he shouts, his cheeks wobble; he has put on weight since his accident, now that he can no longer hunt from dawn 'til dusk.

"I thought you wanted to be loved by the people. What happened to the noble prince you dreamed of becoming? Have you forgotten all that? All ready? Must greed steal away every inch of your goodness? You are not the king I fell I love with."

I turn away from him, shaking my head, hating the argument but determined not to be cowed by him. He continues to bombard me with accusations

"And what was all that nonsense about Solomon and his many wives and concubines? Was that supposed to make me see the error of my ways? If you must scold me about my

246

dalliances then do so in private, not in public, and certainly not in chapel! I will take to my bed whoever pleases me, and you, Madam, have no say in the matter."

I shake my head. A tear drops upon my cheek but I dash it away. He stands before the window, obliterating the light, his spine rigid, his head erect. I know I will not reach him, he might as well be lost to me, and all I can think to do is run away.

I run to find George.

He is waiting in my chambers and when I enter, he springs from his chair. "Anne. That was a stupid risk to take. What were you thinking?"

Even George is against me in this.

"I had to try to make him see sense. Sometimes Henry needs someone to hold up a mirror and show him his reflection is flawed."

George relieves me of my prayer book, takes away my wrap, playing the part of a lady-in-waiting. "I sent the women away," he says, apologetically. "I thought you'd not mind."

I nod, only half noticing how cosy he has made the room in my absence. I sit down and ease off my shoes, kick them onto the floor before the hearth. Holding my toes to the flames, I wriggle them and rotate my ankles. The smile I manage to muster dies before it is half born, and my mouth trembles. These damned tears. Why don't they stop? I feel I've been crying forever.

"What about Cromwell?" George squats at my knee, his hands about mine, our fingers entwined in my lap. "Your distrust of him is out in the open now."

I lay my head on the back of my chair. "It is a relief. I dislike deception. I would rather see my enemy clearly than have him hide behind a friendly face. And it is good for once to be compared to Esther rather than Salome. It makes a happy change."

"Cromwell is an unpleasant enemy."

"I have Cranmer on my side. He should counteract the underhand dealings of the draper's boy."

247

He laughs quietly, straightens up, letting his fingers trail across my face.

"Have I made a huge mistake, George?"

He looks uncertain. "I hope not but next time, tell me your plans before you take action, especially if they are as wild as this one. You know I will always guide you well."

I grab for his hand again, hold it to my cheek. "I know. You are the only one I can trust now." After a pause, I blink up at him through my tears. "I expect he is with her now. I have driven him into her arms."

The court talks of nothing else. I am now officially in opposition to Cromwell's reforms. I stand for neither Rome, nor for total monastic censure. It is an uneasy position to be in. Conversation ceases at my approach, even my most trusted women cannot help but gossip behind their hands. At least they have stopped speculating about Henry and Jane. And at least they know my support is for reform, not suppression. At least it must be plain, even to my deadliest enemies, that I am for the king and what is good for the future of England.

Henry doesn't stay angry with me for long, but he vents his wrath on poor Skip, and then Dr Latimer, who preaches a similar reprimand a few days later. I soon realise that our row meant very little, it was just another marital spat. They seem to be increasing lately.

But everybody has them.

Within two days he is back in my bed, his sulks forgotten in our quest to make another prince. There is nothing lacking in our marriage bed now, and he makes love to me with as much skill as I could ask for. We have been together long enough to know exactly what is pleasing, and what is not. Henry is easily bought and as soon as I begin to feel secure in his love again, I begin to quietly campaign for John Skip's return to favour.

For championing my cause, the poor man has been hauled before the council on charges of slandering the King's Highness, his councillors, his lords and nobles, and his whole Parliament. I work on Henry subtly so he is scarcely aware of my wiles. If a queen cannot support her friends, she is no queen indeed.

18th April 1536 – Greenwich

As soon as we enter the chamber, George and I fall back against the door, convulsing with laughter. The ladies gathered at the hearth look up, surprised to see us holding our middles, tears streaming down our faces.

George recovers first. He goes deeper into the room, among my attendants, wiping his tears. "Oh, you should have seen his face, Jane." For once he is civil to his wife; he places a hand on her shoulder and I see her flush, and glance longingly up at him.

"Who?" She glances eagerly from her husband to me and back again.

"Chapuys. I don't know when I have seen a fellow so ill at ease. He would not have looked more uncomfortable if he'd been tricked into shaking hands with Satan."

I join them, bounce onto cushions, my heart light. Nan scurries forward with a tray of refreshments and takes my gloves and wrap, puts my prayer book on the table. "What has happened?" she asks. "I've never seen you laugh so much."

"Chapuys was finally forced to acknowledge Anne. For years, ever since she came to court, he has shunned her and managed to avoid a meeting."

I interrupt George, eager to give my side.

"His refusal to acknowledge me has always angered Henry. I suggested to him that there might be a way to force his hand, if Chapuys could be persuaded to attend Mass with George."

"And while Mass was being offered the king, with Anne in tow, suddenly emerged from the royal pew on his way to the altar to accept the blessing."

I interject again.

"We came face to face in front of everybody and after just a little hesitation, he bowed and offered me two candles to burn on the altar."

It is a great triumph, my ladies exclaim, and clap their hands at our victory, but they do not see the funny side, having not been witness to his dismayed face, the sweat that popped out on his forehead. It was as good as a play.

As ambassador of Spain, Chapuys' acknowledgement amounts to acceptance from the Emperor. He is now wedged tightly between the disapproval of his Spanish master and the displeasure of the English king. It pleases me greatly to see him so discomforted. The affair has made me very happy. Not the acceptance of a greasy-haired foreigner, but the fact that Henry puts enough store by me to think that Spain's acknowledgment of his queen is worth his notice.

April 29th 1536 – Greenwich

My courses are late but I dare not tell the king lest I be mistaken. I do not think he can bear another disappointment. The whispers about court are not comforting. The gossips say that Henry is tired of me, convinced I cannot bear a healthy child. They say he means to put me aside and marry Jane, although how he can put aside his legal wife is beyond my comprehension.

George swears it is nothing but gossip, for Henry has said nothing of it to him, and they play tennis together every day. The rumours make it hard for me not to run to him and declare I am with child. To prevent myself I have to sit on my hands, mentally tie myself into my seat. I have to be certain. There is no point in telling him until I am sure.

I will wait just a couple more weeks.

To amuse myself I fill my chambers with music and dancing, surround myself with the gayest of companions. When the weather permits we go outside, lounge around the gardens and inhale the scent of the spring blossom. Elizabeth has been brought to court for the Easter celebration, and slumbers with her nurse in the shade of a tree.

I sit nearby so that I can hear her when she wakes. Cautious of dislodging what I hope has taken root in my womb, I rest as much as I can. Although it is hard, I do not dance. I sit with Urien beside me and watch, taking my pleasure in the joys of others.

Mark Smeaton, making cat's eyes at us all, strums his lute, the younger ladies leaping and skipping to the music. The gentlemen vie for their sweethearts' hands, Norris and Weston still compete for my cousin's smiles. Tom Wyatt and Bryan are there with William Brereton, and George is never far from me. He alone knows the secret I may be carrying and is watchful of me, making sure I do not tire.

The only one missing is Henry, still involved with the council about the matters from Spain. I refuse to imagine he may have crept off to be alone with Jane; I just wish he was here and look for him by the minute. My eye is ever straying to the gate, watching for the glimmer of his jewelled cap, listening for the softness of his tread, the bluff sound of his laughter.

Seeing my discomfort, George holds out his hand. "Dance with me," he says but I shake my head, frown at him.

"I have sworn not to. Exercise might trigger another misfortune."

"It isn't as if it's a galliard. Come, I will be gentle," he says, persistently grasping my wrist and hauling me to my feet. With a laugh I give in, and we join the others forming up on the greensward. My fingers rest on his palm, our opposite hands behind our backs. Ahead of us, Madge giggles so hard that her breasts jiggle, her face flushed and warm. Everyone is smiling, the sun is shining. It is a good day.

Halfway through the dance demands that we change partners, and I clasp hands briefly with Norris. As we promenade toward the fountain I look at him sideways, surreptitiously noting his elegant poise.

"Why do you dally with my cousin, Sir Norris? Why do you not just confound everyone and ask outright for her hand?"

He coughs and blusters, a flush growing on his cheek, but he makes no proper answer.

"I hope you are not looking for a dead man's shoes."

He is not interested in me at all and I meant it as a joke, but he snatches back his hand.

"Never, Your Grace, for then I should wish my head were off."

"Don't be foolish, Norris. I was speaking in jest." But he is discomforted and will not look at me, his jaw stubbornly set. Then the dance steps lead me to Brereton, with whom I have never danced before. As he bows to me, my mind is still with Norris. I bite my lip, realising I should never have joked so with a gentle man like him. By speaking so directly I have turned the game of courtly love on its head, and I have shocked him. He is not George, he does not understand my wit.

Then Tom Wyatt is there, his teeth flashing white, his eye kindling with pleasure. He whispers treason in my ear, about my step being the lightest in the land, my lips as tempting as the sweetest honey, my smile the cruellest dart. His heart is bleeding for me afresh. I laugh at him, knowing he is only half in earnest, and then I move on and Francis Weston takes his place.

Finally I am back with George, and as the music ceases he draws me to him, holds me close, and leaves a kiss upon my ear. I tuck in my chin, giggle at the shimmer of pleasure his lips send across my skin. I shiver, smothered in goose-pimples – an unattractive name for such a pleasurable sensation.

My brother leads me back to my seat in the shade where, a little breathlessly, I call for drinks. While I wait I arrange my skirts, pat my moist forehead with a kerchief and crane my neck to see if Elizabeth has stirred. She sleeps still, her thumb fallen from her mouth, a dribble of drool on her chin. Then I look up, and Henry is there.

He is standing with Cromwell by the gate, watching the revel as if hesitating whether to join us. Henry raises a tentative hand to me while Cromwell turns away, casting a smug smile over his shoulder as the king approaches me. I feel a squirm of discomfort and wonder how long they have been watching. I raise my hand and smile, beckoning him into the garden.

Much later, as the moon races through windy skies, Henry comes to my chamber. A jerk of his heads sends my ladies scurrying, and I look forward to a night of love. I move toward him with my arms open, ready for his kiss, but he sits down heavily on a stool on the opposite side of the hearth.

He sighs deeply.

"What is it, Henry?" I lean forward, reach out a hand, but he pulls away. I realise he is angry. "What have I done now?"

Of late, our squabbles have grown worse and more frequent. He is less easily appeased with promises of bedtime games. He rubs his face with both hands, mumbles something into his palm. The few words I can distinguish fill me with fear.

"What did you say?"

He looks at me, his eyes cold, and when he speaks his voice is clipped. "I said, Madam, that your behaviour was unqueenly, today in the garden. You were behaving immodestly with my servants, my friends."

I open my mouth to protest but he forestalls me.

"I saw you, Anne. I saw you flirt first with one, and then with another. Whatever you said to Norris shocked and astounded him. What were you promising, some of the tricks you learned in France?"

"Henry!"

"And Wyatt, drooling over you like a lap dog. Even your brother couldn't keep his hands off you. Were you not content with me, Madam? Do you seek to bewitch us all, stain us all with your vile ways?"

I cannot believe I am hearing this. I can scarcely breathe.

"Henry, My Lord! I do not know what has brought this on. What poison has been dribbled into your ear? You must listen to what you are saying. I am your wife ..."

"More's the pity," he snarls.

I bite back a sob, leap to my feet.

"How dare you speak to me this way? You, who pursued me, would give me no peace until I relented. I could have wed another, mothered twelve children in the time I have spent with you. I tell you, Henry, there are days when I wish to God you'd never laid eyes on me."

"And I you."

We are nose to nose like angry dogs, both of us trembling with the enormity of the moment, both knowing we are trapped in this marriage, for better or worse.

Fear wallows deep in my gut.

The court whispers that he wants to be rid of me, but I never really believed it before. Let him have his whores, his concubines, but he must never tire of me. I am part of him. I begin to grope for firmer ground, searching my mind for a positive aspect to our union. And then I remember Elizabeth.

Turning on my heel, I run into the nursery. Ignoring the protests of her nurse, I wrench back the covers and lift Elizabeth into my arms. Then I march with her back to Henry, who takes one look at his daughter and quietens his rage a little, for her sake.

She knuckles her eye, moans in protest at the rude awakening. She is warm and fat and smells of wet linen. "Look Henry, look at the child we made. Is she not worth all of this? All the pain? All the fighting? Is she not a worthy reason to cherish our love?"

He turns away. "Put her back to bed."

I hold her closer, put my nose to her hair and inhale the wonderful baby smell of her. "If I can give you a daughter like this, imagine how fine our son will be. I will give you a son, Henry. I swear it."

I do not speak loudly, there is no need. I have his attention, and he is listening intently. After a long silence he takes her from me, carries her to the door and calls for the nurse, who appears as if from nowhere.

She has been listening. Tomorrow, our disagreement will be all over court. Our private words bandied about as if they are the property of all men. Henry is quiet now, miserably pensive, defeated, and I think of how alone he is.

In this royal court of which he is king, he has no kin, no family remaining, apart from me, apart from Elizabeth. I risk reaching out and when he doesn't pull away, I stroke the fur on his doublet, take a step nearer.

He smells comfortingly of spice and rosewater, a hint of garlic. When I take his hand he doesn't jerk it away, so I lace our fingers together and sigh deeply. Noting how his glance darts to my swelling bosom, I sigh again.

"Henry." I kiss his fingers. "There is nothing on this earth I'd rather do than give you a son; a prince to follow after."

Am I imagining the growing pressure of his fingers, the increasing depth of his breathing? I lift my chin, look into his eyes. His nostrils flare, he licks his lips, the tip of his tongue is red and wet. On tiptoe I place my mouth lightly on his, my own tongue flicking, inviting a deeper kiss. And, as he engulfs me, I tell myself that everything is all right. He loves me still.

1st May 1536 – Greenwich

"What a lovely day." Nan raises a hand to shield her eyes from the sun as she peers across the tiltyard to see if she can spot her husband, George Zouche, preparing for the joust. Of course, I can spot my Henry a mile off. His splendid clothes mark him from the others. Since the accident in January his leg continues to trouble him, preventing him from competing today, and the inactivity bothers him. His envy is undisguised as, waving his arms around, he advises his friends on the best tactics. I smile at his boyish ways and let my eyes sweep the rest of the field.

It is the sort of day that stays in one's memory. I know I will remember it forever. A perfect summer morning that is surprising, coming so early in the spring. The sky above is blue, as if an artist has over used the lapis lazuli. The birds are busy building nests, and in the hedgerow early bumble bees bounce in and out of frothing may blossom. Above us the pennants snap and strain in a brisk breeze, and sunlight frolics on the knights' armour, dazzling the onlookers.

In the stand, my women and I wait for the tournament to begin. I see George approaching, in full armour. He nods a cool greeting to his wife, his smile spreading to his eyes as he grows nearer to me. I lean over the railing, my veil undulating in the breeze, hovering around me like a lost spirit.

"You do look fine, Sir Knight," I quip. "You are sure to win the hearts of all the ladies, even if you miss the main prize."

His visor is raised, his face flushed with the heat, his hair beginning to stick to his forehead. "Well, since the king does not compete, I may stand a chance. Can I carry your favour?"

"Sorry, George, I promised it to Norris. Ask Jane for hers, do yourself a favour." I laugh gaily at my dreadful pun and George joins in. He leans on the stand below me, his eyes straying to where Jane sits, staring into the distance as if she is unaware of us.

"Go on, George. It doesn't hurt to be nice to her," I hiss. "Do it for me."

He stands up straight, executes a comical salute. "Your wish is my deed, O Queen."

From the corner of my eye I see him approach his wife. I try not to applaud when, after a few moments, she passes him her kerchief. He tucks it beneath his armour and makes an elegant bow.

I wish Mary were here, for she always loved a tournament. I remember her clapping her hands, calling out her support of a favourite. On days like this I miss her more than ever. Last week I wrote her a letter, the first since our estrangement. It was an informal note, asking after the health of her son, born soon after I lost my prince. By all accounts she is living blissfully, in near penury with her horse-master husband. Perhaps it is time to make amends and call her back to court. I owe it to my nephew. I make a mental note to talk Henry round to forgiving her.

The first riders appear, their plumed helmets glinting, their steeds snorting and restive in the sunshine. I can just make out the badge of my cousin, Francis Bryan, who has not been at all hindered by the loss of his eye all those years ago. His opponent is William Brereton. They rein their mounts back, hold them steady, their hooves turning the turf to mush, until the command is given to ride.

Then, like a fury unleashed, they thunder toward each other. In the stand, we hold our breath, hands to our faces, scarcely able to look but somehow captivated by the promise of violence.

They come together in an explosion of splintering wood, screaming horses and clashing metal. For a moment it seems neither will fall; both horses career on, their riders swaying in their saddles, lances tilting. Then Bryan emits a loud curse and tumbles slowly and elegantly from his horse to land with a crash of steel in the dust. There is a brief silence until we are sure he is unharmed, then a great cheer goes up from the crowd and we all relax, chattering and laughing in a mixture of relief and disappointment. Drinks are passed through the stand, pages weaving in and out, tipping jugs, replenishing cups.

As Bryan limps away, Brereton raises his fist in victory and canters past, his horse's hooves kicking up sods.

Next are Norris and Heneage. Norris approaches the stand and I rise from my seat and offer him my favour as I had earlier promised. He tucks it away, leaving just a flash of crimson silk showing bright against the blue sheen of his armour. He rides away. I sit back down, fanning myself and turn to make a comment to Nan.

257

And then I notice Henry. He has taken his seat in the stand a little way from us, and I raise my hand, my mouth stretching in anticipation of his company. He doesn't look at me. His eye is averted, his spine stiffened and his pudgy fingers tightly gripping his knees. I instantly recognise the anger in his stance. What is wrong now? I wonder as I turn my attention to the next match.

Norris gallops past, my crimson kerchief flapping at his breast. For a moment it looks like a splash of blood, a gaping hole in his chest. I shake the image away, clapping my hands as both contestants canter off unscathed. Tension released, a wave of chatter breaks out again, the incomprehensible words erupting like birds freed unexpectedly from a cage.

Henry stands abruptly and, without taking leave of me, heads for the competitors ring. I can see from the set of his shoulders that he is displeased but I shrug it off, used to his bouts of bad temper that have grown more frequent of late.

I am engaged in a light hearted argument with my ladies as to who has the best chance of being crowned champion at the end of the day. Usually it is Henry, whose skill on the field is unsurpassed; today the prize is open. It must be hard for Henry to be debarred from competing by his own ill-health.

Several moments later I see Henry mounted on his horse. For a moment I think he means to enter the list. But just as I realise he is not in armour, he rides swiftly away without bidding me farewell, a cluster of his most favoured attendants about him. Following after, on his already winded mount, is Norris, whom I recognise from my kerchief which still blazons my favour on his shoulder.

"How odd," I remark to Nan. "Norris went through to the next round and still has another bout to ride. Surely he cannot have forgotten. I do hope nothing has happened."

*

Later that evening, George and Madge are illustrating the steps of a new dance in my apartments. It looks complicated but intriguing and I long to join in, but there is no joy in dancing without music.

"Let me take a turn, George. Where is Smeaton? Someone fetch him, we can have the steps worked out and demonstrate it to the king tomorrow."

But Smeaton is nowhere to be found and we have to make do with less accomplished players. Mark Smeaton has a way of blending in with the furnishings and would never speak of anything he heard or saw in my privy chamber. I have grown used to his invisible presence, taking him for granted, and now that he is absent I miss him for the first time.

As the evening stretches toward dawn, my apartments grow quite rowdy with music and laughter. I am pleased to see George including Jane in his circle. She is lightly flushed, her fingers in his palm, her step light. When she smiles she is quite pretty. It is about time George was reconciled with her. I cannot see what there is not to like and, if the Boleyn line is to continue, his duty is clear. When her head is turned away I smile at him, and he winks at me, blows me a kiss.

Morning is not long away by the time I get to my bed. I slide beneath the covers and wish that Henry was here, but he has been closeted with Cromwell and his council for hours. I have not seen him since his abrupt departure from the joust. I yawn and stretch my limbs. Perhaps it is as well to have the bed to myself for once.

I have still not shown any blood this month and I allow my hands to wander down to my belly. I stroke the taut skin above my womb, sending up a silent prayer that I may be fruitful. Just a few more days and I will be certain. Henry will be so pleased. So proud.

Nan is unwell and Jane absent. No one knows where she has got to. I hope she is with George and he is keeping her busy, getting her with child. The women who help me dress do their best, but they do not know my habits so well. Several times I have to reject the proffered petticoats, the jewels they have selected.

When I am finally ready to hear Mass I walk to the chapel, surprised to find that Henry is not there as he usually is at this time. Something bothers me, something nagging at my mind, unsettling and discomforting me, but I cannot identify what it is.

I watch a game of tennis, still missing Nan and Jane, and at noon I wander back to my apartments. I pause at the door and the chatter within ceases. My smile widens as Nan comes forward to greet me, still a little pale after her megrim. Perhaps she is pregnant too. How lovely it will be to share gravidity with friends, and if George is successful, even Jane may join us soon. She will soften once she is touched by motherhood.

"Your Grace, I must speak with you." Nan tugs at my wrist. It is not like her to overstep boundaries but instead of scolding her, I follow, realising she has some important news.

"What is it?" Our French caps touching, she grips my hand tighter, and I am aware she is trembling. She opens her mouth, her voice breathless.

"Mark Smeaton has been arrested."

Before I realise it isn't a joke I give a half laugh, but stop suddenly, my head feeling light, as the gravity of the news strikes me.

"Smeaton? Why, what can he have done?"

She shakes her head. "We don't know. They say he has been with Cromwell all night, and is now in the Tower."

"It must be some mistake … Where is the king?"

"Gone to Westminster."

Stillness settles upon me, a sharp conviction that something is definitely wrong.

"Without me?"

It isn't possible. The unspoken words scream suddenly in my head.

And then I remember Cromwell's scarcely concealed triumph of the day before, Henry's coldness toward me at the joust, the splash of crimson silk on Norris' chest. And last evening Norris and Weston were also missing from my apartments …

The floor beneath my feet dips and sways. A voice is screaming, "Where is George? Where is my brother? Where is George?"

The ornate ceiling comes crashing down, the floor is torn from under me and I lie prostrate. Nan kneels beside me and my ladies are in disarray, squawking and shrieking in alarm.

"Oh, Your Grace, Your Grace. Come let me help you up."

Then I hear the door burst open, running footsteps, a voice breathless and full of fear.

"Cromwell is coming …"

He treads, soft-footed, toward me. "Get out." He tosses the words over his shoulder and some of my ladies scatter, but Nan and Margery falter, clinging to my side until he dismisses them again. "I said, leave us."

Nan looks for my confirmation, her eyes full of fear. With a jerk of my head, I dismiss her.

"Wait in the ante chamber," I say, an unspoken command that she should listen at the door. She nods anxiously. She understands. And then she leaves me alone with Cromwell.

We face each other, all pretence stripped away. For the first time, I glimpse my enemy. He lets me see his detachment, his determination to get a job done, no matter the cost.

I may be the queen but I am in his way.

I stand in the centre of the room while Cromwell circumnavigates, his hands behind his back, his head lowered, like a bull deciding when to charge, where best to sink in his horns. He pauses at the table to run a finger across the strings of my lute, and discordance floods the silence. He picks up a paperweight and puts it down again, raises his eyes to mine. His smile is slow and cold.

My instinct is to tell him to go, scream at him that I am his queen, and he is supposed to do my bidding. But Cromwell is unpredictable, dangerous, and he has always primarily been the king's servant. It is clear that today he works to the king's benefit.

I do not speak. I force myself to keep silent, bite my tongue to stifle my acrimony. I also refuse to weep. I am queen of England and common-born or not, I am determined to behave like one.

Cromwell calmly pries into my private possessions, both of us silent, the only noises are from the gardens, indistinguishable voices from the river traffic that passes close beneath my windows.

"I am in possession of some information."

When it comes his voice is so unexpected that I jump, let out a gasp. I do not answer but I swallow audibly, grapple to keep control of my nerve.

"Information that concerns you ..."

A chess game, abandoned on his arrival, sits half-played. He picks up a knight, moves it across the board, and throws the queen toward a pile of dispensed pieces. She rolls away, falls from the edge of the table.

"... and members of the king's household. Some of them the king's very good friends."

"Indeed." With my fingertip I trace the outline of a flower on a cushion, pretending disinterest, pretending I am not screaming inside with curiosity. He cannot know that fear is already nibbling at the edges of my sanity, corroding my composure. My heart throbs against the constraints of my corset, but I must remain calm ... at all costs. I must remain calm.

"The council are on their way now. There are questions we must ask you. It is important that you answer truthfully."

He levels his dark eye upon me. Even the suggestion that I might lie is an insult. I am nothing to him, just a hindrance to his plans, a blight upon the pretty world he is building for himself. How could I ever have believed this man was my friend? He is no one's friend. He is not working for reform, nor for the king. He is working for one person alone, and that person is Cromwell.

I deign to speak at last, curiosity impossible to ignore. "Of what, exactly, is my musician, Smeaton, accused?"

He props himself on the edge of my table, his ankles crossed, his fingers forming a cathedral, the manicured tips pressed together. It is the most menacing stance I have ever seen and he knows it, relishes the power he has over me. His soft voice is silken with spite.

"Your musician confessed last night to having known you carnally, on at least three occasions."

This is the last thing I expected. The foul words hang in the air like a bad smell.

"What?" I lean forward, thrusting my head toward him. "Are you quite, quite mad?"

***

They rise to their feet when I enter the room, their long faces inscrutable. I glide across the floor and remain standing in the centre of the room while they take their seats again; Sir William Fitzwilliam; Sir William Paulet; and my uncle, the Duke of Norfolk. These men are expected to do Cromwell's bidding, expected to find the allegations worth pursuing.

My uncle peruses the papers before him, tut-tutting at the outlandish accusations, and refuses to meet my eye. In unison they wag their grey beards, and I know then that I am already condemned. They have no need of a trial. What comes next will be a formality.

Norfolk's chair scrapes across the floor as he stands. He clears his throat, his words smearing like muck across my mind's eye as he accuses me of evil behaviour, charging me with having committed adultery with not just Mark, but Norris too, and another whom they have not yet named.

"This is untrue." My French accent is gratingly loud, bordering on shouting, my panic plain to all. "I am, and have always been, a true wife to the king, and I am untouched, totally untouched, by any other man."

They shuffle papers. Norfolk clears his throat, ignores my outcry and begins to speak, his eye fastened on the opposite wall, above my head, as if I am beneath notice. A surge of anger rises in my breast.

"Will you not even look at me, Uncle, while you make these false accusations?"

Paulet, his face flushing red, leans forward across the table. "You will be able to have your say at the trial, Your Grace ..."

My old enemy, Fitzwilliam, interrupts, leers his hatred. "And we have Norris' confession, given in good faith ..."

Norris' confession? He has lied? Perjured himself? For what reason? I remember tales of instruments kept at the Tower, instruments guaranteed to make any man, even the most stalwart, confess to any crime.

"Under duress, I have no doubt."

"Not at all."

He picks up his pen, makes his mark upon a paper, dismissing me as if I am of no consequence.

Paulet intervenes again, clears his throat and informs me that the papers are drawn up and that there is enough evidence for charges to be made against me. Less than five minutes later, flanked by the council guards, I am marched back to my apartments.

The doors are thrust open and my ladies rush to meet me. I am in a daze as they take my arms, usher me toward a chair, their questions falling like rain, like tears.

I do not have the wherewithal to answer. They sit me down, thrust a cup into my hand, but I do not drink. I do not speak. I do not move. I let them do with me as they wish.

Henry will come soon, I tell myself. He will poke his head around the door and declare it has all been a horrible joke. He will take my hands, cover them with kisses, draw me tight into his soft, fragrant chest and I will be safe again.

But he does not come.

I sit unspeaking in the darkening room while fear gnaws at my sanity. I want to run but there is no escape, for a guard has been placed upon my door preventing me from stirring. When they come to take me to bed, I refuse to go. Despite my women's protests I sit there all night long, watching and waiting until morning peeps, clean-washed and pink, over the horizon.

***

It is two in the afternoon and I have begun to think that perhaps nothing will come of it. The king will order them all to leave me alone, remind them that I am their queen and the beloved wife of their king. But just as I am picking up the stump work I have been concentrating on, Norfolk is announced.

He stands just inside the door, a parchment scroll rolled in his fist. He has the grace to avoid my eye.

"Why are you come?" I ask, although I already know what his answer will be. He clears his throat, as he always does before speaking.

"I am here at the king's command, to conduct you to the Tower, where you are to bide during his Highness' pleasure."

His Highness' pleasure? I know well how to pleasure Henry. A fleeting memory surfaces of him succumbing to my bedtime games, his faces flushed at the delicious indecencies I subjected him to. He can't be tired of me, surely.

My mind returns unwillingly to the present, swiftly summing up my options. The Royal apartments at the Tower are sumptuous and warm, only recently renovated and updated for my coronation. There is nothing to fear in a short stay while the matter is cleared up. Even now, George will be pleading my case with Henry. I raise my head, regard my uncle coldly, and reply as if I have a choice. "If it is indeed the king's pleasure then I am ready to obey."

Behind me, one of my ladies succumbs to a fit of weeping, but I silence her with a snap of my fingers, a verbose frown. I call for my cloak.

I am not given time to say goodbye, or to order my possessions packed. Poor Urien is left behind, my needlework is abandoned on the table, my lute placed lovingly against a chair ... until I return. With my chin as high as I can raise it I follow Norfolk from the room, watching his lumpy feet creep along the torchlit corridors until we emerge into a rain-washed morning where a long, low barge is waiting at the wharf.

The river craft bobs and dips in the water. As the men pick up their oars, I crane my neck to look up at the walls of Greenwich and wonder which window conceals the king.

But then I recall that Henry has left already, fled to Westminster, leaving me to the mercy of my enemies. He has discarded me like a soiled kerchief, or a broken lute string, but such flaws can be repaired, washed clean, and taken up again. Soon Henry will realise that and summon me back. My stay at the Tower will not be prolonged.

As the boat glides toward mid-stream I spy a pale face watching from behind the thick green window glass. Not knowing if it is friend or foe, I lift my hand, see a flicker of movement and am comforted, although I cannot tell who it is that dares to bid me farewell.

Erect on the barge cushions, I remember a happier May day when, dressed in splendour, I was taken to my coronation and all the world was wild with celebration.

I remember the warmth of the sunshine, the cheering of the crowd, the pushing onlookers, the exuberant excitement of my sister, Mary.

I remember a child on one of the barges, dressed as an angel. She waved at me and I recall making her day by raising my hand to return her greeting and sending her one of my best smiles. I wonder where that little girl is now, and if she will weep for me when she learns how low I am fallen.

As the river glides along beneath me I have time to think back, try to see what I have done wrong, how I may have offended the king. Every so often a shaft of panic rises, takes up residence in my breast, and it is all I can do to stifle it, thrust it back down again and maintain, at least outwardly, some semblance of serenity. I do not want them to see my fear. I must not give way to panic. Oh, where is George? Why does he not come?

As the outline of the Tower grows clearer, I draw my cloak about me, trying not to shiver in the shadow of the soaring walls. A blast of canon fire sends a dark host of screaming ravens into the sky. I cringe, fingers in ears, my heart hammering, tears springing disobediently to my eyes. The canon signals to London that a person of note has been taken prisoner. Soon everyone will know that the prisoner is their queen. Surely the king will stop this foolishness.

Help me, Henry, I whisper. Help me, George. God send me a reprieve from this nightmare.

The oarsman put up their oars, the barge collides with the wharf wall, and I take my fingers from my ears and look fearfully about me. Upon the slick green steps that will take me to my fate, Mr Kingston is waiting, his hands folded quietly in his sleeves. He is calm, a look of gentle concern creased across his brow. At his kindness the queen in me takes flight, leaving just a terrified girl. I scramble to my feet, grab desperately at his proffered hand and stumble from the boat. "Mr Kingston."

"Your Grace." There is something about his calm manner that vanquishes the last of my dwindling courage. A sob breaks from my throat and his grip tightens encouragingly on my forearm.

"Mr Kingston." I try to smile but my mouth refuses to conform and all I manage is a grimace. "Are you going to put me in a cell?"

He pats my hand. "No, no, Your Grace, you will be lodged in the royal apartments, where you stayed before your coronation. All has been made ready for you, and my wife is waiting to attend you there."

His wife. Mary Scrope is a long-time lover of the old queen and an open enemy to me. Cromwell has chosen well. I wonder what other adversaries await me here. I shake my head, smile my wobbly smile as I take his arm. He leads me on quaking limbs across the inner ward and past the Lanthorn Tower to my apartments.

As my eyes become accustomed to the dim interior I see the chambers are just as I remember, although in my new unstable status they seem somewhat tarnished and chilly, the hangings a little faded, like Henry's love for me. But the familiarity of the apartment reassures me a little. I force myself erect. I am still the queen, still as yet unvanquished.

Cromwell hasn't beaten me yet.

As the door is opened six women turn to greet me, bobbing to their knees, their faces detached and formal. Lady Kingston; Mary Cosyn; and my aunts, Elizabeth, Lady Boleyn, and Lady Shelton, mother of my cousin Madge. But I do not rush into their arms, for they are not my friends and I have no doubt they've been sent here to spy and report any misdoing to Cromwell.

Aunt Elizabeth has made no secret of her allegiance to the bastard Mary, and Lady Shelton resents how, to help save my marriage, George and I manipulated her maiden daughter, Madge, into Henry's bed.

The other two women, the chamberers, are a far more welcome sight. Mary Orchard is my old nurse, and Mrs Stoner an honest woman who loves me well. They come forward to greet me and I am soon divested of my cloak and gloves and offered refreshment.

Barely acknowledging the other women, I toss my prayer book on to the bed and move toward the window to

268

peer through thick green glass. Beyond the Tower walls the river is alive with bobbing craft, as traders and passengers alike cross and re-cross the wide grey stretch of water, all going about their daily lives as if nothing has happened.

I suppose nothing has happened, not to them.

And below my window, on the castle green, the inhabitants act as if there is nothing remarkable in the arrest and imprisonment of an anointed queen. For the first time I realise I mean very little to the ordinary people. If I am locked away here forever, there are very few who will care, and soon I will be forgotten, as if I have never been. All I will leave behind is Elizabeth, and a few unthinking letters, scribbled in haste.

***

Although I have no appetite, I accept when Sir William Kingston invites me to supper. I brush my hair, change my cap and sit at table with him while he serves my wine, carves my meat and selects all the daintiest cuts for my plate. My women wait at a discreet distance, and apart from the two guards who stand like silent sentinels at the door, I can almost believe I am not his guiltless prisoner, awaiting trial for treason against the man I love.

We eat in silence for a while; the food is good but not excellent, and the same might be said of the company. Poor Mr Kingston, I am dull of spirit and cannot pretend to be otherwise, even though I know that each word and gesture will be reported back to Cromwell. I would prefer the spies to bear tales of my confidence, innocence and strength, but it is beyond my capability to live up to such a pretence.

But, at last, I break the silence.

"Mr Kingston, would you speak to the king on my behalf and ask if I might receive the sacrament that I may pray for mercy?"

He dabs his lips with a napkin, chewing his food rapidly to clear his mouth that he might answer respectfully. He nods, swallows, licks his lips, dabs his mouth again. "Of course, of course, Your Grace. I shall make the necessary arrangements right away."

"Thank you. There is no reason why I may not take the Sacrament. I am as clear of the company of men as I am of sin. There is no truth in these charges, you know."

A long silence follows, a silence I want to fill with questions, but I fear the answers too much. "Mr Kingston," I say at last. "Tell me about Mark Smeaton. Have they hurt him?"

He rinses his mouth with wine, presses his napkin to his lips. "I know not, Your Grace."

"Is – is he here? At the Tower?"

He nods, wets his lips, nods again. "And Norris also."

My throat closes up with grief, my voice reduced to a croak.

"Thank you, Mr Kingston."

I try not to react to the news that poor innocent Mark and brave Norris are locked up like felons because of Cromwell's need to be rid of me. Mr Kingston pours more wine, the rich ruby fluid flowing thick into our glasses. I reach out and lift it to my lips, inhaling the deep fruity aroma before letting it loose upon my tongue. I swallow and replace the glass carefully on the table beside my plate.

"Mr Kingston … I love the king very much. Have you seen him? Is he well?"

He shakes his head. "I haven't seen him, Your Grace, not since May Day."

"May Day."

May Day was the last time I saw Henry too, the last time I saw George. I grip my napkin, crunching it into a ball. "And what of my father, and my brother George, have you seen them? Do they plead my case with the king?"

"I know not, Your Grace." His face seems to dissolve a little and I realise that I am weeping, the room swimming in tears. I throw my napkin onto my plate, watch as it absorbs the gravy, the greasy stain spreading as quickly as a plague. My hands are shaking, my chin wobbling.

"Mr Kingston." My voice is high, unguarded, and I know I am on the brink of hysteria. "I have a very great need to speak to my brother. He will help me, once he knows ... Mr Kingston, they say I am accused with three men, but they name but two ..."

I am weeping now, knowing myself to be ridiculous, knowing myself lost. I begin to laugh, place my hand over my mouth, tears spilling over my fingers, my nose starting to run. "They name but two, and those two are lodged here in the Tower with me ... so where is the third? Who is the third?"

I stand up, my chair falling backward, legs in the air. I notice one of the guards flinch, his brow creasing, his eyes no longer fastened on the opposite wall. They are not so blind as it would seem. Sensing his pity, I rush toward him.

"Do you know my brother? Can you send a message to him for me?"

The young guard does not move, even when I hold out my hands, clasp them beseechingly as Mr Kingston takes me by the shoulders and leads me away. I turn toward him as if he were a father, and cling to his robe, plucking the fur at the neck, trying and failing to remain calm.

"You are a good man, Sir, a very good man, and I know you to be my friend. You will tell George, won't you, please? Oh Lord, how my poor mother will weep ... I think she may well die of sorrow ..."

"Hush," Mr Kingston whispers and jerks his head in silent command to my women, who come to take my hand, lead me back to my chambers.

When darkness falls I do not lie easy in my bed. I toss and turn, throw back the covers only to feel cold again and wrench them back to my shoulders. Mrs Cosyn, who has been appointed to share my chamber, sleeps on in her truckle bed, oblivious to my suffering, her snores rattling the casement glass.

I pray for myself, for Elizabeth, for George and for Henry; and I pray for those accused alongside me too. I get

271

up, peer through the dark window to the lightening dawn, and then I lie down again, to toss and turn some more.

Mrs Cosyn is sorting my linen. I watch her sinewy hands smoothing the creases, tucking in the pleats and tidying the lace. Her movements are mesmeric and I find I cannot tear my eyes away from her fingers. "They're questioning young Weston," she says suddenly, and I blink at her, astonished that she should know, that she should break the rules and offer me news of the events outside my prison.

"Not Weston! I fear him more than the others, lest he betray poor Norris."

"Norris? Why? What has that poor innocent ever done?"

"Only loved me, Mrs Cosyn, or so Weston told me once. Norris would never make so bold himself."

Her eyes slide from my face back to her task, and too late I realise I should have remained silent. "As his queen, I mean. His love for me is honourable, as befits the wife of his monarch."

I scramble to undo the detriment of my words, but I don't know if she believes me. I had thought Mrs Cosyn to be gentle. I had believed she was a friend, but now I am not so sure. She might carry my comment to Cromwell and increase poor Norris' trouble. I must remember that I can trust nobody. There is no such thing as a friend, not in these hideous days.

9th May 1536 – The Tower

If I could only see Henry, talk to him, make him forget the poison dripped into his ear by my enemies. Help him to remember only that he loves me. Jealousy twists and tears at my heart as I wonder if he is finding comfort with the Seymour girl. Even now, in the midst of my suffering, he might be with her, stroking her hair, kissing her 'duckies' as he used to kiss mine. A sob escapes me. I sit up and knuckle

272

away more tears, before fumbling for my cup on the night stand. The room is lit only by a dying brazier, and I plead into the dark night, *Henry, Henry, don't forget me. Don't forget your Anne.*

***

"What will happen to me, Mr Kingston?"

He looks so troubled and his face is so lined with care he seems to have aged a dozen years during the week I have been here. He shrugs his shoulders, turns up his palms.

"How can I know, Your Grace? An anointed queen has never been in my charge before. There is nothing to judge your case by."

An anointed queen has never been arrested before, let alone accused of adultery and imprisoned in the Tower. His words are like a death knell, my innocence as inconsequential as that of a gnat beneath a monarch's boot.

"I have to get a message to the king. He cannot know that these accusations are the constructions of our enemies, those whom he believes to be our friends. You must help me, Mr Kingston, to smuggle out a letter."

He backs away, his hands raised in submission, and begins to slide out of the door. "I am not allowed to send messages, least of all to the king, Your Grace."

And all the time the spies are working against me, listening to my ravings, reading and stealing the many letters and notes I try to smuggle out. Mr Kingston is the nearest thing I have to an ally, and even he is not prepared to risk the wrath of the king for the sake of a cast-off concubine. I am alone. Shut off from the world, kept away from George, from my father, and from Henry. I have not a friend in the world.

It is a gilded cage. I have warmth and food, and a soft bed to sleep in, but it is a prison nonetheless. The days seem to drag by and I am beside myself with worry not knowing what is happening in the wider world. The men accused with me could die for crimes they did not commit, and I have learned that Richard Page and Francis Bryan have been arrested, and Tom Wyatt, my oldest friend, has been locked away too. Poor Tom, punished for nothing more than wishing for the moon.

My friends and family will be in torment over my well-being, yet I am not allowed so much as to send a letter to comfort them. Worst of all there is no news of Elizabeth, no news of George or my parents, and nothing from Mary.

The one hope I have is that Henry will come to his senses and put an end to it soon. He will miss me, long for me and demand my release, the reprieve of his friends, and all will be as it was before.

Henry is my one hope but now, after so long in limbo, that hope is dwindling too. All I have are endless hours of waiting and fretting, and in those long dark hours doubt breeds new fears ... and horrors.

They cannot kill me, can they? I am a queen, and innocent of the charges. Yet too vividly do I remember all the others Henry has loved. Thomas More and Bishop Fisher ... Wolsey ... and if Henry could stand by and watch those great men destroyed ...

The trembling begins again. I fall to my knees, clutch at my rosary, and beg God for his mercy.

15th May 1536 –The Tower of London

The King's Hall is crowded, hot. A babble of voices falls silent when I enter and am ushered toward a raised chair in the centre of the room. A great stand has been erected for spectators, those who are eager to see me fall. At first I do not see their faces, but slowly they loom from the confusion. Men I know, men who once professed to be my friends, are now gathered here to witness my collapse.

Ranged along another wall are those come forth to judge me. As I guessed, Henry is not present, but my uncle of Norfolk is here in his place, beneath the canopy of estate, acting as Lord High Steward, a fancy name for an executioner.

He will not look at me but keeps his eyes on the parchment before him, dips his quill before busily scratching away, scoring thick black marks on the page. I wonder what he writes, if he has to battle hard with his conscience to so completely become my enemy.

Close by is Charles Brandon. I could almost laugh. Cromwell could not have chosen more wisely from my enemies as to select that man, who has hated me since the moment of our first meeting. I will have no honesty from that quarter.

Seated beside Brandon are Montague and Henry Courteney, both supporters of Mary the bastard, and enemies both to me and my daughter. A sudden shudder of fear for Elizabeth consumes me. What will they do with her once I am imprisoned? How can I bear never to see her again?

I swallow my fear and examine the men who are sent to try me. This will not be an honest trial, the jury is made up of my enemies and those who love the king and seek only to please him. There will be no justice here today.

And then, huddled at one end of the bench, I see Percy … Henry Percy, my first real suitor. He has aged and is hunched inside clothes that seem too big for him, and his nose is red as if he has a heavy cold. My eyes rest on him for a long time but he cannot look at me and is clearly distressed. Poor Percy is being tested, forced to prove once more that there was never a pre-contract between us, that his feelings for me are long forgotten. If he is wise he will comply with their demands and condemn me, for a life of regret is preferable to imprisonment, or death.

I silently forgive him, and pray that he might have the strength to survive the trials of the day. My throat closes in grief and I am forced to concentrate on staying calm. The armour of arrogance that served me so well when I was queen does me good service once again. Outwardly I am composed. I am glad of my black and white velvet finery, my brazen hat feather. I lift my chin, look down my nose, and inwardly gird myself for battle. Although I am almost certain I cannot win.

As the crimes against me are read out, a ripple of horror echoes around the court. So shocking are the accusations that I struggle to keep calm. I clench my hands together and remain firm although every eye in the house is upon me, judging me before I am heard, condemning me a whore.

My cheeks burn as I am accused of fornication with many of my friends, namely Henry Norris, Francis Weston, William Brereton, Mark Smeaton and, most horrible of all … George.

My stomach lurches and turns, I clench my fists as blood thunders in my ears, tears sting my eyes. It is the greatest crime of all, condemning me not merely as a whore but almost as an anti-Christ. Shame, shame that I should not feel, burns me; my mouth is arid, my tongue swollen, my throat closed with unshed grief.

But I do not weep.

I will not let them see me crumble.

I sit still and listen to their foul words and wonder at the mind that conjured such lies against me, against my friends.

Cromwell.

I look at him; polite, quiet, a dark shadow of a man who now holds us all in the palm of his hand; the hand that wields the axe. The old adage that it is the quiet ones that need the most watching is true. He has been an enemy all along, using stealth and devilish means to undermine me.

In happier times when George showed me the rudiments of chess, he warned me that I must remain composed. When the queen is threatened, only cool calculation can free her, and the courage to withstand the battle. So now, as Cromwell the pawn dares to endanger his queen, I gather all my wits and prepare for the fray.

I pray that George, when his time comes, realises this too, but I fear his anger will be uncontainable and he will give vent to his rage, and in red hot indignation will heap scorn upon our accusers. We must both tread carefully. Right may be on our side but that does not mean we will emerge unscathed, not when the man driving the opposition is a man like Cromwell.

The voice drones on, informing the jury that I co-habited with many men, plotted to poison Catherine and Mary, pledged to marry Norris after the king's death. I can scarcely believe my ears.

"On 6th October at the palace of Westminster... and on various other days before and after, by sweet words, kissings, touchings, and other illicit means ... she did procure and incite ... Henry Norris ... a gentleman of the Privy Chamber of our Lord the King, to violate and carnally know her, by reason whereof the same Henry Norris on 12th October ... violated, stained and carnally knew her ..."

I try to shut out the words, think of other things but his voice intrudes. *"... tempted her brother with her tongue in the said George's mouth and the said George's tongue in hers".*

How can anyone think up such atrocities? How can anyone believe them? But they do, I can see it in their open mouths, their averted eyes, their sorrowfully wagging beards. I am a whore of the lowest denomination and therefore I must be punished.

It takes some time before I become aware that I am being addressed directly, and the time has come for me to answer the charges. I draw in a deep breath, cock my head to one side, making the feather in my hat jiggle, and try to smile. To my surprise my voice sounds normal, there is not a quaver, or a misspoken word.

"I am not guilty, My Lord, of any of the charges you lay before me."

He continues as if I have not spoken, and the woman in the tale he spins is not myself but some horrible parody of me; an insatiable jade who is shameless in her pursuit of sexual gratification; a woman who laughs at Henry, who does not love him as I do; a woman who secretly mocks his manhood and compares him unfavourably to her lovers.

They infer that George is Elizabeth's father, an idea so abhorrent that I cannot answer it. Sir Richard Pollard waves a letter. "You cannot deny that you wrote to your brother informing him of your pregnancy," he yells.

Of course I wrote to George, why wouldn't I? He was as eager for me to give the king an heir as I! That doesn't make him the father; it makes him the king's good servant ... as we all have been.

"Do you deny that you, together with your accomplices, laughed at the king, mocked his manner of dress, his poetry?"

What can I say? He is right, George and I did laugh at the king, but not in a cruel way. Henry's attire is sometimes outlandish, and his poetry shallow and lacking, but that does not mean we do not love him. Surely affectionate teasing of one's husband is not punishable by death, not even in Henry's court.

"I love the king," I hear myself saying, "and have never been false to him."

"The confessions here from Norris, Weston, Brereton and Smeaton state otherwise."

They have accused me? How is this possible? Their faces swim before me, loyal, brave men, devoted to their wives, to their king, and to me, their queen.

"Then they lie, Sir."

"Do you deny you gave Weston money?"

I raise my chin a fraction higher and regard him along the length of my nose—a considerable length George would have said, that any shrew would be proud of.

"I have given many young men money, Sir, should they be in need of it. I am queen, after all, and have plenty. It is part of a queen's duty to be a benefactress to the needy."

It seems hours have passed before a brief interval is called. They shuffle papers and a page brings me a cup of wine. I smile my thanks, and beneath the eyes of the assembled, I take a sip, encouraged by the glimpse of sympathy in the young boy's eyes.

When they proceed to read out the witness statements I almost weaken, I almost weep. Lady Wingfield, as I suspected, Lady Worcester, and Lady Kingston too have spoken out against me. Even my sister-in-law, Jane, George's own wife, has confirmed that George and I are often alone, often intimate. I wonder if she knew what she was saying, if she realised they would twist her words into something so foul.

I decide to believe her innocent, foolishly tricked into saying more than was wise. I wonder where she is now. I have not seen her since my arrest. I hope she thrives without us, once my brother and I are disgraced. Once we are gone.

As I listen to the legion crimes I am accused of, I begin to lose hope of imprisonment or annulment. I begin to fear that I will have to die.

I am yet very young.

They put their heads together, voices murmuring, hands gesticulating, the occasional paper floating to the floor. A pigeon, trapped in the roof space, flaps his wings, sends down a scattering of feathers. Then they turn, my uncle asks for their verdict, and one by one, they give it.

The Earl of Surrey stands up, his face flushed dark red, his eyes bloodshot. "Guilty," he says, and as he quickly takes his seat again, my heart sets up a loud, steady thump.

"Guilty." Brandon resumes his place.

"Guilty." The voices go on, each one condemning me, ending my hopes, exterminating my dreams. And then it is Percy's turn. He shuffles forward, sweating visibly now, his hair plastered to his head. I remember running my fingers through his curls, trying to tempt him to kiss me. Poor Percy. He was as out of his depth then as he is today. Perhaps I am as they say, perhaps I am …

"Guilty …" he groans, almost falling. The page runs forward to help him back to his seat. I had not expected that, although perhaps it is plain he has not the heart to stand up to Cromwell and his ilk.

Norfolk is speaking again, his words a morass of buzzing, "… in committing treason … the law of the realm is this … deserved death … burnt here within the Tower … head smitten off … king's pleasure …"

The words rush upon me, fade away again as I struggle to remain upright. I am clinging on to sanity. It is all I can do not to fall to my knees and scream a curse upon the evil day that brought me to this. Instead, I hear myself speaking, murmuring my regret that innocent men are to die because of me. It is almost as if they are condemning someone else, and this whole trial is something I am not part of.

I remain dry eyed when they bring forth my crown upon a cushion. They rest it on my lap and bid me place my hands upon it, only to take it from me again, publically divesting me of my role.

I am no longer the queen.

I am merely a traitor.

Felon.

16th May 1536 – The Tower of London

Once I was so happy in these rooms, so sure that my future with Henry held only sunshine. Yet today, although a fire roars in the hearth, I am cold, my bones are aching, my head pounding, and food turns to ashes in my mouth.

Will they burn me, I wonder, or will I follow my brother to the scaffold? There was once a prophecy that a queen of England would burn—I used to joke that it would probably be me. But it was just a jest, I never thought it would come to pass, not really.

The women creep around me, casting curious glances, watching and waiting for me to break, to fall into madness so that they can carry tales into the wider world. But I am done with screaming. There is nothing left to do but wait and pray, pray for a swift end. There is no use in wishing for a reprieve.

I see that now.

It is a dead sort of day, the type of day where the sky is white, and there is not even the hint of a breeze. Clouds muffle the horizon and I want to push them away, thrust back the oppression and the fear, and revel for one more day beneath blue skies, feel the wind on my cheeks, the scent of Hever in the air. Instead I am here, in my palatial prison, with no future, no next week to look forward to, perhaps not even a tomorrow.

Just after noon, the door opens and Archbishop Cranmer is announced. He stands just inside the door, his furrowed face dead white. His long fingers are restive, fiddling with the tassel of his book binding. He is the king's servant but a good man nonetheless, and I move forward, breaking convention, to greet him.

"Thomas," I say, grasping his hands that are clammy and cold in mine. It is the first time I have used his given name, usually it is "Cranmer" or "Sir", but today I have need of a friend.

I call for wine and usher him toward a table beneath the window, where the light will fall upon his papers and ease his eyes. "Have you come to hear my confession? I fear it will disappoint Cromwell."

I pour him a cup of wine and hand it to him. He takes it but doesn't drink, instead he places it on the table and runs his tongue across dry, cracked lips.

"Your Grace." He indicates that I should sit, and I do so. He seems more distraught by my approaching death than I, and I have the curious desire to put him at ease, make his task less hideous, although it strikes me that it should really be the other way round.

"Tom, do not worry for me. I know I have to die, whether to suit the king's need or Cromwell's, there is no wriggling out of it. I am ready and if … if George has to die for my sake, then living is a thing I no longer wish for."

"Your Grace," he repeats, leaning forward in his chair, "there might yet be a way. I have instruction from Cromwell that if you agree to certain things, your life may well be granted after all."

Time slows and I can hear the blood thumping in my ears, my heart hammering loud beneath my ribs.

"How? What things?"

Suddenly, life is sweet again. I remember Hever in the sunshine; Mary, George, Wyatt and I crawling through meadows of sunshine, the scent of apples and summertime. I remember Grandmother's horrid little dog, his relentless scratching, his turds curling ripely on the lawn. I remember the boredom, the everyday dreariness of the familiar. I want to experience all that again.

I want to go home.

I want to see my mother.

"How?" I repeat. "Tell me what I must do."

He takes a deep breath and looks me in the eye, speaking all in a rush as though he has little time to say it.

"Admit that your marriage to the king is invalid. Confess to a pre-contract. If you are not the king's true wife, then no crime has been committed."

I do not answer right away. The only sound in the chamber is the crackling flames in the grate. It is so quiet that I know Lady Kingston and my aunt, Lady Boleyn, are listening on the other side of the door. All my life, ever since I came to court, there have been spies carrying tales to my enemies, looking for a way to come between me and the king. Yet even now, I will not whisper.

"And what of Elizabeth?"

"She will be cared for. As a royal bastard, she will receive every honour."

"Like her sister Mary, you mean?"

He does not answer. What can he say? The only person preventing fair treatment of Mary was me. I can only hope that Henry's next wife will be kinder. I slump back in my seat, the brief hope of reprieve forgotten. "She is the king's heir, whatever they may say. I cannot sell her legitimacy for the sake of my life."

He sighs, flicks the edges of his pile of papers, taps his finger as he decides how best to respond.

"She may wish you to do so. You are her mother. Think how she will feel to grow up the daughter of a disgraced and executed queen ..."

"Better to be the daughter of a whore, you mean?"

He closes his eyes against my profanity and we both sit in silence, each thinking our own thoughts.

"Why does Cromwell need my confession to get his annulment? Why not just press some poor innocent into perjury? Why not just promise my sister Mary a fortune in exchange for declaring a pre-contract between the king and herself? Why do you need me?"

Even as I speak I realise that they have already exhausted those avenues. Mary has refused to play their game, and Percy, poor weak Henry Percy, has chosen not to betray me either. Perhaps he is not so weak livered as I thought.

I look Cranmer in the eye. I see pain, discomfort, and much sorrow. I begin to weaken. "If I do admit to a pre-contract, what will happen to me? Will I be free to return to Hever, to marry again and forget I was ever queen, or will I be a prisoner, like the late queen, Catherine?"

He hesitates. "I believe it would be best were you to take orders and enter a nunnery."

I raise my eyebrows. "A nunnery? This has been carefully planned. So I am to be closeted to pray for the king's soul while he continues as before, and is free to marry whomever he pleases ... Tell me, Cranmer, do you think he would ever be able to forget me?"

A long silence, a ragged sigh, a dropped head. "No, Your Grace. There is not a soul on this Earth who has met you who will ever be allowed to forget."

Finding myself touched by his words, I stand up and move to the window, kneel upon the seat. Outside, the castle green is alive with people, and beyond on the river, the world goes on without me. If only I could board a wherry and make my escape upriver, take horse to Hever and never come to court again.

For the first time, a life of obscurity sounds like Heaven. Life is very sweet. It will be less so without George, and I would never know true happiness again, but he would not want me to die.

He would tell me to live.

I make up my mind.

"Very well, Cranmer. You have your confession. I was pre-contracted to many men in my youth, and have lived a disgustingly dissolute life. My marriage to the king has as much substance as gossamer. Go tell him so, and let us be done with this nonsense."

"You will go into seclusion and not seek to visit or communicate with the king, or your daughter?"

"Elizabeth? I must not write to Elizabeth?"

He shakes his head. "But remember, your compliance will ensure her well-being. If you want her to be well cared for and happy, you must remain a stranger to her."

Can I do that? Can I bear to live my life estranged from her, never to share her triumphs, or comfort her in dark times? I would hear news of her, of course, but second hand news is not the same. She is my beloved daughter, I cannot and do not want to live without her.

But life is calling me, singing its sweet tempting song, and I find myself agreeing. If I live, everything else will come right.

I *have* to live.

17th May 1536 – The Tower of London

I am still awake when dawn breaks in a wave of pink sky. Today is the day my brother must die, and our innocent friends along with him. I cannot stand it. How, knowing they die for me, can I continue to breathe, continue to eat, to sleep, to live?

Perhaps I should have stood firm and denied the pre-contract. Perhaps I would be better off dead than suffering a life of torment, without Henry, without Elizabeth, and without George. I wish I could just prevent my next breath from happening, close my eyes, never inhale again, just stop, put an end to everything. Yet somehow my body continues to function, my heart continues to beat … and slowly break.

Why is Henry doing this? Why does he not come and save us? How can he let his friends perish in this way? George, Weston, Brereton, and Norris are men whom he has loved as brothers; men who have served him intimately and devotedly for so many years. What can be urging him to take such a horrible, irreversible step? How can he do this to me, for the sake of whom he took on the mighty power of Rome?

And then I realise. It is all suddenly quite clear. It is not Henry at all. It is Cromwell, manipulating the king to his own ends, and Henry believes it all. He believes I never loved him, that I slept with his friends, laughed at him in secret.

Poor Henry! He must be suffering the most horrible torment. I almost feel his sense of betrayal, imagining me indulging in heinous depravity, laughing at his prowess, his talents, every one of his friends disloyal and spiteful.

He thinks we have made him a fool, but it is Cromwell who does that. Poor gullible Henry, deceived and controlled by the son of a draper; tricked by a servant into destroying his real friends. After this day he will have no one to trust, never again will Henry know the comfort of an honest friend for he is letting them all die.

I cannot sit still; all morning I stride back and forth, chewing the skin around my fingernails, taking neither food nor drink, and speaking to no one. Until, a little after noon, Master Kingston arrives.

"Is the deed done?" I already know the answer for I heard the cannon that signals to the people the fate of all traitors. He nods his head, looks at the floor. "My brother is dead? And the others too?"

"Yes, Your Grace. I am sorry, but take comfort in the knowledge that they died nobly and well."

Nobly and well! What comfort is that? I wring my hands as if trying to wash them clean.

"Tell me," I gasp through dry tears, although part of me has no wish to hear it.

He clears his throat. "Lord Rochford, your brother, went first. He stood bravely, spoke to the crowd of his faith and love for the king ..."

"And his innocence?"

"Of course, Your Grace. All men spoke of that, bar one ..."

His voice fades away.

"Smeaton." I cannot help it, I spit the word.

"Yes, Your Grace, although he had the chance to retract his confession."

"So, he did not clear me of the public shame he has brought to me? Then I fear his soul will suffer for such false accusations."

Kingston accepts my outburst without words. I look at him, sensing he has something more to impart. "Well, what more have you to say?"

"Your Grace, forgive me but ... the council have decided ... your confession regarding the pre-contract ... it is not enough to save you."

For the first time in his presence I almost fall, but swiftly he reaches out and holds me firm, his strong hands clasping my elbows until I am steady again. I slowly raise my eyes to his, hating the truth I discover there.

"So I am to die anyway. I need not have perjured myself?"

He shakes his head once.

"When is it to be?"

"Tomorrow, Your Grace. You must make your peace with God."

Someone is laughing. "It doesn't really matter," I hear a voice saying. "I have lost all that I cared for. My brother is dead, my friends are slain, my daughter is stolen from me. What use is life to me now? Although ... I would have liked to see Hever just one more time."

I come back to myself with a jolt, realise that I am clutching Mr Kingston's collar. I draw back, stand like one chastised, smile an apology for my brief lapse of manners.

"Is it to be by fire, or the axe?"

"The king, in his mercy, has sent for a swordsman from Calais. It will be both swift and painless."

"His Majesty is so kind."

Mistaking my irony, he closes his eyes in silent agreement.

"It is extraordinary, is it not, Mr Kingston, that on paper I am not and never was the king's wife, yet I am still to die for infidelity and treason? How determined he must be to be rid of me."

Mr Kingston bows and asks if there is anything I require, but there is only one thing left.

"I would like to take the Sacrament and make my peace with God."

"It shall be done, Your Grace." Silently and reverently, although I am no longer owed any such allegiance, he bows from the room, softly closing the door, leaving me for one more night, alone.

Just one more night.

18th May 1536 – The Tower of London

Even if the hammering of the scaffold builders stopped, I'd know no rest. It is long since I slept but, somehow, the need for it has passed. I spend my last night on Earth in prayer, reflecting upon my life, what I might have done differently, where I might have taken an alternative path.

Had Wolsey not intervened I might be married to Percy now, and the mother of a dozen boys, but fate decreed otherwise. Had I been made of lighter morals, I might be mistress to Tom Wyatt and likewise a mother to a troop of tow-headed rascals, all looking just like their father. For a few moments I linger happily on the thought, regretting his marriage to Elizabeth Brooke; perhaps we'd all have been happier without it. Perhaps it would have been better to become his mistress, and my mistake was in clinging to chastity. I am to die a whore anyway.

Or perhaps, had negotiations gone differently with the Butlers, I might be mistress of the Ormond estates and mother to a bevy of Irishmen. But instead of all those opportunities I took the eye of a king, and from that moment my path was forged.

I do not regret it, not really. I repent of my behaviour to Mary and Catherine, but only because Elizabeth is now in a similar precarious position. I pray that my actions will not reflect ill upon her, and I pray her step-mother will be kind, whoever she may be.

Ah, Henry. At first you were just the king, a light entertainment; I had not realised you would come to want me in earnest. I had not foreseen you would overturn the country, bring down the Church, and fall foul of the Pope just for the honour of bedding me.

Perhaps I should have been a light skirt like Mary and freely given you my body, thus ensuring life after Henry. Had I done so I might now be living, fat and happy, in the countryside as she is. I can never know and there is no use in dwelling on the might-have-been. I can only hope I have left some good behind me, and that my work for reform is not undone by my successor.

Surely he will not marry Jane Seymour, the pale-faced ninny who loves the Roman Church? That cannot be. Henry will tire of her in the month.

Henry. He runs like a loop in my mind. I wish we could say goodbye. I wonder how he is, if he misses and grieves for me, or if he has cast me out of his mind as well as his life. No news reaches me in my prison. All I can do is hope he is not too unhappy.

Tomorrow—oh no, it is today—I am to die, and I have sought God's forgiveness for all my wrongs, all my small sins, and I pray He is ready to receive me into His arms. It has been a good life, if a little short. I pray that the world treats Elizabeth better.

I dress in my best, most regal clothes. A gown of silver grey damask and a cloak of ermine fur. My hair is tucked beneath a gabled hood, not my usual style but a fine one nonetheless.

After praying a while longer, conscious of each task being for the last time, I pick up my prayer book and rosary and wait for Mr Kingston to arrive.

He is long in coming. My women grow restless and I feel nauseous from nerves and lack of food. There had seemed little point in taking dinner. At noon, long past the hour I had expected to die, Mr Kingston opens the door.

"Mr Kingston, there you are. You are a little late, I had thought to be dead long before noon."

"Your Grace, I am sorry. There has been some delay."

"So I understand, Mr Kingston."

White-faced, with shame in his eyes, he stutters his reply. "I am afraid we will have to postpone it, until dawn tomorrow …"

"Tomorrow?" The word drops like a stone into a well.

The thought of another night like the last is unbearable. I want it over now. I am ready to die now. I cannot go through it all again! But I do not protest too much. I put down my prayer book and disguise my disappointment with macabre humour.

"I had hoped it might be over soon. Not that I desire death, but I am prepared, and have made my peace with God. It will be such a swift and sudden thing for I have but a little neck, and just think, when I am gone the people will refer to me as Anne Lackhead …"

My laughter is loud, too loud, but a glance at the horror-stricken faces of my companions sobers me. It will not do to break down now. It would not be fair on them.

I fumble again for inner calm and when I turn back to Mr Kingston, it is with a peaceful smile. "So, I shall see you on the morrow. God send you rest, Mr Kingston."

And so I am given one more night, a night I neither desire nor relish. I pray again, for so long that I am sure God must be tired of me. Once again, I work my way through a long list, asking His blessing on all my loved ones, on the king, and on Elizabeth too. I ask forgiveness of my sins and failures, and beg that He takes me quickly into Paradise where I might be with George again.

When dawn arrives, my women dress me in the cold grey light. I take a little breakfast and prepare once more to make my end.

This time, I pray God it will be so.

At eight of the clock Mr Kingston returns, and tells me the time has come and I must make myself ready. But I am already prepared, I have been for days.

Dressed in the same clothes as the day before, I collect my prayer book and follow Mr Kingston on my final walk. We leave the Queen's Lodging, pass the Great Hall, through Cole Harbour Gate and along the side of the White Tower. On the green a black-draped scaffold looms, like a monster in the corner of a bedchamber. My steps falter but someone places a hand upon my back, urging me forward.

At the bottom of the scaffold steps, I hesitate. These steps lead me to my death, and my feet refuse to begin the ascent of their own accord. Mr Kingston, seeing my predicament, offers me his hand and I cling to it, trying not to let my terror show.

I raise one foot.

And then another, until somehow I am at the top. I look across the people gathered, men who stand bareheaded in the May morning. I begin to speak but a crowd of ravens set up a rumpus on the battlement, making a mockery of the solemnity of the moment. I wait for them to quieten.

My mouth is dry, my tongue thick and arid, but I know I must address the crowd, as is the custom. I must speak well of the king. I must ignore the truth of his actions and lie for the sake of those I leave behind.

Above the Tower, the ravens continue to screech their mirth, while those men who have come to see me punished wait in silence, only the occasional shouted remark breaking the peace.

I am to die now and my last words must be kind ones. I force my mind to happy times, a place where the grass was tall and the meadows full of flowers.

Mary.

George... and Tom.

A time before Henry.

I raise my head and smile. It is a simple thing to perjure myself to ensure that my family go unmolested. The Boleyns must not be punished any further. I clear my throat and raise my hands.

Hands that no longer tremble.

"Good Christian people, I am come hither to die, for according to the law and by the law I am judged to die, and therefore I will speak nothing against it. I am come hither to accuse no man, nor to speak anything of that whereof I am accused and condemned to die, but I pray God save the king and send him long to reign over you, for a gentler nor a more merciful prince was there never: and to me he was ever a good, a gentle and sovereign lord. And if any person will meddle of my cause, I require them to judge the best. And thus I take my leave of the world and of you all, and I heartily desire you all to pray for me. O Lord have mercy on me, to God I commend my soul."

The masked man stands like an effigy. I turn toward him and hold out a small bag of coin that he accepts, bows his gratitude, keeping his face averted. Then I grasp my women's hands to bid them goodbye and, even though they are Cromwell's spies and have no love for me, they are overcome. Their fingers tremble, their faces are wet with tears as they cling to me and bid me farewell.

"Come," I command for one last time. "You must be strong."

"It is time to kneel." Mr Kingston interrupts our leave taking and I pass my prayer book to Lady Lee, my beads to my aunt. Someone helps me down. I tuck my skirts modestly about my ankles to ensure that in the moment of death, I am not shamed. Then, amid much weeping, my cap is removed. As the blindfold is tied their nervous fingers snag my hair, but I do not scold them, my last words on Earth shall not be a reprimand.

My suffering is over at last, and I trust that Heaven's gate stands ajar. George, wait for me, George, I call silently, hoping that he has not yet passed into Paradise without me.

To my surprise I am no longer afraid, and with one last prayer for my sweet Elizabeth, I begin to pray aloud. The crowd holds their breath while silence screams like a blade around us; even the ravens have ceased their cackle in honour of my end.

"To Jesus Christ I commend my soul. Lord Jesu' receive my ..."

The falling blade is like the sighing of the sea.

***

Everything stops—sound, vision, sensation—but I am aware of everything. I can see back through time to a world where men barely scratched a living from the earth. And I see forward, a hundred thousand years into the future, to a time where royalty is disempowered, to a time when religion is crumbling and only war remains.

War and misery.

But I can still see the present, and realise that this year, 1536, is but a tiny speck in the vastness of forever. From a great height I see my women scrabbling to cover the bundle of bloody rags that was my body, the grisly sphere that was my head.

As they bear their burdens away, Cromwell turns his back, rubbing his hands on his gown as if to rid them of my blood. My uncle of Norfolk and Fitzroi follow him, the king's son snivelling with a cold. And Master Kingston, my jailer, who at the very last became my friend, bids Fitzroi hasten home to bed. Then he turns his sad eyes to his wife, my enemy, Cromwell's spy, and together they pass into the darkness of the keep where, high up in a Tower cell, Tom Wyatt stares blankly into a damp, dark corner.

Life goes on.

Even when we no longer wish it to.

Then my vision shifts and I am in the garden at Lambeth, where Cranmer sits upon a bench, weeping amid the early roses, torn petals scattered at his feet. In a rush of gratitude I reach out to make my farewell, but before I can comfort him, the setting changes again.

I am at Hatfield with Elizabeth. She has not yet been told of my passing and she is laughing, defying her nurses, her face alight with stubborn mischief. She is the king's daughter in temperament as well as appearance.

I see Hever, where Grandmother huddles before a lazy fire. She is still dribbling, still ruled by her noxious little dog, Merlin. She will not comprehend what they have done to me, unlike my poor mother who sobs unrestrainedly in her chamber.

Where is Mary? I search through the mist that separates me from the living and find her at last, praying on her own in a chapel. To my surprise, she is praying for me, and for our brother, George. Poor Mary is left alone, disgraced by those who had thought themselves disgraced by her.

And then, suddenly, I am with you, Henry, speeding along beside your horse as you gallop to Wolf Hall to be with Jane. Filled with a jealous anger greater than any I ever knew in life, I remain at your side as you ride, whispering curses in your ear, denying you happiness, ill-wishing your unborn children.

And I have been with you every day since, my husband. I have seen you change from a prince to a monster. I've witnessed every cruelty, every sin, seen each small betrayal, each moment of joy, watched every discarded wife falter and fall.

And I've wept for every one of them.

What were you running from, Henry? All your life you've been afraid; afraid of failure, afraid of discovery, afraid of the Devil catching up with you. Well, now that time is here. And I have lingered just to see it.

I uncurl my legs and slide from the bed. His breath is scarcely audible now, and soon the rattle will begin again, denoting the end.

The bitter end.

Cranmer clutches his master's hand, praying for his soul, knowing what will come, and fearing it.

The court holds its breath.

The rattling in the king's throat falters, and then stops …tension mounts, he starts to breathe again but I can wait no longer and reach out from the darkness to take back what is mine.

Author's note

The story of Anne Boleyn has been written many times, in many different ways, but I have tried to relate in it a way that Anne might prefer it to be told.

Of all the women in history, Anne Boleyn has to be among the most vilified. Almost from the moment of her death, her attributes were suppressed and her faults exaggerated. Her story, written largely by her enemies, brands her a whore, a witch, an adulteress, and a traitor, and many modern day novelists have followed that path, even embellished the lurid details to make her worse. But despite their best efforts there is nothing in the existing record to suggest any of these things were true.

The damning evidence used at her trial can now be disregarded, and historians have proved that on many of the dates and times when she was alleged to have been with lovers, she was in fact elsewhere; on one occasion recovering from giving birth to Elizabeth. The accusation of incest is unlikely to be true—incest, like witchcraft, was a tag used to demonise a person's character, particularly women, and like many other people, I chose to dismiss it. What I have done is provide a fictional spark to explain how rumours of this nature can quickly burst into flame.

I have chosen to write in the first person, giving voice to Anne's imagined thoughts and fears. In my book she is an intelligent, devout woman with a keen desire to reform the Church. Her relationship with Henry is complex, a love/hate relationship that brings down a queen, resulting in excommunication from Rome and the upheaval of the Church in England. She has many enemies, not least Spain, and it is the records of the Spanish ambassador, Chapuys, which provide the most damaging contemporary accounts of Anne.

We cannot know for certain the circumstances of her fall, but we know it was swift. We know that right up until April 1536, just weeks before her arrest, Henry was as deeply enamoured with Anne as ever. Henry's infidelity was not unusual at this time, and his dalliance with other women should not be read as signals indicating a failed marriage. Something happened between mid-April and early May to convince Henry that Anne was not all she seemed.

Early in her reign she worked in close conjunction with fellow reformer, Thomas Cromwell, but prior to her fall there was a serious disagreement between them. Knowing the king's desire for wealth, Cromwell intended to dissolve the monasteries, fill the king's coffers and his own purse, and sell off ecclesiastic land to the gentry for profit. Anne, on the other hand, wanted to turn the monasteries into seats of learning, close the smaller abbeys and work with them to improve the standards and morals in those remaining. To raise awareness, she caused a sermon to be read in chapel by John Skip in which Henry VIII was compared to Ahasuerus, Anne Boleyn became Queen Esther, and Thomas Cromwell, who was in the process of suppressing the Lesser Monasteries, was Haman, the wicked minister to Ahasuerus. The sermon was essentially a gauntlet thrown at Cromwell's feet. One can only imagine his displeasure.

After that, her downfall was swift and complete. After her death, however, many records were lost. We are not in possession of all the facts, and this has left Anne's story to be interpreted as her enemies wished.

It is easy to write Henry VIII off as a monster, a tyrant, a wife murderer. He has featured as such in many novels; an omnipresent psychopath governing his country with a ruthless hand, dispatching anyone who dared to cross him. It was not until I started my research for *The Kiss of the Concubine* that I began to notice subtler aspects of his character, see him differently and come to have a greater understanding of this Tudor king.

Tyrants aren't born, they evolve, just as saints do, their characters slowly shaped over time, just as ours are. Early chronicles of Henry provide no hint of the embittered man he was to become. On his assumption of the throne, when his future stretched ahead of him in an unspotted landscape of graceful chivalry, he must have seemed the answer to the nation's prayers.

While writing this book I had to forget what was to come later, I had to regard 1536 as a wall beyond which it was impossible to see. So in *The Kiss of the Concubine* you will find a gentler, more complex Henry; a man full of self-doubt, fearful of failure, his need for a son and heir all consuming.

I think, as far as he was capable of it, he loved Anne. He wouldn't have waited and suffered for so long and moved so many insurmountable mountains to obtain her if he hadn't loved her. I think, at the end, he believed the accusations brought against her and it was rage and hurt that turned him against her. I suspect that the belief that his friends, George Boleyn, Henry Norris, William Brereton, Francis Weston, and above all, Anne, had betrayed him drove him to allow such drastic action to be taken. I also wonder if, once the deed was done, and he came to realise his mistake, the enormity of his actions turned his mind. After the fall of Anne Boleyn and those accused alongside her, Henry VIII was never the same again.

The Kiss of the Concubine is based on prolonged historic research, but it is, above all, fiction, and I have ignored some incidents and invented others. I hope you enjoy it.

Judith Arnopp's other books include:

Sisters of Arden: on the Pilgrimage of Grace
The Beaufort Bride: The story of Margaret Beaufort
The Beaufort Woman: Book Two of the Story of Margaret Beaufort
The King's Mother: Book Three of the story of Margaret Beaufort
A Song of Sixpence: The story of Elizabeth of York and Perkin Warbeck
Intractable Heart: The story of Katheryn Parr
The Winchester Goose: At the court of Henry VIII

The Song of Heledd
The Forest Dwellers: and the killiung of William Rufus
Peaceweaver: the story of Eadgyth Aelfgarsdottir